Until We Find Home

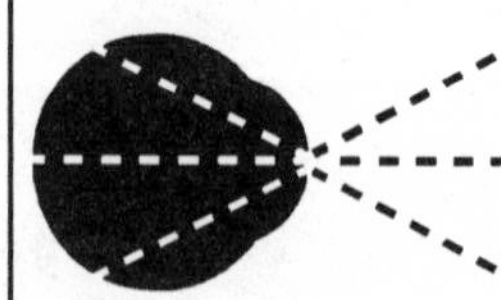

This Large Print Book carries the Seal of Approval of N.A.V.H.

Until We Find Home

Cathy Gohlke

THORNDIKE PRESS
A part of Gale, a Cengage Company

Farmington Hills, Mich • San Francisco • New York • Waterville, Maine
Meriden, Conn • Mason, Ohio • Chicago

Scripture quotations are taken from the Holy Bible, King James Version.
Thorndike Press, a part of Gale, a Cengage Company.

Until We Find Home is a work of fiction. Where real people, events, establishments, organizations, or locales appear, they are used fictitiously. All other elements of the novel are drawn from the author's imagination.
Thorndike Press® Large Print Christian Historical Fiction.
The text of this Large Print edition is unabridged.
Other aspects of the book may vary from the original edition.
Set in 16 pt. Plantin.

LIBRARY OF CONGRESS CIP DATA ON FILE.
CATALOGUING IN PUBLICATION FOR THIS BOOK
IS AVAILABLE FROM THE LIBRARY OF CONGRESS

ISBN-13: 978-1-4328-4946-7 (hardcover)

Published in 2018 by arrangement with Tyndale House Publishers, Inc.

Printed in the United States of America
1 2 3 4 5 6 7 22 21 20 19 18

FOR AIMEE CLAIRE

Whose name aptly means
Beloved and Bright
You are light and joy to me,
Precious Granddaughter
All my love, forever

There is no fear in love; but perfect love casteth out fear: because fear hath torment.

1 JOHN 4:18

ACKNOWLEDGMENTS

With great appreciation and debt to the late C. S. Lewis, for his radio broadcasts and writings, and for documenting his journey from atheism to theism and then to faith in Jesus Christ. At a time when England and the world desperately needed a voice of reason and hope, Mr. Lewis's writings and WWII radio broadcasts reached and provoked the thought and faith of thousands. Those broadcasts, later compiled and edited into his book *Mere Christianity,* continue to reach and inspire millions today, as do his many letters, lectures, and books for adults and children, including his beloved Chronicles of Narnia series.

Special appreciation for the late Beatrix Potter Heelis, the world's bestselling children's author and illustrator, for her wonderful, timeless stories and precious illustrations. What magical, insightful worlds she created! With her earnings, Beatrix Potter

Heelis purchased over four thousand acres of pristine land and farms, which she preserved through national trust in England's breathtaking Lake District. Included is Hill Top Farm, open to the public, which reflects the magic and joy of her tales. In the rooms and gardens of Hill Top, visitors can glimpse inspirations for many of the author's stories.

Thank you to those who keep diaries — especially writers for Britain's Mass Observation Project, begun shortly before WWII, and continued until well after. Thank you to the preservers of historic sites, societies, and museums in England, and to tour guides who love their subjects as much as I do.

Thank you, Natasha Kern, dear friend, literary agent, and sister in Christ, who has believed in, encouraged, and supported my writing and life's journey.

Thank you, Stephanie Broene, Sarah Rische, and Shaina Turner, my gifted and encouraging editors at Tyndale. Special thanks to Sarah Rische for reconceiving the timeline of this story. That made all the difference. Thank you to the entire Tyndale team: senior marketing manager Kristen Magnesen, publicist Kristen Schumacher, and all those who've worked to bring this book to readers. You've blessed me beyond measure. Eva Winters, thank you for the spectacular cover for the original publisher's edition. I love that the handwriting in the sky is taken from the first draft of C. S. Lewis's manuscript, *The Problem of Pain.* You spoke to my heart.

Thank you, Daniel, my son, for translating the French words and phrases in this and my other books. I love you and will gladly meet you for coffee and chats concerning foreign lands anytime.

Thank you, Elisabeth, my daughter, for sharing a lifelong love of gardens and especially *The Secret Garden,* by Frances Hodgson Burnett. I love you and will traipse gardens and traverse books with you always.

Thanksgiving, joyful and abundant, for my two precious sisters in Yeshua/Jesus and my "literary partners in crime" — Terri Gillespie, for brainstorming, for reading this manuscript, and for offering valuable insights into Jewish faith and culture; Carrie Turansky, for brainstorming and sharing an amazing research trip to England and Scotland, and for reading this manuscript. Our adventures in Windermere and the Lake District brought this book to imagination and life. Thank you both for bearing me up through health and writing angst. I cannot imagine this writing or life journey without either of you.

Thanksgiving for Gayle Roper and her insights into widowhood through her book *A Widow's Journey,* and for Lucinda Secrest McDowell, for articulating the joy and freedom of grace in her book *Amazed by Grace.* Both your books appeared before me at a silent retreat the very weekend I prayed for insights into characters within this story. Thank you for your friendship, and for being God's willing vessels and stewards of life through your pens.

Thank you, dear friends, church family, and writing community — with shouts to the Transformational Fiction Fans Facebook group, and to Liz Curtis Higgs and our Scottish Standby Sisters. Carrie Turansky and I joined you for the wonderful trip guided by Liz Curtis Higgs to Scotland's highlands, islands, and gardens. You've all stood in the gap for me, prayerfully interceding. You've showered me with e-mails, cards, and gifts, cheered me on, and believed in my health recovery. God continues to answer your prayers.

Abundant joy and thanksgiving for my dear family — where would I be without each of you? You've blessed me with your love, stories, insights, brainstorming, prayers, encouragement, and patience too precious in times too numerable to count:

Thank you, my dear husband, children, mother, sister, brothers, nieces, nephews, and the generations fast on your heels — all dear spouses included — and my two precious granddaughters. You brighten each new day.

As always, special thanks to Uncle Wilbur Goforth, who, when I was uncertain which career path to take, reminded me that a sure way to know if I'm working in the will of God is to ask, "Do I have joy? Is this yoke easy? Is this burden light?" Uncle Wilbur has spent six decades broadcasting Christian radio, the delight of his heart, to a world in need. His motto: "Radio — the most effective mission tool known to man!" At seventy-seven years, he is still energized by his daily work. It's a family truth and smile that Uncle Wilbur's favorite day is Monday morning. Thank you, Uncle Wilbur, for your shining example!

Above all, joy and thanksgiving to my heavenly Father and Lord Jesus Christ for forgiveness, for preserving my life now, for the hope of eternity, for giving me the gifts of family and story, and for the opportunity to write books containing the very comfort with which I've been abundantly, undeservedly blessed. You are my everything!

CHAPTER ONE

May 1940

Lightning crackled, splitting the night sky over Paris, illuminating letters painted on the bookstore window across the street: *La Maison des Amis des Livres.* Driving rain pounded the loose shutters of Shakespeare and Company, making them rattle so that Claire Stewart dropped the heavy blackout curtain into place.

"It sounds like cannon bursting, like the end of the world." Thunder boomed again. She tugged the belt of her trench coat tighter.

"You must go," Josephine insisted. "The lorry driver won't wait. This is his last run to Calais. He's running on nerves, even now. Arnaud told you —"

"Arnaud promised he'd be here. I won't go without him. I don't even know our British contact."

"You know Arnaud. He'll meet you if he

can — last minute, no doubt." Josephine Ganute — one more aspiring writer, another tumbleweed to make her home amid the burdened shelves of Sylvia Beach's American bookstore — grunted and gently, firmly pushed Claire toward the door. "This is the last group, and the last driver willing to go. He's insane to try. The roads must be packed with people fleeing the city. Calais is a refugee camp — even last week it was so. If you don't leave now, the children will never —"

"But I don't know where to go when we get there!" The pressure in Claire's heart built. Josephine was French and five years older. She couldn't understand how frightened Claire felt.

"The driver knows the fisherman from over the Channel. Arnaud will surely meet you on the shore, if not in Calais."

"But what if he doesn't? What if they've caught him?" Claire pleaded and hated her pleading. But the possibility glared. Arnaud — her heroic Arnaud — took such chances among those sympathetic with the Germans. So many Jewish families he'd smuggled under their noses — from Germany into Switzerland and France. Now, with war declared and German troops on the doorstep, they were no longer safe in France. Arnaud fancied himself — fancied them — the only hope of Jewish children, and Claire loved him for it. *Reconnaissance, smuggling, resistance* — words so romantic in fiction, impossible and dangerous in life.

Josephine stepped close. Her bony fingers clasped Claire's face. "Claire, Arnaud is too smart for that. You read his message. The Germans will take these children as surely as they snatched the Jewish children from their own country if you don't get them out now, before the troops arrive — and they are coming. That's what matters now. Everything else comes later. *Vous comprenez, non?*"

Claire nodded, swallowing the bile climbing her throat. Of course she understood. Goose-stepping Nazis and their tanks plowed westward; the best intelligence had verified it. *Helping these children to safety means everything to me, too, but I can't do it alone.*

Claire stole one last glance at the dimly lit aisles threatened by crooked and towering stacks of novels. At the tables and chairs helter-skelter from the early evening's stilted book tea. The chair Mr. Hemingway — her Mr. Hemingway — once insisted on tipping on its hind legs as he smoked. The desk James Joyce was reputed to have claimed as his own.

She faltered at the door. But it opened, and Josephine pushed her into the dark, into the pelting rain. The click of the latch behind rang final in Claire's ears.

"Vite! Vite!" the lorry driver called from the street, beating his fist against his door. "Come now, or I leave you!"

Claire stumbled, splashing down the puddled alley. She scrambled over the tailgate, into the canvas-covered truck bed, pushing rivulets of rain from her eyes and hair and shivering from the cold water that streamed down the back of her neck.

The lorry jerked forward, bouncing off the curb.

"Pardon, désolée!" Awkwardly, clumsily, Claire climbed over an assortment of small arms and legs — children she couldn't see in the dark, children pulling limbs into huddled forms. Panting, Claire found sanctuary against the wooden wall behind the cab.

She couldn't see to count the number in the transport, couldn't tally the limbs she'd climbed over, but there seemed more room than there should have been. Even twenty would be too few among so many desperate to leave Paris. She must learn their names and those of their parents to write down for the record. *One day these children will return to France and their families — when this madness is over. The list of names and addresses hidden beneath the floorboard of Shakespeare and Company is the only way we'll know to reunite them.*

It was still dark inside the lorry bed when the vehicle finally lurched to a stop. Claire woke, rubbing a crick in her neck. One of the little ones had climbed onto her lap sometime in the night; another slumped a sleepy head against her shoulder. *Do any of them speak English? Ten months in Paris and my French leaves so much to be desired.*

Despite the hammering rain, the scent of sweet Channel air cleared her nostrils. Claire pressed her head against the wooden slats. *At last. Please, Arnaud, be here. Be here and help me get these children to safety.* She hoped for an easy send-off and a speedy return to Paris, where they'd regale Josephine with tales of their latest exploit over a warm fire and a fine bottle of wine in the back room of their dear, familiar bookstore.

Arnaud and I will laugh in the face of the danger we defied and plot our next adventure, keeping our secret even from Sylvia. Owning the bookstore, and employing Jews, she runs risk enough.

Claire's reverie was broken by raised male voices outside the lorry — intense, animated arguments in French so hard and clipped she couldn't catch the words. Claire shook the arm of the child beside her and shifted the little one in her lap. "*Réveillez-vous. Restez silencieux.* No talking, but be ready." She smiled into the dark, hoping to infuse her voice with comfort and confidence, hoping they understood something of her mixed French and English.

She pitied them for being bumped through the night with barely more than they wore . . . pitied them for leaving parents and older siblings they loved and who must love them. She swallowed, trying to imagine such love. *Off to a new country where you'll understand precious little of the language. Poor souls, fleeing home and dear Paris in springtime. Poor, brave little soldiers.*

Knowing time was of the essence, Claire gently pushed the child from her lap and crawled toward the tailgate. She peeked beneath the canvas, eager to glimpse their surroundings and to encourage their driver to move the mission forward.

The engine roared. Tires spun and the lorry jerked to life again. The sudden sharp swerve and the squeal of floored brakes brought cries from every child. Claire's head slammed against the tailgate.

One of the larger children yanked her back into the center of the bed. "Mademoiselle!"

"All right. I'm all right," Claire mumbled, reaching for her forehead. But her fingers came away sticky.

A mile or more the lorry bumped and sped. Finally the brakes slammed again. Still dazed, Claire didn't move from the floor. Five minutes must have passed before the driver lifted the canvas. "*Vite!* Come quickly — now!" He pulled open the tailgate and lifted the children down in the pale light of a shaded lantern. "Get your things — all of them. Leave nothing!"

"Arnaud?" Claire whispered into the streaming rain, her vision blurred and head pounding.

"He is not here." The driver's panic seeped through every word. "The fisherman's contact said he has not come; neither has the children's escort. The tide is turning — not a moment to waste. Run down to the water's edge now!" He pushed the children toward the shore, young ones clasping the hands of older, taller children, all stumbling after a flapping mackintosh–clad fisherman with a feeble torch.

"A fishing boat . . . on the Channel . . . on a night like this?" Claire's temples throbbed and she couldn't stop the world from spinning. "Is it safe?"

"Safer for them than Paris."

"They must wait for their escort. We can't send them off alone."

"Did you not hear me, mademoiselle? The tide is turning. It will be daylight before it turns again. The captain cannot wait. He refuses to come another time." The stale breath of the driver nearly overpowered her. "You must go with them, mademoiselle. *Tout de suite!*"

"Me? No, you don't understand. I'm staying . . . returning to Paris. There are more children to help. These will be safe in England, but I'm needed —"

"They cannot go without an escort. Your English fisherman won't take them alone. There is no one else and there will be no more trips. To wait is madness!"

Claire counted the children's fuzzy silhouettes against the fisherman's torch as they clambered over the side of the boat. Five. Only five souls from one very small to one nearly as tall as Claire. She closed her eyes and painfully shook her aching head. "Surely he can manage five children. I must go back for Arnaud. I don't know what's happened to him."

"Ha! It seems he has left you, *chérie*!"

It was the thing she'd feared each day — that he would leave her, that he did not love her as she loved him. Still, she shook her head, vouching for him. Something warm and liquid seeped into her eye. "Then you must go with the children, monsieur — you're responsible for them. Arnaud paid you. Please, I must get back to Paris."

He slammed the tailgate. "You are crazy, mademoiselle. I will not take you. And I am not responsible for these young ones. I've done what I was paid to do. I'll not risk my life or my family."

Unbelieving, Claire yanked his arm as he climbed into his lorry. "Wait! I'll go with them tomorrow night if the contact doesn't come." She steadied herself against the cab door. "Let me talk to the fisherman — ask him to wait one day — just until tomorrow night. Arnaud will come, I know!"

"I told you: this is his last run. He's a fool to try even now." The driver pushed her away. "You'll be lucky to get through the harbor."

Claire's head rang and swam. The reversing lorry roared to life once more, its spinning tires spraying her with cold rain and filling her mouth with graveled mud as the darkness closed in and claimed her.

■ ■ ■ ■

"Shh, she's coming round," a feminine French face, dancing in the light of a swaying battery lamp, whispered over Claire's pounding head.

"Wipe her forehead now — quick — before she wakens. It will sting more if you don't." A boy, perhaps eight or nine, spit into his soiled handkerchief and passed it purposefully toward the feminine face. "Clean out her eye or she'll go blind from the blood."

"Oh, be quiet," the lovely girl ordered. "You say the stupidest things, Gaston."

Claire groaned and closed her eyes again. The crashing in her head and the rolling in her stomach heaved into one large inner motion. "Where am I?"

"You're on the HMS *Miss Bonny Blair,*" a new voice announced in perfect English with a very French accent. Claire opened one eye to see a taller boy, maybe eleven or so, hovering too close. The boy blushed. "At least that's what Capitaine Beardsley said before we left the shore beyond Calais, though I think it rather more a fishing boat." He grabbed a bar above his head to steady himself.

"Captain Beardsley? A fishing boat?" Claire heard herself moan again.

"Aye, aye." The youngster called Gaston pushed closer. "And we're all his mates. That's Bertram, my brother. I'm Gaston — Capitaine Beardsley's first mate. And you're the lively wench he rescued."

"Gaston! That is vulgar. Mademoiselle is our rescuer," the feminine voice gasped. "I'm Jeanine." She leaned closer, confiding, "We were told never to give our family names, but I will tell you that Elise, here, is my sister. This littlest one came alone and is called Aimee. These boys we met through Monsieur Arnaud."

"Arnaud? He's here?" Claire's heaving stomach skipped into her heart.

"*Non,* mademoiselle," Jeanine sympathized. "He is not. He told us he would come if he could, but . . . You've been calling for him in your sleep."

Claire pulled herself to one elbow and reached for her forehead. "Sleep? How long?" *I must convince Captain Beardsley to turn the boat around.*

"Hours, I'd say," Gaston cheerfully volunteered.

"What?" Panic sped through her veins.

"We must be nearing England's shores," Bertram offered. "Rest easy, mademoiselle.

Capitaine Beardsley said he will find you a doctor once we land."

"It doesn't take hours to reach England."

"It does when you're going the long way round," Gaston declared. "*Le capitaine* said we travel wise as serpents and harmless as doves."

What can that mean? But Claire's head hurt too much to think about it now. She lay back on the makeshift pallet and closed her eyes against the swaying walls and the heaving in her stomach. She hated crossing the Channel in fair weather. She'd never have dared to cross it in foul, much less on the back of a storm-tossed sea. *Mad sea captain — he must be kin to Captain Ahab!*

The last thing Claire heard was Gaston admonishing Jeanine, "You needn't have shushed me. I simply made a mistake with my English. She's not 'lively' at all, not a bit, even for a grownup. But she is quite a 'likely' wench, I'd say — at least that's as Capitaine Beardsley vowed."

Chapter Two

Claire felt the captain's strong arms lift her from the floor, then half carry, half drag her off the boat and through the slowing drizzle, up and off a short, rough dock. Her feet pulled through sand. His scraggly beard scratched her cheek until he deposited her on a heap of sails and nets inside what must be a fishing shack. He left her with the children huddled around her but was back in less than thirty minutes. Despite the predawn hour, as good as his word to Bertram, he'd procured a no-nonsense doctor. The cleaning of Claire's wound and the piercing stitches thrummed painful in her head.

"Rest and a daily change of bandage," the doctor ordered. He looked at the five drowsy children by her side and shook his head at their rescuer. "I won't ask and don't want to know. But I swear by King George, you're in over your head, Captain, and too old by far for such nonsense."

"Aye. I'm trusting you now, Doc. You won't be letting me down, eh?"

"Not a word. Not in these times, poor little devils. Don't make a habit of it." The doctor snapped shut his black bag and pushed out into the dark and rain.

Through her brain fog Claire marveled that in this putrid place the captain somehow brewed tea over a can's open flame. He handed her the chipped and steaming mug, then found her a thick blanket, reeking of fish. Both were welcome. She tried to thank him, but the words muddled.

"Rest easy, lass. There'll be time to talk by and by."

It was good he'd issued the order. Claire couldn't have kept her eyes open another minute.

Morning erupted in streaks of red, orange, and violet across the eastern sky, streaming through the dirty porthole-shaped window of the fishing shed.

"Sailors take warning," Claire whispered.

"A good day to keep beneath the tarps," Captain Beardsley pronounced, handing dry and broken buns and a jar of now-lukewarm tea round the motley group. He must have gone out and come in again with such largesse, though Claire had never heard him.

Claire tried to sit up, to smooth her hair and stir some life into her bones, but her head still throbbed.

"Sit back, now, or you'll be bleedin' all over my tarps, and that won't do."

The tallest girl, the one with the lovely face — Jeanine — was at Claire's side in a moment, supporting her neck with a firm hand and raising a bunch of rags behind her head for a pillow. "Mademoiselle," she whispered.

"Merci," Claire breathed. "I should be looking after you, not this way round. Arnaud?" She'd dreamed he'd come. But Jeanine silently shook her head.

The captain looked away, as if embarrassed. "Don't 'spect he was able to cross."

Claire bit her lip. "Our contact — has he come?"

"No." The captain grimaced. "He should have been here before two this mornin'."

"What time is it?"

"Gone half after five. It's no good. He can't tote five blighters through the docks in broad daylight. You'll have to stay here today, at least until after the night watch. Not a peep. Not one sound. I'll make my rounds, see what I can learn."

Jeanine whispered in Claire's ear, "We all

need the *toilette,* mademoiselle."

Of course they did, and so did she. "Captain, what about facilities for the children?"

" 'Facilities'?" But his bluster faded when he saw tears well in the smallest girl's eyes. He opened the door and a gust of sea air poured in. He was back in a moment with a tin bucket. "Here, use this. I'll empty it when I get back. Not one of you go outside that door, and keep mum. Do ya hear me?"

"*Oui,* monsieur." Five heads nodded, eyes wide as tea saucers.

"And that goes for you, miss. Can't have no woman traipsing the docks. It's like wavin' a red flag."

"I promise. Thank you." Claire had used some primitive facilities in France but never a bucket before a roomful of children. They'd simply have to rig a tarp round one corner and take turns holding it up for privacy.

"If your man don't come by dark . . ."

"Yes?" Claire didn't see how Arnaud could get to England now, but he must, he simply must.

The captain didn't finish his statement. He coughed and harrumphed, but it failed to cover his anxiety. One glance at the children's pale faces and he pushed out his chest. "Rest easy today. No one should bother you here."

"But if the contact comes . . . or if Arnaud . . ."

"Neither will come in daylight."

The captain made to go, but Claire pushed up from the floor with her back to the children, faced him, and whispered, "Have you heard the wireless this morning? Do you know if — ?"

But the captain shook his head. "I'll be back when I can." That quickly he was gone.

By the time the shadows lengthened and the dock settled again for the night, Claire could barely breathe for worry. Had Arnaud been captured? Injured? And what about the captain? What if he didn't return? Could they trust him to help more than he had?

The hours crept by. Moonlight through the grimy window painted worried young faces in an eerie glow. Off and on they dozed. Off and on the younger girls leaned, even snuggled, against Claire. The unexpected intimacy unnerved her. Still, it didn't seem right to push them away.

Deep in the night, the latch on the shed finally lifted. Every eye flew open, but the children remained quiet as church mice. Claire swallowed, pushed the little girls and tarp aside, and stood between the children and the door, ready to face what or whom she must.

Claire sensed each small chest heave a sigh of relief as great as her own when the captain appeared. "What news?" she begged. "I must return to Paris, Captain Beardsley. I must get back to —"

"And how would you propose we do that, miss?"

"You made it through. You could do it again."

"Pity and foolishness on my part. That was my last run. There's ships bringing over some latecomers to Folkestone. Perhaps your young man'll make it yet. Besides, these youngsters are the first order of the day. What do you propose to do with them?"

"I'm not saying I mean to abandon them, but Arnaud had arranged for someone to meet them — you know that."

"Well, it's not my mistake, now is it? And it's not the mistake of these young blighters, neither." Captain Beardsley set down his kit. "I couldn't very well leave you passed out and bleeding on the beach, and someone was needed to mind the young ones for the crossing. There's no goin' back — not till this thing's good and over." He turned away. "It's the trouble with Americans . . . all talk and show and no sticking it out."

If the captain had discovered a magic button, he could not have pressed a more sensitive nerve. "You underestimate both me and my country, Captain. President Roosevelt won't abandon England in your hour of need. You'll see."

"Pray you're right, miss. I'll not be holdin' my breath. Your President Wilson took his good, sweet time in the last war, didn't he? I don't see much difference now. But that's never mind. What these youngsters need is a dry billet and a crust of bread and tea. And that's up to you."

"But I have no contacts here." Claire felt the earth shift beneath her. How could she possibly be responsible for them?

Captain Beardsley sighed, sat down on a barrel, and pulled the cap from his head. He scratched his scalp, vexed or perplexed — Claire couldn't decide which. But the drawn lines of his face and darkened rings beneath his eyes told her he'd used his last reserves getting them across the Channel and keeping them fed and hidden.

"That's a quandary," the captain said at last.

"I've truly no idea where to take them. I mean, we're here illegally, aren't we? If we go to immigration or even the American embassy —"

"No, no, you can't be doin' that. We'd all hang for a good deed." He scratched his head again and waited, staring at his boots for inspiration. "I s'pose I can muster identity cards in time — make these young folk look as British on paper as King George himself. They'll need them to get ration books; there's no eating without. But I've got no place for the lot of you to go in the meantime, and it's no good stowin' you here. Somebody's bound to hear them sooner than later, and the Jerries'll bomb our port towns first once they let go. It'll be no safer here than —"

"*If* they let go. Nothing's certain —"

"Invasion, that's the fear. It'll happen. Could be any day now. Hitler's not satisfied with what's his. He thinks it's all his for the takin'. Anyhow, findin' billets ain't part of my packet. It's yours and that Arnaud fella." He grunted. "Suffer the French."

"Captain, I'm telling you, I don't know a soul here." Claire tried to stick to the point, though the idea of German invasion and what that would mean for her, for the children, for Arnaud, wherever he was, chilled her heart.

"You've been livin' in Paris, but you've

not one relative or friend this side of the Channel? Where were you plannin' to go once Uncle Adolf starts shootin' his firecrackers off the Eiffel Tower?"

A soft whimper came from behind her but Claire didn't turn. She'd no plan beyond escorting the children to Calais because she'd never expected to need one. Arnaud had always said it was safer that she not know other contacts. *What now? What can I do with these children? Where will they be safe?*

Circling her temples with her fingertips, willing the pain and mounting fear to go away, helped nothing. And then she remembered. There was one person, one distant family connection in England. Claire didn't know her and knew little of her. *Aunt Miranda — the one whose letters Mother refused, the one she always said I reminded her of . . . most definitely not a compliment. She lived somewhere in the north of England. Where? Somewhere in the Lake District.* Claire remembered the one envelope with English stamps she'd found when snooping among her grandmother's things after her passing — the one her mother had shredded the moment she realized it existed. *What was the address, the town? Does Aunt Miranda still live there? Might she take the children? Will she take them once she knows I'm behind the scheme? Does she hate Mother as Mother hates her? They've not spoken in years — does Aunt Miranda even know I exist?*

Claire closed her eyes. *What choice do I have?* "I once had an aunt in the Lake District. I've no idea if —"

"The Lake District! Why didn't you say so? Safest place in the Empire!" Captain Beardsley brightened. "Well, if Robert ain't your mother's brother!"

"Excuse me?"

"Bob's your uncle — that's what he means." Gaston popped up, as if he'd been part of the conversation all along, and wiped his sleeve across his running nose. "It's like 'Right you are,' or how they say in the films, 'Just the ticket.' " He tucked himself beneath Claire's elbow and thumped his chest. "Stick close to me, mademoiselle. I'll get you through. I know lots of English."

Claire sighed, exasperated and desperate at once. It was no use. She felt she'd fallen down a rabbit hole as deep as Alice's, and that the hopeful characters surrounding her grew just as fantastic.

In the early hours of the new morning, as the town clock struck three, Claire caught her breath when a key turned once more in the fishing shack's lock. Soundlessly, Captain Beardsley slipped through the door. "Grab your coats and we'll be on our way. Not a word. Not a sound."

With no other preliminaries, the captain lifted Aimee in his arms. On tiptoe the group followed him out the door and down the dock in total blackout, one hand on the person in front with Claire bringing up the rear.

A merciful fog shrouds our fearful band, Claire mused. *A close-knit stream on the heels of our Pied Piper leading us through the backstreets of Hamelin. Why is it that everything reminds me of scenes from children's books I've read? I hope this ends better than that story!* She bit her lip, drawing blood, from nerves stretched taut.

Captain Beardsley, a portly man nearly six feet tall with feet to match, padded softly through puddles and wound deftly round corners, cutting through back gardens. At last they slipped through a space in a low stone wall, where a garden gate must once have stood, less than five blocks from the sea. Before the captain reached the cottage threshold, a woman, squat and semi-stout, pulled open the door and beckoned them forward through the drab moonlight.

The captain pushed the group ahead of himself into a blackened foyer, setting his small burden on her feet at last. Once they were all in and the door closed and latched, the woman opened an inside door, nearly blinding them with light.

"Come in, come in and lay off your things." Mrs. Beardsley, her hair silver streaked and her smile welcoming, herded the troop toward the back of the house.

The cottage smelled to Claire of yeast and freshly baked bread, of soup and that surprise of hospitality that welcomes strangers. Mrs. Beardsley ushered the band into her modest but toasty kitchen, clucking over each face as if they were long-lost grandchildren.

"I'm sorry we've not enough chairs. Here you go, now, take this stool, and perhaps you boys can make yourselves comfortable on the floor with these." She handed Bertram two woolen steamer blankets. Gaston promptly wrapped himself in one and plopped, cross-legged, near the warm stove.

Mrs. Beardsley smiled, ruffled Gaston's unruly curls, then turned to ladle steaming soup into thick crockery. Jeanine passed the heated bowls among the children as Elise handed round a basket of sturdy rolls laced with butter. The kitchen fell silent, except for the steady slurp of soup, the clink of spoons, and deep sighs of satisfaction. Color returned to the cheeks of the ragamuffin crew sitting and standing round the kitchen table.

At last the faces staring back at Claire looked like the faces of children and not miniature wizened old men and women. Even little Aimee, shy as she was, gave a tentative, baby-toothed smile when Mrs. Beardsley pulled her onto her lap and crooned over her tangled golden hair.

"Not so much, not so lavish, Wife. We'll not be keepin' 'em. Neither you nor they must get attached." Captain Beardsley sounded gruff, but Claire marveled at the softness in him once inside his cheerfully lit home.

"What's this?" Mrs. Beardsley fingered the hem of Aimee's dress, resting on her lap. "Have you caught something in your hem, dearie?"

With pleading orbs and worried brow, Aimee pulled her dress from Mrs. Beardsley's fingers but didn't answer.

Mrs. Beardsley hesitated, then patted Aimee's knee. "Well, never mind. There's time for everything. We've beds for everyone, though they're only pallets and comforters on the attic floor," she happily quipped, changing the subject while ignoring her husband's warning. "You'll be wanting to get warmed through and fill your gills right here before you snuggle in, as there's no heat upstairs but the pipe goin' up from the stove."

"We're so grateful, Mrs. Beardsley. I can't tell you what it means that you've taken us in. Your soup is delicious." Claire meant every word. She'd no idea what the knuckle of veal and vegetables had cost the Beardsleys in rations, but knew it must have been dear and sacrificial. Even she and Josephine had been hoarding food for ages. Feeding a group like this would have been out of the question.

"We're not takin' you in, nor the blighters neither," the captain insisted. "It's just a waylay till I can get those papers. Then we'll get you up and on your way north."

"But as I told you — tried to tell you — Captain, I don't know if my aunt still lives there. I don't even know her address."

"You know her name, don't you, and the town where she lives?"

"Windermere, or thereabouts, I think, but —"

"Then you'd best be on your way and ask round."

"What if she's not there now? She could

have moved. For all I know she could have died."

"You'll figure it out, won't you?" he charged, and Claire knew there was no arguing.

"Not tonight," Mrs. Beardsley intervened. "It will be daylight soon and we all need some sleep. Things will look brighter in the morning."

How? Claire wondered.

"You'll keep the children quiet upstairs during the day, Miss . . ."

"Claire Stewart. Claire, please."

"Claire, then." She smiled. "You'll understand that we cannot be explaining the sudden appearance of five French children to our neighbors. I'll send some food up through the day and bring the children down one by one to use the water closet when nobody's likely to pop in, but you must all keep quiet."

"Yes, I understand. Have you heard from — ?"

"Not a word." Captain Beardsley shook his head, not meeting Claire's eyes.

"The news from Paris . . . ?" Claire knew better than to ask in front of the children, but she couldn't bear not knowing.

The Beardsleys exchanged worried glances. The captain rose and ushered everyone, no nonsense, toward the attic stairs. "There'll be time enough tomorrow. It will take a few days or more to get your papers. A wink or two of sleep is what's needed in the meantime."

Mrs. Beardsley led them up the stairs by torchlight, keeping the light to the floor. "I'll leave a torch for you here, but mind you keep the light covered with the muslin and aimed to the floorboards. My blackout curtains are from the last war, I'm sorry to say, and rather moth-eaten. I'd not expected to need them again." She sighed, pulling back an old sheet hung from a clothesline strung across the room. "Boys on this side and girls on this." She pointed, cheerful once more. "Tomorrow we can do a bit of washing. Fresh faces and clean clothes will make you all feel better."

Claire was glad Mrs. Beardsley took over, for she was too spent to think clearly. Yet, when Aimee hugged her dress to herself, Claire idly wondered what the child had hidden in her hem and how it was she'd not noticed before.

Mrs. Beardsley showed Claire to her pallet and whispered, "They're in the Ardennes and have just crossed the Meuse River — that's all we know."

"The Ardennes? But that's . . . too near."

"Not what we expected, not what our boys prepared for. It seems there's no stopping the ruffians, though God knows our men and the French will try. It's invasion we're most worried about now. After France, what's to stop them?" She squeezed Claire's arm and held out a blanket. "Be constant for the young ones. You're their teacher."

"I'm not," Claire whispered. "I'm not constant and I'm not their teacher. I'm not their anything. I was just —"

"That's not what they believe, and they need to believe in something." Gently as Mrs. Beardsley spoke, her eyes insisted. "The captain told me of your young man gone missing. Keep faith, dearie. These things take time and so often pop right in the end."

Claire took the blanket and tried to smile in return. But what Mrs. Beardsley had said wasn't true. Things didn't pop right in the end, not for her. Everyone Claire had ever loved or thought she loved, even those she'd believed loved her, had died or had abandoned or betrayed her in the end. Why should this time be different?

Chapter Three

Days turned to weeks while the cabin-fevered young folks crowded the Beardsleys' attic. They'd endured delays in obtaining the necessary forged papers, then listened for news with bated breath during the British evacuation of Dunkirk. They'd rejoiced with Mrs. Beardsley in the belated return of their dear, bedraggled, and war-weary captain and his shell-shocked HMS *Miss Bonny Blair.*

Once recovered, the captain declared they must go, no matter that they'd become nearly family to the Beardsleys; it was not safe to delay a moment longer.

Finally, Claire stood tall in her sturdy, polished shoes and well-brushed trench coat on the rail platform of London's Euston Station. Mid-June ran balmy, but wearing her coat felt a small armor against all she must face and freed her hands to harness Aimee, the smallest and most wide-eyed of the refugees.

Elise huddled close to her older sister, Jeanine. Bertram, at nearly thirteen, painted the picture of helpfulness and dependability. But eight-year-old Gaston, with all his cleverness and grins, worried Claire. *Can he resist drawing attention to himself? And if to himself, then to us all?*

Soldiers and evacuees swarmed the platform. Duffel bags were slung across soldiers' shoulders, and gas mask kits were slung across the chests of children, including her five French charges. Because she was not a French native, Claire had not been issued a gas mask in Paris. Though her adult version felt clunky bumping against her side, she was grateful for this British issue.

Chaos reigned in the general hubbub, in the shouts made by soldiers above the hiss and whistle of the train, in the fearful glances of children and the anxious goodbyes of parents.

The thrill for a great adventure with chums Claire glimpsed in some — mostly older children — contrasted sharply with the shyness and abject misery she saw in others. Fear and forced smiles marked the faces in Claire's own entourage as they clutched dangling pillowslips or small cases, holding little more than their nightclothes and Mrs. Beardsley's lunch offerings. They'd been able to bring so little across the Channel.

Dozens of English children wore the same painted smiles. Bright eyes looked as if tears might spill any moment. And small wonder, thought Claire. Students filed in crocodile lines behind their teachers to individual platforms and tracks, creating mazes of schoolchildren of all sizes and ages. All wore labels tagging them with names and numbers; each carried meager possessions in satchels or pillowslips.

It looked like Israel's mass exodus from Egypt centuries ago — at least that's what Captain Beardsley had said before giving Claire a hearty "Best of luck" and disappearing into the crowd.

Claire pushed back her worry, resisting the terror that twisted knots in her stomach. She grabbed Aimee's hand, just as the child stumbled and nearly fell, all but causing a pileup in her wake.

More sharp whistle blasts pierced the air. Steam surged and billowed from the train before them, engulfing feet, swallowing the children's knees. Elise squealed. Aimee shrieked, burying her five-year-old head in Claire's hip.

"Shh, shh, it's nothing to be frightened

of," Claire crooned. "Just the noise of the train, getting ready to take us for a long ride."

"I don't want to go on a long ride," Aimee wailed. "I want to go back to Madame Beardsley. I want to go home!"

"But we're not finished with our adventure," Claire resisted stoutly. "You don't want to leave until we've all taken our grand adventure, do you?"

"Grand adventure?" Elise asked. "That sounds like a story."

"It certainly should!" Claire stood on firmer ground. " 'Second to the right and straight on 'til morning!' Does that ring any bells?"

"Ring bells?" Bertram looked confused.

"Sound familiar." Gaston pushed forward, his chin firm now. "That's *Peter Pan.*"

"Precisely! And you remember the story . . . they flew to Neverland! All it took was a little fairy dust."

"Did they fly home in the end?" Aimee still looked as if she might cry.

"Yes, they did," Claire answered gently, hoping that would prove the ending of their adventures too.

"That's all right, then," Gaston affirmed. "We'll go adventuring with you, mademoiselle. You'll be our Wendy."

"But who will be our Peter Pan?" Elise asked, and all eyes turned toward Claire.

"I've no idea," Claire admitted. "I'm sure there will be one when we get to where we're going." She hoped that was true.

Captain Beardsley had said the journey should normally take less than a day. But with all the transport of troops, and with the tide of new evacuees — schoolchildren, old and handicapped people, pregnant women and mothers with young children — and with the stops and the sorting of children sure to come, all that had changed. He'd confided to Claire that they'd no hope of reaching Windermere station before sometime tomorrow at best, and advised her to ration fluids. "There'll likely be no facilities." Still, it would not do to tell the children that, not yet.

Claire shifted her bag and Aimee to her right side. Perhaps the little girl would calm down once they'd settled in their seats. How Captain Beardsley had secured seats for them in close proximity was beyond her ken. She hoped she'd sufficiently thanked him and Mrs. Beardsley for all they'd done. Life for weeks in the Beardsleys' attic with five homesick children had stressed Claire's resolve and nerves beyond reason, and yet kindly Mrs. Beardsley had maintained such cheerfulness while sharing her home and food. Claire had no idea how that good lady had mustered such a spirit.

Claire felt a small hand tug the belt dangling from her coat. "I need to visit the *toilette,*" whispered Elise, mostly in her best English.

Claire groaned inside, knowing that asking Elise to wait would not work.

Suddenly the doors of the train popped open, one by one, and lines of children led by teachers poured into every car, all semblance of order gone in a moment.

Aimee clutched Claire around the leg and Elise tugged her belt all the harder. Bertram hefted the pillowslips and cases for the smaller children. Jeanine grabbed Gaston's hand, much to his indignation. "Come, children," Claire insisted, leading them down the platform to their car, pulling the card with their seating assignment from her pocket.

Elise tugged again, this time more urgently, and said aloud, "I must go to —"

"Hush!" Jeanine all but slapped her sister, whispering something fierce into her ear.

"We'll find one just as soon as we're settled," Claire promised, sorry for the child's teary-eyed misery, and praying this train *had* facilities. *How can I herd them all at once, keep them together and with me every moment, visit the toilet with any child, and make certain they speak no French aloud?* Claire narrowed her eyes, trying to see the children as an immigration officer might see them.

The plan was for them all to pretend they were sleeping most of the time while on the train, or too irritable or miserable to talk. Even if grown-ups asked them questions, they were simply to feign a toothache or, if necessary, abject fear, and point toward Claire, as if she knew everything concerning them. *But will they remember?*

Once they found the correct railcar and climbed inside, Jeanine grabbed the card from Claire and walked ahead with Elise, searching the numbers beside compartment doors. Claire pushed Gaston and Bertram forward and, lagging behind, did her best to keep a grasp on Aimee's hand.

Jeanine stopped and waved the card high, throwing a victorious smile Claire's way and a condescending grin toward Gaston. Claire nodded, grateful for Jeanine's take-charge demeanor. But from the corner of her eye, she glimpsed Gaston shove his fist into his thrust-out hip, stick out his tongue, and fiercely mimic Jeanine's victory smile. Claire drew a deep breath and rolled her eyes.

After a full day of travel and hours of delays, Claire and the children boarded the last late-night train at Oxenholme Station. According to the train schedule, in normal times the trip to Windermere would take a few minutes, but these were not normal times.

Captain Beardsley, who had followed every lead she'd given him with very little information about her aunt, had assured her that getting from Windermere Station to Lady Langford's estate should be no problem. "The buses will be running, though there's no way to know how close they go or if on time. Folks are helping with the 'vacees' all over, and mostly glad to do it. You'll find a lift or walk it. It won't be so bad — you'll see. All of Britain's pulling together, a good example for all."

She'd known that last was a dig over America's refusal to lend a helping hand. After all she'd seen in Paris and the fear running rampant through London, she couldn't help but agree. Claire shook her head. She couldn't do anything about her delinquent countrymen, but she must find some way to return to Paris. The wireless at the Beardsleys' had reported that Germans had marched into Paris on the fourteenth of June. Already, two million Parisians had fled the capital. Swastikas hung from government buildings, including one atop the Arc de Triomphe. Now that the Germans had overrun the city, Claire's ability to move about more freely because of her American citizenship — a woman from a neutral country — could prove invaluable to the Resistance.

At least, that's what she'd tell her aunt. If all she'd heard of her aunt Miranda was true — if she really was a "rebel with a cause round every bend, like that Mrs. Roosevelt" — she'd surely understand. Claire would simply explain that Aunt Miranda and Uncle Gilbert's part in helping with the war effort was to take in these poor, dear children — children at terrible risk whose parents had not been able to get their whole families out of France.

Claire sank into her seat, exhausted. There had been a few close calls throughout the long day when passengers had lifted their heads, listening carefully to Elise's occasional slip into French or to Gaston's retorts to his older brother. But with so many children and troops crowding the aisles, the refugees were largely ignored, blending into the landscape of evacuees —

a small splotch on a great and messy painting.

Claire's eyelids felt weighted, as if someone had dropped large English pennies over them. Her head nodded once or twice before she gave up and it reached her chest. The aisle of the train vanished.

Arnaud, crossing a wide and unfamiliar landscape — something like a desolate moor — marched toward her. Planes emerged over the horizon, like bees from dark clouds. Claire couldn't tell whose planes they were for the longest time, until they tipped their wings, and swastikas glistened in the last light of the sun. Arnaud ran, his legs fiercely pumping. He glanced back, over his shoulder. His face turned forward again, drained of blood. Faster and faster he ran toward Claire's open arms.

She willed her legs to move, but they did not obey. Planes swooped, dove with a vengeance, somersaulting in midair — like an air show — then dove again, strafing the road before and behind Arnaud. He leaped, headlong, into a ditch by the road.

Claire's leaden feet moved at last, pounding the road toward him now. Her heavy eyes struggled to open wider, to see him better. She'd not seen him hit . . . but as she reached the body in the ditch, a bright-red stream spread across his back and into the black dirt.

"Arnaud! Arnaud!" she cried.

"Mademoiselle! Miss Stewart!" Jeanine shook her roughly awake. "You are dreaming," she hissed, pinching Claire's arm, "and shouting."

The woman across the aisle raised her head, glared at Claire, and narrowed her eyes at Jeanine. Claire smiled feebly and turned away, holding her head. The dream had seemed so real. *Thank You, God, it was only a dream.* And then she remembered that she wasn't altogether certain she believed in God. She only hoped, if He was real, that He believed in Arnaud and the work he was doing. . . .

Claire's temples throbbed. She touched the healing scar beneath her hair, the still ever-so-slightly swollen goose egg she'd received compliments of the lorry's tailgate weeks before.

Aimee shifted in her sleep, nestling her head beneath Claire's arm. Claire pulled the little girl's jacket tight around her and snuggled her close. The compartment had grown cold, but Aimee's head felt warm to Claire's cheek. Claire spread her palm across the little girl's forehead. Like fire. Aimee whimpered.

Claire's headache mushroomed. *What now?* Aimee should be home, with her mother. A mother would know how to treat a fever.

The lightbulbs of the compartment, painted blue for minimum light, gave Claire no clue of the time. She lifted the blackout blind hanging down the window. Not even a streak of dawn yet. The face in the dark glass staring back looked older than Claire's new identity papers claimed — more like forty-three years than twenty-three.

Hmm-hmm. The conductor cleared his throat disapprovingly. Sheepishly, Claire dropped the blind into place and shifted Aimee in her arms.

In that shifting, Claire felt a slight weight poking against her leg and moved again. There was something heavy — something narrow and solid — in the hem of Aimee's dress. Claire remembered Mrs. Beardsley's observation of Aimee's hem, the night they'd come to her home. Surely that good lady had investigated, but she hadn't mentioned a thing. "Aimee? What's this?" But the child was fast asleep.

Minutes later the conductor returned, droning, "Windermere. Five minutes to Windermere Station," as he made his way back through the cars.

"Nous sommes où?" Aimee's sleepy voice whimpered again. She stretched her thin

arms high to reach Claire's neck, then nestled back into her embrace.

"Windermere. The Lake District. *On est en Angleterre, ma petite,*" Claire whispered into the little girl's matted hair, hoping, nearly praying, that her aunt would let the children stay.

Two hours and wearier bones later, Claire and her entourage jostled up and down in the back of a white-bearded farmer's straw-laden wagon. Hard of hearing and with one poorly sighted eye, the grim-mouthed farmer, returning from an early morning delivery, seemed more curious than glad to help.

At first skeptical of the notion that children were being delivered to Lady Miranda Langford's Bluebell Wood, he clearly disapproved of Claire. "Another American. Still," he granted, "it's high time her ladyship took some in." He acknowledged the children as England's evacuees, "poor young tykes." Claire simply gave a stiff-lipped smile, offering no response, desperately hoping the children would not speak loud enough for him to hear their French accents. She also desperately hoped she'd not have to beg him for a ride back to the station, five waifs in tow.

Now that the children felt free to laugh and whisper among themselves in the back of the wagon, they alternately stood and tumbled backward into the straw — even the older ones — stretching their cramped limbs. Claire frowned and commanded the children to be seated and quiet. Her head pounded. The last thing they needed was to be ordered from the wagon in the middle of the unknown countryside. She had no idea how to find her aunt's home without the farmer's help.

Gaston seemed a little subdued, glassy-eyed and pink-cheeked, which made Claire wonder if he, too, might prove feverish. She bit her lip. They'd arrive with musty straw and dust in their hair and the stench of urine on the younger children's clothes, but Claire's arms ached and her head had grown so heavy she no longer cared as she knew she ought. She pulled straw from her coat, sure that the itching she felt meant that she, too, had sown straw down her blouse and up her skirt.

Claire urged the fretful Aimee to stretch out beside her and covered her as best she could. It was a relief for Claire to give her brain and heartbeat over to the rhythm of the horse's clomping hoofbeats, to lean her head against the wagon's side, free to drink in the vista as the dark gave way.

Misty dawn crept over the gorse-strewn fells, sweeping a brilliant green and golden landscape — so bright it almost hurt her eyes. The landscape that had, she'd heard and read, inspired poets and painters for centuries. Home of Wordsworth and inspiration of Coleridge.

Claire breathed deeply, wishing it were a different time, a different sort of visit, so she might soak in some of that literary air. She knew the Lake District was renowned for its dramatic skies and pristine lakes, for its high and artful peaks, but she'd not come mentally prepared for one glimpse to steal her breath or mark her soul in this way. She swallowed, her throat painful. *Such beauty . . . unparalleled beauty. No wonder writers and painters spend all they earn to come here and stay as long as they can.*

It wasn't her live-on-the-edge-and-in-the-moment world of Paris or the crowded, musty, provocative, avant-garde draw of Shakespeare and Company. She couldn't imagine James Joyce penning *Ulysses* in such an open environment or that she, here, could write the same as she might in Paris.

But does that mean I wouldn't write in the same voice, or the same stories? Do location and environment bear on the release of imagination or the form it takes . . . the summoning of the muse? Or is that like saying the muse can only visit us in certain times, in certain places, in certain ways?

Claire shifted until she leaned her head against the wagon's seat back and wondered. She loved pondering the philosophical side of writerly questions. Writing, she believed, was her real life, her ultimate destiny. That writing — and all of her life — was destined for Paris, of that she was certain.

She saw Arnaud and herself engaged in saving children in daring, romantic adventures, a noble cause. There would come a time in the very near future when all this would prove grist for her writing mill as well, as the adventures of the Great War had done for a young Hemingway. Just now, however, she'd trade her dreams for the reality of Arnaud beside her.

A long while later, when the farmer pulled back the reins and brought his sturdy draft horse to a halt by the side of the road, Claire felt anything but steady. It was a moment before she realized the farmer was speaking to her.

"The government's taken all those fine cast-iron gates and posts — even the signs for most of the great estates. Shame, really."

And then he seemed to think better of what he'd said. "Mind you, it's the patriotic thing to do — necessary, don't you know."

Claire couldn't imagine why the government would want gates and fences.

"Melting them down for the war effort — munitions and the like, so they say," the man continued. "Make no mistake, miss. Sign or no sign, gate or no gate, this is the place: Bluebell Wood, just down that lane and round the bend."

Claire couldn't make herself move.

"You want I should drive you up to the house?"

"No, no, thank you. We'll walk. It can't be far. It will do us good to stretch our legs." She forced a smile she didn't feel.

The farmer nodded in agreement. "Keep to the path, then, and mind you hurry along. Rain's hoverin'."

Claire stood at the edge of the winding, narrow road and looked down at her five disheveled and dirty charges, at least one of them sick. She felt as uncertain and insecure as they looked. The reassurance they craved, Claire felt totally inadequate to give.

But this was the lane, the drive to her aunt's home, and there was no going back now.

Claire swallowed, pasted on a smile, and

nodded to Bertram to lift the pillowslips and cases from the wagon. She hefted Aimee — who'd cried she was too tired to walk, and who grew heavier with each step — into her arms and marched forward. Gaston walked close as a noonday shadow by her side, content for once to be quiet. Jeanine and Elise silently pulled up the rear.

The graveled drive wound through stately oaks on either side, each looking more than a hundred years old. Evergreen carpets spread the up-hill, down-dale forest floor on either side of the drive, ornamented by towering gray-green canopies beyond. Low stone walls cemented with moss and the occasional creeping fern kept wanderers to the drive. *Yet who,* Claire wondered, *would wander off this lovely path? It's L. Frank Baum's yellow brick road from* The Wonderful Wizard of Oz — *I'd never leave this lane before seeing where it leads!*

Worn though she was, Claire began to hope she might like her aunt very much. *Anyone who keeps such wild beauty barely, cleverly tamed — just enough to delight the eye and lift the soul — must be an interesting person. Even the name, Bluebell Wood, rings mysterious and beautiful. And Mother said her sister fancied herself a poet in her youth. Oh, Aunt Miranda — please, please prove a kindred spirit.*

They'd nearly come to the end of the wood when the drive turned sharply into a wide arc encircling more of the estate. Claire and the children gasped, halting mid-step. Paths, covered in graceful, flowering arches of early-summer pink and cream roses and thick, fragrant, weeping wisteria vines, broke the wide, overgrown lawn. Thick crops of yellow and blue iris provided bright contrast. Scattered, irregular ponds unfolded, strategically placed and dotted in cream and mauve water lilies, bordered by grasses creeping well beyond their bounds. A gangly yew maze edged one side of the gardens. Gigantic animal-shaped boxwood topiaries grown nearly beyond their definitions created something between a circus and a safari on the other. A stallion rearing on hind legs took center stage. Trees and grounds and shrubbery, all somewhat overgrown, perfectly framed a towering gray-stone mansion, complete with turrets and spires.

"It's like a fairy-tale castle," Jeanine whispered.

"It *is* a castle," Gaston corrected.

Bertram turned, his eyes brimming with questions and trepidation. "Mademoiselle?"

But Claire's throat had swollen and gone

dry in the moment. She'd expected a big house — an estate, after all — but not this. Nothing she'd seen on their drive through the Lake District — not even the extravagant distant house their driver had pointed out as Wray Castle — had prepared her imagination for such a place.

She turned, as if to summon the farmer. No wonder he'd not seemed eager to drive them to the house itself. No wonder his curious fascination with the notion of six ragamuffin souls deposited on this regal doorstep. *What have I done?*

Claire could not imagine the owner of such magnificence understanding her plight, let alone that of five homeless French children. *But there is whimsy here, too. What does that mean? Where will I take them when she refuses? Where can we go?*

As if nothing in life could be less certain, the sun, which had dappled feeble rays through heavy leaves along the winding drive, withdrew altogether. Clouds gathered in typical English fashion, darkened, took a deep breath, and spat their wind and rain upon the refugees.

Claire knew nothing about childhood illnesses but was certain that allowing Aimee and possibly Gaston, already feverish, to get wet and chilled would do them no good.

"Run!" she cried, stumbling forward with her load, trusting the others to follow.

The main house lay still another quarter of a mile away. Wind whipped their skirts and trousers, whistling between arches and round trees into the open space, blustering and shoving them forward. Claire heard Elise cry out as she tripped and fell but knew that Jeanine would help her younger sister. Bertram struggled with the cases, dropping one and picking it up, then dropping another before gathering speed. Poor Gaston stumbled, keeping as close to Claire's side as before. She felt the heat rise off his body. *Two sick children! Forgive me, Aunt, but take us in!*

By the time they reached the porte cochere, all six shivered, soaked to the skin, in the dropping temperature. Thunder boomed in the distance and rumbled down the fells, the rain a torrent.

"Jeanine," Claire ordered, squaring her shoulders as best she could with Aimee weighing down her arms, "please knock."

Jeanine lifted the heavy brass ring from the lion's head and let it fall once, twice. But the knock came rather timid. The wind picked up, so Claire urged, "Again, please."

Gaston huddled closer and Elise nestled into her sister's skirt, her thumb slipping into her mouth.

Jeanine knocked again. No one came. Minutes passed. Rain poured.

Claire set Aimee on her feet and stepped forward. The sniffling child clung to Claire's sodden skirt. Just as Claire raised the heavy brass ring and brought it down in a mighty blow, the door fell open and she shot forward, sprawling through the doorway onto the parquet floor. Aimee, clinging to Claire's skirt, flew behind, sliding in the slick track they created.

"What on earth!" A tall, auburn-haired woman in a long, peacock-blue silk dressing gown stepped back from the door.

The gray-haired woman running in her wake squealed, "Sakes alive! You're bringing a monsoon with you! Close the door! Beg pardon, my lady, I was downstairs and didn't hear the door."

"I'm sorry," Claire gasped. "I'm so sorry!" She groped to push herself up, but Aimee cried and clung all the harder, pulling her again to the floor.

Bertram dropped the bags inside the door and dragged Aimee off of Claire, shoving her back toward Gaston, who, wide-eyed and miserable, opened his arms to the smaller child. Jeanine leaned her weight into the door until it closed, Elise whimpering and hiccupping all the while. Painfully, Claire pushed herself up from the floor.

The woman in the blue dressing gown and the gray-haired woman both reached down to help Claire to her feet. Up Claire came, until she stood looking into the face she'd seen in the blackened train window less than three hours before — an older version of herself, but this one regal and lovely.

The women gasped in unison as Claire's mirror image dropped her arm, unsteadying them both.

Claire knew the woman caught the resemblance too — had recognized some echo of herself in another decade. She swallowed. *It's now or never. Be brave.* "Aunt Miranda . . . Lady Langford, I'm Claire Stewart, your niece from America . . . from New Jersey."

The woman gasped again, drawing her hand to her throat. Claire saw immediate confusion and disbelief flash through her blue-green eyes. Then a gradual recognition and a cautious joy. "Claire? Mildred's daughter?"

"Yes," Claire breathed, relieved that her mother's name hadn't brought a scowl.

But Aunt Miranda's sudden warmth stopped cold, replaced by a widening in her eyes. "What's happened? Is Mildred all right? Is she — ?"

"Mother's fine — as far as I know." But Claire didn't know. She hadn't seen or heard from her mother in the ten months since she'd moved to Paris. But then, she hadn't written her mother either. "I should have telephoned or written before coming here, but I didn't know how to reach you — if you were even still living here."

Aimee reached up, whimpering, for Claire's arms. Claire stooped down and hoisted the child to her hip.

Aunt Miranda seemed about to ask Claire something more but looked around, taking in the motley group dripping puddles on her parquet floor. "These are your children? All these?"

Jeanine giggled, out of nervousness or perhaps because the idea seemed so impossible.

Flustered, Claire couldn't catch her composure. "I'm not married."

The gray-haired woman, already pulling a rug toward the dripping entourage, grunted in disapproval.

"Mrs. Newsome, please," Aunt Miranda admonished.

"I mean, they're not mine." Claire flushed. "But they need help, and a home. Their parents —" She stopped, realizing she couldn't adequately explain in front of the children, couldn't say that their parents had sent them away for fear of the coming wrath of Hitler's army simply because they were Jewish.

"English evacuees, my lady!" Mrs. Newsome exclaimed. "I told you they'd not let us off. One to a room, they're saying, counting kitchen and bath. We're lucky not to have been fined already."

"You brought these children to my home as evacuees?" Her aunt pulled back.

"Well — refugees. There's more I must explain."

"More?" Aunt Miranda seemed to grow taller.

Claire felt the ground she'd imagined gaining slip away. "Please . . . may we come in? We've traveled for two days. If the children could just dry off and have something to eat, I can explain."

Mrs. Newsome looked to her lady for instructions, but Claire saw pity fleck the woman's eyes. "They might dry by the kitchen stove, my lady, and Mrs. Creedle could find them a bite to eat, I daresay . . . with your permission, of course."

Aunt Miranda seemed flustered. It wasn't the children she looked to, but Claire, and Claire didn't know how to make herself more pitiable, or more appealing. So she simply cuddled Aimee closer and resorted to her American habit of clasping her hands in praying position, then silently mouthed, *"Please."*

Aunt Miranda lifted her chin, just slightly, drew in a breath she seemed to hold, and moistened her lips. Another moment passed before she pronounced, "Mrs. Newsome is my housekeeper. You will follow her every instruction. Hot baths and breakfast — for everyone."

"Yes, my lady. I'll see to it at once." Mrs. Newsome, clearly gratified by her acknowledged authority, pulled one of the cases from Bertram and motioned for the children to follow.

But Aimee clung to Claire. Claire pushed the little girl gently but firmly away. "Go with Mrs. Newsome, Aimee. She'll get you something to eat."

Aimee buried her head into Claire's skirt. "You come too, mademoiselle."

"Aimee, please!" Claire felt her patience growing thin. Now that someone else could help, she felt near to fainting, incapable of carrying the burden alone.

Mrs. Newsome drew the child away. "Come, now. Such a fuss — why, this child's burning up with fever!" She cast an accusing glance Claire's way. "And there's a rash —"

"I don't know what's the matter. It's just come on while we traveled." Claire felt her own head throbbing, her forehead burning.

Mrs. Newsome clucked her tongue. "I'd best send for Dr. MacDonald, my lady. No telling what they've brought with them."

"You take the children, Mrs. Newsome. I'll telephone him."

"Yes, my lady." Mrs. Newsome hesitated. "I must say, my lady, that dressing gown with its color becomes you."

Miranda Langford blushed, as if the compliment pricked. "You may go, Mrs. Newsome."

"Thank you," Claire said sincerely. She swallowed painfully, ready to follow the housekeeper.

But Aunt Miranda stopped her. "Claire, after you've had an opportunity to refresh yourself, I'll see you in the library. Shall we say at nine?"

"Yes, ma'am. Thank you," Claire breathed. Uncertain she'd said it aloud, Claire said again, "Thank you, Aunt."

But Aunt Miranda had already turned and, head lifted, marched halfway to the grand staircase at the far end of the hall.

Unsettled, Claire shivered. *She's like*

Mother in some ways — that feigned sense of self-importance. Aunt Miranda walks as if she's got a rod up her back and a book on her head. Claire remembered months of training under her mother's strict eye doing precisely that. She bit her lip, no longer certain her aunt would prove a kindred spirit after all.

Chapter Four

Miranda Langford's fingers trembled as she dialed for the doctor from the phone in the library.

The operator responded in her clipped Lakeland accent, "What number, please?"

But Miranda, confused as to exactly what she would say if the doctor answered, hung up. *Mildred's daughter is in my home. . . . Mildred's daughter . . . Claire.* Repeating the information embedded it in her brain, though she would not allow it to penetrate her heart. She didn't dare. *Does Mildred know? Did she send Claire here? Why? You returned my letters, Sister, and yet you send your daughter to my doorstep with five ragamuffin children?*

It made no sense. Nothing her sister ever did made much sense to Miranda. And yet she knew that was too easy a dismissal. She'd not written Mildred in more than twenty years and had never placed a transatlantic telephone call. After five years of posting letters with no response from her sister, she'd given up hope — and every desire — of reconnecting. *You chose to live without me, so I lived without you.*

She sat heavily in the library's wingback chair nearest the fireplace and kneaded the cuff of her black sleeve. *First Gilbert, then Christopher. Wasn't that enough, Lord? Now what does this mean?* After some minutes she picked up the receiver on the desk once more.

Miranda could not say she was sorry for a need to telephone the distinguished Dr. Raibeart MacDonald, even if it was, first and foremost, to examine children who'd nearly fallen from the sky. He'd been her friend, her only confidant besides the occasional sharing with Mrs. Newsome, for more years than she wished to confess. If there was someone who could help steady her, who would understand what another life upheaval meant to her, it was Raibeart.

Miranda wouldn't admit she was flattered when he dropped everything, saying he'd be there within the hour. She knew the good doctor would use his coveted ration of petrol to race to Bluebell Wood. She reasoned that the least she could do was offer him tea in the library by a warm fire this unseasonably cold and wet morning after treating the little girl and examining the older children. What about that younger boy? He looked so lost . . . or perhaps feverish as well. Miranda rubbed her hands across her eyes and forehead. She wasn't up to nursing little boys.

She stood, forcing back nervous tears, and rearranged the tea tray that needed no rearranging. She sat down again. At last the clock in the hallway chimed nine. As if on cue, a timid knock came at the door, a turning of the knob, and Claire peeked round.

"It's nine o'clock, Aunt Miranda. May I come in?"

"Yes, of course, Claire. Come in." Saying the girl's name did not come naturally to Miranda — it felt surreal, like a dream. Miranda had not felt so out of place in her own home in years. Her niece looked cleaner, neater, but her face flared red as beetroot. And yet the resemblance was unmistakable — not to Mildred, as she would have rightly supposed, but to herself. Claire Stewart could have passed for Miranda's own daughter, if she'd had one — flaming red hair that might one day tend to auburn, green eyes that seemed to change in shading and depth with color resting near her cheek. Slender, she stood tall and strong.

"Thank you for the bath and breakfast. We're all so much better for it," Claire offered, smiling tenuously. The girl looked unsteady on her feet.

"Please sit down." Miranda indicated the chair opposite and did her best to smile, unable to take her eyes from her niece's face. *What made you choose me for help?*

"I know I've some explaining to do. Children were not what you were expecting this morning, I realize."

Miranda nearly laughed at Claire's presentation. "No — nor was I expecting you, though that would have been surprise enough."

"Yes. . . . Where to begin?" The corners of Claire's mouth lifted slightly, but the crease in her forehead told Miranda the girl was at a loss.

"Perhaps the beginning. How is it that you're here? And are you here alone? Is Mildred — is my sister with you? Nearby, in England?" Miranda tried to keep the hope and the dread from her voice.

"No. No, Mother's not here. She's in America."

"Your father came with you, then?"

"No — he's not in the picture." Claire visibly swallowed. "I mean, he left Mother and me — soon after I was born."

"Of course, the war. Mother wrote as much. But I didn't realize he'd . . ." Miranda understood the cruelties of the Great War too well. "I'm so very sorry."

Claire hesitated and seemed about to say more, but bit her lip.

Miranda tipped her head. She'd steeled herself to protect her own heart, but the girl looked so pitiable.

Claire heaved a sigh and plunged ahead. "It's tempting to let you think that, that my father died in the war. But that's not what happened. He went off to war, yes, and —" She seemed to reconsider, and stopped. "I'm not the one who should be telling you this. It's for Mother to say."

"You don't have to tell me anything that you don't want to about your parents, Claire. But you must realize that your mother and I haven't spoken in — in a long time."

"Mother told me you and she were estranged. She never told me why, exactly . . ."

Miranda breathed deeply, trying to shut out the pain her sister had caused her over the years, even if it was an estrangement that she'd initiated. But the past couldn't be redeemed, and after all this time . . . It was just like Mildred, to cast blame without ever explaining the separation to her daughter. The only reason Miranda knew Mildred had borne a child was because their mother had written before her death about Claire's birth. "I'm surprised she told you about me at all."

"She didn't . . . not much. Well, not exactly." Claire's red face blushed deeper still. "I read her diary once —"

Miranda felt her eyebrows rise. She'd only just met Claire and the girl astonished her at every turn.

"When I was eleven . . . You know what eleven-year-old girls are like . . . I hope."

Reaching to pour the tea, Miranda held in check a smile born of memory. "I have a vague recollection."

Claire leaned forward. "I only know that you and Mother loved the same man. Uncle Gilbert must be a fine man for you both to have loved him so."

Miranda hadn't expected such directness, let alone an inkling of understanding. Perhaps she'd lived in England too long, acquiring a pronounced lack of obvious curiosity as a social nicety, or grown old too soon. Anyway, shouldn't she be on the offensive with this niece who'd shown up on her doorstep unannounced? But she could not deny the opportunity she'd longed for to mend a long-open wound. *That will never happen with Mildred . . . but what of her daughter? Perhaps . . .* "The finest. He was the best and the bravest." Even now, all these years later, pride filled her voice and nearly burst her heart.

Claire's eyes widened. Miranda realized too late that Gilbert's death would be news to Claire — would have been news to Mildred, in fact.

"I'm so sorry," Claire began. "Uncle Gilbert is . . . not here?"

Miranda pitied her niece. Why she'd come with all those children hardly mattered in comparison with the fact that she'd come. Miranda should do all she could to reach across the room's divide, for she'd certainly failed to reach her sister across the Atlantic. "Gilbert was killed at the Battle of the Somme."

"The Somme? But that was —" Claire gasped, frowning.

"1916."

"Over twenty years ago!"

Miranda nodded. "The Great War. A lifetime."

"Mother doesn't know; I'm certain."

"No, she wouldn't. Mother — your grandmother — had passed by then. The same year, only months before." Miranda would not say that her sister had returned every letter, unopened and marked *Refused.* The only way she'd learned of their mother's death was through the receipt of a small inheritance, handled by the family attorney. Her mother's death had been a devastating and bitter pill — the severing of her last link to home and family, followed shortly by Gilbert's death. *If it hadn't been for Christopher, I would not have wanted to . . . But I mustn't think of that now.*

"I'm so sorry." Claire looked as if she genuinely meant it, but also looked confused. "You must have been married such a short time."

Miranda didn't ask if Claire wanted sugar. She squandered two lumps in her niece's tea and added warmed cream to the cup. "We were married six months before he enlisted. . . . That was our lifetime — my lifetime."

"And all these years, you and Mother . . . Wasted."

Miranda swallowed and looked away. Not even her Christopher had been so direct. "Your mother married, must have found love." It was what she had hoped for her sister, despite the pain of their estrangement, despite the pain of her own widowhood.

Claire sipped her tea before answering. "Mother married, but I don't know that it was for love. I mean, she married because — I think, because — she was lonely . . . and perhaps angry. Mother said my father was a social climber — something Mother craved. If he loved her, he didn't love her long." Claire took another timid sip of the sweet, hot brew and winced as it burned her throat.

"That's a harsh judgment against your own father."

Claire set the cup down and stared into its bottom. Half a minute passed before she looked up. "My father went to war a few months after I was born. Mother thought he was killed, you see — in Belleau Wood. But he wasn't — he just let her think that. He worked it so the Army even thought he'd fallen. He stayed in France, pretending he had no family."

"He deserted? But you — your mother . . . how did you manage?" Miranda thought of all she could have done to ease her sister's plight, if only she'd known, if only Mildred had allowed her.

"Mother learned he was alive through some photo a friend of theirs had — a photo taken after Belleau Wood — and found a way to make him pay. And of course, the Army paid his death benefits to her as his widow."

Miranda could not believe that of Mildred, that she would knowingly take death benefits if her husband had not died. But what did she know of her sister, really?

"He sent money over the years. I'm not sure if that was penance or if Mother blackmailed him. But he wanted nothing to do with us. . . . He has a different family now — had a different family then. A wife and children in France. He never returned to America." Claire looked as if her confession cut her heart.

"I'm sorry." Miranda tried not to look shocked, but she didn't know what to say. "I'd hoped happiness for Mildred, and for you. I was so glad when Mother wrote of your birth. She loved you, loved being a grandmother."

Claire did not answer. She looked uncomfortable with the notion. Moments passed with only the ticking of the pendulum on the mantel's clock before Miranda realized her niece was staring.

"You still mourn him. Uncle Gilbert, I mean."

Miranda stiffened. *My mourning garments.*

"I miss my husband, yes. But to say I mourn him . . . I gradually learned to live again, for the sake of our son."

Claire straightened in her chair. "You have a son? I have a cousin? Mother never told me. I suppose she never knew!"

The lead in Miranda's heart settled all the heavier. *Must I tell the story again . . . explain how England and war once again stole my dearest and best?* "Christopher enlisted, you see — before there was any conscript —"

Before she could finish, the library door shook with a pounding that could only be Raibeart MacDonald. "Are you in, Maggie?"

"Come, Raibeart. Please, come in!" Miranda was relieved for his intrusion. "It's good of you to come on such short notice."

Dr. Raibeart MacDonald's eyebrows climbed dangerously close to his full crop of silver hair. His normal, charming smile turned to a grunt as long strides carried him across the room. He deposited his black bag on the library table. "Thank me now. I've seen the wee bairns. You'll not be thanking me for my diagnosis."

"It's just a little fever, isn't it?" Claire interrupted. "They'll be all right?"

Miranda rose to the occasion. "Dr. Mac-

Donald, this is my niece — from America — Claire Stewart. Claire, this is Dr. MacDonald, our village doctor and an old and dear friend."

"Ach, naw! Another American invading our bonny shores." The doctor grinned, taking Claire's hand. But he turned it over, inspected it, and peered at her flushed face, which made Claire's color deepen. "And by the look of it, another victim."

"Victim?" Miranda stopped short while pouring the doctor's tea.

"Chicken pox," the doctor pronounced, dropping Claire's hand.

"Chicken pox!" Miranda exclaimed, nearly dropping the teapot. "You can't be serious!"

"As serious as the day is long. I have to know, Maggie Langford: did you contract chicken pox as a child?"

"Yes, of course. At least, I assume I did."

"I didn't," Claire all but whimpered.

"Well, I'd say that's taken care of now, Miss Stewart. You've got the beginnings of the rash to prove it, and I'd wager a fever and a splitting head, as do the two youngest of the children, and a third one coming down."

"This is impossible," Miranda sputtered.

"Regardless, ladies, Bluebell Wood is quarantined."

"*Quarantined?* That means they cannot leave."

"Quite so," the doctor quipped.

"But they can't stay here — they can't all stay here!"

"They must. You know that as well as I. One child could infect the entire village. I'll not have it."

"For how long?" Claire's red face paled.

The doctor took his steaming cup from Miranda and paused to consider, before taking a first sip. "Since the rash has already shown itself, I'd say twenty-eight days, thirty-two or -three to be on the safe side."

"A month!" Miranda gasped.

"I can't stay a month," Claire whined. "I must get back to France — as soon as possible."

"France, is it?" the doctor asked. "And what did you propose to do with all these young ones? I venture a guess: I don't suppose Hitler's war zone is the safest place for a passel of Jewish youngsters?"

"No, it's not." Claire rattled her cup in its saucer. "Aunt Miranda, that's what I need to talk with you about."

Miranda felt her carefully ordered room spinning. "Jewish children?"

"Dr. MacDonald is right." Claire pushed

her cup and saucer aside and leaned forward. "Things are bad for the Jews of France now. Some emigrated to other countries months ago — those who could. But many, many more have no resources or connections or sponsors, so . . ."

"So you've brought children from France without any idea —"

"A friend — a dear friend — was supposed to meet us, to line them up with a contact and homes, but . . . something happened."

"What, precisely?" the doctor asked.

"I don't know." Claire spread her hands. "He was supposed to meet us in Calais and there was to be someone in England to take them . . . but . . ." She shrugged helplessly.

"He deserted you and the children?" Miranda wondered if mother and daughter had both chosen poorly.

"No — he would never! But neither he — Arnaud, his name is Arnaud — nor our contact appeared, and it was the fisherman's last run across the Channel. He wouldn't take them without me and I couldn't let them go alone, and besides I'd hit my head . . . But if I hadn't gone with them, they wouldn't have gotten out."

"Are you telling me those children are here illegally?" Miranda couldn't grasp it.

The doctor chortled. "I'd say you've met your match, Maggie. It appears the apple does not fall far from the tree."

"This is not funny, Raibeart. I cannot take in illegals and I cannot take in children. You know that."

The doctor drained his cup, smacked his lips, and set the cup and saucer on Miranda's tea tray. "On the contrary, Lady Langford, you've done just that by opening your door. And for the next month — at least, and if no more in your household come down with it — they'll stay right here. See to their care, and I'll see to their health on my rounds in a day or two. Telephone me if there are complications beyond your ken." He grabbed his black bag and headed for the door.

At the last moment he turned and addressed Claire. "And you, young lady, to bed with you. All the visiting in the world can happen once that fever's down. You should be a fair sight tomorrow with your bright-red spots. Welcome to Windermere."

"Raibeart!" Miranda called, following him through the door into the grand foyer. "Raibeart, I can't have children here. You know how I —"

But the doctor did not stop until he reached the great front door. He set his bag down and turned toward Miranda, taking her face in both his warm hands. "I do know how you feel, Maggie. I've always known. But there's nothing you can do about this, no way I can allow chicken pox to run through the village or a train."

Miranda's heart beat so hard it nearly burst from her chest, raising a sob from her stomach to her throat. "But Christopher —"

"Christopher, above all, would have wanted you to help those hurt by that demon Hitler. Our country's at war now — your own adopted country and mine. This, for this time, is our opportunity to help." He pressed her face with his hands.

Miranda closed her eyes. If she hadn't, she feared he might kiss her or that she might want him to kiss her. But she wasn't ready for that. She'd never be ready for that.

Chapter Five

Mrs. Newsome's grip on Gaston's ear was formidable. Dragging him from the pantry and out of Mrs. Creedle's kitchen amid that good lady's howls and Gaston's French babblings had been no small feat. *The poxed little wretch must have gained five pounds in the last hour.*

Mrs. Newsome had suffered all she could stand at the hands of the small trickster for the past two weeks. She'd worked hard to give Lady Miranda little cause for concern, and Miss Claire the peace and necessary time to heal, but enough was enough. Sick or nearly well, Gaston was more than one body could keep an eye upon.

Gaston tripped and stumbled up the crooked kitchen stairs leading to the main floor, all the while begging for mercy in mixed English and French, but Mrs. Newsome was not in the mood for mercy. "Up and come along, you disrespectful urchin!

Chicken pox suppresses the appetite; that's what the good doctor said — a fact no one seems to have informed your stomach of, now have they, little man?"

Marching him up the wide, crimson-carpeted mahogany staircase to the second floor was easier. Gaston became more subdued as he scrambled up the stairs — likely hoping to keep his ear attached. Mrs. Newsome gathered speed and momentum along with some great satisfaction in her plan to throw the child into Miss Stewart's arms, if not on her mercy.

She rapped crisply on Claire's door.

A weak voice answered, "Yes?"

Mrs. Newsome turned the knob and stomped in, keeping a sure grip on Gaston's ear and knocking over a tottering stack of books beside Claire's chair — novels liberally borrowed from Lady Miranda's library, as Mrs. Newsome knew full well.

"What — what's wrong?" Claire dropped the book in her hands and paled, despite the red splotches still covering her face.

"What's wrong? What's wrong?" Mrs. Newsome felt as if her gramophone needle stuck. "Everything's wrong. This child has utterly destroyed — and eaten — Mrs. Creedle's lovely treacle pudding — a pudding made for dinner today, for the doctor himself, who's coming to examine you all. And the greedy little — little —" She gasped, completely lost for words. "Well, he's eaten himself silly and surely sick! If this selfish little demon spends the night regurgitating his sins, it's you, Miss Claire, that will be cleaning up after him. Not I! I've had my fill."

"I'm so sorry, Mrs. Newsome. I'm sure Gaston regrets — is terribly sorry for —"

"Sorry? *Sorry?* Is he sorry for pulling the feathers from Mr. Dunnagan's best laying hens and frightening them into infertility? Is he sorry for stripping the beds in the servants' quarters and tying their sheets into a rope to climb down from the west tower? I tell you I cannot keep up with this one, let alone play nursemaid to the others."

"I'll speak with Aunt, Mrs. Newsome. Maybe she can arrange for a governess or something."

"A governess?" Mrs. Newsome thought she'd blow a gasket. "It's you that needs to govern these hooligans, Miss Stewart. You brought them here and they're your responsibility!"

"I can understand why you'd see it that way, Mrs. Newsome, but my job was to get them on a boat out of France. I can't actually keep them." Claire's chin wrinkled.

"There are so many more children who need help. I must return to Paris as soon as possible."

Mrs. Newsome stood speechless but did not loosen her grip on Gaston's ear. It took a good fifteen seconds for her to comprehend the audacity of the young woman before her. "Do you mean to tell me you intend to leave them here — all of them?"

"Well, yes, that's my hope . . . my expectation. They are, after all, victims of the war. Children are being evacuated to large estates all over Britain, I understand. You had none here. Now you do."

"English children is what we're to take! Has her ladyship agreed to this?" If she had, well, Mrs. Newsome and her ladyship needed to have a good heart-to-heart. It wasn't like Lady Miranda to go over her head. She'd been conscientious about that in the past, a fact Mrs. Newsome had greatly appreciated.

Claire stood from her wingback chair, albeit shakily. The girl really did not look well to Mrs. Newsome. Perhaps she should take pity and leave Gaston's outrageous behavior for another time — for surely there would be other shenanigans on the child's part. But this impertinence, this idea that five French hooligans might remain at

Bluebell Wood unsupervised and indefinitely was more than she could tolerate. *Best to catch the cat before it's out of the bag.*

"I haven't actually spoken with Aunt Miranda about it." Claire was clearly confessing. "I haven't seen her much — at all, really, since that first day Dr. MacDonald came. I think she might be afraid of catching my chicken pox. She didn't seem to remember if she'd had them as a child."

No, she wouldn't want to be talking to you, now would she? You look enough like young Christopher to be his twin or his female form awakened from the dead. You've probably scared her out of her wits, poor thing. Perhaps it's best if you do go, young miss, but I wager she won't want you leaving this lot behind.

Mrs. Newsome sighed. *But it is war. It's true, there are children being housed all over Britain. How can we not billet them here — an estate of this size? But English children. We should take in English children!*

Mrs. Newsome released Gaston's ear. The boy made a dive to hide behind Claire's chair. Perhaps it would be best if she talked with her ladyship first, before Claire saw her. That way they could come to some understanding.

"I honestly don't know what to do, Mrs. Newsome. I never intended to intrude or force this quarantine on Aunt Miranda — on anyone here. But our contact never came through, and as far as I know, my friend Arnaud is the only one who knew where or with whom they were to go."

How can the vixen look so pitiable? Don't let her pull at your heartstrings, Florence Newsome. She's as winsome as Christopher ever was, and you know how he played you like a Stradivarius, Lord love him.

"Then can't you ask him, this Arnaud fella? Where in all that's holy is he?"

Tears pooled in the girl's eyes. "I don't know. He didn't make it to our meeting point in Calais. And then, on the way to the docks, I got this terrible bump on my head, and the next thing I knew I was in a boat — with the children — on my way across the Channel. I was never meant to come!" Claire burst into tears, covering her face with her hands so that Mrs. Newsome could barely hear the rest. "Aunt Miranda was the only name I knew in England. I didn't know where else to go. I'm afraid Arnaud is — is —"

Gaston crept from behind her and wrapped his arms around Claire.

Mrs. Newsome shook her head. She never could resist a good love story or turn her back on a tragic turn of events. She, too, against all her best judgment, crossed the carpet and wrapped her arms round the sobbing girl. *So frail, so young, so like Lady Miranda when she first came to Bluebell Wood all those years ago. When will you give us peace from the colonies, Lord? Americans will be our undoing if the Germans don't finish us first.* "There, now. There must be some explanation. You love him, don't you?"

Claire sniffed and sniveled, her nose dripping on Mrs. Newsome's sleeve. Mrs. Newsome pulled her handkerchief from her pocket and wiped Claire's nose as if she were no older than Gaston.

"And I'm supposing he loves you too?"

"Yes, I'm sure of it." Claire nodded, her eyes begging Mrs. Newsome to believe her. "At least, I hope so. I think so."

Mrs. Newsome's heart ached for Claire. *Frenchmen. They croon like doves, but in the harsh light of day . . . Well, who am I to know or judge?* "Things happen that we can't predict. He's probably turned up and is wondering where on God's green earth you've gotten to, what's become of you, and what you've done with all these children."

Claire's head lifted. "You're right. I've only been waiting, hoping for word. I never thought about him looking for me."

"He must be worried sick by now, and

whoever'd planned to take these children must be scared out of their wits thinking you've all drowned or some such." She clucked her tongue in disapproval.

"I hadn't thought of it in that way. I wrote to a friend, giving this address. She'll give it to him. I'm sure she will." But Claire didn't look certain about something; what, Mrs. Newsome couldn't divine. Claire pushed her hair back from her forehead as if her head still ached.

Mrs. Newsome thought it surely must. *The lamb's not off the fells yet. These childhood diseases are harder by far on grown-ups, let alone that bump on her brain, and for all her youth I suppose she's a grown-up in fact.* "I think you'd best lie down now, Miss Claire, and take a wee rest. There will be time tomorrow to talk with her ladyship. I simply ask that you keep Gaston with you for the rest of the afternoon. Give him a task, if you will, or insist he sit in the corner. I don't care which. Just keep him out of Mrs. Creedle's kitchen and away from Mr. Dunnagan's henhouse."

"I will," Claire promised. "And if any of the other children give you any trouble at all, please send them to me, and . . ." She faltered. "I'll talk with them."

Mrs. Newsome nodded curtly and turned

to go, knowing that neither she nor Claire believed Claire capable of making any difference in the youngsters. *The girl simply doesn't possess the mettle.* Outside the door she stopped, drew a deep breath, and smoothed her skirt, as if that might smooth the ruffles in her feathers over Gaston. *It will take a fair sight more than talking with that one.*

Dr. Raibeart MacDonald's examination revealed more to him than the progression of Claire's chicken pox. "And how do you know so much of Christopher's death in the short time you've been here? I wager it wasn't your aunt who told you."

"Nancy, Aunt's housemaid —"

"Ach, naw! Talking out of turn, was she?"

Claire blushed. "Not at all. I'm afraid I'm the one who prodded her."

The doctor raised his eyebrows in amusement.

"She only said that he was killed in RAF training, last year."

Dr. MacDonald pulled his stethoscope from his ears. Carefully, he laid the fine instrument in his black bag. He would not look Claire in the face; it was too like seeing Miranda twenty years prior. "Miranda begged him not to join. She'd have marched into the inferno to keep him back, but he was of age and made the choice. He believed in what he was doing, in what needed to be done. The rest of us hoped and prayed that war would never come. Too many of us thought Mr. Chamberlain would make peace with Hitler in the end. Fools, we were."

"But Christopher didn't make it to the war."

"No. It might have been better if he had. An explosion from a backed-up fuel line. Such a waste, and no glory." He snapped his bag shut. "Not that it matters in the long run, but it's noticed by the locals, and somehow harder in the end."

"I don't understand."

Dr. MacDonald felt he was talking to someone very young. "Because your aunt's an American. Because she's always been an outsider. Because the Americans are not coming to our aid in this war, dragging their isolationist heels."

"Aunt Miranda's lived here all of her adult life — over twenty-five years. She's a Brit now."

He shook his head and smirked. "Americans can never be Brits, my dear, any more than I can deny my Scottish roots simply because I've lived in England these thirty-odd years — not that I'd have the least inclination to do so."

"But —"

"You'll find that the locals have long memories, strong prejudices, and short fuses. You'd not be one of them if your family had lived here for two generations."

"That must be so lonely for Aunt Miranda."

"Aye, I believe it is." He looked at her at last and smiled. "And for that reason, I think it's a very good thing that you've come."

"She doesn't seem to want to see me." Uncertainty seeped through Claire's voice and into her eyes. "I would have thought —"

"You look so much like him, lass. Christopher. You're the spittin' image. You could have been twins. I've no idea what your own mother looks like, but you're Maggie Langford at twenty in the flesh . . . as I live and breathe . . . and her son grew straight from the root." Raibeart MacDonald could not keep the years from falling away as he looked at Claire. But she was not Maggie, and it was Maggie who had drawn his heart from his chest the first moment he'd set eyes on her. Not that it had ever mattered.

She'd never given a glance to anyone but Gilbert.

"She can't look at me because I remind her of her son." It was a statement of fact.

There was little the doctor could say. He didn't know Claire's story and wasn't inclined to pry. But he believed — was certain — she could be good for Miranda, if Miranda let her. *And all these young people so in need of mothering . . . they could be the making of both these broken women, if only they'll open their eyes.* "Let me talk with her."

"I need to leave the children here. I need to return to France."

"So Mrs. Newsome said." He stood, looking down at a mouth as stubborn as Maggie's, eyes just as expressive. "You know that the tide has turned, that General Pétain is prime minister, and France has signed the armistice with Germany?"

"Yes, but there must be a way for me to get back. I'm sure Arnaud will think of something."

Dr. MacDonald knew there was no point in talking to the girl — feverish as she was with desperate hope. Current events and the women must sort themselves out. "I don't doubt what she'll say, but I'll do my best."

"Thank you!" Claire's smile was magic.

He couldn't help but chortle, "Two peas in a pod." On the way out the door he paused and turned. "I suggest that you set your mind to compromise, Miss Stewart. I don't believe your aunt will be seein' it all your way."

Dr. MacDonald passed a distracted Mrs. Newsome on her way out the library door. Ten minutes later he'd argued with Miranda until he was blue in the face. He could stand anything — any amount of wheedling or complaining or threatening or temper. But he could not bear her tears. Knowing that she didn't use them manipulatively or freely did not help.

He took her hands in his. "I understand that she reminds you of Christopher. I understand that the children remind you of happy years with Christopher as a child. I know it rips your heart out to hear them laugh and see them running through the garden because your own son is not here to do that, and he'll never sire children to fill these rooms. But I also know you crave that very thing, Maggie — that life, that boisterous exuberance children and family bring. It's what you're missing."

"That life — my life — is gone, Raibeart,

and to have them here now, to see them all so alive and happy . . . it seems a sacrilege, as if I don't care or —"

"Remember?"

She winced.

"Och, but you do remember, with every breath you take. And if anything could honor the life of your bonny lad, it's seeing these children saved from the likes of Hitler. It's why Christopher enlisted. He saw the evil coming before the rest of us did. He was an insightful, compassionate, determined young man. He wanted to fight that injustice."

"He wanted to be like his father, to make his father's memory proud."

"And that he did. He honored Gilbert and carried his legacy. But Christopher was more like you, Maggie. Full of life and vitality, as you were before —" His arm swept the room, the grounds, then dropped to his side in near defeat. "Do you not see that Claire and these children are a gift from the Lord?"

She turned away, but he grasped both her hands once more.

"You may not want to own it, but He loves you. He sees you and knows your name. He's reaching out for —"

"What has He done?" Her sharp anger

took him by surprise. "He's taken away my husband and my son — my only son!"

Raibeart dropped her hands. If she was intent on blaming God for the evils of men and the weakness of their inventions, there was not much he could do. He didn't know why Christopher's time had come so soon, only that it had. And that, he believed, as tragic and sad as it was for all of them, was no mistake. He sat back.

Miranda, her face fallen and eyes nearly closed, reached for him, as if she thought he too might leave her. But he wouldn't, not as long as he drew breath. Not as long as she didn't send him away.

"I see death in my work, Maggie. It's the end of this life, and it comes to every one of us, sooner or later. But those left behind . . . If we spend all our years mourning those who've gone, we miss the life God's given us here and now, the breath to help our fellow beings while we're able."

She shook her head.

"I cannot change your mind. I can only say that these children need you and the gift of your home and love as much as you need them. It's a shame to throw such a gift in the lake — back into the face of God — and walk away. But it's up to you now, my darlin' girl, isn't it?"

■ ■ ■ ■

Miranda spent the remainder of the morning alone, refusing tea and refusing to see Claire, though her niece asked to meet with her. There was so much to think about, to consider. If only she could make them all disappear. If only she could turn back time. In the end, all she could think to do was to ask Christopher.

While the others ate their midday meal in the dining room, Miranda walked to the last door on the third floor of the west wing. She stood in the hallway, key in hand, listening to the great clock in the downstairs foyer as its pendulum swung back and forth, tick and tock, tick and tock.

Once she opened the door to Christopher's room, she knew the memories would flood her heart, her mind, like a storm breaching the banks of Lake Windermere, pummeling the shore, chipping away at its edges. She could stop that flood by not going through, by simply focusing on the tick and the tock, by walking away.

Raibeart was right — Christopher had seen war coming, had seen that Hitler would not be satisfied until he'd wiped every Jewish man, woman, and child from

Germany, and then from the face of the earth. *"He's a madman with a demonic agenda."* Those were Christopher's words. And though she hadn't wanted to believe, she'd read the speeches, had even read Christopher's copy of *Mein Kampf.* If only the world had seen as clearly as her son and stopped Hitler before . . . If only Mr. Chamberlain had not been fooled . . . If only Christopher had not been killed by such a senseless . . .

Miranda leaned her head against Christopher's door. *Why, God? Why?*

She expected no answer. At last she straightened and turned her key in the lock. She opened the door, stepped through, and closing it behind her, reached for the light.

Gaston would never have believed that treacle pudding could make a fellow so sick. If a little made one feel better, then a lot should have put him head and shoulders above the world. But it hadn't. He hadn't needed Mrs. Newsome to forbid him his midday meal; he couldn't have taken a bite if they'd served roast beef and Yorkshire pudding slathered in brown gravy — his favorite since coming to England.

So he wandered the halls of Bluebell Wood, quietly peeking into forbidden rooms

— they'd all been forbidden to him — and taking an inventory of all he saw. He had no plans to pinch or break anything. He was very careful — just wanted to look round.

Some of the doors remained locked. He'd tried them before, so didn't bother now. But there was one, at the end of the hallway in the west wing, that shone a light beneath — a light he'd never seen there. It must not be locked now . . . unless Mollie Taggert had told the truth. Mollie, the scullery maid, had vowed there were ghosts and bogles haunting the north tower, just itching to get their misty claws into wayward boys. What if one had found its way to the west wing? What if one found its way anywhere?

"There's no such thing as bogles, nor ghosts, neither," Gaston whispered aloud, gulping, more to bolster his courage than because he believed it. Slowly he turned the brass doorknob. It didn't even creak. He pushed the door open.

The curtains were drawn wide so the sun streamed in and he could see everything at once. It was a boy's room — not a nursery, but a proper grown boy's room with football pennants on the walls and a couple of trophies on a high shelf. A tennis racket hung beside a cricket bat, and a violin and bow lay on the mantel, as if the owner had just set them down.

Gaston stepped into the room. He hadn't seen any grown boys at Bluebell Wood. The shoes — a pair of soiled tennis shoes and some scuffed golfing cleats — heaped in one corner looked grown-man size. Only a fully grown boy or a man could wield the set of golfing irons in the opposite corner.

So mesmerized was Gaston with this treasure trove that it took several moments for him to see the woman on the floor beside the four-poster bed. So quiet was he — so reverent in a room of such grown-up maleness with grown-up toys a boy would give his right arm for — that the woman didn't seem to have heard him.

As Gaston's eyes adjusted better to the light and shadows in the room, he realized he was staring at the back of Lady Langford. His throat went dry. If he wasn't on her blacklist before, he surely would be now. He'd been told by Mrs. Newsome in no uncertain terms to stay out of this end of the wing, and by Mademoiselle Claire to steer clear of anything that he even imagined might bring trouble. As silently as he could, without daring to breathe, he tiptoed backward toward the door.

He'd just crossed the threshold and was trying to decide whether to pull the door to when he heard her whimper. He stopped. Not a sound.

Gaston took another step backward, into the hallway. Lady Langford began to cry . . . soft moaning sounds at first, as she rocked gently back and forth, and then great, wrenching sobs that pulled at his heart.

She reminded him of his mother, the night before she sent him away to the boat in Calais. Gaston had overheard his parents' deliberations, their arguments about whether to keep him and Bertram at home or send them to England. He was eavesdropping and dared not let them know, but silently begged them to let him stay — to want him to stay with them. He wasn't afraid of Hitler — not one bit. What could a maniac with a nasty little mustache do to him?

His father would have let them stay and taken their chances in hiding together, but it was his mother who'd insisted, who'd said she'd seen her grandparents murdered in a pogrom in Poland, and she wasn't about to watch her children stabbed or shot or set aflame before her eyes. Gaston had never heard his mother use such language or conjure such violent images. All he could think was that she no longer wanted him, didn't want Bertram, either — not enough to fight for them.

That night, when she came to tuck him in, to say good night, he'd pretended to be fast asleep, though he knew she realized he was not. She'd spoken softly to him and kissed him on the cheek, the forehead. But he was angry with her and turned over, pretending to stretch in his sleep. She'd sat there a long time, Gaston knew, until he'd fallen asleep.

It was only toward morning, when the pale light of dawn had crept through his window, that he woke enough to hear her whimpering softly, still sitting by his bed. Even then, he'd not reached out to her. When they'd said good-bye, just before meeting the lorry driver who'd taken him and Bertram and all the others to Calais, Gaston had not kissed her, he was so hurt and so angry.

And this was what he thought of as he watched Lady Langford weeping on the floor, her head resting on the side of the bed. From the back, he could imagine his mother — a similar height and build, her shoulders shaking as she wept.

If he could return to Paris, return to his mother, he would hug her now. He would tell her that he loved her with all his heart and that he was sorry he'd treated her shabbily. It was not how he was raised. It was not what he felt in his heart. He would explain that he had feared she didn't want him, though he realized now that was not true. She was afraid, more afraid than he.

Gaston stepped back inside the room. Lady Langford seemed not to hear. He took another step closer to her, and another. Soon he'd crossed the divide and was standing just behind her back. She held a cricket ball in one hand and had wrapped both arms around a teddy bear, much the worse for wear and perhaps for love. Gaston understood it must have once belonged to the man-boy. It was the kind of thing his own mother kept — things that he and Bertram had long outgrown but once loved best of all.

Still she cried, her face buried in the thin fur of the teddy bear.

Gaston knelt beside her. He was tempted to run away. But that would be the coward's way, and Gaston was not a coward. He would not repeat the mistake he was now so very sorry for. He put his hand on her shoulder and said softly, using his best English, "May I help you in some way, madame?"

Her breath caught. She opened her eyes and for a moment Gaston thought she might be angry with him. Yet she looked like she didn't believe he was there, as if she somehow saw him, but didn't.

"I thought . . . I thought for a moment . . ."

"*Oui?* You thought something?"

She sobbed once more, then sniffed, wiping her eyes and nose with the back of her hand.

Quickly Gaston pulled his handkerchief from his pocket. It was wadded and dirty, but he knew a gentleman should always offer a crying lady a handkerchief.

She looked at the handkerchief, then at Gaston.

He smiled encouragingly, willing her to take it from him.

She looked as if she was about to say something but stopped.

"Allow me," he said, wiping her cheeks and the corners of her eyes.

She closed her eyes, but not rudely, he thought. It was as though she savored his touch — something his mother used to do. "Gaston."

"*Oui,* madame, that is my name. You remembered!"

"Where did you come from?" she asked, her eyes still closed.

"From Paris, of course," he said, most

seriously.

She smiled and, after another moment, opened her eyes. "I meant just now."

"Ah, *oui,* I understand. I came through the door."

"Yes. You weren't at table?"

"No, madame." Gaston reddened. *Does she know about the pudding?* "I was not hungry."

Her eyebrows lifted toward her hairline. "That seems most unusual for a boy."

"*Oui,* madame. It is not my usual state of affairs."

"Ah." She looked as if she was trying not to smile. "I believe you."

"*Merci,* madame."

"*Merci* to you, Gaston."

"But of course, madame. I am pleased to help in any way that I can."

She hefted the cricket ball in her hand. "Do you know who this belonged to?"

"A very lucky boy, I think."

She looked at him quizzically.

"To live in such a place as this, to possess such — such toys and tools for the sports. It is a dream come true."

"A dream come true," she echoed, another tear escaping her eye.

"*Oui,* madame . . . the room of a very lucky boy," he repeated.

"Yes." She looked around at the room. "A very special boy — my son."

Gaston sat back on his heels. He now felt certain he had intruded on a private moment and wondered if he should leave.

But the lady stood, not looking at him. She sniffed again and pulled the cricket bat from the wall. "I think there are wickets in the carriage house. Mr. Dunnagan will know." She turned the bat over in her hands, then picked up the ball once more. "Would you like to have these?"

"Pour moi?" Gaston stood, unable to believe such good fortune. Was she testing him? Should he thank her politely but say no?

"For you and the other children . . . well, I suppose mostly for you and your brother."

"Bertram."

"Yes, for you and Bertram."

"*Mais oui,* madame! That would be most wonderful! But your son — will he not object?"

She smiled sadly and placed the ball into Gaston's hands, wrapping her own around them. "I think . . . I think he would be happy for you to have them."

"We will take most special care of them, madame." Gaston did not fully comprehend, but felt as if he'd received something more sacred than a ball and bat. "And we will not make noise . . . I promise."

"No, that will not do."

"*Non,* madame?"

She looked at him very carefully, deep into his eyes. "You must make noise, Gaston — in the garden. Make all the noise you want."

Chapter Six

Though Claire's spots had not completely faded, her fever had long gone. The spots still itched, but not violently, and that was a relief.

Looking and feeling stronger, Claire believed it was high time she talked with her aunt about returning to France. It couldn't be more dangerous in an occupied country than in one under incessant bombing and daily threat of invasion, could it? If she could find a way to reach Paris . . . If her aunt, who must surely have connections in high places, would help her . . . If she'd finally agree to keep the children long-term . . .

According to Mrs. Newsome, Aunt Miranda had committed only to keeping the children through the extended quarantine.

Claire waited until after breakfast, when she knew her aunt would be in the library, and knocked on the door.

"Come," her aunt's voice answered.

Claire squared her shoulders and pushed open the door, giving her best and most confident smile.

Aunt Miranda straightened uncomfortably but graciously welcomed her. "I'm so glad you're feeling better, Claire."

"Thank you, Aunt. I owe you a great debt. I can't imagine what the children or I would have done without your generous hospitality."

"I'm glad you've enjoyed the respite."

Claire breathed. *Perhaps she does understand that I'm leaving. Perhaps Dr. MacDonald and Mrs. Newsome have cleared the way.* "It's been a saving grace for the children, especially . . . having to leave their homes and families. You've really made them welcome."

Aunt Miranda tilted her head. "I was just about to pour a cup of tea — chamomile, actually. Now that our tea is severely rationed — much to Mrs. Creedle's dismay — we've resorted to drinking weeds from the lawn at odd times," she joked. "Would you like some? It's not bad with a dollop of Mr. Dunnagan's honey."

"Yes, thank you." It seemed the civilized and friendly thing to do. This was going better than Claire had anticipated, but she rushed on. "Bluebell Wood really is a perfect wartime home for them — safe from the bombing, all the running and playing space they could possibly want, good food from the gardens and your livestock, fresh Lakeland air."

Aunt Miranda nodded slowly. "Yes, no matter that no place in England is truly safe just now, I've been thinking the same. Of course —" she smiled — "Dr. MacDonald and Mrs. Newsome have had a hand in helping me see the light."

Claire sighed, a great weight falling from her shoulders. She sipped the tea, smooth and velvety in her mouth. "I'm so glad, Aunt. I don't know what would become of them if you didn't take them. I'm so grateful you understand."

"I'll take them for the duration of the war as long as I have help," Aunt Miranda said carefully.

"Of course — you'll need help. I was telling Mrs. Newsome the same, that perhaps you could hire a governess and maybe even a tutor . . . if the cost isn't too dear. I think Aimee might need a nursery maid still, but Elise and Gaston could attend school."

"I won't be hiring a governess." Aunt Miranda was firm.

"Oh. Well, I suppose there's the village

school. No one will know they're not children you took in of your own volition, will they? I heard that a great many French orphans were evacuated just before Dunkirk. Under the circumstances, with evacuees running all over the north of England, the constable's not likely to come round to collect them!" Claire laughed nervously at her own joke. When Aunt Miranda didn't smile, she rushed on. "Of course, now that we know so many have been taken in, they'll be able to get identity cards and ration books in their own names. I've collected the children's full names, their parents' names, their birth dates and addresses. I assume that's all you'll need."

"Obtaining identification and ration cards won't be difficult. I've already discussed our need with the local authorities."

Claire smiled, relieved. "Great!"

"I don't see why they would need the village school, though that is a possibility. It would give you a few free hours each day, though Aimee might need a nursery maid. I can see that."

Claire wasn't certain she liked her aunt's use of words. To make things perfectly clear, she said, "I promise to keep in touch as best I can. I don't know if there is any way to get civilian mail through from France now.

Perhaps I can send letters to someone in America — Sylvia Beach's parents live in New Jersey — and from there to here. I'm sure they wouldn't mind. I've no idea how long it will take letters to reach you. I'll let you know what I learn of the children's parents, of their families, as soon as I can."

Aunt Miranda stared at Claire a long while, then spoke slowly and deliberately. "I'll take them as long as you remain here and supervise them, Claire."

Claire felt sudden heat rise from her heart to her face. "You know I can't do that, Aunt Miranda. You know I must get back to France — to Arnaud and the work we're doing. I thought you understood that."

"It seems you've done the work of getting these children out; now you must do the work of helping to care for them, to see them safely through this war."

"That wasn't why I brought them here," Claire sputtered. "I never intended —"

"Neither did I, but here we are."

Claire saw her mother's grim mouth and resolute eyes in Aunt Miranda's face. "That's not fair."

"Life is rarely fair. But I think you need to reconsider what you're calling 'not fair.' "

"Paris is overrun by Nazis. We can't send Jewish children back to France."

"No one is suggesting that we should. I'm simply saying that you showed up on my doorstep with five children in need of food, shelter, and so much more. They're not puppies to be deposited with new caregivers and left. You brought them, Claire. They're your responsibility."

Claire felt her anger growing, her indignation ready to fly through the roots of her hair. "You don't understand the importance of our work. I don't even know if Arnaud is dead or alive. I can't just up and not return." She knew she should not throw the deaths of Aunt Miranda's husband or son in her face, but she was desperate. "You must remember what it is like to love someone, surely . . . to not know if he's alive, or if he desperately needs you, if he's calling for you."

Aunt Miranda paled, her eyes flashing pain.

Claire felt if she could just push a little harder, she might get through. "Imagine if —"

But a knock came at the door, three sharp raps in quick succession.

"Come," Aunt Miranda said, her voice no longer strong and confident.

The door pushed open and Nancy, the housemaid, slipped in, a paper in her hand.

"Pardon me, your ladyship, but it's a telegram come directly. The boy's waiting by the door, in case a reply is wanted."

Claire knew telegrams rarely meant good news, especially in wartime. Despite her own building war with Aunt Miranda, she pitied her. What more bad news could one woman bear?

Aunt Miranda stood, as if ready to march before a firing squad. She reached out her hand. "Give it to me."

Nancy looked between Aunt Miranda and Claire, confusion on her face. "Yes, your ladyship. But — but —"

"But what?" Aunt Miranda asked, looking as if she very much needed to get whatever it was over with.

"It's for Miss Stewart."

Claire felt the world spin, slightly off-kilter. "Who would send me a telegram?"

"Who knows you're here?" Aunt Miranda looked as astonished as Claire felt.

"I don't know — I —" But there was one person, perhaps two or three. None of them could be sending good news . . . unless Arnaud was alive and well . . . unless he was on his way.

It took but a moment for Claire to retrieve the envelope and rip it open.

MUTUAL FRIEND SERIOUSLY WOUNDED — STOP — AUTHORITIES SEARCHING FOR ACCOMPLICE — STOP — DO NOT RETURN — STOP — J

"Claire? Claire, what is it?"

But Claire could not speak or stand. The telegram confirmed in block letters what she'd most feared but would not admit, not even to herself: Arnaud had been captured. He might die. And for her, there would be no going back.

Chapter Seven

Chicken pox had proven trial enough for Aimee. At least Dr. MacDonald had come to visit her every few days after her spots had bloomed. Aimee loved the doctor's benevolent smile and the twinkle in his eye. She believed no grandfather could have been kinder.

But just when it seemed that everything might turn right, Mademoiselle Claire had fallen ill again. At least, Aimee supposed she was ill. She'd kept to her room for almost a week, and Madame Langford was the only one, besides Nancy and Mrs. Newsome on occasion, allowed in and out her door.

Aimee didn't know what was wrong with Mademoiselle Claire and no one could tell her, or no one would.

The little girl sighed as she pulled back the blackout curtain from her bedroom window, peeking out to the front lawn. It was barely nine o'clock and Gaston and Bertram were already out playing with the cricket bat and ball Lady Langford had given them, Gaston's knees mottled green from the wet grass.

Aimee shook her head and clucked her tongue. Mrs. Newsome wouldn't like that and Nancy would scold. Nancy scolded about so many things, like the bed linens.

Aimee was very careful to get out of bed the middle of each night and use the chamber pot, sometimes trying so often she barely slept, but Elise couldn't seem to wake up. Although she and her sister, Jeanine, assured Nancy and Mrs. Newsome that Elise had never wet the bed at home — not for years — Elise could not seem to stop now. Each morning she woke crying over her shame, and each morning Nancy scolded. Finally one morning, in a fit of temper, Nancy smudged Elise's nose into the sheets and made her sleep on a rubber mat that night. Elise had cried herself to sleep, and still wet the bed.

Aimee had touched the rubber mat in the morning, and it gave her shivers — so cold and hard. She wouldn't want to sleep on that.

Elise stuck very close to Jeanine, like a shadow. Where the two went in the day or what they did, Aimee was not certain.

Hours stretched between breakfast and luncheon, and the time loomed even longer until tea. Bedtime quickly followed. Mrs. Newsome insisted Aimee go to bed even before the sun had set.

At home, in France, the evening meal was served late and Maman never made her go to bed early. It was always dark when her mother tucked her in, and the candles were lit, shining like stars in her bedroom window. *Such good company, candles and stars,* Aimee thought.

But no candles shone in the windows of Bluebell Wood at night. Mrs. Newsome had explained that every window must be covered and blacked out. No candles could shine out and no stars could shine in.

Aimee missed her mother and her home in France, especially at night. It was then that she would sneak the mezuzah from its hiding place beneath her mattress and kiss it. Her mother had pulled the treasure from the doorpost of home and told Aimee to keep it with her always — had sewn it into the hem of her dress, to help Aimee remember her home and her parents, and most of all to remind her that she must look to and love Adonai with all her heart, that He would watch over her. Mrs. Beardsley had found it the first night they'd come to her home but, after washing her dress, had sewn it back into the hem and given Aimee a kiss.

Aimee wasn't at all sure Nancy would do the same, so she'd torn the stitching from her hem and hidden the precious mezuzah beneath her mattress. Someday, her mother had said, she would live in a place that wanted her, a place glad to have the mezuzah posted by the door. Aimee was not certain Bluebell Wood was that place.

So it was with more than a little delight that Aimee unexpectedly met Dr. MacDonald on the stairs late that morning.

"Well then, and how's my little mademoiselle today?" The big doctor leaned down, his silvery whiskered face very close to Aimee's.

"Very well, *merci.* No spots."

"No spots? At least, almost no spots. I'm very glad to hear it, to see it is so. And where are you off and about to this fine morning?"

Aimee shrugged. She wasn't off and about to anything, anywhere.

The doctor stood and looked up the stairway, then down into the gallery below. "I saw the lads playing in the front garden, but where are the other children — Jeanine and Elise?"

Aimee shrugged again.

The doctor frowned. "So, you've no one to play with — for the moment."

It was a statement of fact, not so much of sympathy, but it pulled the tears from somewhere inside Aimee's chest and up into her eyes. They almost spilled over, but she wiped them away, lifted her chin, and shrugged once more.

The doctor still frowned. Aimee hoped he wasn't unhappy with her.

He knelt down and placed his hand on her shoulder. "We must do something about this, you and I."

She nodded in agreement, though what he meant, she didn't know.

He squeezed her shoulder. "Leave it to me." And then he took the stairs two at a time.

Aimee felt a little better, hopeful, and followed Dr. MacDonald up the stairs. She knew he was bound for Mademoiselle Claire's room, where Madame Langford had gone even before the doctor arrived. She also knew she would not be admitted.

When she reached Mademoiselle Claire's door, it was closed again. But she could hear Dr. MacDonald and Madame Langford inside.

"What can you be thinking, leaving the child to roam the halls with no one and nothing to do?"

"I have my hands full with the running of the estate, Raibeart. All our men, save poor Mr. Dunnagan, have either joined or been called up, and Mollie and Nancy are run off their feet. I thought to hire a nursery maid, but most of the local girls have signed up for war work. The children are housed and fed and well cared for. Under the circumstances, how can you expect more?"

"You've given them a house, Miranda, and I applaud you for that, but they need a home. They're children taken from their parents and they need love, affection — even chores would help. Don't tell me you don't know that. You lavished love on your own. Have you none to spare for these motherless children?"

"I had a son, not daughters. What do I know about girls?" Lady Langford sounded defensive, and Aimee cringed. It was not a good thing when grown-ups got defensive. Aimee wrapped her arms around herself and scrunched down by the door, still listening.

"Were you not a girl yourself once? And you, Miss Stewart: is it too much to ask that you get yourself out of this room and mind them — read them a story, take them for a walk, tell them a tale?"

"That's not quite fair, Raibeart. Claire's received horrible news. It's too soon —"

"You're both reading the worst possible into a few lines of text. That telegram did not say he was dead, woman, and even if he is, do you not think he'd want you to do your very best for these children, as he did? I canna understand either of you!"

Aimee didn't understand either — not the shouting or why she'd been brought here, or even what a war was, not really. Had her mother sent her away because she'd been naughty? She'd tried very, very hard to be good all the while she'd been with Mademoiselle Claire, and quiet as a mouse once they'd arrived at Bluebell Wood. Maman had cautioned her about not talking too much, about keeping herself clean and being respectful to those who took her in.

Maman, I promise I will be good. Please, please let me come home!

"I — I simply have no strength." Mademoiselle Claire's voice came through the door.

"You have no strength because you've been lying about, letting your muscles atrophy and your will to live go to slaughter. There's not a medical thing I can do for you, but to urge you to get yourself up and out that door and help those in need — the very ones you brought here. It's the best medicine. 'Twould be the best medicine in the world for all of you."

"You're pushing too hard, Raibeart. I agree Claire needs to rally herself and help with the children, but we've needed to give her a little time."

"Time, is it? Time is what you've taken, Maggie — a lifetime mooning over your loss of Gilbert. Now you've started a second stanza for Christopher. Has it served you well? Are widow's weeds and a long face the life you want for your young niece here?" The doctor's voice grew louder. Aimee knew he neared the door. She crept back, but stopped when he spoke again. "You might have left those wee folk in France if you've no heart to help them."

"That's unfair. Claire may have saved their lives. The children are all old enough to take care of themselves for a time — to make their own entertainment."

"The wee one is not much more than a bairn, Maggie. I'm done talking. You may as well send them all to the woods to be raised by the animals. At least they'd give a sight more attention and communication."

The doorknob turned. Aimee scampered behind the long curtain in the hallway and climbed into the window seat, hoping she was quick enough not to be seen.

The doctor paused outside the door, and Aimee heard him say, impatience in every word, "Yes, yes, I'll stop in a week. I expect to see roses in those cheeks and a spring in your step, Miss Stewart. Do not take your grieving lessons from your aunt. She doesn't know how to close one book, nor open another." He shut the door, harder than Mrs. Newsome would possibly approve.

After he'd gone, Aimee sat in the window seat a long time, looking out on the lawn and thinking. What had Dr. MacDonald said? Something about going to the woods to be raised by the animals and com — com-something. Aimee didn't know the English word he'd used, but she understood that it meant talking. Animals talking. Aimee would very much like to see that.

Going to the woods was another thing entirely. She'd never gone there alone, and Mr. Dunnagan had told her to plant her feet firmly in the gardens nearest the house and take not one step beyond. Mollie had said that bogles roamed the woods, looking for wee bairns to eat, so she must never go there.

But if going into the woods meant that she could truly hear the animals speak, that they would want and welcome her . . . well, it was something to think about.

Claire closed her eyes and rolled over after Dr. MacDonald and her aunt had gone from her room. She wanted only to sleep, to shut out the world. But Dr. MacDonald's words frightened her. *"Are widow's weeds and a long face the life you want for your young niece?"*

Claire shivered beneath the covers, despite the heat of the fire set to ward off the unseasonably cool morning's damp and chill. She could see how grief had possessed her aunt. She didn't want to close herself off or hold herself aloof like that. She didn't want to grow too soon old, or alone. She didn't want to copy Aunt Miranda's behaviors any more than she wanted to copy her mother's.

Arnaud, where are you? We had so many plans. Arnaud — so full of life, so bold and daring in your rescue exploits.

Claire, in all her previously sheltered existence, had craved such a life, one she'd only ever imagined and lived through the pages of novels.

Arnaud had laughed when she'd asked him if he wasn't afraid, wasn't terrified they'd be caught. "I live ready to meet my Maker at a moment's notice, *ma chérie.*

Why would I not laugh in the face of death? Until that time comes —" he'd shrugged — "I will live each day, each hour to the fullest."

And he had. Every moment had seemed filled with urgency when she was with him . . . urgent and beautiful and free.

Why he'd been drawn to Claire, she didn't know. She saw herself as a mouse of a person — a fearful mouse that dreamed of wearing cat's boots and a sword, but had neither the gumption nor the confidence.

All her daring to help the French Jews, and even her boldness to approach well-known writers visiting Shakespeare and Company, to pursue the writing of her dreams, had come from Arnaud's zest for life, from his belief that anything was possible. She'd felt more alive working with Arnaud, running dangerous missions with the children, than she'd ever experienced.

With him, she'd lived what she wanted to write — a life of adventure, rich in meaning. It was the kind of life Ernest Hemingway had spoken of casually over drinks when he'd talked of his time in the Great War . . . those late afternoons when he'd stopped by Shakespeare and Company to visit with Sylvia.

It was Arnaud who'd made her believe in

herself — not so much by what he'd said about her, or even her abilities, but by simply shrugging and invigorating her with his *joie de vivre.*

Claire bit her lip. She'd never been honest with him, but had hidden her insecurities, certain he'd find them unattractive. By pretending — by playacting — she'd hoped to become more of who she wanted to be in his presence. *Did he know?*

But Arnaud is not here. So now who will I be? What am I without him?

Claire pushed back the eiderdown. Swinging her feet to the floor, she sat up in bed. She'd gone to Paris to pursue her long-nurtured dream that her father would welcome her as his family, and to pursue the literary life of the great writers of this age in the hope that one day, she too would write a great novel, the great American novel.

Neither dream had come true. Her father had not wanted her, had sent her packing in no uncertain terms, pleading only that she not reveal herself to his family and almost threatening her if she did. And writing . . . What could she write without the avant-garde literary lights of Shakespeare and Company to emulate?

Arnaud was gone — if not forever, for a

long time. Life as she'd known it those few months in Paris was gone. *What is left?*

A life of meaning, a purpose greater than your own.

She straightened, not knowing where that thought came from. What did it mean? Helping these children, perhaps?

Claire sighed and closed her eyes. *What do I know of children?*

As if summoned from her muse, images from Charlotte Brontë's novel *Jane Eyre* filtered through Claire's brain. Jane tutoring the lively young French girl, Adèle. Jane doing whatever needed to be done, whether that meant "buckling down" to teach or investigating the cries of mad Bertha or even running away from it all. And then there was Mary Poppins, who'd made every chore for the children a lark, an adventure.

Claire considered the possibilities, the challenge, and, pleased with the literary inspiration, opened her eyes. She doubted she could muster the courage or fortitude of Jane Eyre, or the creativity of Mary Poppins. Still, the adventure could begin only when she placed one foot firmly in front of the other. That was a position she knew Arnaud would expect and applaud.

Chapter Eight

Claire hadn't expected her resolve to be tested so soon. The heat and mugginess of August did nothing to enhance the moods of Mrs. Creedle or Mrs. Newsome. Even Aunt Miranda, who'd taken more interest and time with the children of late, grew short-tempered when they'd trampled her prizewinning poppies to fetch a stray ball during a cricket match.

Claire determined the most helpful thing she could do was to keep the children from Mrs. Creedle's kitchen, from Mrs. Newsome and Nancy's realm of duty within the house, from Aunt Miranda's library and front gardens, from Mr. Dunnagan's kitchen gardens and henhouse . . . but where and what did that leave?

Perhaps a traipse through the local graveyard to do stone rubbings. Stone rubbing was a thing Claire could do well — a hobby she'd enjoyed while growing up not far from an old cemetery in Princeton. The project had a "Mary Poppins-ish" appeal in a morbid sort of way. They might even gather some local lore from the groundskeeper in the process.

Claire collected all the leftover butcher paper Mrs. Creedle was willing to spare and thick pieces of charcoal from Mr. Dunnagan. She never bothered to explain the outing to Aunt Miranda or Mrs. Newsome, certain those good ladies would be glad to find the house and grounds quiet for a change.

After breakfast, before the heat of the day, Claire mustered the troops and marched them down to the village church and graveyard.

"What are we doing in the Christian cemetery?" Bertram wanted to know.

"We're going to do stone rubbings."

"Stone rubbings?" Jeanine sounded incredulous.

"Now watch this; I'll show you how it's done." Kneeling before the first stone she came to, Claire placed a portion of butcher paper over the chiseled epitaph. Leaning in with flexed muscles, she rubbed the charcoal briskly and methodically across the paper.

"Look!" Elise pointed. "You can see the writing!"

"Precisely." Claire sat back on her heels, satisfied. "Now I want each of you to take some paper and charcoal and find the most interesting epitaph or some of the most interesting names you can. Then we're going to make up stories about who those people were and what they did."

"But we don't know those people," Jeanine objected, "and paper is precious. You want us to use it for pictures of tombstones?"

"It looks as if they've been dead a very long time," Gaston observed.

"Of course they have," Claire agreed, ignoring Jeanine's frugality, "but we're going to use our imaginations."

Jeanine and Bertram exchanged worried glances, and Claire could see from Bertram's crossed arms that he disapproved.

"What's the matter?"

"When we visit graves, we do so out of respect for the loved ones buried there. We might bring a stone of remembrance, but we take nothing away. We do not scribble over their grave markers."

Claire felt heat rise up her neck. "I'm showing no sign of disrespect and I'm stealing nothing. In fact, it's just the opposite. I'm appreciating the stones and remembering the lives of people who've been gone for generations."

Jeanine stepped forward, spreading her hands, clearly trying to bridge the gap between Claire and Bertram. "But we aren't remembering them, don't you see? We never knew these people."

Claire heaved a sigh. "You're missing the point entirely."

Bertram looked away and Claire knew there was no way to reach him. It was one more thing she didn't understand about their Jewish culture, one more reason she was not the person to teach or govern them. "Look, you don't have to do the rubbings if you don't want."

"I'll do them!" Elise stepped forward, eager to please.

"All right." Claire forced a smile. "Those of you who want to do them, come with me. The rest of you wander through and see what you can learn from what's written on the stones. You'll be surprised how much you can learn about the village."

"Whispers among the dead?" Gaston wiggled his eyebrows.

Claire tried not to grin in return, especially when Bertram pinched his younger brother's arm.

"Not exactly. But when you find several family graves with common death dates, you know some tragic event must have taken place — a fire, a flood, maybe a raging epidemic. When you find an infant's grave of just a few days, or less than a year, you know there was a sad and grieving mother behind that story."

Claire wasn't sure the children appreciated all she said, and sharing her thoughts felt like losing something sacred . . . but she continued. "When I discover a little lamb atop a tombstone, sometimes I cry. I think that lost child must have been especially sweet and dear to their parents."

Aimee looked as if she might cry too, which was not what Claire had envisioned for any of them.

"Aimee, you might look for flowers that grow in the cemetery. I see some forget-me-nots over near the church's nave. Pick some especially pretty ones so we can press them in a book."

Aimee smiled, looking relieved, and trotted off toward the church. Bertram and Jeanine wandered in the opposite direction.

"Elise and Gaston, come; I'll show you how to begin."

"I saw." Gaston grabbed some paper and a charcoal. "I can find my own way, mademoiselle."

"We'll meet at the gate when the town

clock strikes eleven!" she called after him and gratefully turned back to Elise.

Claire helped Elise rub the chiseled wool of a particularly old lamb on a stone and idly wondered what Aunt Miranda might think, if she'd ever haunted cemeteries in search of stories or imaginings. Claire's mother had always complained such fascination was morbid, but Claire didn't see it as such.

So many of the village stones were ancient, some crumbling. Two were newer, more freshly dug graves with no grass, changing the landscape. When she and Elise stood, Claire glimpsed a tall monument near the far edge of the cemetery, flanked by similar sculptures. "Let's see what's over there."

They'd not taken three steps when Aimee's terrified scream pierced the air.

"Aimee? Aimee! Where are you?"

"Mademoiselle!" The scream came again and again. Claire, the children, a groundskeeper Claire had not seen before, and even the vicar raced toward the child's screams.

Claire couldn't see Aimee anywhere but ran toward the horrified faces of the vicar and groundskeeper, who stopped her short with a mighty jerk before she plunged headlong into an open grave.

"Mademoiselle!" Aimee wailed from six

feet below, Gaston standing guiltily beside her.

"Aimee! Gaston! Are you all right?" Claire all but fainted from terror and embarrassment.

"*Oui,* mademoiselle," Gaston affirmed, "no broken bones. The ego, however, it is damaged, and Aimee is not happy."

The vicar raised his eyebrows. "These are yours, Mrs. — ?"

Claire felt her color rise from more than the encroaching heat of the day. "Miss Stewart. I'm responsible for them, yes. They're evacuee children, you see, from Bluebell Wood."

"I do see." The vicar did not smile.

"I sent them exploring and I'm afraid they must have —"

"Aimee dropped her flower into the hole, and then lamented its loss," Gaston shouted unnecessarily from below. "She stepped too near the edge to retrieve it and — *voilà*! I jumped in to save her."

"Gallant lad. And now there's the both of you prime for planting." The groundskeeper shook his head, but the creases near his eyes inclined to laughter — an impulse the vicar didn't share.

"We've a funeral here this morning. The casket should have already arrived. I sincerely hope —"

"Never mind, Vicar." The groundskeeper seemed to enjoy himself entirely too much. "It's my fault, if any. I staked no rope round the opening. Reckon I wasn't expectin' guests. I'll have them out in your mother's blink."

"I'm so, so sorry," Claire appealed.

"I don't know what they do in America, Miss Stewart, but the cemetery here is no place for children to play."

"I know that, Vicar, and again, I'm so very sorry."

"It's a mercy these children didn't break their necks, and you can tell Lady Langford I said so."

"Yes, Vicar." Claire wanted to step into the open grave herself.

The vicar turned to go, then faced Claire once more. "Dr. MacDonald tells me Lady Langford has agreed to take in German children. Make certain they stay out of the cemetery as well."

German children? Surely there must be some mistake! Claire didn't know whether to cry or simply let the groundskeeper bury her.

Much to Miranda Langford's relief, Dr. MacDonald settled the children's education in September, over a stroll through Bluebell Wood's rose garden.

"There is a Miss McCoy, a teacher from Liverpool, here with twenty evacuees from her school — all spread through the village, billeted as best they can be. Miss McCoy's made arrangements with the schoolmaster to share the school day and premises. Local children have lessons with their own teacher at the schoolhouse in the mornings until luncheon. Evacuee children will have lessons with their Miss McCoy in the afternoons. It's only half a day for each, but better than naught."

"They won't mix them and work together?" Miranda thought it rather typical English snobbery to separate the children. She plucked a rose hip in irritation.

"Too many of them, for starts, but they've found the children in very different levels of learning. . . . Best to keep them advancing with their own teachers."

"I don't see how that helps us." Miranda had always been put off by the formalities of British education, for both the elite and the masses. She'd longed for Christopher to be educated at home or nearby in the village school, but neither the village nor her peers had thought that proper for a boy bound to fill his father's shoes as Lord

Langford. It was Eton and away for him, something she regretted even more now that he was forever gone.

"I've asked if she'd be willing to take your children in her classes, and she's quite willing as long as they're well behaved and able to keep up."

"But those are English children she's teaching. Will she take French children — or German children when your evacuees arrive?" Miranda hoped he took the point that these proposed newcomers were his idea and his evacuees, no matter that they would be billeted at Bluebell Wood. She was already losing her determination to avoid attachment to the French children; her heart dared risk no more.

"Aye, as long as they speak enough English to learn and obey, and not disrupt the rest of the class."

"Well, there's no way to know about the Germans until they're here. Bertram and Jeanine are certainly prepared. Elise can probably just manage the English as long as Jeanine helps her. Gaston considers himself a native from birth."

The doctor laughed. "A native tongue with hot French blood!"

Miranda sighed. "I can't imagine getting Gaston to sit still long enough, but it will be a blessing to Mrs. Creedle to have him out of the house and off the grounds for a few hours each day."

"It will be good for the boy. Discipline is needed in the ranks." The doctor raised his eyebrows at Miranda, a thing she rarely appreciated and didn't now. She chose to ignore it.

"I don't think Aimee is quite ready."

"Nor do I. A bit wee yet. Perhaps next term." The doctor hesitated, opened his mouth to speak, but turned away.

"Raibeart?" Miranda didn't welcome his interfering, but she'd known him a long time, after all, and valued his insights and advice.

"I'm concerned about your niece."

"Please, don't start again. She's doing the best she can. She knows nothing of governing children, which she's embarrassingly and abundantly proven. I know you disapprove —"

"It's not that, Maggie. I'm concerned for her. She's sunk since being here — something neither you nor she wants, surely."

"She's unhappy, but she is trying. Her young man is hurt or possibly dead, at the very least a prisoner by now. She misses her friends, her work, her hopes of writing. All of that was so bound up in her life in Paris."

"I understand all that. I do. And there's nothing can be done about her friend, not until we know more. But perhaps she doesn't see what's before her."

"A war. For someone Claire's age, it looks like a lifetime. As much as I need her help with the children, I understand that. I remember."

"Has that served you well, Maggie?"

Miranda bristled, as she always did when Raibeart MacDonald pointed out her weaknesses.

"Don't get your back up. I only want to help your niece. I'm a doctor, after all, as well as an interferin' old friend . . . both are what I do." He snapped the stem of an apricot rose in the blush of new bloom and handed the fragrant beauty to her, a conciliatory gift.

Miranda couldn't help but smile. "What do you suggest?"

"Just this: that you encourage Claire to get on with her writing. She's filled with some romantic notion that the only way to do that is to return to Paris and her American bookstore."

"She said there's great literary inspiration there — writers she admires. I sympathize."

"And there is great literary inspiration here. Wordsworth and Carlyle came to the

Lake District for that very purpose. And most of all, my friend, there is you."

Miranda inhaled. Raibeart MacDonald was probably the only person alive who knew of her longing to write, a longing she'd never fulfilled beyond bits of poems that no one saw and journal entries for the Mass Observation Project — a project that he had suggested for her.

As if he could read her mind, the doctor smiled. "And how is your Mass Observation journal coming?"

Miranda twisted the rose he'd given her until she broke the stem. "Not well. Not since Christopher —" She couldn't bring herself to say more.

Kindly, the doctor went on. "Claire is in a similar boat, Maggie. She needs to wrench the grief from her spirit. If putting it on paper would help, then perhaps that's a project for her."

"I imagine London has all the grief-stricken writers it can stand these days." If she was sarcastic, even cruel, who could blame her?

"That's just it, isn't it? We're a nation at war. Understanding the horrible effects on the populace — the people who must survive while everyone else is off bombing the living daylights out of one another . . . Well, perhaps that understanding could lead to fewer wars, to no wars one day."

Miranda hadn't wanted to write of her grief after Christopher's death. But for Claire it might be needed to vent her soul; Miranda conceded that writing had helped her after Gilbert's death. "Perhaps you're right. I'll speak with her about it."

"Perhaps you'll take up your pens together."

"Now you're being pushy."

The doctor smiled. "So I am." He donned his hat and lifted it again in farewell. "On that note, I'm off. I'll stop when I've word of our new evacuees."

Miranda didn't correct his use of "our evacuees," nor did she suggest he telephone her with the news rather than squandering his petrol ration to visit.

Claire was not at all certain she wanted to accept her aunt's invitation to the library for afternoon tea, a formality they'd rarely indulged in since a light evening meal was served so early for the children's sakes. At least that was what her aunt had explained, though Claire realized Aunt Miranda was not inclined to spend time not required with her. According to Dr. MacDonald she bore a strong resemblance to her cousin, Christopher. Her aunt might also find her a reminder of years of estrangement with her own sister. But could it really be because Aunt Miranda found Claire herself disagreeable, disgusting in some way? Claire didn't know, but the price for clarity ran high.

The smile that greeted Claire when she entered the library was brave but tentative. That's how she thought of her aunt mostly — brave but tentative.

"Good afternoon, Aunt." Claire infused as much cheer into her voice as she could muster.

"Good afternoon, Claire. You look lovely today."

Claire started. It wasn't like her aunt to compliment her. But in anticipation of the tea Claire had taken special pains with her hair, winding its thick and unruly tendrils into victory rolls. She fingered it self-consciously. "Thank you; so do you."

Aunt Miranda looked as if she didn't believe her, but indulged her niece's attempt at flattery. "Will you take tea?"

"Yes, thank you. Is this a special occasion?" Claire didn't want to be caught unawares if something more lay on the horizon.

Her aunt looked up after pouring. "No, at least it shouldn't be." She set the pot down.

"I'm sorry it's taken me so long to see that. I want to right the situation, if we can."

Claire's stomach tightened.

"I won't make excuses. I simply wasn't prepared for . . . for you or the children."

"We descended on you out of the blue. I never intended it to turn out this way. I'm sorry. And I'm sorry about the vicar and the cemetery — and everything."

"I know you are. And I'm sorry I didn't welcome you. It's just . . ." Aunt Miranda looked as if she wanted to continue but couldn't.

"We're a great burden, I know. Even with making things legal and ration books for the children —"

"No. Truly, that's not the case. Everyone is doing their bit now, taking in someone or many someones for the duration. I can't expect to be any different. I'm not even certain, now you're all here, that I would want it to be different."

Claire felt her mouth drop and forcibly closed her teeth. Her aunt rose from her chair and walked to the window. What she saw through the ancient paned glass Claire couldn't be certain, but she heard Elise's squeal of delight from somewhere out of doors.

"It's been a long time since children

played tag or hide-and-seek in these halls, since children climbed the trees or played in the mazes or overran the orchard or the gardens."

"I'm sorry. I'll try to keep them quieter, less into things."

"Please stop apologizing. I'm not sorry. I only mean to say that it's been too long. Raibeart — Dr. MacDonald — is right. This is the perfect place for children . . . and for me to have them. I'm glad they're here."

Claire felt as if she might fall off her chair. To calm her nerves, she took a sip of tea and had nearly set the cup in its saucer when she boldly asked, without thinking, "And me? What about me?"

Aunt Miranda turned and looked at her. Claire couldn't read what she saw in her eyes. But she didn't have long to wait. Her aunt moistened her lips. "You're more difficult."

The frank rejection called up tears Claire hated but couldn't control. *What about me is so unlovable, so repulsive?* "My mother found me difficult. It's natural that you would." Claire tried to make light but couldn't stop the wells from overflowing.

"You've misunderstood me again. We can't keep doing this to one another, Claire." Aunt Miranda shook her head. "It's only that you look so much like him, so much like my Christopher."

"Again, I'm sorry, but I can't help that."

"Of course not. It's just that sometimes I see you, and for a moment — just a tiny moment — I think he's here again."

"And then it's just me."

"And then it's you — not *just* you, but you. It's you I must get to know and not expect you to be like him, not expect you to be him."

"I don't know what to say. I'd leave if I could."

"Which also makes me afraid to know you, to — to love you. I know you won't stay longer than you must. I'm not sure how much more loss my heart can take."

Her aunt seemed to want some sort of response, but Claire still didn't know what to say. To stay tortured her aunt. To leave frightened her. Leaving, if she couldn't return to France, frightened Claire, too. *Where can I go? Who wants me now?*

Aunt Miranda sighed. "That's my problem, not yours. Your challenge is to face the life you have now and make the most of it."

"I've taken on the children as best I can, but I'm not a teacher."

"No, and it was unfair of me to expect it. Dr. MacDonald helped me see that we need more help in that department and the children need to continue their education. We've no idea how long they'll need to remain here or what shape their future will take after the war."

Claire agreed wholeheartedly that more help was needed. Despite her desire to prove the perfect governess, she had little idea what she was doing. Getting more attached to the children terrified her. Claire refused to love another person who would surely walk away from her, who found life elsewhere more appealing, even if returning to their homes and parents was the most natural conclusion. But Aunt Miranda was right. Who knew what the world of these children would look like after the war or what would become of them? "I'm afraid for their parents."

"So am I, with good cause. But I also want what's best for you."

"You do?"

Her aunt smiled and shook her head as if she couldn't understand Claire's thickheadedness. "Of course I do."

Claire swallowed.

"Dr. MacDonald has arranged for the children to join the evacuee school in the village weekday afternoons from one to five. There's a teacher from Liverpool in charge of her own pupils then. She's agreed to take ours as well."

"That's wonderful!"

"Yes, well, as long as the children are not disruptive and as long as their English is fluent and won't hold the other children back."

Claire's heart dropped. "I don't know if Gaston can go an entire hour, let alone four, without being disruptive."

"He'll need some coaching or the threat of no dinner if he misbehaves, but I'm certain he can learn. Food seems to be a powerful motivator for him. Aimee can spend the afternoons with Mrs. Newsome or with me after her nap. That will give you a bit of free time for yourself. I'll need you to continue being a den mother to the children in the evenings, and you'll need to work diligently with them in the mornings to improve their English and make certain their lessons are accomplished for school."

"Free time? For me?" Claire was certain she'd not heard correctly.

Her aunt smiled knowingly. "I thought it might give you opportunity to dust off those literary ambitions of yours."

"I don't know what to say — or how I would even do that."

"Say yes, and take this letter. Read it over.

Britain has embarked on the Mass Observation Project. I think you'd make an excellent candidate for one of their writers."

"I've heard of that — the recording of daily lives — but I'm not even British. The few villagers I've met turn away the moment I open my mouth. There's little love for Americans here."

"Well, they took me, and I'm American, though I've not been very faithful in my contributions for the last year. I think they'd find the observations of a young American woman caught up in the French Resistance absolutely fascinating."

Claire's heart rose at the notion, then thudded. "I'm not doing anything about that now."

Aunt Miranda knelt before her, taking both Claire's hands in her own. "Claire, look at what you are doing, not what you imagine you should be doing. Life is not a drama on the stage with cued entrances and exits; it's messy and unpredictable.

"You're a den mother to five French children you rescued and will soon add who knows how many German children to that mix, some of them already orphans for all we know. What you're doing is a desperately needed contribution to the war effort. It matters. You matter."

Claire felt her head spinning, confused both from the things Aunt Miranda said and from the strength she poured into her hands. "It's only happening because you took them in — took me in."

Her aunt sat back on her heels. "So I have the privilege of being part of the story. *You* have the privilege of being part of the story, of writing it down from your own perspective."

Claire tried to comprehend that.

"I dare you." Aunt Miranda rose and resumed her seat. "Now, drink your tea."

Chapter Nine

On the first afternoon, Claire walked the children to the village school and introduced herself to Miss McCoy. The teacher, shorter than Claire by a few inches, seemed similar in age, but much more sure of herself.

"You'll need to work with your children at home, Miss Stewart. I'll not have them holding back my own students; is that clear?"

"Perfectly." Claire bristled, determined that "her" children would not hold anyone back, though she wasn't entirely sure how she would ensure that academic achievement.

That ought to have worried her, Claire knew, but from the moment Miss McCoy closed the school door in her face, she felt free — swept away and gloriously, giddily free. *Four entire hours to do just as I please!* She'd squandered time as a child with no idea of its meaning or value. But now, it was as if someone had handed her mountains of gold and she couldn't imagine how to spend it, although the pen and sheets of lined paper planted in her pocket gave her a very good idea. She nearly skipped down the road to the village proper.

She toured the village in search of a tea shop or a nook — a safe and quiet place to write — which took far less time than she'd hoped or imagined, especially since the local shopkeepers kept their eye on her as though she were bent on pocketing merchandise from their shelves.

There was little to buy, which didn't matter. The frosty, "Another American, eh?" from the greengrocer sent her scurrying, and truth be told, she had no money except for the shilling Aunt Miranda had given her to splurge on her afternoon of freedom with a cup of tea and a scone. Still, Claire did her best to ignore the cold shoulders and luxuriate in the lazy browsing and walking alone, something she hadn't done in ages.

She looked for a bookstore but found the only books available at the chemist's shop — few and of little interest. Claire realized four things: how differently the English viewed Americans than did the French, how difficult it was to find a quiet place to write, how desperately Windermere needed its own bookstore, and what a treasure trove her aunt's library boasted. She'd taken too little advantage of it since her recuperation. If she was going to be here for the duration — though they all hoped that wouldn't be long past Christmas — perhaps she'd best take note.

Claire rounded the long walkway to the church guarded by wide-spreading yews, grateful for their shield from the all-seeing eyes of the vicar, and made her way to the cemetery. No stone rubbings today, for certain, but perhaps she could find a bench or some quiet place to write. Surely no one could object to that.

Despite her earlier cemetery faux pas, Claire was comforted, even spellbound, by the old tombstones and their unique epitaphs. Many were older by far than any she'd seen growing up in Princeton.

She'd long romanticized the idea of finding intriguing characters — at least their names — among the stones, and loved to imagine stories of the lives those people had lived, or the ones they might have lived had they taken different paths. She was glad now that she'd not shared that fancy with the disapproving Bertram.

She spotted the tall monument near the far edge of the cemetery — the one she'd planned to investigate before Aimee's screams. Claire glanced guiltily over her shoulder. As near as she could see, she was quite alone, so she pushed open the gate and headed for the solitary bench positioned near the graves — and the solitude to write. Only when she'd rounded a corner boxwood hedge could she read the name on the monument: *Langford.*

Ripples of goosebumps ran up and down Claire's arms and legs. She felt she'd inadvertently stepped on sacred ground. It was all sacred ground, she realized, but this was Aunt Miranda's family, her family.

Gilbert Langford

Beloved husband and father

Served his king and country well

November 9, 1884 — August 23, 1916

This was the man her mother and aunt had fought over, had divided their tiny family over. *You must have been someone quite special, Uncle.*

Claire kept staring at her uncle's monument, almost afraid to move on. She knew whom the next stone would belong to:

Christopher Langford

Beloved son

Served his king and country well

April 12, 1914 — November 17, 1939

Ironic that the epitaphs are nearly the same, that they say next to nothing about the men they commemorate. Did Aunt Miranda write these, or was she so distraught that someone else chose these words for her? Bitter words, or bittersweet?

And what of you, Arnaud? Are you alive and well, or are you buried somewhere in France — somewhere in the cold, dark ground? Claire knew her Arnaud would have no monument set above his plot, not if he'd been given a choice. He saw himself as one of the people of France and would not want what he would surely label a bourgeois monument.

If he'd died in a German prison, would there even be a stone to mark his grave, a place for her to visit in years to come? Or would the Nazis have thrown him into an unmarked mass grave? There were rumors of such in Poland, even before she'd left France.

Claire sat on the low stone bench, the heaviness of the place a weight on her spirit. *Where are you, Arnaud? What's become of you?*

Where the afternoon went, Claire wasn't sure. The air turned cooler as the shadows lengthened. Sorry she'd not brought a jacket, Claire pulled her cardigan tight about her chest and began her trek back up the long hill, sadder, more sober than when she'd walked down.

She passed the village school just as the students turned out for the day. Gaston burst through the door, delighted to be set free. Claire smiled. He seemed as glad to walk beside her as she was to have him, a young boy living and breathing and full of chatter and teacher imitations bordering on the disrespectful. *Perhaps this life — this joy of life — is what Aunt Miranda has been missing, what she's decided is good about having us all here.*

Perhaps, Claire considered, *it's good for me, too.*

The German evacuees had been scheduled to arrive in October, the day after the bombing of the east end of the Henry VII Chapel in London's Westminster Abbey, and the day they learned of a German prisoner escaped from the nearby POW camp. The three impossible events became, in Mrs. Newsome's mind, inseparably linked.

Mr. Dunnagan brought the news to Lady Miranda at the breakfast table. "No doubt about it, my lady, a German prisoner of war escaped from Grizedale Hall earlier this month. Hidin' among the fells and in caves and such, he was."

"Is he still at large?" Lady Langford drew her fingers to her throat.

"Nothing to worry there, my lady. A farmer over the way caught him sleepin' in his barn — took 'im by surprise a week or more ago. By the time he telephoned the authorities, the scoundrel'd got away again, but they caught him for good and all last night. He's locked up tight and I wouldn't be surprised if they've sent 'im off to a higher security prison. Grizedale Hall's not much of a fortress, if you ask me."

"Have they many prisoners there?" Bertram wanted to know.

"That I don't know . . . except to say they're mostly naval officers and those nabbed off captured submarines and such. They're callin' it the U-Boat Hotel. Fancy that!"

"Why have we not heard of this before now? We could have all been taken unawares."

"That's just what the locals are sayin', my lady — up in arms they are, and demandin' to be kept abreast of such things in future. The officer from the hall said he didn't want to alarm the village."

Mrs. Newsome plunked another bowl of porridge on the sideboard. "It's more alarming by far to think we could all be murdered in our beds because we don't know —"

"Mrs. Newsome, please, the children."

Mrs. Newsome straightened the toast on the rack. It was very well for her lady to hush her, but Claire and the children should think of these things. *What if one of them is accosted on their walk to and from the village school, or in the woods or orchards, where they've all taken to roaming freely?*

"You don't suppose those prisoners will try to make contact with the German evacuees coming here, do you?" Gaston wanted to know.

"What a stupid thing to say," Bertram reprimanded his younger brother. "The evacuees are children — like you."

"Like us!" Gaston retorted. "You're a children, too!"

"Boys!" Lady Miranda admonished. "That's quite enough. May I remind you that we will welcome the children arriving today in the same way you wished to be welcomed."

After breakfast Elise stood beside Mrs. Newsome as she scraped the plates.

"They're Jewish, these new children coming today?"

"Yes, they are, like you. And like you, they've been through a great deal already in Germany — perhaps more than we guess — and are likely to still be afraid. They might find it hard to trust us at first. We'll all be strangers to them. We must remember that and be patient with them. They've had to leave their first English homes along the coast because of the German bombing."

"But they are Germans," Elise ventured.

"Yes."

"Then . . ."

"Yes?"

"Can we trust them?" she whispered.

Mrs. Newsome wondered the same thing, though she was ashamed to say so. It was nothing more than a feeling born of fear of Hitler and his hateful swarm of bomb-wielding Messerschmitts that terrorized England night and day, but a feeling just the same. Still, it wouldn't do to pass her fears to Elise.

"These are children, Elise, escaping the

claws of the Nazis, just like you young ones from France. They'll be missing their parents fiercely, just as you miss yours. We must be very kind indeed to them and make them feel at home."

Elise nodded uncertainly.

Mrs. Newsome didn't blame her. It was hard to understand, this war and the throwing together of refugees from hither and yon. Mrs. Newsome hardly understood it herself, could barely separate her inclinations and prejudices from facts. How could she expect a child to do so? "I believe we'll all get on once we've gotten to know one another. Dr. MacDonald will be bringin' them by this afternoon, so you'll meet up after school. Perhaps I'll ask Mrs. Creedle to prepare us a little welcome tea. Wouldn't that be nice?"

Elise nodded, smiling tentatively.

Mrs. Newsome stroked the little girl's hair and gave her back a pat, sending her on her way. She hoped that all she'd said was true and that her own fears were unfounded.

Lady Langford asked Mrs. Newsome to combine the boys into one large dormitory room and the girls into another, despite the vehement protestations of the French children.

"There'll be no national divisions in this household; do I make myself clear?"

"Perfectly, Madame Langford." Gaston crossed his arms, pouting. "But there is a line that cannot be crossed."

Bertram sent his brother a look Miranda classified as "daggers."

"No Maginot Line here, Gaston; just remember that. These children are in the same plight as you were when you came, and I expect you to make them at home and welcome, as I did you."

Gaston colored slightly, but did not nod in agreement. He simply looked the other way.

Miranda thought it best to introduce the German children to Claire and the French children in the library, just before tea. As Miranda introduced Claire and Mrs. Newsome to the newcomers, the two groups of children stood off like small armies, neither giving the other a welcome or acknowledgment, but sizing up their new housemates as if planning military strategy.

"My name is Peter, and I am thirteen — I will soon be fourteen." The tall and muscular teen gave a small bow, eyeing Bertram with an air of superiority, then clamped his hand on the shoulder of a younger boy. "This is my brother, Jo—"

The boy, near Gaston's size, shrugged the hand from his shoulder and pushed in front of Peter. "I am Josef, eight years old, and I do not need anyone to speak for me, *danke.* This, on the other hand, is Franz, Ingrid and Marlene's cousin, and he is . . . awkward with girls."

"I am not awkward," Franz hissed. "I am, perhaps, not confident of meeting so many at once. I am seven."

"He's shy," Elise interpreted, smiling. "I'm Elise, and I don't bite."

Jeanine poked her sister in the side, whispering, "Don't be so familiar." She hesitated, blushing. "I'm Jeanine. Elise is my younger sister, and this is Aimee, the smallest among us."

Aimee ducked behind her curls, and Franz nodded, barely looking up from the floor. Josef's glare softened.

A sturdy young girl with two thick, dark braids down her back stepped forward. "Ingrid, ten."

"And I'm Marlene, twelve," a tall but quiet girl spoke softly. "Ingrid and I are sisters, and yes, Franz is our cousin."

Miranda thought Bertram's eyes lit up when Marlene flipped her long brown braid over her shoulder and couldn't help but notice the defensive lift of Jeanine's chin.

"Bertram, thirteen," Bertram offered, standing straight.

"I am Gaston." Gaston spread his feet and crossed his arms with the scowl of a young Napoleon.

Miranda did her best to ignore the overtones, nodding to Mrs. Newsome to ring for tea — a tea that proved the quietest and most orderly of any they'd taken in the house for four months as the competing nations scowled or flirted with one another.

The peace was such a reprieve from all she'd anticipated in combining the children that Miranda smiled and began to think they just might make it through the war . . . until the boys destroyed four goose-down pillows and an eiderdown in a blistering dormitory pillow fight that night.

Chapter Ten

Despite the constant digs of the boys against opposing nationalities — primarily Josef and Gaston — Claire began to find a rhythm to her days. Mornings were spent tutoring the French children through homework, Aimee seated at her side drawing or coloring pictures, while Claire worked with Gaston and Elise. Bertram and Jeanine appeared competent in their studies as well as their English, so needed very little help.

Aunt Miranda tutored the new children in English, brushing up on her rusty German as she did so, much to Claire's relief, for she spoke no German. The German children already understood a good deal of English, and most spoke well.

Josef, though young, was an especially quick learner. It wouldn't be long, Claire thought, until he might join the village evacuee classes. Even now he made noble efforts to communicate with her in full

English during teatime.

Bertram seemed energized by the daily routine of school and the challenge of studies in English, tackling each of his subjects with a will.

Jeanine took a different view of Bertram's enthusiasm. "I believe he is more excited about a certain English girl from the village than he is about King Henry VIII."

Claire noticed that Jeanine emphasized Bertram's interest in English girls in front of Marlene and wondered if she might be a little jealous of the German girl. The thought made her both smile and pity Jeanine. *Why is it boys don't notice when we like them?* It was a problem Claire had experienced time and again growing up.

Elise thrived on Claire's personal attention, especially when they worked on reading together. She'd not seen Elise smile so much or respond so happily before, and the young girl's blossoming pleased Claire. Elise had stopped wetting the bed at night, a fact that pleased not only Mrs. Newsome, but especially Nancy, the housemaid.

"This is my new primer, mademoiselle." Elise proudly showed Claire. "Teacher say I have progressed to a new reading level."

"Teacher *said,*" Claire corrected.

"*Oui* — yes — Teacher said," Elise repeated, smiling.

"That's wonderful, Elise. I'm so very proud of you."

"See my picture, Mademoiselle Claire?" Aimee interrupted, pushing her coloring between Elise's book and Claire's face, giving Claire an inadvertent bump across the bridge of her nose in the process. "It is of the trees near the orchard now, all red and gold!"

"Aimee! Please! That's very nice —" Claire rubbed her nose — "but I'm working with Elise now. You must wait your turn."

"*Oui,* mademoiselle." She turned away and whispered, "But when is my turn?"

Aimee's pitiful plea was not new to Claire. She felt sorry for the child who wanted only to join in the activities and attention of the older children, but Claire was one person and there was only so much of her to go around. The little girl would simply have to wait, or amuse herself.

"Mrs. Newsome will help you this afternoon, Aimee, when she's done her morning's work. You know that. Now sit and color or go play by yourself until luncheon."

Claire tried not to notice the child's trembling lip.

The afternoon hours Aunt Miranda had planned for Claire to write, to journal for the Mass Observation Project, had completely vanished. By the time the German children's afternoon lessons ended, the French children were out of school and it was time for a group tea, which had replaced the evening meal. Then chaos reigned in three languages until bedtime.

Claire counted herself lucky to find twenty minutes for a short walk through the grounds after lunch to clear her head and ten minutes to scribble a few lines of her would-be novel before falling asleep at night, pen in hand, ink staining her coverlet. The lack of solitude and focused time, and the lack of sleep, made her grumpy. She knew she shouldn't take it out on the children, least of all little Aimee, and that made her grumpier still, especially when Mrs. Newsome clucked her tongue.

"Come, Aimee," the housekeeper said. "You may help me haggle with the greengrocer. Mrs. Creedle can handle the puddings. We'll collect your pictures and make a nice book of them, shall we? This afternoon we might take a stroll over to Auld Mother Heelis's farm. My niece Ruby works there as housemaid. Perhaps Mrs. Heelis will take a look at your drawings, if she's not out traipsing the fells, checking on her sheep. In any case, you can see some of her pictures.

She likes to draw bunnies and lambs, just as you do. You'll enjoy her sheep, and there's always ducks about the place."

Aimee brightened. *"Vraiment?"*

"Thank you, Mrs. Newsome. I appreciate it." Claire felt both the burden and the guilt leave her shoulders.

"It's a trip you'd enjoy, I'm quite certain, Miss Claire, if you find the time. You're welcome to join us."

Claire bristled. Mrs. Newsome knew perfectly well Claire's schedule.

" 'Twas just a thought," the older woman said, taking Aimee by the hand.

The afternoon trip seemed to have done Aimee a great deal of good, much to Mrs. Newsome's apparent delight and Claire's relief.

"Mrs. Heelis said that Aimee shows great promise as an artist!" Mrs. Newsome crowed over tea that evening.

"Did she?" Aunt Miranda seemed pleased beyond Claire's comprehension.

"Oh, madame! She showed me pictures of her bunnies, and the naughtiest squirrel I ever saw!" Aimee all but squealed, unable to stay in her seat.

Aunt Miranda's smile widened. "You're a very lucky little girl to have visited Mrs.

Heelis. She doesn't often take time for children — or adults, for that matter."

"*Oui,* madame!" Aimee beamed. "She said the bunny was created for a boy long ago — he is now a man all grown and an air-raid warden in a bombed London parish; and the squirrel, he lived on the shore of Der— Der—"

"Derwentwater," Mrs. Newsome helped, grinning all the while.

"*Merci!* Derwentwater, the lake near Keswick."

"My goodness," Claire said. "What an imagination your Mrs. Heelis has."

"Mademoiselle Ruby, the niece of Madame Newsome, said there are others straight from Sawrey — the talking duck, and the frog with a waistcoat, and . . ."

"Talking animals?" Claire smiled indulgently. That was more imagination than she had summoned since childhood.

"Ah, *oui,* mademoiselle! And there is a fairy caravan where the Girl Guides used to camp high up in the hills — but of course now they cannot go there because of the war and the bombing — and some other sort of camp and something about a footpath, but I cannot remember what." Aimee's forehead scrunched, but she was wound like a spring and barely stopped for air. "I think perhaps it is hidden in those blue and green hills above her farm — Troutbeck, I think she said . . . or some sort of *poisson.*"

"I think you'd best calm down now and eat your soup. You've had quite a day, what with talking ducks and fairy caravans and towns named after fish."

"Oh, and the bunny chased by a garden rake!" Aimee clapped and laughed, her voice rising like the tide.

Claire shook her head. "That's enough, Aimee."

"*Oui,* mademoiselle." Aimee stopped, crestfallen, and ducked her head. Still, she whispered, "I should very much like to see the fairy caravan."

Aunt Miranda smiled at Aimee but gave Claire a disapproving raised eyebrow. Claire lifted her chin, turning her attention to her meal. She couldn't say why she found Aimee's prattle annoying. She knew she should be glad that the little girl had enjoyed her day. Something about it made her a little envious, including Aimee's strengthening bond with Mrs. Newsome, who always seemed to have time for her, no matter how busy she was.

I can't be all things to all people. Why do I care what she does as long as she's busy and happy?

"Claire? Claire, did you hear me?" It took Claire a moment to realize her aunt was speaking to her.

"I'm sorry; what did you say, Aunt Miranda?" Claire wiped her mouth with her napkin.

"I have a ten o'clock appointment here tomorrow morning, and I must ask you to work with all the children for a couple of hours. In the drawing room would be best. My meeting is in the library."

"All? A couple of hours?" Claire thought she might burst a blood vessel.

Aunt Miranda must have seen Claire's panic. "I'll take your afternoon group while the other children are in school, if you wish. That will give you a few hours of free time. Would you like that?"

Would I? "Thank you, Aunt Miranda. That will be wonderful." Claire nearly swooned at the thought. *That more than makes up for throwing us all together for the morning. Three hours — at least — to escape! If only it won't rain!*

Claire could barely keep her mind on the children that night. Marlene, the oldest of the German evacuee girls, had become a right hand at tucking the young ones into bed, including her younger sister and cousin, ten-year-old Ingrid and seven-year-old Franz. Of course, Peter, at nearly fourteen and having celebrated his bar mitzvah before leaving Germany, was too old for tucking in. He and Bertram had become fast friends, if competitive at games and debates.

It was eight-year-old Josef who tried Claire's patience, who stated flatly that he was too old for tucking in and clearly despised Gaston for claiming such a baby's attention from Claire. The boy adored her, she could see, but the antics he performed to capture her attention left Gaston's pranks in the dust. *Which is probably quite the point,* Claire conceded.

Morning lessons dragged for Claire. Verb conjugations and points of English grammar for the German children swam in her head along with the mix of times tables and reigns of British monarchs for the French children. By luncheon she was ready to explode and convinced her aunt and Mrs. Creedle that she would prefer a picnic lunch and a long walk.

Aunt Miranda looked a little perturbed to lose her additional table referee, but Claire no longer cared. She'd kept her end of the bargain. Mrs. Newsome could assist through lunch and in getting the schoolchildren out the door and on the road in good time.

Claire changed her shoes into her aunt's loaned Wellingtons and belted her trench coat. Once outdoors, she pushed her pen and paper deep into her pocket, tucked her lunch and tea thermos beneath her arm, and left the maze path. She'd explored little of the orchards or other gardens and, in fact, had told the children never to stray beyond the front lawn and maze.

Mrs. Newsome had suggested that her ladyship might not like the children traipsing willy-nilly through all the woodland paths, though her aunt had said no such thing. Claire had asked her why not, but Mrs. Newsome had simply said that "some things are not meant to be shared."

Claire never knew what the children were up to when turned loose out of doors. *Would I have obeyed a "keep away" mandate at their age? Would I obey one now?* She shook her head in recognition of the truth. *Can I expect more of them?*

The afternoon air sprang glorious after the early-morning rain. A cobalt-blue sky rode high, and the sun's brilliant rays shone through the leaves of brown beeches, emerald yews, rusting larch, and ancient oaks that Claire believed must have towered even in King Arthur's time. Lime trees dripped gold and green, their fallen leaves forming a thick carpet over the lawn she walked. Trees and shrubbery — brilliant, but different from any Claire had known in New Jersey — burned in shades of crimson and orange. Claire spent her first hour trekking the perimeter of the lawns and musing over the overgrown topiaries before turning to the woods.

Her aunt had told her that most of the trails wound through the gardens and the forest, coming back on themselves in meandering paths, creating the illusion of two, perhaps three miles of special haunts — that it was easy to become confused. Claire knew it must have taken years — decades — to create such splendor. What a shame, she thought, that now there were not enough men left to tend this treasure.

Wooden doors and arbors leading to individual gardens and new vistas beckoned each way she turned: kitchen gardens, flower beds, herb gardens, orchards, berry thickets . . . Her favorite was the garden she'd discovered the first month she was quarantined at Bluebell Wood, the one dubbed the Secret Garden by an old, lopsided sign, a board nailed awkwardly with the letters scrawled in a childish hand. Of course the sign made it secret no longer.

The curious thing was, the lock had been cemented. It was nothing more than a tease. She imagined the frustration of the children upon finding they were not admitted to the "secret garden" no matter what they did. Of course, they could try climbing over the wall if one lifted the other, but it was high, and such a feat seemed unlikely, even for Gaston.

She was about to turn away when it occurred to her that there might be another entrance for such a large walled area.

Remembering a similar story from childhood, Claire, with new energy, walked the perimeter of the walled garden, pulling back vines every few yards. Nothing. She'd nearly made it to the back wall of the garden when she found a slight indentation in the stonework. Pulling back the thick vines covering the space, she found built into the wall, a foot or so above ground level, a heavy wooden door painted to look exactly like the stone.

Claire's heart tripped, then picked up a beat. There was a lock in the door, but no key. She ran her fingers round the heavy sill. At the top, she grasped the cold iron of a heavy, old-fashioned key — just the sort she might have imagined for such a place.

Claire swallowed, glanced furtively around

as if she might be caught, and inserted the key.

Everything about stepping through the door reminded her of the book she'd loved as a child, *The Secret Garden* by Frances Hodgson Burnett. From the moment she crossed the threshold, Claire knew she'd traversed worlds — time and space.

Inside was a fully functioning but riotously overgrown Victorian garden, summer-spent and needing to be tidied for winter. Rose hips, full and red, burst beneath late-season blooms opened to shades of pink, coral, and butter yellow. Thick wisteria vines, their blooms long past, wound tentacles up and round aged tree trunks. A winding trail through an untrained wooded patch created magic beyond anything Claire had seen or explored. The garden appeared even bigger on the inside than she'd imagined from her trek outside the wall.

Round one curve she found a swing large enough for two — built from a sanded board hung with thick and twisted ropes. She tested the weathered ropes. The swing could certainly hold her, and made the perfect perch to eat her lunch and drink her tea. Back and forth, back and forth she pumped her knees. Claire had forgotten how she loved to swing, how she loved to chant aloud the rhyme of Robert Louis Stevenson:

How do you like to go up in a swing,
Up in the air so blue?
Oh, I do think it the pleasantest thing
Ever a child can do! . . .

A canopy of honeysuckle and wisteria vines grown wild covered a section of treetops — so thick and sturdy a child might climb them and pretend he'd hoisted the sails of a great ship. She imagined Gaston, and perhaps Elise or Franz — if they could be coaxed — climbing and swinging across the tops of those vines for hours. Josef would need no coaxing.

Claire knew she should work her way back toward the house soon. The children would be home for tea in an hour or so, and she dared not desert Aunt Miranda again.

But a little brown bird Claire didn't recognize chirped, hopping from branch to branch — probably, she thought, desperate to lure her from its perch for the evening. She knew she should ignore the bird and hurry back, but something drew her deeper into the garden. Claire still believed, or wanted to believe, in magic and the charm of thin veils between worlds. What better place to find such a veil?

She took a deep breath and followed the bird, just as Mary Lennox had followed the robin to find the key to her secret garden. She walked slowly at first, then tripped over tree roots in her speed and eagerness to keep pace with the flighty creature. Apparently having lured her sufficiently away, the bird chirped ferociously, beating the air with its wings, then took to the sky, flying back the way they'd come.

Claire was at last ready to give up her fancy and return too. But as she turned, she saw on the tree from which the bird took flight another sign — another board awkwardly nailed to its trunk.

She stepped closer, parting the tangle of wild vines wound round the tree. The words, painted in the familiar childish script, had long faded, but were still legible: *Christopher's Secret Place — KEEP OUT — THAT MEANS YOU.*

Claire's breath caught. The moment was like walking over her cousin's grave again. She glanced round as if afraid of being caught breaching the sign's security. *Silly,* she thought, knowing she was the only one in the walled garden.

Just above the sign hung an old rope, thick and pinned to the tree by more wisteria vines. It took all of Claire's strength to yank it free. It appeared to be tied from the lowest sturdy limb — barely eight feet off the ground. Knotted every ten inches to a foot, the rope appeared intended for climbing. She walked round the tree and looked up. Just above the sturdy limb was another board, smaller and more evenly nailed, and another above that. The tree's leaves had shed enough to see that much, but no more. What more could there be? Her curiosity was too great to let her walk away.

Claire glanced over her shoulder once more and pulled with all her weight on the rope. Despite its apparent age, it didn't seem the worse for wear — certainly not frayed or likely to break. She hiked her skirt into her belt and slipped her aunt's loaned Wellingtons from her feet.

Thankful she'd worn thick and double socks for her trudging, she climbed the rope, one challenging knot at a time. Claire grunted from the effort. Her strength was not in her arms.

When she reached the second board, she discovered more, leading high into the tree. She pulled the vines to the side and climbed, the going easier. Just above the wisteria canopy, the tree's branches thrust open — far and wide to all points of the compass. In that great, thick neck between the tree's head and shoulders and multitudinous arms sat a lean-to — a wide, flat board overhanging thick branches, creating a sturdy floor to sit upon. Overhead, another board, placed across higher branches, sheltered the occupant from rain.

Claire climbed onto the board, astonished by such a find. She leaned against the thick tree trunk. From her hidden perch she peeked between the branches, and nearly the entire estate — the grand house, the maze of gardens and outbuildings, the topiaries in the front — spread before her.

From her perch she realized that the topiaries, though not chessmen, had been laid out like figures on a chessboard. *How clever! How ingenious!* It was something she'd never have known had she not climbed so high and found her aerial view.

A person could be truly alone here, with her thoughts. She could think things and write things that no one would ever know. The idea surprised her — surprised her that she'd thought it, as if it was something she desired.

This must have been my cousin's favorite place as a boy — his hidden, secret cove. She wondered if he'd come here as a grown man. She'd no idea how long it took wisteria vines to grow, to pin such a rope to a tree, but she imagined it had been many years since anyone had climbed to the nest.

Claire sat on the board until the sun lowered itself in the sky. Convinced it must be past time for tea, she gave her bird's-eye view one more search and reluctantly climbed down, careful to cover each of the footboards and tuck the knotted rope into the vine as high as she could reach. She covered Christopher's handwritten sign and pulled a bit of brush back onto the path she'd plowed in getting to the tree.

Exactly why she did this, she couldn't say. No one knew it was here.

But she wanted to save this place. She didn't want the children, as much as she wished Bluebell Wood to be their home for the war's duration, to know about it, to desecrate it. *It belonged to Christopher, and now it belongs to me.* Claire gasped at her own presumption, but it fit, and was precisely what she meant.

Chapter Eleven

November brought stark trees, thunderous skies, and ever more chill and pelting rain to Bluebell Wood.

Life seemed gray enough to Miranda without adding the news that the Germans had nearly flattened beautiful Coventry in nonstop bombing raids. More than 550 people lay dead, 1,200 injured, more left homeless, and their magnificent old cathedral all but obliterated.

Closer to home was the one-year anniversary of Christopher's death. All that day Miranda kept to her room, kept the blackout curtains drawn, and refused to eat.

She sent word, asking that Claire and Mrs. Newsome handle the children from dawn to dusk. Every member of the household walked on tiptoe, including Gaston and Josef, respecting the terrible grief of Lady Langford for her son and mourning, with Mrs. Newsome and Mrs. Creedle, the decimation of their beloved Coventry.

But when the dark night passed, Miranda washed her face and sleepless eyes, packed away her mourning garments, and brought out a deep-green dress, seamed and belted, if a little loose. It wasn't so much that the year had turned over on itself, that the time of mourning had officially ended. What did Miranda care for conventions such as that? It was more that the anniversary marked a turning of her heart.

Sitting in front of her dressing table, she closed her eyes. She imagined for a moment that Christopher stood behind her, his hand on her shoulder, saying, "It's all right, Mother. The children here need you. It's time."

Twin tears escaped the corners of her eyes as she reached for the hand upon her shoulder, but the precious grasp wasn't there. Miranda swiped at the rivulets on her cheeks and blew her nose. A moment later she caressed an old and favorite gold brooch at her neck, given her by her late husband, then stood, smoothing her skirt. Five minutes later she astonished her new and makeshift family at breakfast.

"Praise God," Mrs. Newsome whispered, barely able to hold on to the bowl of porridge she carried to the sideboard.

"What's that, Mrs. Newsome?" Miranda asked, taking her seat.

"I said you look lovely, my lady. Somehow, that color makes the horrible war news and even our rationing of everything from bacon to butter more bearable." Mrs. Newsome bent to check the milk pitcher on the sideboard. "Thank heaven for our faithful cow and Mr. Dunnagan here to milk her."

"What would we do without either of them?"

"I've no idea, my lady. With all these children, the milk, the cream, and the extra butter make for blessing beyond blessings."

"We do have much to be thankful for, don't we, Mrs. Newsome?" Miranda smiled tentatively.

"That we do." Mrs. Newsome's kindly face bolstered Miranda's courage.

"Green is my favorite color," Gaston announced, breaking the awkwardness as no one could.

"I'm very glad it is," Miranda approved. "It was my son's favorite color too."

A hush fell across the table, one Miranda had not intended. She looked to Mrs. Newsome for support.

"We've a guest coming soon, I believe you said, my lady — an American, is it?"

"Yes." Miranda had nearly forgotten,

though she was astonished she could do so when David Campbell's plans had raised such unexpected ire in Raibeart MacDonald. She realized now she should have known. Nearly two hundred and fifty years was clearly not enough time to erase the Scottish feud or the stench of the massacring Campbell clan from the nostrils of the unsuspecting MacDonalds.

"An American?" Claire dropped her spoon.

Miranda smoothed her napkin over her lap. Now was as good a time as any to make the announcement. "Mr. David Campbell, from West Virginia, though lately from Edinburgh. He's an engineer of sorts and has some war work to do in the area for a time."

"He's staying? As in, he's going to live here?" Claire's astonishment was reflected in the faces of the children.

"For the time being," Miranda conceded. "He needs a billet. The request came from the War Office, so I really can't refuse."

"Aren't we full up?"

Claire's impertinence annoyed Miranda. Bluebell Wood wasn't her niece's house, though she'd certainly started a parade of her own guests traipsing through.

"We don't know how long he'll be with

us, but we'll all work to make him welcome." She looked pointedly at Claire. "It will be good to have one of our countrymen among us."

After breakfast, Claire cornered her in the hallway. "He's coming here because no one else will take him."

"We Americans are not tremendously popular among the British at the moment. You've experienced that in the village, surely."

"Bringing another American here won't help. We've just settled the German kids in school; the village is angry enough about that. Can't he stay somewhere else?"

"I rather think that's why I was asked to take him. Well, not exactly 'asked.' I thought you'd be glad of a fellow Yank for company."

"It's not helpful — in the village or here. The children are just getting adjusted to one another. Things will change now that Mr. Roosevelt's been reelected. He'll push to enter the war; I'm sure of it. But we ought not rub the village noses the wrong way now," Claire challenged as if her concerns were all political. What lay at the heart of her niece's outburst, Miranda couldn't imagine, but she had no time and little patience for Claire's behavior.

"I hope Mr. Roosevelt does come to

Britain's aid. But that's not our affair. Hospitality in this situation is, and I expect you to be a gracious host." Miranda prayed they all would, if only she could keep David Campbell and Raibeart MacDonald from killing one another.

Four days later, Mrs. Newsome vowed that of all times for Mrs. Creedle and Nancy to fall ill, this was the worst. It was already six fifteen. Despite her own splitting headache, she hurried up the stairs to Claire's room and rapped on the door. *At least it's a Thursday and not much going on until after tea.*

A sleepy "Yes?" responded.

"It's Mrs. Newsome, Miss Claire. I need your help. May I come in?"

"Yes, of course."

Mrs. Newsome didn't give Claire a chance to sit up or wipe the sleep from her eyes. "I'm sorry to call you so early, but we're in desperate straits. Mrs. Creedle and Nancy have both come down with influenza in the night. I've been nursing them back and forth since the wee hours, and a right mess it is, too."

"Oh no. Does Aunt Miranda know? Have you telephoned Dr. MacDonald?"

"Yes, on both counts. It seems it's spreading through the village like brush fire."

"That means we're all at risk."

"That it does, and we're without cook or kitchen help. Even Mollie's looking poorly; she may not be far behind. You understand what this means."

"It means we must be very careful not to spread germs."

"It means you and I are the last defense against starvation for a household of hungry youngsters. Do you know how to cook, Miss Claire?"

"Cook?" Claire looked as bewildered as Mrs. Newsome feared she might.

"Can you prepare anything at all?"

"I — I made pancakes once."

"That will have to do for luncheon, then. Perhaps you can fry up some rashers to round it out. I'll get together some porridge and toast and coffee for breakfast. You wake the children and see that they're dressed and downstairs for eight."

"All of them?"

Mrs. Newsome thought she might collapse from weariness. "You'll have to get Bertram and Peter to carry up some coal and stoke the heaters. Josef and Gaston can fetch firewood for the library — it's a damp day; we might as well have the extra heat. It won't hurt them to help and they're certainly strong enough. I don't know why we've not had them help more before." She was nearly out the door, leaving a wide-eyed Claire, when she stopped. "If Aimee has that rabbit hidden amongst her bedsheets, you'll need to put them to soak, no doubt, and insist she take it outdoors to feed it."

"A rabbit in her bed?"

"You didn't know? She's been sleeping with it ever since our trip to Mrs. Heelis's." That Claire knew so little of the child annoyed Mrs. Newsome more than she could say. "Have the girls lay the table . . . and tell them to be quick about it — please." Mrs. Newsome closed the door behind her, exhausted, but with a satisfaction she hadn't known before. *They should all be helping. We're not a house as we were before the war; we're a makeshift family. Well, we should makeshift the work and share it, too. I'll speak to Lady Miranda about that as soon as things settle down. In the meantime, I suppose we'll all see what we're made of.*

It was one thing to tuck children into bed at night, but Claire had never overseen their morning washing and dressing. Even through those first dark days in the Beardsleys' attic, Mrs. Beardsley had done that with the pleasure of a storybook grandmother.

Claire knew nothing of tearful children who accused her of heartlessness while clinging to frightened rabbits who'd messed the bed. Her mother had never allowed a pet in the house, let alone one intended for food. *Heaven help us all the day Mrs. Creedle serves rabbit pie!*

And Claire had never cooked a meal for a crowd. The pancakes she'd made — once — were enough for her mother and her; they'd come out soggy, a fact she'd failed to share with Mrs. Newsome. Even in Paris, Josephine had cooked every meal in their flat. Claire had washed the dishes, pots, and pans, but that was the extent of her housekeeping knowledge.

Midway through the morning, Aunt Miranda excused Claire from lessons with the children. "I'll take charge here now. You'll want to familiarize yourself with the kitchen, Claire, and make sure you have whatever you need for the meal. Mrs. Newsome said Mrs. Creedle wasn't able to do her normal shopping yesterday. I suppose she was already feeling poorly but didn't realize what she was coming down with."

Claire made her way downstairs and stood in the midst of Mrs. Creedle's vast and spotless kitchen. She knew enough of Mrs. Creedle to know she dared not create a disturbance or smudge she couldn't erase before that lady's return to duty. *Let it be soon!*

"This is a project," Claire said aloud to the kitchen, bolstering her confidence. "I must look at this as a great adventure . . . a wartime assignment." She plopped a canister of flour on the worktable and removed the lid, pulled a bowl of fresh eggs from the pantry, no matter that Mrs. Creedle had insisted they should be carefully rationed, and laid out the rashers Mrs. Newsome had told her to use. What to do next, Claire wasn't entirely certain, but she squared her shoulders. "I'll not be intimidated by pancakes. I won't."

At that moment Aimee's brown rabbit, Mr. Cottontail, tore through the silent kitchen, so close to Claire's feet that she screamed and jumped, knocking the canister of flour from the table and covering her skirt, her shoes, and the spotless kitchen floor in a thick layer of powdery snow.

Twenty minutes later Claire had retrieved what she dared and swept the rest of the precious but useless flour into the waste bin. She opened a new flour sack, Mrs. Creedle's predicted tirade ringing in her head:

"Wasteful! Wasteful!"

There was no time to mop the floor. Claire's floury footprints accompanied her every move.

At long last she covered sizzling rashers in a skillet heavy enough to rival cannons. She whisked eggs as she'd seen Mrs. Beardsley do, pulling bits of shell away. She knew the lady had added salt and pepper, perhaps even a little milk?

Claire couldn't remember the recipe for pancakes, and Mrs. Creedle apparently worked without a book or recipe file of any sort, so she guessed. "Eggs, milk, flour, salt, maybe some baking powder and soda and butter . . . What more could there be?" Claire had no idea, so she dumped all that together and mixed it up.

She heated another skillet, ladling the hefty batter in dollops, hoping the puddles would expand and do what they must to look like thin pancakes. But they expanded very little, and bubbled to a height Claire knew no pancake should, then fell like rocks. What had she done wrong? The clock ticked ever closer to noon. Luncheon could not be late or the children would miss school. Having them all home the full day loomed worse than one questionable meal. Claire cooked the eggs to a rubber shine.

"Mademoiselle?" Jeanine, Marlene, and Ingrid appeared in the kitchen doorway, their mouths open wide.

Claire looked up, trying to see what they saw, what it was that they tried so hard to hide in their faces. Her apron was covered in flour and smears of batter; the flour on the swept floor still looked like marble dust. Claire squared her shoulders once more, trying to appear as if she had everything under control.

"Madame Newsome sent us to carry the meal upstairs," Jeanine offered.

"Well then, just as soon as I dish up the eggs, we'll be ready."

Ingrid sniffed. "What is that strange smell?"

Marlene elbowed her.

"The bacon!" Claire grabbed a tea towel, wrapped the skillet handle, and pulled the blistering pan from the stove onto the wooden worktable. She yanked off the lid. Black smoke billowed to the ceiling.

"Ohhhh," all three girls lamented.

"It's just a little over-browned, a little well done," Claire affirmed. "It will be all right. Everything will be all right."

The girls glanced at one another as if they didn't believe her.

"Stop standing there! Jeanine, carry up

the pancakes," Claire sputtered, pushing damp hairs from her forehead. "Ingrid, take the eggs. Marlene, carry that tray with butter and marmalade. I'll see if I can find some honey or syrup."

"What about the milk, the tea?" The girls looked around the room.

Claire's heart stopped. She'd forgotten to put the kettle on or bring Mr. Dunnagan's new milk jug in from the cooler. "We're not drinking with our meal today."

"Nein?" Ingrid gaped in disbelief.

"No, it's common with this meal. Now, go along. I'll bring the meat platter when I come." Claire waited until the girls left to address the burned rashers. *A pound and a half of ruined meat! What will Mrs. Newsome say? What will Aunt Miranda say?* Claire swiped a tear of frustration from her eye. *Well, they shouldn't have had me do it. I know nothing about cooking.*

What do you know about?

Claire had no idea where that thought came from. If it was God — if He was really there — then His timing was bad. She couldn't have felt worse than she did. Claire bit her lip and speared the burned meat onto a platter with a vengeance. *It's a little extra chewy today; that's what I'll tell them. American bacon cooked like this is called crispy. This is the British version of crispy.* She sighed. She doubted even the children would fall for that. She knew her aunt and Mrs. Newsome would not.

Claire wiped her hands on the ruined tea towel, untied her apron, and smoothed her hair as best she could. The clock struck twelve. "It's now or never," she said aloud and, hefting the platter, headed for the stairs.

Miranda didn't know how she could have misunderstood Mr. Campbell. He'd said his train should arrive in Windermere in time for him to make dinner at Bluebell Wood on Thursday, November 21. She'd been certain that meant the evening meal. But as he was standing in the foyer before her, she remembered the American Southerners she'd known in her youth. Many of them spoke of their noon meal as dinner and their evening meal as supper, a holdover from days gone by. She prayed that whatever Claire was preparing would pleasantly astonish them all.

"Mr. Campbell, we're delighted you're here, but must ask your indulgence. We're a little at sixes and sevens at the moment, you see."

"Oh? Is my arrival inconvenient?" He set

his cases to the side of the stairway.

"No, not at all. Of course we were expecting you. But our cook and her assistant are unwell today, and we're rather more short-staffed than usual. As a matter of fact, my niece has stepped into the kitchen to prepare luncheon."

"That's fantastic!" Mr. Campbell smiled, not the least bit discerning of Miranda's worries. "You said your niece is American, so this is her day, after all."

She smiled, not sure what he meant, but hoping it would be wonderful. The looks on Jeanine's and Ingrid's faces as she'd passed them carrying covered platters and bowls to the dining room looked more frozen than anything. She'd heard no gong or bell but supposed Claire might not think of that, handling so many new things on her own.

She took Mr. Campbell's coat and laid it across the banister. "We'll show you to your room after luncheon. With things as they are, I need to make certain your room is ready."

"You'll find me very adaptable, Lady Langford. I appreciate your taking me on — or in, as the case is."

Miranda relaxed a little. She'd forgotten how easygoing young American men could be. "We'll go through, shall we? I'm sure luncheon won't be long." She thought she'd best prepare him. Even if the children were on their best behavior, they were an unusual lot. "*Adaptable* is precisely what we require, as you'll soon see. I think I mentioned to you that we've taken in a number of refugees. Five of our charges are German children, three of whom arrived on an earlier *Kindertransport* and two smuggled into the country more recently. Five more are French Jewish children my niece rescued just before the invasion — quite an adventurous story."

"Admirable indeed — my curiosity grows. I'll be happy to help, in my spare time, in any way I can."

From the peals of laughter and ungentlemanly snorts coming from the dining room, Miranda was afraid his admiration was mislaid. She laughed. "You don't know what you're saying."

Before she could open the door, she heard Claire's shrill command of "Put down that rasher now — before I thrash you with it!"

Opening the door didn't help. The children were seated — barely — at the long table, poorly set, while Josef gleefully shot what appeared to be strips of blackened shoe leather across the table toward Gaston, who batted them back with the energy of a grouse-shooting bush beater. Elise and Ingrid twirled stiff, round discs from their forks and giggled uncontrollably.

"Did you hear me?" Claire's voice reverberated from the corners as she shook a threatening serving spoon in midair. Wide-eyed and pale, Aimee crawled beneath the table.

Miranda coughed as she entered the room. Peter and Bertram stood immediately, each doing his best to harness his younger brother. Jeanine pulled Elise's hair, sending up a yowl until she turned to meet Miranda's eye. Aimee peeked over the table's edge.

Miranda realized that Claire, her back to the door, mistakenly took the calm to mean that the children respected or at least feared her. "That's better. Now you'll all sit in your seats and eat this meal, and you will like it!"

"Claire," Miranda whispered, mortified.

But Mr. Campbell clapped. "Hear, hear! Lady Langford, I applaud you. You're lucky to have a sergeant major at the helm of this unruly lot."

Claire, her face still livid, whirled to meet her aunt's frown and the deep-brown twinkle of David Campbell's eyes. Miranda saw the connection in a flash and knew those eyes and that grin were her niece's undoing.

For that she was grateful. Claire sank dumbstruck into her chair.

Miranda knew she must deal with the disruption and its cause sometime, but for now she chose to rise above it and focus on their newest member. Perhaps she could salvage something of her own dignity, if not her niece's. "Claire, and children, I would like you to meet Mr. Campbell. He comes to us from Edinburgh most recently, and from the United States before that."

"Like you and Fräulein Claire," Josef enthused.

Miranda smiled. "Yes, like Fräulein Claire and me."

"Bonjour!" Gaston bowed, clearly not to be outdone by Josef. "Welcome to our table."

"Well, *bonjour,*" Mr. Campbell intoned in a truly Southern Appalachian accent, "and I thank you. I'm pleased to join such grand company."

Miranda sighed. "You're very kind and gracious, Mr. Campbell."

"Please call me David."

"Monsieur David," Gaston offered.

"All right then, children, you have permission. Let's have our prayer, and while we eat you may each introduce yourself to Mr. David."

"May I offer thanks on our behalf, Lady

Langford?" David Campbell seemed not a mite perturbed.

"Please, and thank you very much." Miranda could not be more relieved.

"Shall we bow our heads? Dear heavenly Father, we come before You with joy and great thanksgiving for this feast lovingly prepared, for this company gratefully gathered, and with deep appreciation for our safety in the year that is past. It's been a hard year for most of us in one way or another, and we know that the days ahead are likely to test our mettle, to test the strength of our character as well as the safety of our families. We stand ready to do and be what You will, by your grace and strength, Father. We know we can't do it alone. We need each other, and most of all we need You. On this Thanksgiving Day, we remember those who have gone before and the strong examples they set in forging a new life in a new land. We ask for that strength and that fortitude now. Through Jesus Christ our Lord, amen."

The silence around the table belied the presence of ten children. Miranda wasn't sure whether it was awe for David's prayer or discomfort on the part of the Jewish children that he so clearly called upon Christ Jesus in faith.

She could not believe she hadn't realized the day. She glanced at Claire and one look told her that it had not occurred to her niece, either.

"Happy Thanksgiving." David smiled at her.

"Happy Thanksgiving," Miranda replied.

"Happy Thanksgiving, Miss Claire," he said.

Claire looked too upset to respond. Even so, the children took up the enthusiastic chant.

"Is this the meal you always celebrate for your Thanksgiving Day in America?" Josef wanted to know as he tapped the table with his solid pancake.

Miranda saw that Claire was ready to burst into tears. "Not every family celebrates in the same way, Josef. Now, please, eat your lunch and, beginning with Jeanine, stand and share your name with Mr. Campbell."

"*Oui,* madame."

The children stood with respect to make their introductions. David Campbell seemed genuinely interested. When the introductions came round to Claire, Miranda wondered if she'd need to speak for her niece, but Claire surprised her again.

"I apologize for the scene you witnessed when you arrived, Mr. Campbell."

"Call me David, please."

Claire nodded. "And I'm Claire. Cooking is not my — my normal —"

"No, I understand you are a rescuer of children, something I greatly admire. Lady Langford explained you are short-staffed at the moment. If you'll allow me, I can help out by roasting a few sausages over an open fire. I can even whip up a pot of Scottish porridge or a hearty fish chowder — a bit of Cullen skink, if you like. What I can't do is come close to claiming the important thing, the lifesaving thing you've already done."

Miranda was as speechless as Claire, and the children turned to view Claire with new respect.

"It is true, Monsieur David. Mademoiselle Claire saved us from the Germans. She has been most brave." Jeanine wrapped her arm around her sister beside her. "I do not know what would have become of us had she not."

Silence followed, interrupted shortly by the ringing of the telephone in the hallway. Claire, her face already flushed, jumped up. "I'll get it."

Miranda thought that the best exit possible. While Claire was out of the room, Aimee whispered, "I don't think I can eat this, madame."

Miranda nodded. “No, it’s all right, Aimee. We’ll have something hearty for an early tea. You children may prepare for school now. We’ll —”

But Claire burst in before Miranda could finish. “That was Dr. MacDonald. He said the influenza is everywhere in the village. The school’s been closed for the remainder of the month to help stop the spread.”

Miranda thought she might faint.

CHAPTER TWELVE

Aimee went to bed happy that night, despite Mademoiselle Claire's insistence that Mr. Cottontail sleep outside. Tonight, all Aimee's thoughts were of Monsieur David. She considered Monsieur David a most beautiful man — nearly as beautiful as her father. A man of great understanding and appreciation for lovely things . . . like her sweet rabbit. He'd understood completely when she had introduced him to her furry Mr. Cottontail and whispered that the bunny slept with her. Of course, she'd told him, he must keep her secret; she could only slip him upstairs after Mademoiselle Claire thought her fast asleep. Mr. Dunnagan was her cohort and had agreed to leave the bunny in the mudroom. Mademoiselle Claire did not approve of bunnies in bed.

Monsieur David had crossed his heart, promising that he would never tell, and confided that he'd had just such a bunny when he was a boy. It was his best friend.

Aimee pulled the mezuzah from beneath her mattress as she did every night, kissed it, and rubbed the familiar lines of its engraving with her thumb. She turned over and sighed in great contentment. Monsieur David was a man that Maman and Papa would approve. Perhaps, if he would wait until she grew up, Aimee would marry him . . . if she didn't marry Papa or Dr. MacDonald first.

Not only had David Campbell brought order to their miserable luncheon table, he'd helped with arithmetic lessons all afternoon, much to the delight of each of the children he'd worked with. He'd stepped in and organized the older boys to whip together a heavy tea of fish chowder and grilled cheese bread, satisfying even Mr. Dunnagan's voracious appetite.

But Claire discovered his most astonishing accomplishment after she'd tucked Aimee into bed and come down the stairs. She had heard of hamboning but had never seen it performed until now. The older children sat in a horseshoe, delighted and mesmerized by his rhythmic knee and body slapping while stomping to Appalachian mountain music sung in a high, lonesome tenor, sometimes through long nasal tones and interspersed with yodels.

"He could be our Alpine yodler!" Peter laughed.

"He *is* our Alpine yodler!" Josef crowed.

"*Non! Non!* He dances with the joy of the French!" Bertram asserted.

"Joie de vivre!" Gaston cheered.

Claire edged closer to her aunt and whispered, "He's a one-man circus!"

Aunt Miranda laughed. "He's a godsend."

Claire looked at her aunt. She wasn't eyeing David as she might a prospective suitor. He was too young for that — more Claire's own age. She was embarrassed now that she'd pictured some middle-aged American who would be smitten with Aunt Miranda's beauty and wealth — and she possessed both in spades — leaving Claire abandoned yet again.

It was good to see her aunt laugh. It was good to see the children laugh. It was amazing to feel that urge bubble up within herself. And yet, how could she? Merriment felt disloyal to Arnaud — not knowing where he was, if he was alive. It was disloyal, wasn't it?

After the children said their good-nights and had been tucked into bed, Aunt Miranda invited David and Claire into the library for a drink, something Claire and her aunt had never done. Claire hesitated, tempted to refuse. Even a small glass of wine reminded her of her mother's addiction, though she would never say that.

"I think it's only appropriate that we offer you a toast, David. You've put in a full day's work that I'm sure you never bargained for — one surely more taxing than engineering. We can't thank you enough. You've brought joy and order to our chaos, and we've not even shown you your room."

David laughed. Claire found the creases by the corners of his eyes most attractive, a thing as disturbing as the wine. "It was my pleasure. I don't know when I've had such a good time. Not since the war started, that's certain. They're a great bunch of kids."

"They are," Claire agreed, then sobered, closing her eyes. "I can't believe we didn't realize that today is Thanksgiving. It never even occurred to me. I must be turning into a real Brit."

David's smile faded a little. "Thanksgiving was my favorite holiday back home when I was their age. I guess it's a thoroughly American holiday . . . no British version here."

"Not precisely," Aunt Miranda agreed,

"although there are harvest celebrations and days of thanksgiving offered through the church. I remember as a child in New Jersey we'd celebrate with turkey and cranberry sauce and my mother's apple and pumpkin pies."

"I remember those recipes." Claire was glad for the family connection with her aunt. "Mother always said they were Grandmother's, though it was our cook who made them."

Aunt Miranda nodded, a little wistfully, Claire thought. To change the subject, Claire asked David, "What traditions does your family keep for Thanksgiving?"

"Oh, it's been quite some years since I've lived in America. That's why I'm here now. I've been living in Scotland with my uncle since I was a boy — first school and then work. But I remember, before my dad passed, that we'd go around the table, and he'd ask everybody what we were most thankful for."

Aunt Miranda stared into her wineglass. Claire swallowed, not certain how to respond to that.

"Maybe we can do that now," David continued. "I'll start. I'm thankful to be here, to be with Americans again and new friends while I do the work I'm assigned.

And I'm thankful to find myself in a house full of young people. That's quite a change for me." He grinned. Claire thought she'd never seen such white teeth or such deep dimples in a man's cheeks. "It's an unexpected blessing and one I don't take for granted."

He waited, Claire knew, for her or Aunt Miranda to speak. A minute passed. The fire Bertram had lit for them to chase the chill fell low in the grate. Little sparks flew upward.

"I'm afraid I haven't expressed thanksgiving for some long while now. I'm a bit out of practice." Aunt Miranda set her glass on the table beside her chair.

David nodded. "I understand that better than you might realize."

Aunt Miranda tilted her head. "That surprises me. But I rather think you're full of surprises, Mr. Campbell. Cheerfulness and thanksgiving seem to be easy habits with you."

He sighed. "If only that were so, Lady Langford."

Aunt Miranda looked about to speak, possibly to ask more, Claire thought, but he turned to Claire. "And what about you? You've saved five French children and are helping your aunt keep open a house full of refugees. Life must be very satisfying."

Claire started. No one had ever summarized her life in that way. She wouldn't have. "Life is . . . uncertain." She could say no more. He was a stranger, after all.

Aunt Miranda stood. "I think it's time we all said good night. Tomorrow will come earlier than we wish. Neither Mrs. Creedle nor Nancy will be up to working, and Mrs. Newsome's come down with it now."

"I can take the breakfast shift if you like," offered David, "and can help with the other meals, if I'm not in the way. I won't be starting my work here for a couple of days."

"Bless you," Claire said, and meant it. He grinned again.

Aunt Miranda turned off the lamp. "I'll check on Mrs. Newsome before I go up. Claire, would you show David to his room? I asked Peter to ready it for him. Make certain there are towels, and show him the bathroom on that floor. I'll see you both in the morning."

David stood. "Thank you, Lady Langford, and good night."

Aunt Miranda, tired around the eyes but still the gracious hostess, left the library.

"I'll get my bags." David was quick to head for the stairs as well. Claire couldn't blame him. He must be as exhausted as she, and the wine had made her sleepier still.

"What can I carry?" she offered.

"How about my briefcase?"

She didn't argue. His suitcases looked formidable, and the briefcase must have contained a load of books, heavy as it was.

Aunt Miranda had stationed him on the third floor, west wing, near the boys' room. The girls and Claire were on the second floor, east wing.

"The bathroom is through here, second door on the left from your room. I'd advise you to make good use of the lock. Neither Josef nor Gaston is likely to spend time knocking."

"Sounds like normal boys." David smiled, and his smile weakened her knees, annoying Claire more than pleasing her.

"This is your room." She opened the door. "Be careful with the blackout curtains. But you know that."

He nodded.

"Well, the room looks fine; the boys did right by you." She set his briefcase on the writing desk by the window. As she did so the latch flipped open and several books slipped out and to the floor. "Oh, I'm sorry."

"It's not your fault. That latch is weak."

Still, Claire felt embarrassed as she bent to pick up the books. "*The Holy Bible, The*

Problem of Pain — some light reading?" she tried to joke.

"I guess you can never get enough Scripture. This one is a new author to me — C. S. Lewis, an Irish transplant to England. He says he was inspired by one of my fellow Scotsmen, George MacDonald, who has long been a favorite." David shrugged. "Thought I'd give him a try." He took the books from her but hesitated. "My guess is we all have some kind of pain . . . don't we?"

His empathy almost undid her. To hide that, she replied, almost flippantly, "Pain's a problem; that's for sure." It was hard for her to imagine that a man who smiled so much knew anything of pain. "Good night, David." She crossed the room without waiting for him to reply.

Claire took the stairs down to her floor, eager to close the door on David Campbell and this long day. Arnaud was her love, the threat of his loss the rip in her heart. And yet she realized, as she clicked the latch on her bedroom door, life held a new concern.

David Campbell is an enigma. A handsome, insightful, and charming enigma . . . and therefore a potential problem. She bit her lip, determined not to let him become her problem.

Chapter Thirteen

The air-raid siren wailed just before midnight, the first week of December.

"Out! Out, and down the stairs to the cellar!" Miranda burst through the door of the boys' room first, jerking blankets from the beds of five sleepyheads. David was at her side in a moment, hustling the boys from the room.

Miranda tore down the stairs to Claire's room and the girls' dormitory. She knew Mrs. Newsome would rouse the staff. "Hurry, girls! Leave your things. There's not a moment to lose!"

Mrs. Newsome met the troops at the bottom of the stairs, holding her lantern high. Miranda shone her torch over the stairs, praying none of the children would trip in the dark.

Aimee whimpered, but Claire grabbed the little girl's hand and did her best to shush her.

"We'll all be safe and snug downstairs in a moment. Follow Mrs. Newsome." If only Miranda could keep her voice from quavering so she might not frighten the children.

The German children were down the stairs in record time, their training and experience from previously bombed sites apparent. The French children cowered together. Miranda and Claire pushed them forward.

"I don't want to go into the cellar!" Aimee cried. "It's dark — it's a hole, like — like . . ."

"We must go!" Miranda had no time for this.

"She's afraid, madame," Gaston insisted. "It's a hole — like the grave she fell into."

Miranda's nerves stretched taut, nearly to the breaking point. "Get downstairs, now!" Far worse than the fear of open graves, she feared the house, if bombed, would bury them all.

Once they made their way to the cellar, Miranda lined the children against the wall, the place both she and David deemed safest, and drew Aimee onto her lap. "It's all right, my dear. It's all right. I didn't mean to scold, but we needed to get downstairs quickly. Whenever you hear that sound, run to the cellar."

The screaming siren finally stopped, but there was no return siren for the all clear. Even beneath the earth they could hear the droning of German planes far above.

"Best turn off your torches," David ordered. "Save the batteries."

"Keep the lantern!" Claire insisted.

"Of course." David's voice came calm. Miranda breathed a sigh of gratitude.

"In London, in the Underground station, we sang songs during air raids," Ingrid offered.

"That's a splendid idea." Mrs. Newsome's cheer sounded forced. "Who will begin?"

But no one volunteered.

"Should have pocketed my harmonica," David mumbled.

"That would have been just the ticket, Mr. David," Mrs. Newsome agreed. "Next time."

The French children looked at her in horror.

"There will be a next time?" cried Elise.

"You know nothing of war," Josef chided. "By the docks there were raids every night . . . nearly every night, and bombings and explosions — and fires! This is nothing but planes."

Franz pushed Josef. "Be quiet! You tempt fate!"

"Josef might be right." David nodded. "They might just be returning from delivering their loads south."

"We can go upstairs now!" Aimee sniffled.

"No, not until we hear the all clear, dear." Miranda stroked the little girl's hair. "Then we'll know it's safe."

Aimee moved her hands nervously in front of her face, making shapes.

"What is it, darling?"

"I'm making shadow puppets. Maman told me to do that whenever I'm afraid. Can you make shadow puppets, madame?"

"Oh, my." Miranda tried to laugh. "If I've not forgotten how."

"Make them in front of the lantern," Gaston insisted. "They'll make shadows on the wall."

"Gaston, you and Bertram show us how," Mrs. Newsome urged.

Josef turned away, as if watching Gaston do anything to entertain Aimee might smack of approval.

Miranda smiled a thank-you to Mrs. Newsome and settled in for a long night. At last, Aimee's eyelashes fluttered closed, and she whispered, just before falling asleep, "They're friendly shadows."

"Yes." Miranda nestled the girl closer yet. "Yes, they are."

■ ■ ■ ■

Mrs. Newsome thanked the Lord that the weeks of December passed with no direct bombing of the Lake District. *Plenty of planes overhead at night, and too many trips to the dark, dank cellar, "just in case."* The children hated hiding in the dark, nearly as much as she. Elise began wetting the bed again, though not every night. Gaston, despite his daytime bravado, jumped at sudden noises — mischief Josef gleefully precipitated and exploited. For Mrs. Newsome, it brought back too many memories of the Great War, a thing she hated most of all.

"But we've still body and soul together, unlike those poor, poor people in London. I mustn't complain," she muttered as she walked to the Heelis farm. "We're all healthy and we've everything we need."

Still, they weren't without their sorrows. Dr. MacDonald had not been to a meal at Bluebell Wood since David Campbell had crossed its threshold. Mrs. Newsome missed the good doctor and knew her ladyship missed his companionship.

Mrs. Newsome considered grudges, particularly carrying the grudges of forebears, a terrible waste. Especially so now, since she could count on one hand the evening meals David Campbell attended. He was out long and late with his war business, whatever that was. Lady Miranda said it was all most hush-hush. But Mrs. Newsome learned the lay of the land from her niece Ruby over tea that Saturday while Mrs. Heelis was out.

"They're wantin' to put in a flying boat factory, that's what — make airplanes that can land on water and take off from the very same!" Ruby gushed. "The Germans already have them, so we must too. There's a factory in Rochester, nearly bombed — the Jerries missed it by a quarter of a mile, so I'm guessing Mr. Churchill's not wanting to put all our eggs in one basket now. Anyhow, it's a grand deal — factory and hangars and such, and there's to be housing for the workers and their families, a canteen, a hall for meetings. The locals hope for dances and concerts and lectures, even a store. They'll build a proper little town. That's what Mrs. Heelis is up in arms about, her and all the local conservationists. They say those poorly built sheds will spoil the beauty of the Lake District."

"Slow down, Ruby. Come up for air, dear!"

"Well, I'm that vexed about it because

Mrs. Heelis comes home in such a state after every one of those meetings — and she takes it out on me and everything I cook. And it's your Mr. Campbell what's workin' betwixt Short Brothers' Sunderland flying boat factory and the government, overseeing the surveying of the land and setting up the building and such. She's not got a kind thing to say of the man, that determined for the cause, he is. If she knew he was staying at Bluebell Wood there'd be the devil to pay."

"I don't think she or the villagers would want an American anywhere closer, do you?"

"No, not unless that Mr. Roosevelt gets off his fat — I'm sorry, Aunt Florence; I'm not myself."

"Let me make you a cup of tea, Ruby." Mrs. Newsome was concerned for her niece's blood pressure but glad to know that the young man had not been stepping out with local girls. Hard at work for the good of Britain and the war; that's just what she'd expect of him. She smiled. She might just let that slip to Miss Claire, who seemed to have taken a particular interest in him, despite her wish to pretend she had not.

"Thousands of incendiary bombs dropped

over London again last night, the paper says. Those poor, dear people. How do they stand it?" Miranda waved away Mrs. Newsome and poured her own morning coffee. It wasn't like her to share war news first thing in the morning, but the knowledge of relentless bombing troubled her heart and had kept her awake that night.

"Not all do stand it," David replied, setting his spoon down. "I read that there's more pouring out of the cities every day."

"More homeless than ever we could have imagined." Mrs. Newsome clucked.

"The worst is the planes overhead at night," Ingrid spoke up, standing suddenly in the doorway. "I'm afraid they'll drop bombs right on our heads."

"They've only been dropping them over the fields and fells so far," Gaston asserted, pushing past her to the dining room table.

"But how do they know where fields and fells are, and no houses — especially in the dark? It is only — how do you say it — *luck* that they've not hit us," Ingrid retorted.

Miranda broke in. "You needn't worry, my dear. We have the cellar, and it's well equipped. The moment we hear the air-raid siren we'll be down those steps — as always."

"I was thinking," David offered, "that

perhaps we could — I could — help make that a bit more cheerful . . . add an electric light or two. It would be easy to run from the upstairs. And maybe bring some of the children's books and games in to play. Maybe store some tea biscuits or —"

"Rats!" interjected Josef. "The rats would eat them."

"Mice," Mrs. Newsome corrected. "We've not got rats, just field mice, as any great house would have in their cellar."

Miranda clamped her lips, though she knew full well there were rats, also as in the cellar of any great house — country or town.

"Mr. David is right," Mrs. Newsome conceded. "We could store some there — in a tin, so no worries about vermin. The vermin I'm more concerned with eating them are you and Gaston!"

The boys grinned wickedly and kicked each other beneath the table.

"I was wondering, Lady Langford," David spoke quietly, "if you have a wireless I might listen to. I need to stay abreast of the news."

Miranda shifted in her seat, not certain she wanted to bring the war into her home by live broadcast.

"If you don't, I'll see about sending for one."

"It's in the drawing room, behind the

door," Gaston offered.

Miranda sat up. "How do you know that, Gaston?"

Now Bertram kicked his younger brother, who kicked him back.

"You might as well tell her," Peter said.

"Tell me what?"

Jeanine spoke up. "At night, after you have all gone to bed, madame, we come downstairs and listen."

"What?" Miranda gasped.

"We must know what is happening in the war, in France — and in Germany. What becomes of our families," Bertram defended.

"You sneak downstairs in the middle of the night?" Claire set down her fork.

"Oui!" Gaston boasted. "Like the Resistance, we are very quiet, and no one knows we are there."

"We do not mean to offend, madame," Jeanine pleaded, "but we are desperate to know what is happening . . . and you do not tell us."

"I was trying to protect you — all of you. Listening to the news each night brings the war home, makes it come alive again and again. You don't know what you're playing with, what it is to lose someone in this war . . . the nightmares."

"Begging madame's pardon," Peter spoke quietly but without reservation, "we know." He glanced quickly round the table at each of the children, resting his eyes on Claire. "We all know."

"I hardly know what to say," Miranda began. "But you can't all be tripping down the stairs in the middle of the night. That's unthinkable."

Claire looked as if she were to blame for the children's presumption. "I'm sorry, Aunt Miranda. I had no idea."

"You are right, Fräulein." Peter looked at Claire squarely. "You have perhaps lost your lover, but you have no idea what it is to fear for your mother, your father, your grandparents, your brothers and sisters — everyone you've known in life."

Claire's face flamed.

Out of the mouths of babes, Miranda thought.

"No wonder you're all so difficult to rouse come morning," Mrs. Newsome interjected.

"May I make a suggestion?" David offered. "Since several of us feel the need to listen, may those who wish gather for the earlier broadcast? I could tune the radio. If we hear difficult news, at least we'd be together to help one another through it. Sometimes," he added more quietly, "not knowing and imagining the worst is worse than knowing the truth."

"Oui," Jeanine whispered, "this is so. Please, madame."

Miranda thought her heart might break for the desperate hearts and worried minds of the children — a need she'd recognized too little. *Thank You, Lord, for David. He's a level head with eyes wide open . . . a skill I'm sorely lacking these days.*

Claire hurried down the stairs, lesson books in hand. Now that the village school had reopened and all signs of influenza had been swept away with the bitter December cold, she looked forward to her first free afternoon in nearly a month. The difficult breakfast discussion and Peter's accusation that she understood so little had settled her plans in her mind.

Preoccupied, she bumped into David as she rounded the banister at the bottom of the stairs.

"I'm so sorry!"

"No harm done." He smiled. "You're in a hurry this morning."

"On a mission." She smiled as best she could, on her way once again.

"By the way," he called after her, "I have some time off this afternoon. I wondered if you'd like to take a walk. I haven't seen the grounds and thought I'd go exploring. Mrs. Newsome says the mazes and trails are enough to intrigue Sherlock Holmes."

Claire's heart skipped a beat, but she wasn't about to go off walking with David Campbell. It would be disloyal to Arnaud. Besides, she had her own plans and wouldn't share them with anyone. "I'm sorry. I've got my hands full." She held up her lesson plans to plead her case.

The nearly imperceptible slump in David's shoulders spoke rejection. "Understood." He turned to go.

Claire had meant to reject him, but contrarily didn't want to leave that impression. "I just want to say . . ."

"Yes?" He stopped, apparently eager to hear anything she might say.

"What you did, what you offered for the children this morning about the radio — the wireless — was very kind of you, a good thing. I'm sorry I didn't think of it."

He shrugged. "You didn't know what they were up to in the dark of night. Sounds like they pulled the wool over everybody's eyes."

"But I didn't understand their need, and . . ." She didn't know how to continue.

"And that worries you?"

She nodded, a confession. "You have a

way with them, and I might as well say I admire that."

"They just want to live in the real world, to know what's happening to their families."

"But you understood that, and you're nearly a stranger to them. I've been with them for months, at least with the French children."

"Guess I have something more in common with them."

"What?" Claire didn't understand. A need for European news? "Your family's in America. They're safe. Nothing can happen to them there."

David blinked and turned away. "I'm going for a walk. Tell Mrs. Newsome I won't be back for lunch."

Claire didn't know what she'd said to offend David. It niggled at the back of her mind, but she forced it aside through the morning routine.

Bertram and Peter had promised to make sure the younger students reached school in time and to keep Josef and Gaston from torturing each other, which meant that Claire was free even sooner than she'd expected. Four glorious afternoon hours spread before her.

Under her trench coat, she layered on an extra vest Mrs. Newsome loaned her, wrapped a thick muffler round her throat, and pulled on her aunt's Wellingtons over double wool socks. Claire had just opened the front door to make her escape when she met the elderly postman on the doorstep.

"Deliveries, miss. Fine day it is — cold, but fine."

"Yes, it is. Thank you, Mr. Kendall!" Claire took the mail but did not stop for small talk. She threw the bundle of letters to the receiving table in the foyer, pulled her gloves over her fingers, and nearly beat the postman to the drive. She cut through the maze trail and off toward the gardens.

It had been too long since she'd found the time and freedom to visit her treetop, and her heart was ready to burst for want of its sanctuary. If inspiration struck, she might even begin a story of life in Paris before the war — romance, suspense, a bit of life at the brink of Nazi invasion among the elites in Parisian literary circles. It was a story she'd been conjuring in her brain in that place between sleep and awake, that veiled spot where magical things happen. Was that memory from *Peter Pan* or somewhere else? Claire didn't care; she was only glad for the bit of muse.

She'd almost reached the secret door when she heard whistling, somewhere not far beyond the garden. She froze. When it came nearer, she stumbled back into the shrubbery. *Who is so close to the secret garden . . . my secret garden? The children are all in school. Mr. Dunnagan? What would he be doing here?* She burrowed deeper into the shrubbery as the whistling came closer, then stopped.

"What the devil?" and a chuckle. " 'The Secret Garden.' How great is that?" The sound of the locked door handle shaking rattled Claire's heart.

David Campbell! What are you doing here? Oh, please, please don't find my way in.

But she knew he wasn't stupid and wasn't easily discouraged. For the next several minutes she heard him doing exactly what she had done, following the wall, pushing back ivy, grunting in frustration, and making his way around the outside. It wouldn't take long until he found the indentation. If she made her way back to the path and called his name, as if she were looking for him, as if she wanted to take that ramble he had offered, she knew he'd come, perhaps be deterred from finding the entrance as she had done.

Claire walked quickly, determined, frantic, back toward the maze. She must be far enough from the garden to alleviate his suspicion, close enough for David to hear when she called. She'd reached the edge of the maze — just far enough — when she heard her own name.

"Claire! Miss Claire! Come quickly!" It was Nancy on the other side of the maze. "Lady Langford wants you. She said it's urgent. Can you hear me? Miss Claire!"

Claire closed her eyes in frustration. She couldn't call David and pretend she hadn't heard Nancy, so close at hand. *So little is mine. Please, please don't let him find my garden!*

Claire sat by the library fire opposite her aunt, holding the envelope in her lap for several minutes, her heart beating wildly, like a caged bird. She knew she would open the letter, but she was afraid. Whatever it said was final. Either Arnaud was in custody or he was free. Either Arnaud was alive or he wasn't. And if he was alive, either he'd penned the words himself and declared his love or he hadn't. She closed her eyes, waited until she heard her own breathing, and felt very much alone.

At last she slit the seal with her thumbnail. A quick line on the outside of the envelope came from Mrs. Beach: *I hope this brings good news. Write your mother when you can.*

She's terribly worried.

Claire felt her face warm. *Mother? Worried? I don't believe it. And I can't think about that now.* She unfolded the inner letter. From Josephine. Claire's eyes smarted. She scanned the lines . . . so much white space, so few words:

> Our beloved friend is well and recovered, lighthearted as a bird in flight, as merry and busy as always. Never worry, dear Claire. I take good care of him.

Claire's heart fluttered. "He's alive."

"Thank God, most truly," Miranda said, leaning toward her niece.

Claire swallowed, doing her best to come to grips with the paper in front of her, what little it said and all it didn't say. She understood the lines to mean that Arnaud was alive and well. He was "busy" — which must mean he was free again and working with the Resistance. *Free because he was freed or free because he escaped? Either way, is he too busy to write me himself?*

"Yes." Claire looked up and tried to smile. "So much to be grateful for." What she didn't understand was the second line. It might mean nothing, or everything. Arnaud flirted with all the girls. Josephine was nearer his age than Claire. Yet Josephine knew how she felt about Arnaud, what she believed he felt about her. Claire had always hoped, even trusted that Josephine and Arnaud's feelings for one another were more like brother and sister, or comradely friends. Arnaud had reassured her that was so — then.

But Josephine is working with Arnaud in dangerous and exciting missions. She probably nursed him back to health. She's the one he confides in now, the one he shares his exploits with over a glass of wine in the back of the bookstore. Josephine is there . . . and I am not.

Chapter Fourteen

Gaston missed Shabbat. He missed his mother lighting the candles, praying, and pulling the flame toward herself. He missed his father's prayers and the long, leisurely meal they would enjoy after. He missed temple.

Gaston understood that in a Christian home they would not celebrate Shabbat, though it seemed a shame, a great loss for all of them. He wouldn't have realized the days for Rosh Hashanah or Yom Kippur had passed if Bertram had not told him. It was a solemn revelation. How could the new year begin and he not know it? What of their parents? Did they forget too?

But despite the fact that Lady Langford observed no Jewish holy days, despite the fact that neither he nor the others dared to ask for such a thing from the Christian lady who gave them sanctuary, he would not forget Hanukkah. All year he waited for the festival of lights, and no one could make him miss it.

He'd looked in every drawer in every room but the kitchen and never found a menorah. Tonight, the second of his midnight raids, he found candles, enough to represent all the days, in the back of the pantry. He might have felt chagrin at pilfering Madame Creedle's pantry. After all, that fearsome lady had insisted each child stir her Christmas pudding and offer a wish, saying it was "a tradition for all the children in a house, Christian or not." Gaston had steeled himself against her last comment and wished for his parents to come to England, though he hadn't believed they would. Now he shook off any misgiving about taking candles. This was too important.

"What are you doing in there?" It was Josef, always nosy Josef, out of bed and trailing him, sneaking about in his bare feet.

"This is my business."

"Not if it means you are stealing tomorrow's dessert. I will tell Frau Creedle."

Gaston smirked, knowing that was a lie. Neither of them willingly spoke to Madame Creedle; neither dared come within twenty feet of the monarch of the kitchen.

"Frau Newsome, then. I'll tell and you'll

be banished from tea."

"It's nothing to do with food. Go away."

"What, then? Tell me or I'll knock on Frau Newsome's door now."

Gaston sighed heavily. Such a chore it was to put up with Josef and his meddlesome, wheedling ways. He was the same age in years, but Gaston believed the boy stunted in intelligence, though he knew Josef did not see it that way. "Can't you mind your own business for once? Your curiosity will be the undoing of you."

"You heard Frau Newsome say that. You're just repeating; nothing clever in that."

"I'm not trying to be clever. I'm trying to be left alone!"

"They'll hear you if you shout. Now tell me, what are you doing?"

Gaston stood, undecided. If he refused to tell Josef, the boy would surely sound the alarm. If he did tell . . . well, could he trust him? "I suppose a German Jew is still a Jew."

"What? What did you say?" Josef raised his fists, prepared for a fight.

"I said you are a person, a Jew, like me."

"That is not what it sounded." Josef lowered his fists.

"Dig the potatoes out of your ears."

"Frau Newsome says that, too."

"*Oui,* she is clever, that good lady." Gaston handed Josef the candles. Now he would be a conspirator and less likely to tattle.

"What are these for?"

"Do you not know what tomorrow is? What happens at sundown?"

Josef's facial muscles tightened, Gaston could see, but he could not read the boy. "Frau Newsome said it is their Christmas Day."

"*Oui!* It is their Christmas Day. It is our first day of Hanukkah."

"Is it?"

"Bertram said almost never do the two fall on the same day, but this year it is the same."

"You're going to light the candles? Let me help. Let Peter help. Peter's good at carving. He will carve a menorah for us if I ask him . . . or at least holes in wood for the candles. They must all be the same height, you know. You don't want to simply stand candles on a plate."

Gaston considered. He'd only planned to let Aimee know. She was the one most needing Hanukkah light, the most lonely and forlorn of them all. But having Josef and Peter, having them all, would make it a proper celebration. Half the fun, the joy, was in seeing the flame reflected in other smiling eyes, and having a real menorah, or even a semblance of one would be best. "In France our *shammash* was always higher. Tell him to carve it higher than the rest. And Madame Langford must not know. She has forbidden Monsieur David the Christmas tree. I think she does not like the celebrations."

"*Ja,* this is true. I heard Herr David ask if they could not at least 'kill the old red rooster,' but she did not answer."

"What old red rooster?"

"I do not know. I asked, but he said it is an expression, and to never mind."

"These Americans, they always say to never mind but do not explain." Gaston had had quite enough. "*D'accord.* You and Peter, and we will invite the others to come — after Mademoiselle Claire thinks we are in bed tomorrow night, after they have all gone to their rooms. When the hall clock strikes ten. You ask Peter about the carving in the morning."

"*Ja,* and a dreidel. I know he will do it. Where shall we meet?"

Gaston thought for a moment. It must be somewhere safe, out of hearing from the others, but with a window to shine the candle's light into the night to bear witness to the miracle — a window the night warden on his rounds would not see. "There is a tower on the far end of the house."

"I know the one you mean. But it is locked," Josef asserted. "Impossible. I've tried to get in."

"*Oui,* it is locked." Gaston smiled, glad for this opportunity to exhibit his superiority. "*Mais ooh-la-la!* I found the key."

Josef blinked, nodded slowly in admiration, and stuck out his hand. Gaston grasped it and they shook in agreement.

Christmas night, after the children were in bed, Claire offered to pour tea in the library for her aunt and David. She knew her aunt was still vexed with Mrs. Newsome about the Christmas crackers at dinner.

"But they're children," Mrs. Newsome had begged, aggrieved. "They must be allowed some pleasure, my lady. They're so very far from home and it is the holidays."

"They're Jewish children, Mrs. Newsome. I don't believe they mind missing Christmas celebrations," Aunt Miranda had retorted.

Mrs. Newsome had had her way with the meal, and for that Claire was glad: roast chicken and stuffing flavored with onion, rosemary, sage, and something scrumptious Claire couldn't define. Mr. Dunnagan's favorite carrot and turnip mash, plus potatoes, split and roasted brown in their jackets, creamed celery, and brussels sprouts steamed in such a way as to make them buttery and sweet rounded out the meal. Claire sighed. Mrs. Creedle was truly a wonder in the kitchen, and her Christmas pudding with hot custard sauce had melted in Claire's mouth. *You'd hardly think there was a war on.*

Still, the tension had been thick enough to slice, and neither Aunt Miranda nor Mrs. Newsome had said another word during the meal, at least not until Josef pulled a Christmas cracker with Aimee. Though Josef earned the prize — a metal puppy — he'd gallantly presented it to Aimee, bringing a smile to the pale little face.

That had opened the meal and the remainder of the day to merriment, including David's hamboning and harmonica playing. He'd even played Christmas carols, which most of the children did not know. The carols brought a few solemn moments to the group. He'd ended with "Silent Night," a carol that Claire had always found peaceful and comforting.

Claire smiled as she poured cream into the tea, remembering Aimee's adoring gaze up at Josef after the Christmas cracker gift. Josef had surely grown two inches while straightening his shoulders. It was the single most healing gesture between the German and French children that Claire had seen. She wondered over the ability of simple gifts to bring peace and change.

"Thank you, Claire." David smiled, accepting the cup she handed him. "That was something to see — Josef giving that token to Aimee."

"I was thinking the same," Claire agreed. "And what a surprise. They never cease to amaze me. First it's pranks enough to make you tear your hair out, and the next thing I know they do something . . ." She shook her head.

"Something kind and wonderful," Aunt Miranda sighed. "And to think I almost ruined it."

"But you didn't," David affirmed.

"I must apologize to Mrs. Newsome tomorrow. I don't know why I was so hard on her."

"I suppose those things are reminders of earlier days."

Claire's stomach tightened. David had been at Bluebell Wood little more than a month, but he rarely hedged from saying things she longed to say to her aunt, things she didn't even know how to frame into words.

"Yes, they do." Aunt Miranda sipped her tea. "Christopher loved the crackers. When he was young we had a much larger staff here, even though it was just the two of us. My husband always felt it his duty to employ as many as our income allowed, that it was a way of giving back in gratitude for all we'd been given."

"He sounds like a wise and generous man."

"He was. You would have liked him. He would have liked you . . . and you, Claire."

Claire smiled in return, hoping that was true.

"After he was gone, I broke with tradition — too often to suit Mrs. Newsome — but always at Christmas, at least if we had no guests or were not away on holiday. Christopher and I went below stairs and ate with the staff. What a merry time we had, and what hilarity when the crackers were pulled and popped and the crowns came out! Of course many traveled to their homes, or they did after luncheon, to spend time with their families. But some lived in, and . . . we were a sort of family then."

"That's why Mr. Dunnagan and Mrs. Newsome ate with us today." Claire had wondered — glad they'd come — but she bristled at the notion of a makeshift family.

How her aunt could pretend like that was beyond her ken.

"I wish they would every day. I've invited them, and Raibeart — Dr. MacDonald. He would often come for Christmas, even in years past."

"I think my presence is the reason for the doctor's absence. I'm sorry." David sounded as if he meant it.

"It's not your fault."

"The fault of my name and lineage." David's brow creased. "I've met the doctor at a couple of the town meetings about the new factory — a good man. I'd like it if we could get acquainted. I think he'd find I'm not the bloodthirsty, murdering sort my ancestors were."

"I'm sure he would." Miranda smiled wearily. "That, and all these British formalities and separations, seem silly, especially now that we're so few, what with the war taking our young men for soldiers and even most of the young women for lumberjills or factory workers. I do understand that by the time the meal is served, Mrs. Creedle wants a rest, and Mr. Dunnagan prefers to slurp his coffee from his saucer in peace. He doesn't think we'd like that. But I wish Mrs. Newsome would eat with us regularly."

David laughed. "Sounds like my grandpa,

my mother's dad. He always preferred the saucer to his cup."

"What about your family?" Claire asked, curious. "Have you heard from them? What are they doing for Christmas?"

David shifted in his seat. "My uncle passed away last spring. He was the last of our part of the clan in Edinburgh. So it's just me."

"I'm sorry. What about your family in America? In the mountains where all that good hamboning the kids love so much originated?" Claire meant to be amusing, but David didn't respond. She exchanged an uncertain glance with Aunt Miranda.

David stood, setting his cup and saucer on the tea table. "Think I'll go for a walk before turning in. It's mild for a Christmas evening. Thank you, ladies, for today."

Claire hadn't meant to break the friendly moment. It felt as if she'd snuffed a candle without knowing how she'd done it. "I didn't mean to pry. I'm sorry if —"

David was nearly out the door. He hesitated only a moment. "I don't know what they're doing. Good night."

"The mails are so slow now, what with —" Claire began, but he'd gone, the door closing behind him. Startled, Claire looked at her aunt. "I didn't mean to upset him."

"You couldn't have known. I certainly don't. He hasn't received any letters, except for business, since he's been here."

"You looked?"

Aunt Miranda colored. "Mrs. Newsome sorts the mail. I asked her." She shrugged, guiltily. "I was curious."

Claire understood. So was she.

It wasn't until after Aunt Miranda had gone to bed and the fire burned low in the grate that Claire decided to go upstairs. As she turned out the light, she noticed that David had left his book behind. *The Problem of Pain . . .* the book that had fallen from his briefcase the night he moved in.

Claire turned the book over, reading the dust jacket, and over again. She sighed. *I could certainly use some help with the problem of pain.* She returned the book to the table, hesitated, looked over her shoulder at the library door, then picked it up again. David wouldn't be back for it tonight, in any case.

Claire closed the library door behind her and took the stairs to her room slowly. This Christmas Day had been like none other in her life. Even last year, so far from home, she'd celebrated by sharing little gifts with Arnaud and Josephine in the back of the bookstore, toasting the day. The year ahead had loomed uncertain, but rich with adventure.

Now what? Claire saw no end to the day-after-day lessons and schedules and needs of the children, and no soon end to the war, no matter how stiff the British upper lips around her. That also meant no knowing how long until she could return to Paris and Arnaud, or if he would be waiting for her.

The clock in the hallway bonged nine. Claire switched on the lamp and sat on the edge of her bed. She turned David's book over in her hands, knowing she should not have taken it. *I'll read it as quickly as I can and leave it again in the library. He won't even know.* With a prickle of guilt, and no longer certain precisely why she'd taken it, Claire tucked it beneath her mattress.

She reached for the leather journal she'd found slipped beneath her door when she'd come up after dinner. The leather was soft as doeskin and the linen-quality pages a beautiful cream. Inside, she'd found a note:

For Claire —

Writing is a gift. May you know and enjoy it in full. May this journal help you make sense of all that surrounds us.

Love,

Aunt Miranda

It was an astonishing gift — astonishing that there *was* such a gift in wartime, and then that it was the perfect gift, a special place to pen her novel, though that writing was going anything but well. Somehow, her characters didn't ring true, and every bit of dialogue sounded forced and artificial, even to Claire.

She picked up her pen, then put it down. She wanted to mark this day, to begin her writing right away. Perhaps this time, in this beautiful, literary journal, she'd be able to write the words of her heart. But it didn't seem enough to begin it here, in her room. She wanted to begin somewhere more likely to beckon the muse. Perhaps in her secret place, in Christopher's secret place. What could be more fitting, more truly a new beginning, than to climb the tree by moonlight and write in this journal from his mother on Christmas Day?

There was still time, and David had said the evening ran mild. He was probably back inside by now and the children fast asleep in their beds. She'd take her torch and muffle the light with a cheesecloth cover.

That was allowed in the cities; surely in the country as well.

Claire's heart beat with renewed purpose and a twinge of excitement as she crept down the carpeted stairs. Even Mrs. Creedle and Mrs. Newsome must be sleeping by now. No one need ever know. That thought appealed to Claire and made her shiver. *My own secret adventure to close this day.*

She had just slipped through the front door and pulled it silently behind her when she turned, bumping headlong into David. "Oh," Claire all but squealed, then slapped a gloved hand over her mouth. "You startled me!" she whispered. "I thought you'd gone in for the night."

"I was just on my way. What are you doing out here?"

"I decided I need a walk too." She lifted her head in the dark, hoping she sounded confident, brave, offhanded, and not guilty for stealing his book.

"It's a wonderful night. Just look at those stars." His hand swept the night sky.

"Amazing." She meant the stars, but her heart beat faster than the sky allowed.

" 'The heavens declare the glory of God; and the firmament sheweth his handywork. Day unto day uttereth speech, and night unto night sheweth knowledge. There is no speech nor language, where their voice is not heard.' "

"That's beautiful — what you said, and the stars."

"From the Psalms. When I see the night sky, when the stars light the world like this, I know beyond any doubt that God is there."

"Even in the middle of war?" Claire looked at the sky above her and might believe in anything. But doubts, she knew, dawned with daylight.

"Especially in the middle of war." She could hear the strength and smile in his voice. "It's a bit late. The Home Guard will be making their rounds before long. Are you sure you want to be out?"

"I'm quite safe. I'll stay on the grounds. Good night." She'd already started moving away, not wanting to be questioned or deterred.

"Claire?"

"Yes?" She stopped.

"Would you like me to come with you? The planes haven't started, but on such a clear night, they're bound to come." He sounded worried and possibly interested. She didn't want that — didn't want to want his company, though the image of walking the maze paved in starlight, David Campbell at her side, appealed.

"No, no — but thank you. I'll be fine. I won't be long. Good night." She hurried on before he could say more, before he convinced her not to go at all.

Claire stepped quickly through the maze, cut through the orchard, and made her way toward the gardens. The wall around the secret garden, so high and shadowed, looked almost forbidding. She shivered, eagerly following the ivy curtain around its perimeter, coming at last to the indentation in the stones. Her fingers ran over the lightly frosted lintel. She grasped the cold key, turned the lock, pushed the heavy wooden door that creaked in the night on its hinges, and stepped inside. *My garden — my own secret garden.* She reveled in the thought and in the joy of it.

Claire flicked off her torch. Starlight bathed the barren garden as if it contained its own light. She raised her hands in freedom, in success, then spread them wide. A perfect night. A romantic night.

She breathed deeply and exhaled, watching her breath rise before her, warmth rushing to her cheeks and her imaginings. The face that sprang before her was David's. Alarmed, Claire pushed the image aside, forcibly bringing Arnaud to mind. But Arnaud's smile faded quickly. Confused, she didn't try to conjure it again.

Claire shook her head, annoyed with her own fickleness, and headed for the winding path on the other side of the garden that led to Christopher's tree. She'd nearly reached the center of the garden when she stopped. Her eyes blinked, trying to focus on exactly what she was seeing through the dark.

The small evergreen, a tree perhaps six feet high that stood in the midst of the garden, shimmered and tinkled softly in the faint breeze. She flicked on her covered torch. From top to bottom hung beautiful, old-fashioned ornaments. Claire approached cautiously, circled the tree, reached out, and touched one. She pulled off her glove and reached again . . . glass.

Each ornament was as beautiful as the one before, and each different — starburst centers or hand-painted globes; exquisite, tiny scenes painted in hollowed-out glass bowls; glimmering stars; silver and golden bells. On top sat a multi-pointed star. Claire recognized it as Moravian, popular in Bethlehem, Pennsylvania.

David . . . David must have done this. How on earth did he get all this? Did he send for it? At first the thought thrilled her, made her heart race that he would invest himself in creating such beauty. But then she realized, *That means he found the key that day. He's made himself at home in the garden, my garden.*

Claire swallowed. It felt a violation, a theft, no matter that the garden wasn't rightfully hers. Before she'd discovered the entrance, it was an abandoned garden. *Well, it's not abandoned anymore.* The thought was rueful and, she knew, ungenerous.

He must be terribly lonely to have done this. If Aunt Miranda had only allowed a Christmas tree in the house, he probably wouldn't have. Claire sighed, not sure whether she was more frustrated with David or Aunt Miranda. *I can't feel sorry for him when he's discovered my special place . . . but this tree is magical and beautiful . . . and romantic.* Perversely, Claire wished she'd thought of it.

At least he doesn't know about the treetop — Christopher's and my tree. I hope. Oh, please, let it be untouched!

Claire picked up her pace and made for her tree. She pulled back wisteria vines. Nothing seem changed from the last time she was there. Even with the light of heavenly bodies, she needed her torch to find the knotted rope, and higher, the boards for her feet. She tucked her torch into her coat pocket and began to climb.

Clambering up and onto the board was trickier in the dark. But she found her footing and, at last, her resting, nesting place. Claire adjusted her coat, pulling it tight for warmth, and leaned back against the thick trunk of the old tree. *A haven. This is my haven. Thank you, that it is mine.*

Claire's heart swelled in gratitude for this sacred spot, for the clear and brilliant sky, for the gift of the journal in her pocket and the knowledge that however little her aunt understood her, she'd understood enough to give it, and cared about her.

Aunt Miranda loves me. Claire sat a little straighter, startled and pleased by the thought. She held it close to her heart, daring to let it past the inner shield she'd built, and blinked moisture from her eyes.

On such a night, in such a place, Claire could almost believe there was a God. But believing was too big a jump to commit. If she did, she'd no longer be able to ignore Him, to push Him aside. And what would that mean? *A changed life.* Changed for knowledge, for some kind of inner joy and relationship, for duty of some kind, if David was an example. But even with his apparent believing, David still seemed distracted, sometimes almost tortured. *Shouldn't believ-*

ing change that?

Claire shook her head, hoping to free her mind. Beneath the crescent moon, she pulled her pen and the precious journal from one deep pocket, her torch from the other. Even needing her muffled light pleased her. *Like a writer in her garret, creating by candlelight. Or like Jo in* Little Women, *writing her bloodthirsty tales and plays in the attic, late at night. Delicious!*

She opened to page one, took up her pen, remembered Paris and the avant-garde writers who'd frequented Shakespeare and Company, and began to write as she believed they would.

She struggled through five pages, but the lines came stilted, deliberate, the dialogue forced, as before. She crossed out several lines, then half a page, then the opening scene, tempted to rip and crumple the desecrated pages from the binding of the beautiful book. *Why is my story not coming? It all sounds so false . . . worse than vaudeville.*

All Claire could do was compare her life to the life she wanted to write about — the flamboyant and heroic characters she wanted to pen. Real life came up short, and frustrating. *The Mass Observation Project . . . I wonder if that's why Aunt Miranda gave me the journal, if that's what she intended. But it's not what I want. By the time I return to Paris, I want a novel in hand, a novel that will make Sylvia Beach sit up and take notice. A novel she will champion as she championed Mr. Joyce's* Ulysses.

Claire felt herself blush in the dark. She'd never framed her wish so clearly, and she would never write a book like that. The desire to go to such places in her mind, to peruse those avenues with her pen, made her shudder, though she wasn't sure why. She certainly wanted to write something grand, something the world would read and remember.

She heaved a sigh, her intensity spent. When her back hitched, she sat straight again and stretched, realizing she'd been huddled in a cramp all the time she'd written, or tried to write. She leaned back against the tree and flicked off her torch, which had steadily dimmed, the battery waning. It didn't matter now.

That's when she saw the light . . . high in the north tower of Bluebell Wood. A candle burning brightly, steadily. Or was it two candles of differing heights? Claire frowned, squinting her eyes to better see. No one would burn a light like that, not with the strict blackout regulations. It made a pinpoint for German Messerschmitts. The ARP and Home Guard would rage. Aunt Miranda would surely be fined, not to mention ridiculed and further harassed by the locals.

Claire's skin prickled. Fear of invasion ran rampant through the village, as it did through all of England. Every man, woman, and child kept on high alert, on the lookout for spies said to send signals to German planes in the night. Lake Windermere and its banks were a prime concern, constantly patrolled. German flying boats could land right on the water, sending ashore troops under cover of darkness in a matter of minutes. Planes that never left the air might fill the sky with parachutists.

It would be just like Hitler to send his minions on Christmas — a terrible "gift" to the people of England, the people whose lives and morale he'd vowed to grind into the dirt. Hadn't they heard the bombers on Christmas Eve?

Who from Bluebell Wood would wreak such vile betrayal? The few servants had been loyal members of the household for years, some for multiple generations. The idea of Aunt Miranda betraying England was unthinkable. That left David, of whom she knew so little.

Claire's heart constricted. She couldn't

reconcile such betrayal with a man who secretly decorated a Christmas tree in an abandoned garden. She also knew she couldn't let romantic notions keep her from her duty. If it came out that she'd seen the light and done nothing — if Bluebell Wood was bombed because she'd hesitated — Claire couldn't live with the repercussions or guilt of either.

She pocketed her treasures and made her way down the tree as quickly as she dared. Not covering Christopher's boards or his tree sign, Claire stumbled through the garden, raced past the Christmas tree and to the garden gate. She took time only to lock the door and replace the key before groping her way around the garden wall and heading for the path.

Nearing the maze and lawns, she stumbled over a stray tree root. Pain shot through her knee, reminding her of the night she and the children left Calais . . . the sudden bump on her head . . . the sick feeling that the world had taken a turn she didn't want and couldn't stop.

She pushed through the maze. Out of breath, she had nearly reached the porte cochere when a deep-voiced command stopped her cold.

"Home Guard. Hold on, missy!"

A second man added, "Who are you? State your business here."

Both terrified and relieved, Claire bit her lip to keep from screaming. "I'm Claire — Claire Stewart. I live here, with my aunt, Lady Langford. Thank goodness you're here!"

"I'll wager," the first huffed. "Trust the Yanks. In a bit of a hurry? There's a curfew, young lady."

"I was out for a walk. Look, it doesn't matter —"

"I'll be the judge of what matters, miss."

Pompous! Insufferable! Claire had hoped to investigate on her own, but perhaps it was better this way. If someone was sending signals, especially if that someone was David, it might be best to have two strong men with her, though they weren't really tall nor did they look so very strong. "Please, I need you to come with me. I was out for a walk, but I saw a light burning from the north tower."

"A light?"

"It could be anything, but everyone should be asleep by now."

"Signals!"

"And with a clear view of the lake!" Both men, past their prime, took on new energy.

"Show me!" the thinner one ordered.

"This way." She turned back to the path she'd just left and took them to the edge of the maze. The light in the tower still shone.

"I'll be —"

"That's a pinpoint for the Jerries, by gum."

"I can show you how to reach the tower if you come with me."

"Lead the way, miss."

She found the front door still unlocked, proof that Mrs. Newsome had gone to bed before Claire had slipped out. *At least she'll be off the grill list. Surely there will be a grilling. I hope I've not made a mistake!*

Inside, protected by the blackout curtains covering every window, a soft lamp burned in the foyer. A brighter light gleamed beneath the library door.

Aunt Miranda must have come back down. Should I alert her or take the men upstairs first?

"Take us directly, miss. No time to waste."

"Right." She knew that was true and raced up the stairs, the Home Guard hot on her heels. She'd only been to the north tower once. It was a convoluted route ending in a high and steady climb. Aunt Miranda had said the rooms were locked ages ago — no need for them now, and certainly no need to clean or heat them. Claire realized that once the Home Guard saw those empty rooms, Aunt Miranda was bound to receive a visit from the local billeting officer. *Plenty more room for evacuees.*

At last they reached the stairs to the tower. A light, barely visible, filtered onto the high wall at the top of the stairs, just as they reached the last winding.

The Home Guard officer behind Claire grabbed her wrist, pressing a finger to his lips, and pulled her back.

Please, please don't let it be David. She swallowed, hating to be the one to turn him in. She waited, holding her breath, behind the edge of the stone wall, as the Home Guard took over. That's when she heard the door at the bottom of the tower open and new footsteps — heavy, rushing upward.

A moment later, one of the Home Guard exclaimed, "Well, by gum!"

And the other, in tandem: "What in the name of King George do you think you're doin'?"

The unholy howl of a child's scream didn't sound like spies to Claire. She rounded the wall just as David appeared behind her.

A circle of nine wide-eyed, panic-stricken, pajama-clad children stared back at them with open mouths, while Aimee screamed, clinging to Jeanine. Two brightly burning candles in a crudely carved menorah, sitting on the tower's window ledge, illuminated a homemade dreidel, just finishing its spin on the floor between them. Claire saw all this in a flash, just before the heftier of the Home Guards swatted out the burning candles, leaving them all in total darkness and sending Aimee into high-pitched hysterics.

Chapter Fifteen

It was two o'clock in the morning, long past curfew and the time all mortals should be asleep, when Dr. MacDonald opened the library door of Bluebell Wood. Lady Langford and Claire, still dressed in their Christmas Day clothes, had both fallen asleep in chairs flanking the fire.

He wanted nothing more than to gaze on Maggie Langford's sleeping face, to watch the low firelight play across her cheek, but hearing footsteps in the hallway, he coughed discreetly. Maggie's sleepy eyes flitted open and met his. He saw the smile of relief there, the assurance that she saw him as her rescuer. He wanted that, and more.

A moment later David Campbell pushed open the door with his foot, balancing a tray laden with tea and sandwiches. The doctor sighed, at once appreciative and regretful. He set his bag on the table.

"The children?" Maggie whispered.

"Asleep at last."

"And Aimee?"

"Sedated. The wee bairn was mightily upset."

"That's why I telephoned. I didn't — none of us could calm her."

He nodded. "Aye. She should sleep through the day. A little supper and a great deal of loving is what I prescribe. Stay with her until she falls asleep again. I'm concerned she might be coming down with something more. I don't think it's influenza, though there've been some new cases in the village. I'm trying to contain it, but it's too early to know."

Claire opened her eyes, blinking against the light. "Oh, I hope it's not that again."

"We'll do our best." Maggie smiled, though she looked very tired to the doctor, unnaturally tired. "Do you have time to sit with us, Raibeart?" Her invitation eased the taut muscles in his neck and he sank into the chair nearest her.

David set the tray on the table. "Doctor, have a sandwich and a cuppa."

Raibeart glanced at David as he accepted both, annoyed to like the younger man. Even at this late hour, he, a near stranger, was up and helping in the best way he could. It was the second time that long night the doctor had received a steaming cup of tea at the man's hands.

Maggie pushed the hair from her eyes. "They were all so terrified, especially when the Home Guard pretended to arrest them. Their fear worries me more than that the wardens saw their candles burning."

"I hope you'll feel that way when they fine you, Aunt Miranda," Claire chided, pouring tea for the rest.

Dr. MacDonald knew Claire meant to be amusing, but he didn't find it funny.

"We're giving them a home — a place to live — but I feel like we're failing with them." Maggie spread her hands. "I don't know what else to do."

"They're missing their families and everything they've known. I don't see how we can help that." Claire's honest assessment eased the doctor's annoyance, but only a little.

He set his nearly drained cup in its saucer. "Though it goes against my grain, I'll have to agree with the Campbell." He'd never expected to be on the same side as his clan's sworn enemy. But the child's hysterics were more than enough to know that something must be done, and David's suggestion had seemed a good one.

"What do you mean?"

The doctor looked to David and nodded.

"We can't do anything about what they endured before they came here, but I think you're right that they're missing their families," David began. "I think tonight was about trying to hold on to a remnant."

"Of their families?" Claire asked.

"Of their families, but also of their identities, and their memories." David paused. "They're Jewish, and I think most if not all of them come from practicing families. Their years are defined by religious festivals, even more than our years are defined by holidays."

"Are you saying we've taken their Jewish identity away from them? We don't insist they attend church, and this is wartime, after all."

"Maggie, be honest with yourself. They don't attend church because *you* don't attend church, something that wouldn't harm either of you women. If you expected it of them, they'd go to please you."

Maggie bristled, but Raibeart wasn't sorry he'd said it. She'd sealed herself off from the world too long, and from the church ever since Christopher had died. Perhaps having David Campbell to help plead the children's case would move Maggie in a way he'd failed to do.

"I'm just saying they need the stability of their heritage and the faith they've been raised in." David spoke with more authority now.

"But I don't see how —"

"I know the rabbi in Penrith," the doctor cut in. "A patient of mine before he moved out that way. Regular services are held there."

"Penrith must be thirty miles or more! However would we take them all that far? Petrol is rationed, and we don't —"

"Let me talk with him. If you're willing, perhaps he'll come here . . . or he may know someone closer to teach the children on occasion. If I don't miss my guess, those older boys have either been bar mitzvahed or are missing it, losing out on their Hebrew lessons, or whatever it is they do. Not a thing to be overlooked in their faith, not even in their culture."

"The stepping into manhood." David nodded. "Peter said he celebrated bar mitzvah in Germany — even brought his grandfather's prayer shawl with him. But I think Bertram may be ready or even just past the appointed age."

Maggie sighed. "We don't even know what they're missing."

"No, we don't," David agreed, "but we

can learn. I'll help in any way I can, any way you wish."

"While you're here," Claire stated flatly, then crimsoned. "I mean, you're planning to leave once the factory's village is built, right?"

"Well, I don't —"

"I'm just saying that whatever we start is something those of us who are here must be able to carry on. If you're not staying and the doctor can't be expected to help, well then, it's just Aunt Miranda and me."

"And would it hurt you to welcome a stranger into this house to help those children?"

"Raibeart," Maggie soothed, "Claire is just being practical. They're not ours to raise. They're only here temporarily."

"Temporarily? There's a war on, Maggie, and no end in sight. They're apt to spend their childhoods here."

"Or be gone tomorrow."

"Aye, but we all know that's not likely. And if they were gone tomorrow, would you not want them to go back to Germany, or to France, with a stronger faith? Won't they be needing that faith in a world that may well have ripped their families from them forever?"

Raibeart knew Maggie understood and

had always embraced the importance, the deep necessity of faith. Grief still weighed her down, had made her blind. There was no shortchanging that journey, but how he wished he could shake the darkness out of her, for her own sake and for the sake of the weeping children he'd just quieted. Had he made a mistake in bringing more youngsters to Maggie? He hoped not.

He glanced at David, his ally in seeing things as they stood, and shook his head. Wartime made the strangest comrades, and the oddest foes.

CHAPTER SIXTEEN

1941 dawned. As mysteriously as the ornaments on the tree in the secret garden appeared, Claire found they had disappeared by late January.

Dr. MacDonald was as good as his word and brought the rabbi from Penrith to Bluebell Wood himself. Rabbi Meir patiently explained to Mrs. Newsome the importance to Jewish people of keeping a kosher kitchen, and his understanding that such a thing might prove impossible for Bluebell Wood in wartime. Significantly, he instituted the keeping of Shabbat and tutored Aunt Miranda and the children in their duties for the weeks he would not be able to preside — duties their parents had assumed in bygone days.

The first evening the family observed the Shabbat meal under the direction of the rabbi, tears coursed down Jeanine's cheeks and Peter's eyes filled. Aimee's eyes glowed like the candles they burned, and each head, German and French, reverently bowed in prayer. Claire realized, once again, that David had understood and reached out to the children in ways she had not — that she had not even realized their deep need.

How does he know? How does he see these things? Why don't I?

Valentine's Day had long been painful for Mrs. Newsome. Not so much for herself — it had been many years since her husband had died in the Great War, and she'd learned to live and love her life. But seeing her ladyship grieve through February for the past two decades had been hard. And now her American niece took up the moping vigil. It was nearly more than Mrs. Newsome could stand to see the two mooning over past loves, imagined loves, and neglecting the cheeks and eyes that needed brightening around the breakfast table.

She ladled porridge from the tureen on the sideboard and handed bowls to the children, one by one. "I noticed that Valentine's Day is just round the bend."

Lady Langford blinked, her mouth a straight line, but did not reply.

"I was thinking that our fine young artists might like to engage in a particular project."

"Mrs. Newsome, whatever are you talking about?"

"Why, about making valentines to give, and perhaps to send to the district hospital, for recovering soldiers. They might bring a bit of cheer for the lads."

"May we?" Jeanine enthused. "Do you think they'd want them — homemade ones?"

"Mr. David thinks so. He thinks it a splendid idea."

"I don't know . . ." Lady Langford hesitated.

"Please, madame!" Gaston clasped his hands together as if praying.

Mrs. Newsome barely suppressed her smile. The lad, knowing or not, had picked up that habit from Miss Claire. "It's a war effort project, my lady. It will show the men that we care about them and appreciate all they've sacrificed. I hear that some of the wounded men have lost their sweethearts, if you can imagine it — girls turning their backs on men because they've lost a leg or an eye. How could they at such a time?" Mrs. Newsome knew Lady Langford would agree. Perhaps it had been unfair to bait her in front of the children, who immediately took up the cry, but they all needed cheering, and if a bit of lace and ribbon and colored paper with a sentimental line or two could do that and help the poor fighting lads at the same time, well, who was she to mind the wheedling?

"You're in charge of this project, Mrs. Newsome. You may go ahead or nip it in the bud, as you wish."

"Thank you, my lady."

The breakfast table sent up a cheer, all except Aimee, who seemed even more withdrawn than usual. Mrs. Newsome made a mental note to remind Aimee that she needn't know how to write; she could simply draw a picture to send. She hoped that was all that ailed the child.

During the next week every meal was served à la carte in either the drawing room or library, for the dining room table became a veritable assembly line of plain and colored paper, ribbon, lace, pen, and ink.

Mrs. Newsome had expected industry and creativity but was more than a little astonished by the romantic and amusing verses penned by the roomful of laughing youngsters, particularly Peter, who kept his last valentine to himself, no matter how much the others cajoled him to show it. Ingrid proved to have a fine hand with calligraphy. Mr. David offered to collect the colorful missives to deliver to the hospital staff, who'd promised to distribute them according to perceived need.

But Aimee held one valentine behind her back.

"Don't you want to send it to the wounded men, Aimee? It will mean so very much to them to receive a pretty valentine from a sweet young girl," Mrs. Newsome encouraged the child. Aimee had made very few, and each one had taken her a long time — each one that much more precious in the housekeeper's mind.

But Aimee firmly shook her head. "This is for someone."

"For whom, dear?"

Aimee flushed and looked toward Claire. "For mademoiselle." She brought it from behind her back and ran toward Claire at the far end of the table. Aimee stopped suddenly, as if uncertain how to proceed.

Mrs. Newsome wanted to pinch Claire. *Take it! Don't you see what it means to the child?*

But Claire sat, stilted, and as uncertain as Aimee. Finally, she said, "Thank you, Aimee," and took the valentine, but as if afraid it might set her fingers on fire. She set it on the table and pushed it closer to Aimee. "That's very nice, and thank you, but I think it would be best to give it to the wounded soldiers. They need it most."

Aimee did not blink, did not move, did not retrieve the precious gift. Her face faded from tentative to flat, as though someone had washed a slate clean.

Mrs. Newsome couldn't be sure, but she thought she saw a heave in the child's chest before she turned and ran from the room, tiny fists clenched.

Josef had pleaded, even begged Peter not to go. Sneaking out and meeting the pretty Fräulein beside the lake at night could bring nothing but trouble. "Can you not give her your valentine tomorrow — hand it to her before our school session and after hers?"

"Mine must be the first she receives. Besides, she may not come. She did not promise. If she does not appear, I will return the way I came. I am not a *Dummkopf,* Josef. I know enough not to get caught."

All the same, Josef tossed and worried all the while Peter was gone late that night.

Josef's eyes were barely open when Peter finally pulled aside the blackout curtain and slipped back into the room. His older brother was not humming under his breath as he'd done before going out. Josef could tell by the slump in his shoulders that the meeting had not gone as planned. Rather than ask, Josef turned over, closed his eyes, and gave his brother the privacy he surely needed.

The breakfast gong had just sounded when the pounding on the front door came. Mrs. Newsome sent Nancy to answer. "Who could it be at this hour, and in such a state?"

She hadn't long to wonder. Two booming male voices echoed up and down the foyer.

"I told you they're nothing but scum! Children, my eye! Arrest the bloomin' Hun, Foley! Be quick about it."

Mrs. Newsome reached the hallway at the same time Claire raced down the stairs, trailed by the children and nearly bumping into David.

Lady Miranda, still in her dressing gown, her face the color of watered-down milk, placed a trembling hand on the banister at the top of the stairs. "What is it, Mr. Firthman? What is the trouble that's brought you to my door?"

"It's them bloomin' foreigners you're harborin' here! Nazi informants! Caught red-handed! And if you don't have him arrested you're in it for treason . . . my lady!"

"Whatever are you going on about, Douglas Firthman?" Mrs. Newsome had had quite enough of the man, and she didn't want Lady Miranda standing in the chill. Her lady had never quite come down with the influenza as had some of the staff and children, but she'd not looked well — as if fighting something off — for some time.

"Mrs. Johnson saw that tall blond one signaling across the lake last night, caught him leaving German messages for the invaders."

"Peter?" Claire sounded incredulous.

"The very!"

"There must be some mistake, some misunderstanding —" David broke in.

"Show him!"

Sergeant Foley pulled a smudged and dog-eared paper from his pocket, the very paper the children had used to print valentine messages. "It's German writing, all right. Mrs. Johnson lives just by the road. Said she saw him signaling with a torch, bright as can be, then stuff this into the rock wall a block or so from the schoolhouse. Figured him to be signaling an accomplice."

"And did you see this accomplice?" David all but sneered.

"No need to be high-handed with me, Campbell. I'm doin' my duty for king and country, not to be deterred by anyone, even the likes of you."

"What about the likes of me?" Dr. Mac-

Donald thundered behind him. "What are you on about now, Douglas Firthman?"

"Espionage! Traitors! Treason! That's what it is."

"Please, my lady, come and lie down." Mrs. Newsome took the stairs as quickly as she could and placed a supportive hand under Lady Miranda's arm. "They'll sort this out. It's surely a lot of thunderblus. You know what Douglas Firthman is." She whispered the last. Her ladyship, though weak and trembling, did not budge.

Peter appeared on the stairs, his face flushing at the sight of Mr. Firthman.

"You! There he is! Arrest him, Foley."

"A wee bit of sanity, if you please, Sergeant Foley." Dr. MacDonald pushed into the midst of the group. "May I see the paper you found?"

"Well, Doc, it's a bit of evidence. Don't know that I should."

But the doctor snatched it from Foley's hand and opened it. He read it slowly, then read it again, the hint of a smile reaching the corners of his eyes, which he appeared to suppress. "And just who, young Peter, were you planning to translate this for, to woo? Not the Nazi paratroopers, I suspect."

Peter turned scarlet.

"What's that you're sayin'?" demanded

Firthman.

The doctor handed the paper back to Foley. "Would you send a love poem to the high command?"

"A love poem?"

"Aye. My German's a mite rusty, but I know enough to see that's what it is. Why don't you have the boy translate?"

"He'd lie!" Firthman blustered.

"Then one of the others, or Lady Langford. I'm sure she knows enough of the German tongue to tell. Or one of you. Firthman? Sergeant Foley? Didn't you learn a smidgen in school? Or didn't you bother to read it before you came stormin' in here?"

Firthman colored and snatched the paper in return. "Lady Langford, I ask you to translate."

"Must she?" Peter looked miserable.

"Aye, I'm afraid so, son," the doctor commiserated. "To clear your name of these vile suspicions."

Foley grabbed the paper from Firthman and squinted. "I can make out a word here, there, a line or two. Perhaps it's as you say, but I want to know who you intended this for. Speak up, lad!"

Peter looked as if he'd bite bullets first.

"Who were the torch signals for?" asked Foley. "That's something I must know. It's already in my report, lad. We don't take infringement of the blackout lightly."

"They were for the girl!" Josef stepped forward.

"Be quiet!" Peter jabbed his brother in the ribs. "It's none of your affair."

"It is if he arrests you! What's the honor of your lady if she's betrayed you? If she didn't even take up for you with — with him? Tell him, or I will."

Claire groaned.

"Emily." Peter looked at the carpet, his face as miserable as a boy's could look. "It was Emily."

"*My* Emily?" Firthman sputtered. "You nasty cur, sneakin' out to lure my innocent girl —"

"She didn't meet me." Peter looked up, his flashing eyes angry, hurt. "I wouldn't have left the note if she'd met me, would I?"

"It was a valentine," Josef spoke out. "He only wanted to give her a valentine."

Peter jabbed him again, softly this time.

"You must tell them. It's better than him thinking you a traitor." Josef stepped forward. "We'd never help the Nazis. Don't you know that? We're Jews!"

Now Douglas Firthman's color deepened.

"The lad's got a point, Firthman." The

doctor scratched behind his ear. "They've escaped Hitler and his SS by the skins of their teeth. What would any of them have to gain in aiding the enemy?"

"That's enough for me," Foley said. "No more signals, young man, or I'll be running you before the magistrate and fining her ladyship what houses you from her charity. And I'd advise you youngsters to leave off pushing notes in the stone walls. This is not the first worry by villagers that you're sendin' notes to enemy conspirators, and I'd rather not be runnin' down every schoolgirl rosy-posy. Understood?"

But Mrs. Newsome objected. "Sergeant Foley, schoolchildren have left notes for one another in the stone walls for generations. How can you ask them to stop?"

"For their own good, mum, and for mine."

"Will you ask the same of the village children?" Lady Langford lifted her chin.

"No, I will not, madam, for the simple reason that they're not Germans. Folks here have had all they want of Germans, and rubbin' their noses in it by joinin' in the common culture won't help. Keep out of local affairs. I'm sayin' it for their own well-being."

"And stay away from my Emily!" Firthman jabbed a fierce finger toward Peter.

"I'm warnin' you for the last time."

Peter lifted his head and spoke clearly. "Because I am German, yes? Or because I am Jewish?"

"I want neither sniffin' round my girl!"

"Get out." Lady Langford's voice trembled but commanded. "Get out of my house, Mr. Firthman, and do not return."

Firthman crimsoned once more but narrowed his eyes at Lady Langford, enough to make Mrs. Newsome swallow. He slapped his cap against his knee and turned on his heel, storming out the open door. Sergeant Foley touched his fingers to the brim of his cap and left quietly. David closed the door behind him.

"I know you meant no harm, Peter," Dr. MacDonald spoke low but firmly. "I know you did it for love of a maiden, and despite my venerable age and silver-hued hair, I understand that." He almost smiled. "But I speak to all of you now. Give the locals no reason to fear or doubt or mistrust ye, insofar as you are able. It will go better for you and for Lady Langford. It could be a long war, and you do not want to make enemies of your hosts. Do I make myself clear?"

Crystal clear, Mrs. Newsome thought. Though by the look in the eyes of the children it was unfair persecution, another singling out, an ostracizing with which they were all too familiar.

Once the crisis and shouting were past, and Dr. MacDonald had fussed aloud over her ladyship needing to go back to bed and taken her by the hand, Claire herded the children to breakfast.

In the quiet, as she walked down the stairs, Mrs. Newsome caught the sound of a soft whimpering. It took but a moment to find the little form huddled behind the covered table nearest the door. "Aimee! What in the world are you doin' here? Ach, child, whatever is the matter?" Mrs. Newsome bent down and took the little girl in her arms. But the child couldn't stop her sobbing.

"Did all that shouting frighten you, love? Is that it?"

Aimee nodded.

"Well, never you mind, lamb. It's over now. They've gone. That Douglas Firthman is nothing but hot air, and Dr. MacDonald meant well by Peter. He stood up for him as best he knew. And don't you worry about our ladyship; the doctor will take good care of her. He loves her with all his heart, and he's just that worried for her; that's all." Mrs. Newsome was worried too.

Chapter Seventeen

Dr. MacDonald pronounced Aunt Miranda a new victim of the influenza — "a veritable bad case, and here I'd hoped it had passed her by" — and took to spending wakeful nights on a cot in the hallway outside his Maggie's room for the remainder of February. Claire didn't believe he'd have removed himself an inch through the trauma if he hadn't been urgently called away for births and mumps or injuries accompanied by significant blood loss.

In sharp contrast to bleak February, March brought brilliant branches of forsythia into bloom, reaching sunshine arms to the sky.

Next, tiny emerald blades pushed from beneath the soil and, by April, sprouted buds. At last daffodils lifted golden trumpets while crimson goblets bowed in the wind. Claire tried to get away to her secret, special haunt each day, just to see what new thing had emerged.

But change came not only to the garden. Springtime swept the woods and fells. Sapphire bluebells carpeted the forest floors while rhododendron rioted in every color. Gorse and broom bloomed in golden patches amid tender grass, rich and green thanks to the winter's snows. Lambs barely a month old dotted the hillsides, rolling and frolicking one minute, then butting their mothers' sides the next, demanding they let down their milk.

The influenza that had crept through the Lakeland village all winter was finally gone, as if the sudden sun scorched it and the fierce spring wind whisked it away. Even so, Aunt Miranda did not rebound with the strength of the others.

Unable to remain indoors or demand that the children should, Claire led her unruly troops on daily outings, trudging through the woods, into the orchards, and over the fells, encouraging each one to create a nature diary and mark the changing features of the season in words and drawings.

It was a practice that Aunt Miranda had said was popular, even expected, in Victorian and Edwardian days, but no less inspirational now — one that would get them all out of doors.

Just as valuable to Claire, the exercise thwarted the children's irritability and long-winter cabin fever, bringing roses to all their cheeks.

Claire was astonished to discover the scientific bent, but even more, the serious enthusiasm of the older children for growing things and the laws of nature. It was as if someone had drawn aside a curtain. For the first time they seemed truly eager in their studies, as if entering a new world of their own outside of school or the house.

Ten-year-old Ingrid demonstrated particular gifts in drawing and painting, in addition to her fluid calligraphy. Her joy in collecting flowers, leaves, and bird feathers — in sitting for hours to draw and paint them with just the right hue in the changing light — fascinated Claire.

But it was Aimee who surprised her most. All winter the child had waned, pale and sober, especially since that frightening Hanukkah night. Claire knew Aimee blamed her for the bad men coming, like soldiers, to snuff their candles and march the children from the tower.

Dr. MacDonald had surmised there must have been something in Aimee's experience or memory, perhaps something she'd seen before leaving France or overheard about the fearful workings of Germany's Gestapo or brownshirts that had fueled her mind and fears when the officious Home Guard had pretended to arrest the children. He had no other explanation for the change in Aimee.

Aunt Miranda had tried to love and cuddle the child, but she'd not responded and continually squirmed from her arms. Now Aimee was beyond delight over the newborn lambs. She romped and played alone, petting the lambs whenever able to get near, as the other children collected specimens and drew. She picked wildflowers and arranged them in pretty bouquets, often whispering secrets to herself or nearby birds. It was as if she wore two faces, one for humans and one for wildlife.

Once, Claire glimpsed a rare and tentative joy in Aimee's face as she approached. The child headed directly for her with a lovely bouquet, but Claire in that moment turned, needing to stop a fist cuffing between Gaston and Josef. When she'd turned again to Aimee, the child was gone, her pretty bouquet strewn across the ground.

Claire, remembering her faux pas with Aimee and the valentine, which Mrs. Newsome had brought to her attention in no uncertain terms, tried to approach Aimee later that afternoon. But the little girl remained sullen and intent on drawing newborn lambs under Mrs. Newsome's care. She would not even look at Claire. "They are for Mrs. Heelis. She will want them," Aimee insisted to Mrs. Newsome, covering her picture so Claire could not see.

Claire sighed. She couldn't help but feel she'd failed the child again.

"I've no idea how to connect with her," Claire complained that evening to Aunt Miranda over tea in the library. "I can't seem to do the right thing by her, and I don't even know what that thing is."

"Nor do I." Aunt Miranda pushed an auburn tendril streaked with silver from her creased forehead.

Claire hadn't noticed when her aunt's hair had begun to gray.

"Raibeart and David were right. I think the rabbi's visits and the regular Shabbat meals are a help to the older children — they seem more content and purposeful. Bertram seems so pleased and committed to his bar mitzvah preparations. But I worry for Aimee. Mrs. Newsome said she found her behind the sofa yesterday, crying for her *maman,* and that she's taken to hoarding food in her pockets from mealtimes. She's not eating enough."

"She needs her mother." Claire had known this from the first, known because Aimee had said so often and because that's how she'd felt at Aimee's age. She could still remember desperately needing attention and affection from a mother who, though just in the next room, remained preoccupied with her own concerns, particularly as they related to the amber-colored liquid in crystal decanters.

"Yes, she needs her mother, poor child. And we're all she has."

"I'm not her *maman.* I can't be that for her, and it wouldn't be right." Claire's heart beat faster. She felt the need to justify herself before Aunt Miranda. It was one thing to care for Aimee's needs, to be kind to her, but quite another to mother her.

One day the child would go home to her real *maman,* and Claire would be left alone again.

"No." Aunt Miranda frowned, pensive. "No, I suppose not."

Passover and Easter came and went. Claire had never attended a Passover meal, but the rabbi's explanation of the feast's origins and the reason for each of the foods gave her much to think about.

Later, David pointed out the biblical accounts in the Old and New Testaments for Passover and the Last Supper and showed her how one led so naturally into the other, how Jesus offered Himself as the Paschal Lamb.

No one had ever explained that to Claire before. No one had explained so many things. Now she wondered if she didn't believe because she truly disbelieved or if it was because she lacked information. Could information equal faith? Could it establish faith?

The thing she did know was that she dreaded the completion of the factory village at Calgarth, for surely David would relocate there when the time came. And that, she was not looking forward to.

How will we manage when he leaves?

April downpours gave way to May showers and to the heavenly fragrance of cream and purple lilac bouquets that filled every open window at Bluebell Wood. Each morning Claire thought the land, the lawn, the gardens and orchards, the woods and fells could not possibly grow more lovely or more green. Each glorious afternoon proved her wrong, and she reveled in nature's instruction.

But Claire knew that not all at Bluebell Wood was beautiful. She noticed the deepening circles under her aunt's eyes, saw the way her aunt quickly wearied. Claire did her best to absorb more of the children's time. But the more she took over, the more Aunt Miranda seemed to want the children near her. Claire didn't know which way to turn.

Perhaps it was her worry for Aunt Miranda, but Claire felt her impatience with Aimee's moping and churlishness grow. The little girl would not respond to either of the women, and with the other children needing Claire more, with Aunt Miranda depending on her more and more to keep the children busy, with bad news from France increasing and less time to steal away and write . . . Claire felt herself slipping away, as if there were not one moment of each day to call her own.

Evenings, after tucking Aimee in, brought both relief and worry as those eager to listen sat round the wireless, intent on the day's news. It was a close-knit time, one Claire knew the children relished as much as the adults. Entertainment came in the form of concerts and comedy programs during the week, and in the form of church and cathedral broadcasts on Sundays.

But this evening they all sat in a tense circle, even the younger children forgoing their normal pinching and punching. Aunt Miranda had heard earlier in the day that there was to be a special announcement from France.

David had just come in from the factory and was loosening his tie. Bertram moved over, beckoning David to sit on the bench beside him. The voice over the wireless began:

> "Today, 14 May, in Paris, over 3,700 Jewish men of foreign nationalities were rounded up and arrested in what has been termed *'Rafle du billet vert,'* or 'Roundup of the Green Ticket.' Ostensibly, these men are being transported to a convocation to check their situation as foreign Jews currently residing in France. Contrary to expectations, the men have not been released, but were transported by bus to the Gare d'Austerlitz, where they boarded trains. No word as to where the trains are bound has been released."

Aunt Miranda switched off the wireless. Not a sound was heard until Elise pressed her sister's arm and whispered, "Does that mean they took Papa away? Papa is not French, not really. He came from Poland; Maman always teased him so."

Jeanine had gone pale. "I do not know. How can I know?" But tears filled her eyes.

Gaston and Bertram exchanged dark glances. Claire could see in their faces that they were afraid. She understood. As much as she hated her father for not wanting her, she was relieved to know he wouldn't be arrested . . . not now, not for his nationality, anyway.

"What about Aimee's father? Is he French?" David asked.

"I've no idea," Claire replied, "but it won't do her any good to know about this."

Mademoiselle Claire might not know if Aimee's father was French, but Aimee knew. She knew that her father and even her mother were born in Belgium — a thing her parents made certain she was proud of and would never forget.

Now, as she hid behind the library door to listen to the wireless and the grown-ups talk, she wondered. *Does being Belgian mean the bad men have come and taken Papa away? If they have taken Papa, how long before they will come and take Maman?*

Aimee knew there were many things she didn't understand about the war, but she knew about people disappearing and never being heard from again. That had happened even before she left France with Mademoiselle Claire. Aimee remembered the night angry men had broken into their home and dragged her *oncle* from bed, beating him all the while with sticks — clubs that looked like those the Home Guard had carried when they arrested her on Hanukkah. When she'd asked the next day what Oncle had done, tears escaped her papa's eyes and he'd said, in a voice dull and flat, "My brother was born. He was born Jewish." Oncle Pierre never walked into the house again.

That was war, Aimee knew. People disappeared in different ways for different reasons. She knew too well about them being smuggled through the night to faraway places. Wasn't she one, after all?

If Maman and Papa were taken, Aimee knew she could not find them again, and they would not come for her, no matter that they had promised.

It was frightening and horrible to imagine all of life without Maman and Papa. But truth be told, even though Aimee kissed the mezuzah each night after the lights had gone out, she'd been having a much harder time remembering the faces of her parents. She remembered more the smell of Maman and the warmth of her body as she had cradled Aimee in her arms. She remembered the sound of Maman's voice as she sang over her before bedtime.

Mademoiselle Claire was nearer her mother's age than anyone, but she never held her, never sang over her. Madame Langford had tried, but Aimee knew her heart was torn. Madame longed for her own boy who had gone away and never returned. Sometimes when madame held her, she cried, and that made Aimee feel worse. Mrs. Newsome was kind, but she was so very busy with all the children and the household.

Twice since living at Bluebell Wood, Aimee had heard Dr. MacDonald say the animals in the forest took better care of their children than Mademoiselle Claire did. Aimee didn't know much about the animals in the forest, but she knew about the lambs on the fells. She'd seen how the mother sheep never turned her children away, no matter how rude, no matter how hard they butted up against her sides demanding their dinner. Perhaps living with the animals might be a good thing.

It was not a new idea to Aimee. She'd been thinking of it all the winter, had even saved a bit of food for when the time was right. She knew just where she'd go. Auld Mother Heelis had given her the idea. Aimee was certain the old lady would never lead her astray, and that she knew things other grown-ups did not.

Aimee had even whispered her plan to the little lambs on the fells that spring whenever she saw them. They hadn't responded, but Aimee hadn't supposed they would. It wasn't up to them.

Now that Papa had likely been taken away, Maman would need her more than ever. Until she could find a way home, she could live with the sheep. The days were warm and the nights mild. The moon shone bright enough she could probably make her way without a torch, even in the dark.

Aimee crept back upstairs and into bed, making certain no one saw her. She fell asleep, dreaming of laying her head against the soft, warm coat of a newborn lamb.

Chapter Eighteen

Claire counted the sober, sleepy heads of ten children at breakfast. She wouldn't have been surprised if they'd slept in, if last night's news had kept them awake until the wee hours. But they were all there, as much because they needed one another more than ever as because they needed sustenance, she thought.

Only Aimee seemed animated and hungry beyond her usual self. Claire was glad the little girl knew nothing of last night's broadcast. Whether Aimee's parents were French or foreign Jews, life in France these days did not bode well for them. It was not something for one so young to know or worry over. There was nothing any of them could do. The truth would out in time, and they would face it then.

It wasn't until luncheon that Aimee was missed.

"I've no idea where she's gone," Mrs.

Newsome confessed to Claire. "She asked for a tea party for the dolly I made her and said she'd like to play in the orchard this morning. I was glad for her to be out in the sunshine, and in truth, it gave me a moment's peace."

"I can't imagine she'd miss lunch with the other children, even so. She must have heard the outdoor bell." Claire felt more annoyed than worried. Aimee had never wandered far.

"I will see if she is in our room," Jeanine offered.

"She's not," Elise said.

"How do you know?"

"I just came down from there. I saw her go out soon after breakfast. I think she might have run away."

"What?"

Elise shrugged. "I've heard her talking about it with her doll for ages. But I didn't think much of it. We've all run away, haven't we? She'll come back when she's hungry. I did."

Claire looked at her aunt, helpless. *Do all children run away? Where would she go? Will she know her way back?*

Aunt Miranda set down her teacup, which had frozen in midair all the while Elise spoke so philosophically. "I think, just as soon as we've eaten — as quickly as we can — that we should all search for Aimee. She's too young to be wandering around unchaperoned."

"*Oui,* madame!" Gaston asserted. "We will miss the school today and form a search party! Not a problem, as Monsieur David says."

Claire and her aunt made eye contact again. Claire feared turning Gaston and Josef loose to search posed a greater threat than Aimee's disappearance. "No, I'm sure that's not necessary, Gaston. We'll find Aimee and make sure she's safely home before you return. You can all keep an eye out for her on the way to the village. If you see her, bring her directly home. In the meantime, we'll look here. Before you go, each of you search your room."

"Bertram —" Lady Langford took the reins — "if you will, please check with Mr. Dunnagan. See if he's seen her about the stables or gardens, or if she's been in the orchard this morning."

"*Oui,* madame."

"Look under the beds," Josef dictated. "That's where I go when I want to be alone."

"A very good idea," Gaston approved. "You should stay there."

Bertram rolled his eyes and punched his younger brother's arm.

Franz stood. "I'll check the north tower."

"She'd never have returned there." Claire was certain. But Franz shrugged, as if to say, *You never know.* Claire nodded, thankful others were thinking too. She'd have to give Aimee a talking-to when she found the little girl. She couldn't be running off and worrying everyone. There wasn't time or manpower for this.

Later Claire wished she'd kept the children home from school and enlisted their help. Afternoon teatime neared and Aimee had not been found. Every member of the household, upstairs and down, had been put on high alert and freed from their duties to search. The grounds had been covered and searched again. Claire had even gone to the secret garden and climbed Christopher's tree to get a better view of the landscape. No Aimee. *Where can she be?*

"There are only two more hours of daylight. The temperature is dropping and a storm is brewing," Aunt Miranda whispered to Claire and Mrs. Newsome when they'd gathered with the children for tea in the drawing room. "I need to telephone the constable."

"And the vicarage," Mrs. Newsome suggested. "The vicar can call together a search party in no time. They'll all come for him. And Dr. MacDonald. Perhaps he's seen her on his rounds."

"Yes, yes." Aunt Miranda nodded. "Raibeart might have some ideas."

"And David," offered Claire. "Aimee's fond of him. She might have confided in him."

"Where is David? He's usually home by now."

She thinks of this as David's home. He's won his way into her heart. Claire bit her lip. He'd crept into her heart too. "I don't know. Probably still at the factory. He's there so much now."

"Shall I telephone, my lady?" Mrs. Newsome asked, clearly wanting to move things along.

"No, I'll do it. You and Claire see that the children are fed and that they stay in the house. I don't want to lose any more."

"I need to search, Aunt Miranda. I can't stay home and do nothing."

"I'll mind the young ones," Mrs. Newsome offered. "I think Bertram and Peter might be of help to you."

Josef broke between them. "I want to search for Aimee. She is small and needs our help."

You are also small and need our help, Claire thought. Before she could say so, Aunt Miranda replied, "I need you and Gaston and Franz to man the front lawn and gardens for me until dark. You can post yourselves beneath the folly canopy in case the storm breaks. If Aimee comes back, you must ring the outdoor bell three times so that those searching will hear it and return. This is important work. Can we count on you boys?"

Josef narrowed his eyes, as if he guessed he was being sidelined, but pushed back his shoulders. "*Ja,* Frau Langford. You can count on me."

"And me," seconded Gaston, his cheeks bulging with soda bread.

Franz nodded vigorously.

Mrs. Newsome made certain the children were well fed and that those continuing the search were clad in mackintoshes and Wellingtons. It was the only practical thing she knew to do, and the supplying kept them all busy for a few minutes.

She'd racked her brain and grilled each of them for anything Aimee could have said or implied that might give a clue as to where the child had gone. All the little girl's associations were either in the house with the family or out among the growing things — gardens, orchards, woods, or sheep on the nearby fell. Even the depths of the little fishing pond had been prodded by Mr. Dunnagan, though Mrs. Newsome's heart leapt to her throat with every swish of his pole and net. No Aimee.

As a last resort she telephoned her niece Ruby at the Heelis farm. Auld Mother Heelis wouldn't like her serving girl getting a phone call in the evening, but perhaps Ruby could remember if Aimee had said anything — or even if Mrs. Heelis had any notion of where the child might have gone. Aimee nearly worshipped Mrs. Heelis and her paintings and stories, though the old lady barely gave her the time of day.

"What is it, Aunt Florence? You know I'm not to be taking telephone calls."

"I know, dear. You can apologize to Mrs. Heelis for me. But it's Aimee — she's disappeared. Run away, most likely. She's taken her best dress and dolly, and her pillowslip's missing. I can't think where she's gone but she's away since midmorning, and we've no way of knowing if someone picked her up or what might have happened to her since. Have you seen her, or do you remember anything at all she might have said about going away?" Mrs. Newsome was breathless, but she might as well get it all out in one go.

"No! Well, no, I've no idea at all, Aunt. Poor little mite, and on a night like this! The wind's up and howling and the rain's sweepin' down the fells in sheets! She's like to freeze or drown, no matter that it's May!"

As if I don't know! As if my heart's not breaking already! "If you hear or see anything at all, you'll telephone, no matter what Mrs. Heelis says about usin' the phone?"

"Of course I will, Aunt. I'll explain it all to her. She'll understand, though I've nothing to suggest. I'm that sorry."

"Not so sorry as I." Mrs. Newsome hung up. Ruby had been her last hope.

Raibeart hated that Maggie's hopes soared when she heard his voice on the other end of the line, then fell just as far when he revealed that he was only calling to see if Aimee had been found.

"No, nothing, no news at all. The vicar and the constable and half a dozen men were out looking for her, but there's been no word. With the rain and the blackout, they've called the search off until morning. They can't see a thing in the dark. Oh, Raibeart, I'm frantic!"

The telephone click-clicked, click-clicked, and the operator came on. "Terribly sorry to interrupt, but there's an emergency call coming through for Bluebell Wood. Will you hang up, sir?"

"Yes, of course."

"And will you accept the call, madam, for Bluebell Wood?"

"Yes! I'll call you back right away, Raibeart."

"I've stopped at Harris's to telephone. The operator will give you the number."

The doctor waited by the phone, never touching the steaming cup of tea Mrs. Harris pushed upon him.

"Have a bite while you're here, Doc. It won't hurt to keep up your nourishment, 'specially on a night like this." Randolph Harris urged the doctor to accept the plate of bread and jam his missus had brought near the phone.

But Dr. MacDonald shook his head. "That's kind of you, but I've no stomach for anythin' but findin' the wee one." Truth be told, the doctor had had time to think. He had no doubt why the child had run away. She believed she wasn't wanted. He'd seen it in her sad little face each time he'd visited. Those enormous blue orbs swelled in gratitude whenever he tweaked her cheek or took a bit of time to talk with her. She wasn't like the older children, off to school and making friends. She needed mothering, and she needed it badly.

He wished he'd never set eyes on Claire Stewart. She'd been nothing but trouble for her aunt since she'd stepped foot in Bluebell Wood. His railing had done nothing to help Claire become the motherly figure she was not, perhaps could not be. The girl simply didn't see life staring her in the face. She was a dreamer and a chaser of dreams, just as her aunt had been at that age. Maggie hadn't seen him, no matter that he'd have given her the world if she'd looked his way. Perhaps that reminder, that memory, was what angered him most about Claire, and it wasn't even the girl's fault.

Raibeart pushed the damp hair from his forehead and ran his hands through his thick mop in frustration.

Rrrrrinnng! Rrrrrinnng!

The doctor didn't wait for Harris, but grabbed the receiver. "Maggie?"

"It was Ruby, from Mrs. Heelis's. Mrs. Heelis remembered telling Aimee about a fairy caravan, something about the high buildings being a good place to shelter in a wild rainstorm. She said that Aimee was certain that was the place animals could talk."

"Talking animals?"

"Ruby said Aimee is convinced animals talk, that you told her so."

"I?" Dr. MacDonald had no idea what she meant but knew enough to know that didn't matter. "Where on God's green earth is the shelter for the fairy caravan?"

"There isn't one, of course, but Mrs. Heelis thinks that Aimee might believe it's near her — in those blue-green hills above her farm, near Troutbeck. There are shepherds' shelters there. I can't imagine Aimee could make it that far, but she does know the way to the Heelis farm."

"I'm on my way. I'll phone you the min —"

"No — David's returned. He and Claire have gone to search. But if she's hurt or sick, we might need you here."

"Neither of them knows the fells. They're dangerous enough in good weather and daylight."

"But, Raibeart —"

"I know those paths like the back of my hand; I'm on my way. If she's there, we'll get her home to you. Rest assured, Maggie."

He hung up the phone before she responded, before she fussed that he was too old to be traipsing slippery, rocky fells in a thunderstorm. He pulled his collar up the back of his neck, shoved his hat over his forehead, and headed into the night.

Claire had never pushed through the heart of such a storm. Even the night they'd struggled across the Channel from Calais was nothing compared to this relentless beating of wind and rain. The temperature had sharply dropped, and she was certain ice prickled her cheeks.

Poor Aimee! Oh, please, God, if You're there, help her, shelter her! Let us find her!

David pulled Claire along, having given up his insistence that she stay in the car. They both carried torches, their lights shielded by cheesecloth. Dim light was better than no light.

"Aimee! Aimeeeee!" David called into the wind.

"Aimeeee! Aimee, dear!" Claire echoed, begging. "Answer us, Aimee! We want you to come home! Aimee, please!"

David gripped her hand all the tighter and pulled Claire up the hillside, both of them slipping and stumbling over wet moss and slick rocks.

Brakes squealed and a motor gunned in

the valley below. Another torchlight emerged. "Aimee!" a voice called.

"Dr. MacDonald! We're searching this side. Can you take the distant path? Mrs. Heelis said there are two!" David shouted through the rain.

There was no answer, but the soft light bobbed quickly in the opposite direction, making its way across the bottom of the fell and gradually up the other access to the shepherds' path.

Claire could barely see, was frozen to the bone, her teeth chattering so she could hardly speak, let alone call out anymore. *How could Aimee have come so far, and all alone? We don't even know if she did, if she's here. She could be anywhere. She could have gone to the lake. She could have drowned in the stream or stumbled off the cliff in the dark. She could have —*

"Aidez moi!" the plaintive cry came from above.

"Aimee!" David called. "We hear you! Where are you? Call again!"

There was no sound but the wind and rising storm.

"Aimee!" Claire called. "It's Claire — and David! We want you to come home. Please tell us where you are!"

Still no answer came.

Lightning crackled across the sky, splitting an oak on the fell and shooting sparks, streams of fire, upward into the dark.

A terrified scream rent the storm, and in the moment before the light from the burning tree died, Claire glimpsed a sodden waif cowering on the cliff above them.

"David! There! There she is!" But it was too late; the light had died.

"Where?"

Claire pointed her light, ripping the cloth from the torch. No blackout could keep her from getting to the child. She pushed past David and groped her way up the hillside, slipping, falling, clawing upward.

By the time she reached the ledge, Aimee's screams had stopped, replaced by heaving sobs.

"We're coming, Aimee. I'm almost there."

"Help me!" the child cried.

Claire slipped again just as she reached Aimee, and they both fell to the ground, a tangle of arms and legs. David scooped Aimee up, and steadied Claire as she stood, reaching out to his precious load.

Claire's tears came as fast as the soaking rain. It was her natural inclination to scold the child, and from terror and genuine relief combined she nearly did.

"She's freezing, Claire. We've got to get

her home and out of these wet things. Signal to Dr. MacDonald. We'll need him." David swept past her, leaving her to make her way down the path in the dark.

Claire felt as if someone had slapped her awake. What was she thinking? Aimee was found, but far from danger. She waved her torch toward the faint light making its way up the hillside, and called, "We found her!"

The light opposite stopped. Claire called again, "We found her! Meet us at Bluebell Wood!"

The light bobbed in recognition and turned. Claire stumbled after David and Aimee as quickly as she could.

Chapter Nineteen

Miranda had the boys build a roaring fire in the library fireplace, hoping as much to chase the raw chill of fear as the damp edge of night. All the children had gathered and remained long past their bedtime. Between the horrific news from France and the terrifying loss and final recovery of Aimee, no one wanted to be alone. Miranda couldn't blame them. Aimee was off the mountain but not out of the woods.

Dr. MacDonald had been with the child this past hour, insisting that Miranda sit by the fire and calm herself, stay warm. His solicitude nearly drove her mad. She would much have preferred to be by Aimee's side, holding the little girl's hand, stroking her brow — anything, rather than be left outside the sickroom door.

Claire and David had changed their clothes, and David had sent a dry set to Dr. MacDonald, insisting that it would do none of them any good if he came down with pneumonia.

Ever the pragmatist. What would we do without him? What will Claire do without him? That last was a new thought to Miranda, but she didn't dismiss it. The two seemed as natural together as peas in a pod, and yet at times as unlikely to mix as oil and water. *So much like Raibeart and me . . . too much like us. I hope Claire doesn't make the same mistakes I have, waiting for someone who will never return.*

Why she was thinking of this now, Miranda didn't even know. She needed, intended, to focus on Aimee, and vowed to do so fully, if the little girl survived her ordeal.

Mrs. Newsome handed Miranda a warm brandy, barely two swallows in the bottom of a teacup. "Drink this down. You know the doctor would order it."

Miranda smiled. What would she do without Mrs. Newsome?

But Mrs. Newsome voiced her worry too. "It fair took my breath away when David carried that child over the threshold. White as a sheet, she was, and barely breathing."

Miranda handed the brandy back to Mrs. Newsome. "I think you need this more than I do."

Mrs. Newsome didn't demur. She swallowed the thimbleful in one go, shuddered, and breathed deeply. "Thank you."

Miranda reached for the older woman's hand. Mrs. Newsome nodded in understanding, then glanced significantly across the room toward David and Claire, whispering near the piano.

"I see," Miranda replied, "more than you know." She squeezed Mrs. Newsome's hand and stood, thinking it time to send the older children to bed. Gaston and Elise, Franz, Josef, and even Ingrid were fast falling asleep as they stretched over carpets and chair arms. "There's nothing more we can do tonight, children. Aimee is home and Dr. MacDonald is caring for her. Mrs. Newsome will see you up. Please, Mrs. Newsome, tuck each one in tonight, even the boys."

Bertram grunted his disapproval, but Franz half smiled.

Mrs. Newsome clapped her hands. "It won't hurt a one of you, and it will do my old heart good. I might even be compelled to kiss you."

At that, the boys all groaned aloud, except Gaston, who sleepily and gallantly offered Mrs. Newsome his arm to escort her upstairs. "Madame," he said in his most courtly French.

Mrs. Newsome patted and looped his arm, winking her appreciation.

They'd just stepped through the door when Claire thanked her aunt. "I should have seen them to bed, Aunt Miranda. I'm sorry. I'm just not thinking."

"Nor should you be. Our concern tonight is for Aimee. You've done wonderfully, Claire. If it hadn't been for you and David —"

The library door opened again and Nancy scooted through. "She's awake and calling for you."

Claire flushed and set down her teacup and saucer. "Thank you, Nancy!" She was halfway to the door before Nancy could get the next words out.

"Not you, Miss Claire. She doesn't want you." Nancy crimsoned. "Doctor was most specific that Lady Langford is the only one to be allowed in the room now."

The blood drained from Claire's face.

"I'm sorry, miss." Nancy sounded as sorry as David looked shocked.

"Surely she wants to see Claire. Claire found her. She —"

"No, sir. The doctor said to tell you there will be time for that tomorrow or when she recovers, that Aimee's had a terrible shock and is suffering from hypo— hypoth—"

"Hypothermia," David offered.

"Yes, sir. That's it, sir. He said we should do just as he says for the child."

Miranda squeezed Claire's arm as she followed Nancy from the room. "I'm sure she'll be asking for you soon. I know she will."

Claire swallowed and stepped back, allowing her aunt to pass. She couldn't look at David. This was too much, too agonizing and too humiliating. Yet Claire knew she'd brought it on herself. Each time Aimee had reached out to her, she'd turned away, held the little girl at arm's length. She'd told herself, told Aunt Miranda and Mrs. Newsome, even Dr. MacDonald, that she wasn't Aimee's mother, that she didn't know anything about children.

But that wasn't true. She knew just what it was to be a child forgotten and pushed aside. Claire hadn't been an orphan, hadn't been ripped from her mother's arms, but her mother had pushed her as far away as she could, so often lost in the stupor of her drink.

Life in New Jersey had been filled with nannies when she was very young, then before- and after-school care, classes of every imaginable sort to keep her busy through the evenings, camps so she would be out of town during the summer holidays. Twice Claire remembered spending Christmas with neighbors and once with the Beach family as her mother had trotted the globe or visited friends for skiing trips, anything to keep her from home and Claire.

And Claire had done much the same to Aimee. She'd not sent her away physically, but she'd emotionally distanced herself. *Why? Because Aimee wanted me and I wanted to hurt her as my mother hurt me?* Claire knew that was not true. As quick as she was to berate herself, she was not sadistic. *Because that's all I know, all I've experienced. I don't know how to love her.*

Claire dug the heels of her hands into her eyes. *Pain! That's all I know and all I give! How does a person love?*

And then something she'd read in David's book, something C. S. Lewis had written, played through her mind. . . . Something about God using pain for a purpose.

"Are you all right?" David was by her side.

She hadn't even noticed him cross the room. "Yes." She tried to smile, though she couldn't keep the tears pooled at the corners of her eyes from leaking down her face.

He pulled a handkerchief from his pocket

and handed it to her. She fumbled, trying to unfold it. He took it back, unfolded it, and tenderly wiped her cheeks, dabbed at her eyes, and tweaked her nose. His kindness, his sympathy, unleashed a faucet, and Claire found herself sobbing in his arms.

Dr. MacDonald didn't know if he should step backward out the library door and knock, or if he should discreetly cough. Neither David nor Claire seemed the least aware of his presence, and he wasn't entirely sure what the embrace he witnessed meant. Two friends in need? Lovers? He couldn't simply leave, not without saying what he'd come to say. He coughed, twice, and closed the door, louder than his wont.

Claire and David split apart as if someone had shot them. Both looked a mite guilty and surprised by that realization at the same time. It was all Dr. MacDonald could do not to smile.

David spoke first, while Claire wiped the last tear from her cheek. "How is she, Doctor?"

"She'll mend. It will take a wee bit . . . she'll be a week or so on the puny side, I wager. She survived some fearful moments out there in the dark. The cold and rain did her no good. Ach, but she's a spry little thing and I've no doubt she'll pull through."

"Thank God," Claire whispered.

"Aye, thank God, and you, Claire Stewart . . . and you, David Campbell. I'd not have found her in time. That lightning hitting the tree scared her half to death. It's a wonder she didn't tumble down the crag then and there. You reached her before she tried to run again. You likely saved her life."

"I think that credit goes to you, Doctor. Thank you for searching for her, for being there . . . for being here." Claire spoke but looked as if she wanted to hide beneath the carpet. "Did she say anything . . . about why she ran away?"

"She's fair out of her head, poor mite. Going on about talking animals and fairy caravans and taking a boat home to Paris. She'll come round, but she's got some sorting out to do. You can help her with that. Help her see that there's a difference between reality and imagination. She's young, but she needs to draw those lines. 'Tis all too easy for the mind to slip under the pressures of war. I've seen it in adults. It can happen to children just as well."

"Yes, yes, I'll do anything I can . . . anything she'll let me." Claire meant it, the doctor was certain. What she'd be able to do, he didn't know.

"There's something I needs must say to ye, lass." The doctor's brogue came thicker than usual.

"I think I know everything you'll say, Doctor, and you're right. I haven't done right by Aimee."

"I think you've said everything to Claire on that subject that needs to be said, don't you, Doctor?" David stood ready to defend her.

"A gallant knight you've got there," Dr. MacDonald chided gently. "But I'm not here to dress you down, Claire Stewart. I'm here to apologize. I'd no right to say the things I did. You can't help that you're not something you weren't born to be."

Claire paled. He could see her swallow, but she didn't speak.

"That's all I've come to say, and now I've said it, I'll check on the bairn one last time before I leave. I'll stop by tomorrow." He turned to go, then stopped. "Oh, I've told Nancy that someone's to stay the night with the child, keeping watch. I don't expect a problem, but it would be best if someone was there. Call me if anything's amiss. Trouble is, Nancy's that dead on her feet, so I'm wonderin' if you might spell her sometime in the night."

Claire's wary eyes met his. "Nancy said

Aimee doesn't want me."

"When she first opened her eyes, she wanted only Mrs. Newsome. I convinced her to let Miranda come in, for I knew Miranda needed that. The child's terrified — of being alone in the storm, of being punished, of never seeing her mother and father, of everything imaginable. I've given her a sedative. She'll not know who's there through the night. Watch over the bairn." That was all he had to say. He nodded to them both and was gone.

Claire sent Nancy to bed directly and sat by Aimee's side until dawn, refusing every offer to spell her, including David's. Nothing could pry her from the child's side.

Claire had never believed in prayer or that there was anyone there to listen, let alone answer. But a miracle had happened on the fells that night and Someone was responsible; Claire couldn't let it pass. When she felt certain everyone had gone, Claire knelt beside Aimee's bed, the child's tiny hand clasped in both of hers.

I still don't know if You're there, God. I was always so certain You weren't real, that You were a crutch, a fantasy like Aimee's talking animals and fairies. But I asked for Your help tonight and something happened. We found

Aimee on that crag, just in time. What Dr. MacDonald said was true: she could have fallen and injured herself terribly, could have been killed. I couldn't live with that. I couldn't live knowing I'd . . .

I'm so sorry for the way I've treated Aimee, for the way I've pushed them all away. I don't understand why I'm like I am.

Dr. MacDonald sees I'm no good at mothering and he's right. I'm just so afraid, so . . . Oh, help me, God. If You're there, help me. Help Aimee to forgive me and let me have another chance. I promise to do better. I don't know how, exactly . . . but I'll learn to love her, if You'll teach me.

Claire stopped praying. It was as if Someone jogged her memory. At last she brushed the hair from Aimee's forehead and slipped from the room, retrieving *The Problem of Pain* from beneath her mattress. Lewis had written about how God uses pain in people's lives. Claire felt as if she'd earned a PhD in the school of pain. If only that pain could be used to help Aimee in some way, perhaps it had merit. She needed to find the passage. She knelt once more by Aimee's bedside and flipped through the pages by torchlight, reading softly aloud, " 'Pain insists upon being attended to. God whispers to us in our pleasures, speaks in our conscience, but shouts in our pains: it is His megaphone to rouse a deaf world.'

"You have my attention! You've roused me. . . . Now what?

"I don't want to hurt Aimee — I don't want to hurt anyone by what I do or by my neglect! But caring — loving — must mean more than caring for bodily needs . . . more than I know to do. Please, God, show me how."

A footstep near the door caused Claire to look up. *David.* She brushed the tears from her eyes, frustrated that he'd caught her like this and upset that he'd likely heard her pleas.

"You're hard on yourself. This is not your fault."

"Yes, it is. I know you mean well, but it is my fault. Aimee would never have run away if I'd given her the attention or love she craved." Even now Claire wasn't certain what that meant. There was no point in pretending she had a plan. She sat back on the floor. "I've no idea how to give her what she needs from me."

David said nothing. Claire didn't know if he was shocked or disappointed, but she didn't care. Even his opinion didn't matter compared to Aimee's need. "I never had siblings. My mother didn't have time for me. I know what I missed, but not how to give it."

"Then give what you are, what you know."

There was that urging — a question — again, the one Claire had no answer for. She all but grunted. "I'm nothing. I know nothing. Do you have siblings? Do you know what to do?"

But David only asked, "What do you love?"

"I — I love Arnaud; you know that." It was the only thing Claire could think to say, the only thing that came to mind. Even as she said it, she knew that might be a fantasy too.

"I didn't say *whom;* I said *what.* What do you love, Claire?"

She pushed the disheveled hair from her eyes. "I was reasonably good at sports. I did well in most subjects . . . Art was my weakest class."

"You're not hearing me. Tell me what it is that gives you joy."

No one had ever asked her that. "Books." She sighed. "I've always loved stories. I've lived through stories, imagined myself in stories, succeeded in stories. That's part of the problem, I guess. I see life as if it's a story."

"And you're the heroine?" He grinned.

"Sometimes." But she couldn't smile in return. It was a painful confession. "Tonight I feel the villain. I suppose you think that's all silly."

"Not silly at all. Give them that."

Claire closed her eyes and counted to five. She stood and straightened her skirt, then took a seat in the rocker beside Aimee's bed. "You heard Dr. MacDonald. Aimee doesn't need more fantasies; she needs to understand real life, to learn to cope with life as it is."

"But stories have helped you do that. That's what stories are for." David threw out his arms. "If characters can succeed in a story, if they can overcome their dilemma, then it stands to reason that the reader can too. Stories give us a way to make sense of the world. Understanding that, demonstrating that, would be an incredible gift to these children."

Claire stared at him, skeptical.

"Life has dealt them a terrible blow. They need ways and means to cope modeled for them. You and your aunt can't model everything. Let stories help."

"What stories?" Claire challenged, though a tiny recognition of the truth he spoke, a minuscule hope, struggled to life within her, alongside a vague memory of rallying the children through the example of *Peter Pan.*

"Give them the stories you love; they will love them too." He grinned. "If I don't miss my guess, you're probably quite a hand at voices."

"I can do all the voices." Now she couldn't help but smile. It was something few people knew about her.

David nodded. "They'll see that time, that investment, is made just for them. You wouldn't do it if you didn't love them. That love is what they'll take away." He hesitated. "As long as you're all in, as long as you don't hold back."

CHAPTER TWENTY

"It was David's idea, really," Claire said as she and Aunt Miranda entered the library, "but it makes sense to me. He said it will help them pass the evenings — that even if the news is bad, at least this will be something they can count on."

"That's true. Still . . ." Her aunt hesitated.

Claire well understood her aunt's reservations — that sharing something so personal, so precious as the stories of their hearts, knowing the children would not stay, was anything but easy.

"I don't know how that man got to be so wise." Aunt Miranda sighed. "He's young. He's not married. I don't even think he has siblings."

Claire wondered the same thing.

Morning sun poured through the far end of the library, illuminating the fairy-tale figures Jeanine and Ingrid had drawn and pasted — outlined in crosshatched tape to prevent flying glass in case of a bombing. The most creative windows in the village, Claire was certain.

"This hand-woven carpet, this rounded room of the turret, with all its windows, was Christopher's favorite spot to play as a child. We pretended it was a magic carpet that would 'take us lands away,' just as Emily Dickinson said about the ship." Aunt Miranda began the recitation. By the second line, Claire joined in:

"There is no frigate like a book
To take us lands away,
Nor any coursers like a page
Of prancing poetry.
This traverse may the poorest take
Without oppress of toll;
How frugal is the chariot
That bears the human soul."

Claire and her aunt smiled in unison, a rare comradely smile.

"As long as we kept the room warm enough, we spent hours here, reading, talking. And then I'd sing to him. He'd fall asleep in my arms . . . in this rocker." Miranda faltered. "I know it doesn't go with the other furniture at all. I'd always meant to replace it, but now . . . now I never will."

Claire reached her hand nearly to her aunt's arm in sympathy but pulled back, self-conscious. *Love is what they'll take away, as long as you don't hold back.* Surely David's words applied to her aunt, too. She reached again.

Aunt Miranda started, clearly surprised by Claire's touch. She smiled tentatively and placed her hand over her niece's. Claire's heart fluttered. *How did David know?* Again she had no clue.

Aunt Miranda pulled a handkerchief from her pocket and wiped her eyes. "Well —" she forcibly brightened, leading Claire to the lower children's shelves — "what would you like to start with? It will be a challenge to find something appropriate for all ages."

"The Secret Garden." Claire had thought of nothing else all morning.

Aunt Miranda stiffened.

"The book, by Frances Hodgson Burnett," Claire added quietly. "I thought that might be a good one, especially for this time of year . . . seeing everything come alive in the gardens and on our walks through the woods and over the fell." Claire worded her statement carefully. She would not violate another of her aunt's memories. "I think, perhaps, Aimee feels a bit like an orphan, like Mary Lennox when she came to Misselthwaite Manor, before she found the garden."

"Yes." Aunt Miranda's voice came strained. "I'm sure you're right."

"I read it when I was Ingrid's age and have never forgotten. I've always longed for a garden of my own."

" 'Might I have a bit of earth?' " Aunt Miranda quoted, her expression far away.

"Yes. Exactly."

Aunt Miranda turned. Claire could see the battle behind her aunt's eyes, the struggle to maintain her secrets and the desire to breach those walls. "Perhaps," her aunt ventured, "we're more kindred spirits than we know."

Claire's heart swelled. She knew she shouldn't allow it, would live to regret the breach in her own walls, but a tiny flame of hope flickered and she didn't put it out.

Miranda slipped into a chair by the library fire, its grate empty now that warm evenings were upon them. It was the perfect perch to observe Claire and the cluster of unruly children surrounding her in the circular turret.

" 'When Mary Lennox was sent to Misselthwaite Manor to live with her uncle everybody said she was the most disagreeable-looking child ever seen. . . .' "

Hearing Claire read to the children, seeing their roving eyes transform to rapt faces or the intent posture of their backs as they leaned into the story, turned back years for Miranda. So easily could she imagine Christopher sprawled there among them, chiming in favorite, familiar lines as she'd read them aloud.

Aimee nestled into Claire's side, beneath her elbow. Now that her dark night had passed, and once the little girl learned of Claire's search and vigil for her, she seemed to have opened her heart to Claire and attached herself in a new way. Miranda knew Claire still stood wary, fearful of being hurt, but to her credit she made deliberate efforts to reach out to Aimee, to include her and even single her out sometimes.

Miranda breathed deeply, grateful to witness such change in her niece and in the children, even in herself. Watching Claire grow into her role with the children, albeit haltingly and not without its setbacks, felt like passing the torch to her niece.

I'm nearly fifty, but feel eighty or more. Is it the grief . . . the desperate missing of Christopher? It was almost too painful a question, and yet, surprising to herself, Miranda didn't think it was her grief. She found herself smiling and even laughing at the antics and quips between the children, loving them as she'd not planned. She wished to enter into their games and songs. Even now, a part of her longed to sit on the floor, cross-legged, in their midst, absorbing *The Secret Garden* with them. She wished to dream, to plan what they'd plant and grow together . . . but her emotional and physical energy seemed entirely drained. She felt old and tired. A good night's sleep made no difference. She always needed more.

Miranda fingered the brooch on her dress. Something was wrong — she knew it. But she didn't know what and couldn't explain it. Perhaps if she didn't mention her unsettled feeling, if she ignored it, in time it would pass.

May turned into June. Aimee loved the early-summer evenings best. She waited all day for the moment Mademoiselle Claire would open the book and begin to read about Mary Lennox and her formerly grumpy cousin, Colin Craven. She loved how Colin was being transformed by the garden, how he stretched his limbs and did all manner of things he'd believed impossible.

Best of all, she loved Dickon — good, kind

Dickon, who could speak with the animals. How she wished one of the boys in the house were Dickon. She could imagine Mr. Dunnagan as Ben Weatherstaff, but she could never imagine Nancy as kindhearted Martha. Even Mademoiselle Claire could not live up to that.

Mademoiselle Claire was unpredictable, and that worried Aimee. Sometimes she pulled Aimee close beside her as she read. There were moments when it seemed she spoke and lived the story only for Aimee. Other times mademoiselle seemed very far away, her brow wrinkled over things that could have nothing to do with the story. Aimee no longer felt that Mademoiselle Claire didn't want her, but she didn't understand her teacher.

Some of the words in the story were difficult. They weren't as clear as Mrs. Heelis's stories, which had pictures to help. And although Dickon seemed well able to communicate with the animals, they didn't speak in a language Aimee could comprehend, not as they did in Mrs. Heelis's stories. Aimee confided this to Claire one afternoon as she sat, coloring, in the library.

"Do you miss your visits with Mrs. Heelis?" Claire put down her pen and tilted her head.

"Oui, certainement," Aimee sighed, looking up, "but Madame Langford said it is better if I don't go there." A flush rose over Aimee's cheeks. "It is because I went searching for the fairy caravan, you know. She said such things aren't real, that fairies are pretend, that animals do not speak, and I should not go to such dangerous places alone."

"You can understand that, surely. She has your best interests at heart."

"Oui, je comprends, mais . . . ," Aimee whispered, "I think she is wrong. I think she has forgotten, as the grown-ups did in *Peter Pan.*" She shrugged. "I miss Madame Heelis. I miss her house and her stories. I miss Mademoiselle Ruby. She gave me jam and bread anytime I visited, you know."

Claire smiled. "Yes, so I heard."

Aimee nodded, sighed dramatically, and went back to her coloring.

Claire received no quarter from Mrs. Newsome in the matter of tucking into the picnic basket early. The older woman gently placed a tea towel filled with warm and fragrant currant buns and a little jar of Lyle's Golden Syrup in Claire's knapsack, a gift to give their unsuspecting hostess.

"Can't we eat some on the way?" Claire

taunted, childlike.

"There's a Peter Rabbit bun for each of you in this napkin. You may stop for a picnic with Aimee along the way, but don't dawdle. I've telephoned Ruby, and she's expecting you both for early tea. Mrs. Heelis should be home from checking on her lambs by then. She's all about breedin' those darlin' Herdwick sheep of hers these days, but you'll find her fascinating. Try to get her talking about her young days."

"Peter Rabbit buns?" Claire smiled. "That's cute. I'm not sure they won't be lost on our neighbor. You said she's ancient and grumpy, that all the children call her Auld Mother Heelis behind her back."

"She still writes stories now and again — she's written a dozen or more — and her paintings are marvelous. You'll love them, even if your personalities are not precisely what they call 'kindred spirits.' "

Claire didn't expect "kindred spirits." She just hoped to get through the afternoon.

They walked the back road, hand in hand, nibbling their currant buns, and passed silver birches waving lithe and graceful limbs. As they climbed over the fell to the Heelis farm, Claire knew she'd no cause to grumble. It was a lovely day, one of the few in the Lake District with brilliant blue skies and no afternoon shower. Aimee licked the glaze from her fingers, then pulled her picture from her pinafore pocket. She smiled and skipped, parading her drawing of newborn lambs for Mrs. Heelis up and down the path, so excited that Claire laughed despite herself.

"Wait until you see the pictures, mademoiselle, and her farm animals! They are lovely — the most cunning little rabbits and, oh my, the sly fox! And, oh, what a stupid, stupid duck lives there!"

Claire smiled at the child's chatter, not always certain whether Aimee meant the animals on the Heelis farm or in the owner's drawings. She wondered if Aimee knew where to draw the line, either. But something about her reference to the "stupid, stupid duck" struck an ages-old memory for Claire. Just as they approached the farmhouse, Claire asked, "Aimee, do you know what Mrs. Heelis's first name is? What her Christian name is?"

"*Oui!* But of course! Don't you know?" Aimee laughed.

"I've never met her." Claire knocked on the door.

"But you've read her books! Mrs. Newsome reads them to me all the time. She says they were the very favorite of Master

Christopher when he was a boy no older than me." Aimee leaned conspiratorially toward Claire and gently chided, as if Claire should know better, "Mademoiselle, children all over the world know Beatrix Potter!"

Ruby flung wide the door.

"Welcome, Miss Claire, little Miss Aimee! We've been expectin' you!"

But Claire had not expected to be ushered into the home of Beatrix Potter, renowned children's author and illustrator. Such a privilege had never occurred to her.

While Aimee was interviewed and her drawing critically received by the famous lady, Ruby took Claire on a tour of the home. Each room held mementos and figurines, practical pieces of everyday childhood and housekeeping that had inspired well-loved and classic stories. There were the dolls, Lucinda and Jane, and even the wonderful dollhouse that Mr. Warne had built for his niece, the very one that had inspired Beatrix's *Tale of Two Bad Mice.* The gardens ran amok with kittens and ducks just like those that had crept into the stories of Tom Kitten and Jemima Puddle-Duck.

Stories and bits of stories lingered in every corner — on the mantelpiece, in the parlor, in the kitchen. After tea, Mrs. Heelis invited

Claire to join her upstairs in her inner sanctum, to see where she wrote and drew and to tell about her own writing — for she'd heard from Aimee that Claire was a great novelist. Claire felt as if she'd swallowed shoe leather. What could she say? That she wrote shallow stories with forced dialogue set in worlds of which she knew nothing? That she copied ideas and plots from literary lights?

Before they sat, Mrs. Heelis was called to the door to speak with her head shepherd — something about a Herdwick that had fallen into a ravine.

In that lady's absence, Claire boldly ran her hand over Beatrix Potter Heelis's writing desk and marveled at the stories that had been composed there, the countless letters written, the imaginings that must have come while sitting in the very chair behind it.

To think that Beatrix Potter Heelis had not traveled to exotic lands or rubbed elbows with literary giants like those frequenting Shakespeare and Company, but had taken her inspiration from such humble, everyday surroundings . . . It gave Claire a great deal to ponder.

All this time Aimee had been entertained by the world's most beloved children's writer and illustrator, and Claire had not given her the time of day.

"Do you like my desk, young woman?"

Claire started. "I'm so sorry, Mrs. Heelis. I was just — just . . ." What could she say? But the truth was simple. "I wanted to touch the desk of a real writer. I've loved your stories since I was a little girl."

Mrs. Heelis sank into her desk chair. "You're not a real writer?"

Claire stepped back, groaning inside. "No, ma'am. Aimee was misinformed."

Mrs. Heelis raised her eyebrows and waited.

"I want to write. . . . I scribble." Claire nudged the braided rug with her toe. If only she could slide beneath its bound edge. "I mean, I write, I do . . . I journal for the Mass Observation Project, and I've tried writing fiction. But it simply isn't going anywhere." She shrugged. "It doesn't sound real — not like yours."

"My stories are full of talking squirrels and ducks and rabbits that wear clothes, take tea."

"I mean what you write sounds true to your stories — true to your characters. My characters are real people, but they — they aren't like any people I know. They aren't like the characters or stories of writers I admire."

"As I was growing up, my brother and I weren't allowed many acquaintances, let alone friends. My pets and those animals I observed in nature became my friends. My animal characters are my friends. They are just who and what they would be if the animals in your garden could really, truly talk."

Claire tried, but she wasn't sure she understood.

"Young woman — for to me you are a very young woman — listen carefully and remember what you will: Write stories of those you know, the life you live, in your own voice."

"I can't imagine anyone would be interested in that."

"Of course they will not, if you are not." And Beatrix Potter Heelis turned toward her desk and took up her pen, as clearly dismissing Claire as if she'd walked out of the room.

It was just as well. Claire had no idea how to respond. She believed she'd been told something profound, perhaps obvious — at least to Mrs. Heelis. But Claire needed time to think about her words. "Thank you for seeing me, Mrs. Heelis, for taking the time . . ."

But Mrs. Heelis was deep in thought, her pen moving quickly across her page.

Claire slipped from the room and down the stairs. Ruby stood with one hand on the banister, beside Aimee, already dressed for her journey, holding their empty basket over her arm.

"I'm so sorry, Ruby. We've stayed longer than we should. Thank you for having us. Please thank Mrs. Heelis when . . ." Claire didn't know how to finish.

"When she comes up for air — I know." Ruby smiled.

Dusk was creeping in by the time Ruby ushered Aimee and Claire out the door and down the lane. Aimee chattered on and on about the praise Mrs. Heelis had given her drawings, about her insistence that she never allow grown-ups to tell her how to draw, that she must always draw with the joy and whimsy of her nature, though Aimee wasn't altogether certain what that meant. Mrs. Heelis, she said, had advised that she study the fur of animals, the wings of the smallest birds, the way a fern bends toward the light, for herself, then draw just what she saw.

All the while, all the way home, Claire silently berated herself. If she'd only known, if she'd only listened to Aimee and Mrs.

Newsome, if she'd not assumed that no important thing could happen in the Lake District now that Wordsworth and Coleridge and Ruskin were dead and buried.

If she'd opened her eyes to real life around her, she might not have missed forming a vital relationship with a real-life author. Despite that good lady taking the time and pains to receive her, to give her writerly advice, Claire had gotten the distinct impression that Mrs. Heelis didn't much like her.

Why should she? She surely knows I've resisted bringing Aimee to visit and that Aimee is in need of love and attention. And beyond that, I clearly know nothing of writing, not real writing. Claire sighed. She was trying to do better on all fronts, but in the midst of trying she'd worn blinders, focused on her to-do list.

Claire squeezed Aimee's hand, taking note of the little girl's bright eyes, her dimpling smile, the way she leaned into Claire's side as they walked. *Is this what Mrs. Heelis meant — this writing about the life I know, the life I live? It's personal, intimate, and yet who will want to read about that?* Claire forced herself to return to the moment.

"Aimee, your pictures are so much better than I ever realized. I'm not really an artist, you know —"

"But you are, mademoiselle! I saw your nature journal. *Il est superbe!*"

Claire smiled. She could kiss the child. "What I mean to say is that I could bring you some flowers and ferns from the high fell to draw as Mrs. Heelis suggested, the next time I go out climbing with the older class."

"When I must nap," Aimee pouted.

"Well, yes, but that's necessary, isn't it?"

"*Non,* I am too big to nap. I could keep up with the others. You would see if you allow me to try."

"Well, perhaps you and I should try on our own first, to make sure you can keep up. How would that be?"

"*Oui,* mademoiselle! That would be splendid!"

Claire's heart lifted, and she vowed to make certain she found the time — made the time — for this expedition. *Is loving and being loved like this? A leap of faith followed by a reaching out and taking in?*

They'd crossed over the fell and trooped through the pasture, nearly reaching the road when goose bumps prickled Claire's skin. A sudden thrashing in the brush across the road and a flash of dark movement brought her up short. The jerk nearly pulled

Aimee off her feet.

"What is it, mademoiselle? What is the matter?"

"I don't know. Nothing, maybe nothing, but . . ." Claire peered through the dusk. "Is anyone there?" No sound. "I said, is anyone there? Show yourself!" She spoke in her most authoritarian voice, though she knew it quavered.

"Who is there, mademoiselle?" Aimee whispered, her voice trembling.

Claire knew she must not frighten the little girl.

"Maybe no one. Come, I think we should hurry along."

Twice more before they reached the grounds of Bluebell Wood, Claire felt as if someone was near, someone was watching. *Surely this is the product of my overactive imagination! An afternoon of talking ducks and mischievous squirrels and dolls in houses that come to life could do that to anyone! Couldn't it?*

Chapter Twenty-One

Twice in July, the Home Guard alerted Bluebell Wood of German prisoner escapes from nearby Grizedale Hall. Josef begged Fräulein Claire not to go out walking alone, to allow him to accompany and protect her. His offer, made public at the luncheon table, only infuriated Gaston, who proclaimed himself Mademoiselle Claire's official protector.

"What do you two suggest?" Jeanine teased. "A duel?"

Josef ignored her. "We need to make certain that women and children are safe within these walls, that any escaped prisoners will find themselves in deep regret if they cross these boundaries."

"Well, I do lock the doors and windows come evening," observed Mrs. Newsome, clearly trying not to smile.

"That is very good," Gaston agreed. "But we need to do something about the grounds.

I concur this time with Josef."

Lady Langford raised her eyebrows, but Josef ignored that, too. "We must not only concern ourselves with escaped prisoners; we must remain vigi— vigilant in case of invasion."

"The Home Guard is patrolling," Bertram said. "They're trained for such things; you are not."

"*Ja,* trained, this is true, but they cannot be everywhere. I am talking about protecting our land and our women."

Lady Langford raised her eyebrows once again.

"Do you, Madame Langford, give us leave to protect the women and children of Bluebell Wood? We could prepare this afternoon."

"It might take longer than one afternoon," offered Gaston. "I have a plan."

"And I have another." Josef was not to be outdone.

"Claire? What do you think? Could you spare these young soldiers for an afternoon or so?"

"Yes! I mean, I think that could be arranged." Claire sighed in apparent relief. "I'm fresh out of ideas to keep everyone bus— productively employed since the school holidays began."

"I don't suppose David will be home in time to supervise?"

"Herr David is consumed with his most vital war work at the factory," Josef spoke knowingly. "He would be most useful in helping to fortify the grounds, but he is not here. Do not worry, Frau Langford; we will protect you. We will not let you down."

Gaston nodded in full support, a thing so rare even Josef blinked.

Aimee whispered, "May I help? I can do something, can I not?"

Josef straightened. "It is you most of all, Aimee, that we wish to protect. But you may bring us sandwiches."

The little girl flushed with pleasure, while Elise huffed in disgust.

Five hours later, Mrs. Newsome witnessed two weary, mud-covered boys creep through the kitchen door and down the hallway to the stairs, carefully avoiding Mrs. Creedle and her spotless tiles. She'd heard them stash their spades and surrender their muddied boots to Mr. Dunnagan outside the back door, promising to scrub both down after tea.

"Well now, young soldiers, how are the fortifications coming?" Mrs. Newsome could not resist the tease.

"It will take us a day or two more," Josef avowed, "but we should finish before the invasion, wouldn't you say, Gaston?"

"*Oui,* Hitler and his minions will not get past us; this is certain!"

Mrs. Newsome's mouth dropped open as they marched up the servants' stairs. Not only had the two rivals spent an entire afternoon out from underfoot without creating mischief, but they'd apparently become comrades in arms, as well. *Will wonders never cease?* She clucked her tongue as she headed upstairs with the teapot. *War certainly makes the strangest bedfellows.*

David was home in time for tea, cause for rejoicing by all the children, big and small. Claire counted herself among the jubilants.

"How is the project coming, David?" Aunt Miranda wanted to know.

"The canteen's finished. They're working on the hangar now — almost ready. It will be a while before staff can be housed on site."

"Good." Aunt Miranda flushed. "I mean only that we don't want you to leave. There, I've said it."

"None of us want you to leave, Monsieur David." Jeanine was nearly breathless. Claire realized for the first time the girl's affections might be more than platonic. *And why wouldn't she be head over heels for him? He's dashing and kind.*

David smiled. "I'm in no hurry to go. It's nice to be where I'm welcomed. Being an American here is as foreign as —"

"As being French?" Bertram suggested.

"But not the stench to the English as being German," Peter said more quietly. Franz nodded soberly.

David tousled Franz's hair. "It's good to be war misfits together, isn't it?"

Franz grinned.

Claire marveled again at the easy way David had with the children.

"Say, what's for entertainment tonight?" David rubbed his hands together.

"Mademoiselle Claire is beginning a new book, *Great Expectations*!"

"Ah, Dickens, always a favorite."

"*Oui!* We know his stories in France." Bertram took a seat across from David.

"And what's the news here today? I'm behind on the home front."

Claire caught the quick exchange between Josef and Gaston, but contrary to their natures, neither boasted of their anti-invasion plans. David apparently saw the guilty glance between the boys as well.

"They've been digging Hitler holes," Elise

reported in the spirit of tattling.

"Digging what?" Aunt Miranda looked as puzzled as Claire.

"That reminds me: I ran into Ed Foley today," David moved on.

Josef lit up like a Christmas tree. "Did you know that there are now thirty members of the Home Guard in the Lake District? That is, thirty adult members. Gaston and I have formed the youth brigade. We will be ready, as soon as we are called, to join forces with Sergeant Foley and his men."

"Oui!" Gaston refused to be outdone. "They have four speedboats, two houseboats — all equipped with machine guns!" The boys turned to one another, raising imaginary guns in imaginary combat. *"Rat-a-tat, rat-a-tat-tat! Rat-a-tat!"*

"Boys!" Mrs. Newsome yanked both their ears, setting off yowls.

"Yes," David said slowly, "he said to tell you boys to stay out of the tunnels by the lake."

"Lake Windermere?" Aunt Miranda gasped. "What on earth were you doing way over there? What tunnels?"

Now Gaston and Josef quieted, ducking their heads.

"Apparently there are tunnels no one is

supposed to know about. But our explorers —"

"Anti-invasion team. We are the Youth Anti-Invasion Team," Josef insisted.

"The Youth Anti-Invasion Team has apparently been spying on the Home Guard, whose work and training are meant to be top secret, according to Sergeant Foley."

"We were not spying on the Home Guard." Josef stood, planting fists in his hips. "We were in training ourselves, and helping them by clearing hooligans out of the air-raid tunnels and secret pits."

"Hooligans?" David sounded skeptical.

"*Oui,* courting couples — kissing in the tunnels," Gaston spat in disgust. "We shone our torchlights on them and chased them away. They should not place our Home Guard at risk by discovering tunnels and revealing them to their lovers. They could be followed there. There are spies everywhere; that is what Sergeant Foley said!"

Following the first enticing chapter of *Great Expectations,* after the children were all tucked in for the night, David asked Claire to join him and Lady Miranda in the library.

"Foley's quite concerned about the boys' antics. They bring attention to things the Home Guard's not wanting to publicize;

they're deeply concerned there may be German sympathizers in the area. Between the prisoner escapes from Grizedale Hall and the recent bombing near Troutbeck, there's concern that communications from the area are reaching Germany, and that our factory may have been targeted. Of course, it might have been nothing more than a returning flier jettisoning his bombs, but fear of invasion is extremely high now."

"I had no idea they'd even left the property; had you, Claire?"

Claire shrugged, shaking her head. "I knew they were outdoors most of the day, but they mentioned spying on courting couples — does that mean they're sneaking out at night?"

David shrugged in return. "Could be anytime, especially in this summer weather. The tunnels, after all, are dark. But I take it from Foley that this was not their first offense. He's convinced they're trying to prove themselves patriots, but it's got to stop."

"I can't keep track of them all." Claire spread her hands. "I'll try to do better, but even with insisting they help with some domestic chores, I don't know how to keep them all busy or under observation at once. September and school are not exactly around the corner. I can't keep them sitting at a table or under lock and key."

"No," David said, "but I've had an idea."

"Anything," Aunt Miranda begged.

"They need friends."

"They have a houseful to plot and scheme with. Isn't that part of the problem?"

"No disrespect, ma'am, but they need friends from the village. You heard them tonight. They see themselves as outcasts. If they made friends with the village kids, they could join in community efforts — paper drives, scrap collections, truly helpful efforts for the war that they're only playing at now."

"Or getting into trouble with," Claire agreed.

"Exactly."

Aunt Miranda shook her head. "I don't see how they'll do that with school closed. Not one family has invited any of these children to their home. You know how most of them feel about the French. They'll not tolerate Germans, and even though they pity the Jews, they don't trust them. I'm afraid our children are blacklisted at every turn."

"I heard you tell Elise the other day that the way to have a friend is to be one."

"My mother used to say that to my sister

and me." Aunt Miranda smiled.

"So, be friends to the community children. Invite them here."

"Here?"

"Why not? A school chum or two to start. It can't hurt, and if you invite them for a meal, well, no mother is going to turn down the chance to have her child eat off somebody else's ration book."

"But what would we have them do?" Claire nearly cried. "I really don't think I can keep track of more."

"Confine Gaston and Josef to the grounds. Tell them they can work out their war tactics as long as everything is focused on keeping Bluebell Wood safe, that they're our very own Home Guard. If I don't miss my guess, that will keep their imaginations and new friends busy for quite a while. Maybe, in time, some of the other kids' mothers will reciprocate."

Aunt Miranda sighed. "I hope you're right."

"It was a good plan, in theory." Mrs. Newsome determined not to make her ladyship feel worse. She kept a tight hold on the ears of Josef and Gaston as she dragged them into the library and before their tribunal. "Asking the vicar's son first was just the right diplomacy, if I do say so myself. We simply had no idea the number of holes these boys could dig, or that the vicar's wife would cross the garden with her beef tongue aspic rather than keep to the road."

"They're Hitler holes, Madame Newsome," Gaston insisted. "Intended to catch parachutists and members of the invading army. They were never intended to catch English vicars' wives, or beef tongue aspic."

Josef shuddered. "I'm glad we didn't have to eat it."

Gaston kicked him.

"But tripping her into a four-foot hole is just what they did, now isn't it?" Mrs. Newsome fumed.

"How bad is it? Did she sprain her ankle? Oh, I hope not!" Lady Langford wrung her hands.

"Broke it clean, my lady. Dr. MacDonald's plastering a cast even as we speak."

"Ohhh, noooo," Lady Langford groaned.

"I suppose it could be worse," Gaston observed as he shoveled dirt into the very hole he'd dug out and so carefully camouflaged with branches, leaves, and a light layer of soil that morning. "I suppose Madame Langford could have court-martialed us."

"*Ja,* that would be worse," Josef agreed. "But now . . . this is a waste of our labor. How will we catch Nazis now? We've no weapons to speak of . . . only these protective strategies. Women do not grasp such things."

"We could not very well have posted signs: 'Keep off the grass. Watch for Hitler holes.' That would have alerted the enemy."

"*Ja, ja.* The English take down their road signs and village postings for the same reason, but they take offense when one civilian is injured because we have done something crucial to save them." Josef threw down his spade and wiped his brow. "Ha! I heard from the vicar's son that more English pedestrians are injured or killed on the motorways now than before the war."

"The blackout — no headlights," Gaston agreed. "It is a thing most dangerous."

Josef picked up his spade again and the boys dug in silence.

Shortly before noon, Elise, trailed by Aimee, appeared with a thermos of tea and two sandwiches wrapped in brown paper. "Madame Creedle sent these. She says you are to eat out of doors and get back to work."

"I didn't want to go in anyway," Josef huffed.

"Exiled," Gaston moaned. "Will we be allowed in for tea?"

"Only if you've finished filling in the holes. Madame Langford said to tell you that she's paid a visit and apologized profusely to the vicar's wife, and that you must begin weeding the vicar's garden first thing in the morning, including all the paving stones on the pathway to the church."

"The paving stones! That's a quarter mile if anything!"

"Exaggeration won't help." Elise shook her head. "You've brought it on yourselves, you know. Still, it is a pity, and I am sorry for you."

"*Merci,* Elise, that is kind of you. I, too, am sorry."

"Don't be sorry for me." Josef threw back his shoulders. "I'm not sorry — not one small bit — about digging the holes. It was a good idea. They'll be sorry we've filled them in when the invasion comes."

Elise shrugged. "Perhaps, but those are the orders from above." She smiled sweetly at Josef. "But I am glad you're here, Josef. I know I am safe with you."

Gaston glanced between Josef and Elise and back again. *"Ooh la la!"*

Elise did not bop him on the head, but smiled again at Josef, then turned on her heel, head raised high, and walked back toward the house, Aimee following behind.

"She's sweet on you, Josef!"

"*Ja,* well, I cannot help that. It is nothing to me." Josef tore into his sandwich.

"I wouldn't mind Elise being sweet on me," Gaston said regretfully, "though I would much prefer the affections of Mademoiselle Claire."

"There is no time for such things. We must think again how to prevent the invaders." Josef set down his sandwich, eager to take Gaston's mind off of Fräulein Claire. After all, he had his own sights set on that special lady.

Chapter Twenty-Two

By mid-July Claire was at her wits' end.

The vicar's wife had proven more than gracious, all things considered, but the congregation's leading gossips had erupted in fury over the "conspiracies of foreigners." Not another invitation to Bluebell Wood had been accepted by village mothers on behalf of their sons or daughters. Claire walked on eggshells, all but pleading with the children to help forge peaceable relations with the villagers, until she learned that when given increased freedom for the summer, Elise and Ingrid had joined two local girls in spying on Mrs. O'Reilly, certain the arthritic old Irish lady was a conspiring member of the IRA. The girls had watched her mail, followed her, listened to her conversations in town, keeping track of her purchases and whereabouts, and even been seen listening beneath her window. Mrs. O'Reilly's tearful telephone call to Bluebell Wood made

Claire's humiliation complete.

"I'm so very sorry, Mrs. O'Reilly. Yes, you're absolutely right. They have no call to do any such thing. I'll speak with our girls right away. I promise you they will apologize and never do that again." Claire pleaded for understanding, pulling out the foreign-orphan-and-war-victim cards she'd mentally vowed never to use.

That night, after the BBC wireless news and the latest reading of Pip's encounter with Miss Havisham in *Great Expectations,* with all the children safely abed, Claire met with her aunt and David in the library. Dr. MacDonald stopped by, late from his evening rounds, and joined the conversation.

"The trouble, I daresay, is that our locals still see all of you as the enemy. Being Jewish and that fiend's victims in this war has not elicited the sympathy one might rightfully expect among many of the villagers, I'm that sorry to say, even though they be children."

Aunt Miranda sighed. "I'd just hoped for better things and better attitudes . . . from everyone. And I'd not anticipated the antics all these children get up to."

"You wouldn't be so surprised if you knew the antics of your own lad at that age."

"No, I suppose not. In those days I would

have been mortified."

"Now ye'd relish the laugh, I'll wager."

"Aye, Raibeart MacDonald, I would." She smiled a comrade's smile.

"If that's the trouble," David mused, "if they see us as the enemy, we must join forces with them."

"I'm not so sure your idea of making friends with the locals was the best," Claire worried. "You can see what our gang did with that!"

"Not friends, not chums, exactly — more like allies in the fight against evil."

"So you said before — more or less," Claire reminded him.

"Out with it, friend. I've come to expect outlandish but suspiciously sound doctrine from ye." Dr. MacDonald exaggerated his brogue.

David grinned. "What is the thing that the village and everyone here is united in?"

"The war against Hitler, against the Nazis," Aunt Miranda went along.

"And what do the locals do that we don't do here at Bluebell Wood?"

"We're already rationing like everyone else. We're digging victory gardens," Aunt Miranda defended.

"Not to mention 'Hitler holes,' " Claire huffed. "We're sharing the school with the village, just like all the English evacuees."

"Those are homeland preservation activities," David urged.

"But not activities that unite us in fighting the war, to bring fathers and brothers and sons home." The doctor nodded. "I see where you're headed."

David leaned forward in enthusiasm. "The village children, the families, are collecting fats and scrap metal. They're hosting or supporting fund-raisers — dances, sing-alongs, plays, orchestrations. All sorts of things to raise money for Spitfires and ambulances. The local Women's Institute — including Mrs. Newsome — are knitting their fingers to the bone making mittens and socks and helmet caps."

"I've tried, but I'm the worst knitter in the village." Aunt Miranda frowned. "I was all but expelled from the church knitting group for newborns years ago."

"But what you do have is the most interesting grounds far and wide. The mazes here, the orchards, and the unusual layout of the gardens and wooded acreage are amazing."

"The perfect backdrop for . . ." The wheels in Claire's head began to turn. "I think I see where you're going too."

"Invite the enemy into the camp?" David

grinned.

Dr. MacDonald took out his empty pipe and tamped it. "Rather like the MacDonalds offering hospitality to the Campbells and finding themselves slaughtered in their beds, isn't it?"

David's color rose. "That was a diabolical event, and I'm ashamed of my ancestors."

"Aye, it was." The doctor's firm and low note sent a warning.

"But that was nearly three hundred years ago and had nothing to do with me or the plan I'm suggesting. We'd not be asking anything of the villagers, but sending an offer to become allies, partners to get us all through this war."

The men stared each other down.

Claire held her breath as long as she could. "I see what you're saying, but I don't think inviting the locals to a singsong or a picnic will do — not this time. It has to be something everyone can participate in for the sake of winning the war — and our children need to be seen as the hosts, much more than the grown-ups."

When David's eyes lit in appreciation, Claire smiled, the blood pounding in her veins in a way it hadn't for ages. "I have an idea — a splendid idea."

■ ■ ■ ■

Mrs. Newsome thought Claire's idea a splendid one indeed and presented lists of orders to the children the next morning in military style without even consulting Lady Langford. If a thing was to be done, it must be done right and no shilly-shallying. She placed the oldest boy and girl among the French and oldest boy and girl among the Germans in charge of their task forces, then sent them out the kitchen door, ignoring groans and mock salutes.

Getting the grounds in shape for the fund-raising fete Miss Claire had schemed would take the rest of July and most of August. They'd best get started. If Mrs. Newsome didn't miss her guess, this veritable army of competitive youngsters might do what three grown men had been challenged to keep up. *A bit of fun, a strong work ethic, and killing two birds with one stone* — now that appealed to the Scottish housekeeper.

At eleven o'clock Mrs. Newsome poured tea for Lady Langford in the library.

"I just worry that we're expecting too much of them. They're children, after all. I would never have expected Christopher to labor in the gardens like this."

"Ah, but he did, and with you, my lady, despite Mr. Dunnagan's protests."

Lady Langford smiled, her eyes glassed in memory. Mrs. Newsome smiled in return at the image of her lady and the young master covered in garden dirt and drenched from sudden downpours as they'd rushed through the kitchen door, laughing — not once, but many times. "If memory does not fail me, those were some of your happiest days . . . and his."

Lady Langford blinked back moisture that Mrs. Newsome politely ignored. "Yes. Yes, they were. We did it together . . . that's what made it so special. It wasn't work at all, for either of us."

"And it needn't be work now, my lady." Mrs. Newsome waited a moment more.

"Are you suggesting I join them?"

"I'm not suggesting anything at all, my lady. But that does sound like a bonny idea. The sunshine and fresh air might do you a world of good. You've always loved gardening and growing things."

Lady Langford gave a self-conscious laugh. "I'm not sure how much digging or clipping or weeding I'm up to these days."

Mrs. Newsome's brow wrinkled. She'd seen her lady's loss of strength, and it worried her. "Mind, you must be careful not to overdo, but I think if we set a chair in the shade for you, you might find it pleasant, and enjoy watching their activity. I daresay those youngsters will labor their hearts out trying to impress you."

"What are they working on today?"

"You should see them! The older boys climb those ladders like young monkeys, a true blessing for poor Mr. Dunnagan. Under his veteran instruction they're learning to trim and shape the topiaries."

"I can hardly imagine that."

"Bringing those gigantic animals back to life will inspire everything to come. The younger children are picking up brush, raking leaves, and I believe Mr. Dunnagan will set some to trim grass. Even young Aimee's out weeding the flower beds. Mr. Dunnagan has gone and fashioned her a child-size spade, and Peter's shown the patience of Job in teaching her to dig and plant."

"You're certain we're not expecting too much of them? Not only are they children, but they're here as our guests."

"They're evacuees and refugees, my lady. It's high time they were gainfully employed and helping. This is their home for the duration, after all. Children relish learning new skills. They take pride in becoming capable. 'Twas all that idle time that gave way to mischief and shenanigans in the first place . . . a common enough trouble among adults and children alike, if I do say so." Mrs. Newsome knew her lecture sounded disapproving. Lady Langford's notion of coddling youngsters was one thing when that meant coddling her own son, the young master, but quite another for ten active and imaginative foreign-born children bent on mischief.

"Miss Claire and the children are conspiring on a play from one of the books she's been reading them; she'll write and they'll perform. It turns out that young Franz is the son of a tailor back in Germany and reared in the family trade, for being only a mite. He's prepared to turn some old drapes I found in the back of the linen cupboard into costumes with the help of Marlene and Ingrid.

"Mr. David's promised to work on some props with the young ones, and he's working up a bit of his hamboning. He and Miss Claire pulled out the gramophone. Mr. David has quite the collection of recordings. They're going to teach the children American square dancing — that should be a sight — and a bit of those gyrations they call the jitterbug." Mrs. Newsome shuddered at the thought. The jitterbug was a vulgar dance in her mind. But she daren't say that to her ladyship — an American, after all. "They'll finish up with a rousing singsong."

"British tunes, I hope."

Mrs. Newsome laughed. "British, through and through. Miss Claire says she'll pick them out on the piano, though I think Jeanine is the one to play them. That girl's got music in her fingers and toes. Mrs. Creedle and I can handle the food. She's agreed to save back most of our sugar rations and fats and such until then. Things will prove a bit meager during the saving, but that's as it is."

"The events of the day must be finished long before the blackout."

"They'll all be on their way home before the gloaming. We'll do an afternoon bonfire, if the day isn't too warm. Miss Claire's fete and the money it will raise will provide a real wartime lift. It's a great lot of work, I agree, but I believe Miss Claire is right: it's worth the doing. Preparations will keep the children busy and out of mischief, and the villagers will relish a day on the grounds. Raising funds for another ambulance is a cause we can all get behind. It just might forge a bridge between."

"What we might call 'mutually beneficial'?" Lady Langford laughed.

"Aye, 'mutually beneficial'!" It was worth all the fuss and bother just to hear her lady laugh.

Claire waited while David fiddled with the wireless dial on Sunday night. She and the children had finished the washing up after tea, listened to an early news broadcast, and enjoyed a shortened reading of *Great Expectations.* The BBC broadcast of Norwegian news was just finishing. None of the children seemed eager to break the domestic circle. Aimee nestled close to Claire's side, and Claire gladly drew the little girl in.

"Quarter to eight on Sunday nights, C. S. Lewis will broadcast," David explained. "This is his first one. I'd like to listen, if you don't mind. He's the writer whose book I was reading a while back. Never finished it. Don't know what I did with it. He's writing another, I heard just the other day. Becoming quite well known."

Claire squirmed. She'd never returned David's copy of *The Problem of Pain,* never even told him she'd taken it. She'd read it through — twice — and wasn't ready to let it go, as if holding on to it might make the things Lewis said about life and God come clearer or deepen the comfort his writing gave of recognizing her inner being. *Nothing else has made that much sense in a long time.*

Claire's sense of guilt was ill-timed, she decided, or maybe it was fate. Lewis spoke for fifteen minutes on the topic of common decency.

It was going along fairly well, until Lewis reached his main point:

> "I hope you will not misunderstand what I am going to say. I am not preaching, and Heaven knows I do not pretend to be better than anyone else. I am only trying to call attention to a fact; the fact that this year, or this month, or, more likely, this very day, we have failed to practice ourselves the kind of behavior we expect from other people. There may be all sorts of excuses for us. That time you were so unfair to the children was when you were very tired. That slightly shady business about the money — the one you have almost forgotten — came when you were very hard up. And what you promised to do for old So-and-so and have never done — well, you never would have promised if you had known how frightfully busy you were going to be."

Claire groaned within, but Aimee squeezed her hand and smiled up into her eyes. Claire knew that Aimee, young as she was, understood what Mr. Lewis had said, and that the child forgave her.

Though she tried to focus on the broadcast and the children before her — what common decency meant for her treatment of them — her mind kept returning to her own hurt, closer to the surface.

She'd received another letter from Josephine on Friday. It had taken five weeks to reach Claire from Sylvia's mother in America. Josephine had mailed it from Paris six weeks before that. Two and a half months. Josephine wrote that she hoped Claire would understand that she and their mutual friend had been working side by side these many months and grown closer. It was natural, she supposed, but felt the need to let Claire know, to never betray their friendship.

Claire knew Josephine did not write those words to taunt her, but to forewarn her, to practice common decency in the way she could. Josephine had fallen in love with Arnaud, Claire was certain. Even now, Claire felt her heart pound, the heat rise up her face. *Well, why wouldn't she? All the girls fall for Arnaud. The question is, has he fallen for her in the same way?*

In the past, when Claire had asked him

about their mutual close friend, Arnaud had laughed, saying, “Josephine? She’s too old — she must be nearly my age! *Non, ma chérie!* She’s like a sister to me. You, on the other hand, are not like my sister.” And then he would smile and wink in a way that sent chills up Claire’s arms. Surely, she’d believed, they were made for one another.

In two and a half months, anything might have happened. Still, Claire could count on Arnaud to be loyal . . . couldn’t she?

Chapter Twenty-Three

By late August Claire's play rehearsals for *The Secret Garden* ran full length. Franz and the girls had finished the costumes in time for dress rehearsals, and Marlene had created a veritable flower garden in pots, ready for the outdoor makeshift stage. David had directed the building of an arbor, and even a swing. Mr. Dunnagan and David had orchestrated the moving of a downed tree to stand in the center of the "garden" and hung the swing from its lowest branch. The girls had fashioned paper blooms, dyed from vegetable peelings and the petals of the summer's wildflowers.

It was the dancing that worried Claire. The children loved the music and seemed to catch on easily to the American square dancing. Jigs and reels and folk dances of all sorts ran native through their blood. Though jitterbugging tangled the feet of the youngest, and they were quick to give it up, especially when they found it meant holding on to one another through the entire dance, the older children were as eager to learn as David was to teach them.

But there came the rub. David wanted Claire for his partner to teach the children, and that meant they needed to practice, with the children and without.

"I can't pretend the lady's part while doing the gent's," David protested as he spun Claire out in a dramatic twirl. "Don't you like dancing? Don't you like dancing with me?" he teased, pulling her back, a little too close.

Claire loved jitterbugging, but doing it in David's arms sent chills up her spine, set her mind to racing, and discombobulated her nervous system . . . all of which apparently pleased David to no end. Her pleasure felt disloyal to Arnaud. And yet, that confused Claire too. Was Arnaud loyal to her? And if he wasn't, why did she fear betraying him?

I won't be like my father! He was far away from Mother and me, but he should have remained true — not thrown us over for another woman, a second family! The revelation of her concern — the connection — shocked her, but there it was.

"That's it, Peter!" David cheered. "Step,

step, rock step . . . step, step, rock step. Once we've got that, we spin the lady out, like this —" he twirled Claire again, her mind still whirling — "then twirl her back and under your arm, two arms linked, and rock step, step, step, repeat the rock. You keep the same basic step all the way through, even while you spin her. Got it?"

Peter wiped the perspiration from his brow. "I think Bertram would be better at this. I'm two left feet, as you say. I need something slower."

Jeanine's face fell, and Claire's heart, in recognition of rejection, hurt for her, but Bertram stepped up to the plate and took her hand from Peter's. "Shall we?"

Claire's mouth dropped open as Bertram spun Jeanine out, spun her back, and rock stepped in perfect rhythm. Without waiting for David to place the needle on the record, Bertram spun her out and back once more, then lifted her for a perfect flip.

Mr. Dunnagan stopped in the drawing room doorway, nearly dropping the potted geranium he carried. "Well, I'll be a — I mean to say, suffer the French!" He grinned from ear to ear. "Well done, young Bertram! Well done!"

"Where did you learn to do that?" Claire gasped.

"Mademoiselle, you were not the only one who knew Americans in Paris," Bertram teased, suddenly older than his years.

David laughed. "Mademoiselle Claire, I believe we have a show!"

Claire laughed too, relieved that Bertram and Jeanine could be the center-stage jitterbugging couple. At the same time, she was astonished to realize how much Bertram and Jeanine had grown in the year they'd all lived at Bluebell Wood, how much all the children had grown and changed. Had she changed too?

Dr. MacDonald insisted that a Scottish reel be included in the festivities, and Peter's suggestion of something slower was echoed by Elise's unexpected request for waltzing lessons and a fox-trot.

"It seems we're now official dance teachers, mademoiselle," David whispered in Claire's ear as he took her in his arms to begin a fox-trot. Was it the music's sultry saxophone or David's breath on her hair's damp tendril, tickling her ear, that sent the shiver down Claire's spine once more?

"I haven't danced in ages," Aunt Miranda objected as Dr. MacDonald pulled her to her feet. "I'm not sure I can, or that I have the breath."

"Of course you can, lass." The doctor

would not take no for an answer. "You're the lady of the manor; you canna remain seated and expect the villagers to commence. You must open the dance and lead the day! We'll take it one step at a time."

Claire marveled at the way the doctor could convince her aunt of almost anything, though she sometimes wondered if it was more a case of him giving her the permission she craved to step beyond the grievous choices she'd framed for herself, or the lethargy into which she'd sunk.

Yet when the doctor spun his laughing partner out and back again and she stumbled, bumping him shoulder to chest, Claire saw a sudden spark fly between the older couple that she'd not seen before. Claire had known, ever since the doctor's attendance to her aunt during her bout with influenza, that he loved her. But the brilliant light in her aunt's eyes told Claire that the passion was not one-sided.

Aunt Miranda, don't waste another minute holding him at bay. It's not betraying Uncle Gilbert's or even Christopher's memory. They're gone, and we're all interlopers into your life. We won't stay . . . none of us. Don't be alone. You need him and he loves you!

Oh, to be loved like that!

Each of those thoughts raced through

Claire's mind in a moment. Each made her wonder if they applied to more than her aunt.

For all the snide remarks Claire had received in the village shops, the day of the fete seemed to turn the tide — at least for some — as she and Aunt Miranda welcomed cheerful villagers to Bluebell Wood.

"They're more than curious; that's all," Claire whispered to her aunt between guests. "They've been longing to walk the grounds and see the inside of your estate for ages."

"This is our opportunity to respond graciously and prove ourselves generous," Aunt Miranda reminded her. "We're here for a greater cause. And it was your idea." Her aunt smiled widely as she turned and warmly greeted the now-walking vicar's wife.

Claire knew Aunt Miranda was right, and as the day progressed her own heart opened to the laughter of children and the dry wit of some of the locals.

She clapped with everyone else, praising each act of the performance of *The Secret Garden.* Watching Gaston as Colin rise from the wheeled chair, unsteady and halting in his crippled steps, and stumble across the makeshift secret garden from Mary — Elise — to Dickon's waiting arms — Peter — Claire could almost believe in magic and new beginnings, could almost believe in anything.

The conclusion of *The Secret Garden* brought rousing cheers and foot-stomping approval. Mr. Dunnagan's bow as Ben Weatherstaff pulled the adults to their feet to clap. He was a longtime villager, after all, and Claire thanked all the stars that be that she'd cast the crusty gardener in his role. It was written just for him.

"Forging new relationships takes time." Dr. MacDonald nodded his approval. "You're doing right well, lass."

"That affirmation was worth the day," Claire whispered to David when he brought her a heaping luncheon plate and forced her to sit down and eat.

"Wait until your aunt counts the money and bestows the kitty for the new ambulance on the WI. They'll all come round."

By the time Claire and David stepped onto the dance floor, Claire discovered that David was lauded as a bit of a hero by some of the workers who'd been invited from the factory, while disdained by a few. Men slapped him on the back in welcome and more than one girl batted her eyelashes, rolling a shoulder in coy invitation.

One man bumped his shoulder deliberately. "Sitting pretty on these grounds, are you, Campbell? You Yanks stick together and glide through. Parties and fetes won't win the war."

Claire stood ready to challenge the man, but David pulled her away. "Don't get your dander up."

"He's all but calling you a coward."

"It's nothing to do with me," he whispered, taking her by the arm. "It's because the US is taking so long to come into the war. The people here have waited a long time for Roosevelt to act. I can't blame them for feeling the way they do. In fact, I'm feeling a coward — a hypocrite, sitting comfortable here, working at the factory, while Brits are giving their lives left and right. I'm thinking about joining up."

Claire nearly tripped in her heels.

"I talked it over with my supervisor yesterday. I can't sit here and let other men do my fighting. Not when everything we know and love is at stake."

"You came here from Scotland to do your bit because America hadn't joined the war. What you're doing is invaluable to the war effort — you said so yourself. You've been trained for this very thing." Claire no longer felt like dancing. She pleaded for David's sanity.

David drew a long breath and released it, leading Claire into a fox-trot. His breath near her ear and his hand on the small of her back raised the hairs on the back of her neck. "That's what he said — that I'm more needed here."

"You agreed, right?"

"I told him I'd think it over. Look, I'm sorry I said anything now. Guess it's just on my mind. Let's forget about it and enjoy the afternoon." He begged her with his eyes. "Please. I want to dance with the prettiest girl in the Lake District."

Claire smiled as best she could and pinned her gaze to his shoulder. But she couldn't stop the rapid beating of her heart. *What will I do if you leave?*

She couldn't answer that question, but carried its weight in her heart around the dance floor through the fox-trot, even the fast-paced jitterbug and jive. By the time they reached another fox-trot, a brazen village girl walked up and tapped Claire on the shoulder.

Claire was so surprised she stepped aside, despite the question in David's eyes.

She found a seat at a nearby empty table and watched, determined to keep the smile pasted on her lips. The couple had barely made it round the floor when another girl tapped the first one on the shoulder and pushed herself into David's arms. *Is this a game? Some invention to humiliate the American girl or compete with one another?*

Claire watched, undecided.

"Your boyfriend seems to be in high demand." The voice behind her was deep, suave, with a trace of Irish.

"He's not my boyfriend. We're just friends."

"Ah, well, then you'll not mind me joining you."

Before Claire could answer, he claimed a seat on the other side of her. "Ian Kennedy, at your service. Can I get you a drink? A little whiskey?" He pulled his jacket aside to reveal a pocketed flask.

"No, thank you. It looks like you've had enough for both of us. We're not serving alcohol here, you know. There are children present."

"Beauty and a quick wit. What's not to like about American girls?" He laughed and leaned too close.

Claire stood. "Excuse me."

"Ach, no, lass. Where are you off to? And us just getting acquainted."

"I'm off to retrieve my dance."

"Ach — your dance, but not your boyo."

"No, he's not my 'boyo.' " It was a recognition that both steadied and unsteadied Claire.

She walked directly to David and tapped the bleached blonde in his outstretched arms on the shoulder.

"We're not finished with our dance," the girl objected.

"Yes, you are." Claire squeezed between the village girl and David, pushing him gently backward.

"At last, a woman who knows how to lead!" He grinned. "I thought you'd never come rescue me."

Claire felt a blush rise to the roots of her hair. "I wasn't sure you wanted rescuing. The girls here are mighty brazen."

"The first one was my boss's daughter."

Surprised, she stopped midstep and they both tripped, laughing. "You're serious?"

"Never more!" He spun her out and back into his arms.

"Ohhhh, sorry I interrupted. What about the last one?"

"The boss's cousin once removed." He grinned, and she swatted his chest, just as he pulled her close, his chin resting on her head for a slow dance. "Stay close, Claire. I won't let anybody step between us again."

Claire swallowed. *Does he know about Josephine and Arnaud? Did Aunt Miranda tell him? Or is that his wish?* Regardless, Claire closed her eyes and determined to give herself over to the music, to hear only the sweet romance of "A Nightingale Sang in Berkeley Square." Every moment in David's arms turned to moonlight and magic, despite the afternoon sunlight that dappled through oak limbs. She wouldn't have been surprised to hear that nightingale break into song, or to see the moon rise from the punch bowl.

She looked up into his face. David winked, smiled, and closed his eyes, then nestled his cheek against her hair. The pressure of his hand on hers, the moment when he pulled her closer still and rested his chin on her head — melted into one long, sweet memory. *Let this never end. Let it always be like this.* The thought was real and honest enough, Claire knew, but was it right? She closed her eyes and, breathing deeply, pulled away, ever so slightly, determined to remain true to Arnaud.

Once they'd played through David's collection of gramophone records, a man from town pulled out his fiddle and a few of the villagers stood for impromptu sings. The crowd joined in, swaying in time to the music. A trio of sisters belted out perky war songs in perfect harmony. Feet picked up the beat the moment the sisters began "Run, Rabbit, Run."

David pulled Claire to her feet once more and she gladly followed in a less-romantic quickstep. "This song reminds me of Aimee and her bunny. I'm so afraid Mr. Dunnagan will forget one day and shoot Mr. Cottontail for rabbit pie!"

"Oh, man — hope I'm far away the day that happens!" David lamented.

"I hope you're never far away," Claire whispered.

"What's that?"

"Nothing. Nothing."

And then the fiddle music slowed again. Love songs became the order of the afternoon. Men and women and teens danced toe-to-toe and cheek-to-cheek. Despite the war, despite the brazen village girls, the austerity and rationing and uncertainty of all her tomorrows, it was the happiest day Claire could remember.

Josef had agreed to participate in the Virginia reel, as long as Aimee was his partner. He felt a certain protective care for the younger girl, and it was one of the few dances she seemed able to learn. But he'd stoutly refused when Elise begged him to try the fox-trot with her. He'd no notion of returning the girl's flirtations and didn't want her fawning over him.

Children vied for the honor of taste-testing the jam and tarts made by local ladies, but those privileges went to the doctor and the vicar. The girls loved the flower arrangement competition, but the real action, Josef felt, came in the intense marble game a group of boys from the village had set up beyond the maze. They'd heeled a dirt circle out of the lawn. Mr. Dunnagan wouldn't like the destruction, Josef knew, but he'd never played marbles before and was drawn to the game like a moth to flame.

"Teach me," Josef ordered, standing behind the group, doing his best to sound confident.

The game stopped. The boys, who'd been hunkered down and cheering one another, turned. The boy with the largest marble only lifted his head. "Oh, I don't think so. No Nazis allowed."

Josef felt the blood drain from his face. "I am not a Nazi . . . no more than you."

The other boy stood slowly and, squaring his shoulders, turned. "Don't you ever say that about me. Me brother's over there, fightin' back those Jerry Huns."

"And mine is here, because they killed *mein Vater,* and if we'd stayed, we would have been next." It was the thing Josef feared, the thing he dreaded. He knew his father and uncle had been arrested, beaten, and taken by train to some faraway work camp, somewhere in Poland, the German police had said. They'd not heard from either of them for three long years before leaving Germany, and Josef had decided it was easier to pretend his father was dead than to wonder and worry. After living through that, he wasn't about to back down from an English boy who knew nothing.

"You're Jewish. It's because of you we're in this war. If it wasn't for you —"

"Hitler. It is because of Hitler."

Another of the boys nudged the first and cupped his hand to whisper in his ear. The bigger boy cocked his head and challenged, "He says you been diggin' Hitler holes, settin' traps for the invasion. Show me."

Josef stared him down. "The vicar's wife stepped in one and broke her ankle. We had to fill them in and reconnoiter. New tactics are in order."

"It's true. I seen her with her leg plastered up and him and that French boy weedin' the paving stones at the church . . . clear to the road and back toward the vicarage as penance."

"That's a lot of weedin'," the older boy gave grudging respect. "Me mate and me had to do it a couple o' years ago. Got caught pinchin' the Communion wine."

"There's a lot of paving stones," Josef agreed.

The two stood, staring at one another until the older boy held up the large marble. "I'm Wilfred Cooper. This here's me tolley. You knuckle down, like this, and flip your thumb, sending the other chap's marble clear of the ring. As long as you clear the ring, you're good, and you capture that marble. You keep goin'. Miss that, and the turn goes to the next. At the end of the game, whoever has the most marbles wins and gets to keep what he wants — keepsies." He looked back at Josef, hefting his leather pouch of marbles. "You can't play without marbles."

Josef swallowed. He hadn't thought of that. But he knew where he might find some. "I'll be back."

Once Josef had followed Gaston into the room Frau Langford kept locked, the room belonging to her grown boy, now dead. He'd seen a leather pouch with a red drawstring — just like the one Wilfred Cooper held. He'd bet his last teaspoon of Marmite that the bag held marbles.

Josef made it into the great house and up the stairs without a word or second glance from anyone. Everyone knew he belonged there, which pricked his conscience just a little.

The sun had already traveled to this side of the estate, and the light through the window at the end of the hallway shone on him like a spotlight. He swallowed, but pulled a slim blade from his pocket and inserted it into the lock, twisting gently, lifting — just barely — until he heard the tumblers click into place. He pulled the blade from the door and turned the high knob.

The room was dark, blackout curtains drawn taut, even in daytime. It didn't matter. Josef knew exactly where to find the pouch. The moment his fingers clasped the lumpy form, he smiled. Marbles, certainly.

Josef silently closed the door, not bothering to lock it. He'd return the marbles before the others came in from the fete. They'd never be missed and his borrowing would never be known.

Five minutes later Josef and Wilfred stood on either side of the ring, a great pack of marbles clustered in its center. Wilfred lifted his chin, planting his solid brownish-red tolley on the tip of his nose, then let it roll down, dropping into the dirt. It rolled within three inches of the ring before it came to a stop. "Now you do it — tolley off. Whichever tolley lands closest to the ring goes first."

Josef solemnly nodded. He stood straight, lifted his chin, and let Christopher's agate tolley, brown and shot with bands of light as it rolled, drop from the tip of his nose. It rolled toward the center of the ring, catching sunlight as it went — a thing of beauty.

Wilfred licked his lips. "I go first."

Josef nodded again, suppressing a smile. He didn't mind Wilfred going first. He could learn a great deal of strategy from the older boy.

Wilfred squatted, dropped one knee to the dirt, and took aim. He shot off the edges of the pack, sending one, two, three . . . ten marbles easily outside the ring.

And then Wilfred's magic streak broke: His next shot grazed the pack but didn't send the intended marble from the ring.

Josef knuckled down, just as he'd seen Wilfred do, and flicked his tolley. It wasn't much different than the skill required for a game he and Peter played with coins. The first marble barely crossed the ring. Wilfred grinned. Josef's mouth formed a grim line, and he flicked again, this time from the position of the tolley. One, two, three, four marbles and counting sped outside the ring.

By the eighth marble Wilfred's smirk had gone. Other boys shifted their stance. Josef did his best to ignore them. On the eleventh marble his tolley missed. Wilfred's sigh of relief came audible.

Seven marbles later it occurred to Josef that if he lost Christopher's marbles, he must confess that loss to Frau Langford. She had been generous with her son's cricket ball and bat, but taking her son's precious marbles without permission — breaking into his room and "borrowing" them — was another thing. *Borrowing?* Nein, *she will see it as stealing.* Sweat beaded above Josef's lip. He might have prayed, but something about praying over stolen marbles smote his conscience.

One of the boys coughed, and Wilfred fumbled. His tolley missed the marble altogether.

"You made me flick too soon! I should have a do-over!"

"*Nein.* That's surely not the rule," Josef challenged.

"He's right." One of the village boys crossed his arms. "Hard luck, but there it is."

Josef breathed. Wilfred dared not go against his peers, but mumbled, "Cheaters," under his breath.

Josef bent to his task. Five marbles outside the ring before he missed. *Fifteen!*

Wilfred again, and the tension increased. The marbles rolled. At last he missed.

Josef did his best. Seven more. He needed three to win. Just as he flicked, Wilfred clapped and stomped near his ear. Josef's tolley ran wild, flying outside the ring. A groan of disbelief rose from the watchers.

"Dead. Your tolley's dead."

"What does that mean?"

Wilfred smirked. "It means you can't use it. It means you must flick and shoot without it."

"Oh," sighed Josef. "That's not so bad."

"That's part of it. Your tolley's like any other marble shot outside the ring now. Winner can take all, if he's a mind."

Josef froze.

"You can't. They're not mine."

"I recognize that aggie. Every bloke in school's wanted it since me older brother played Master Christopher in primary school. Lady Langford's not likely to have given it to an orphan, now is she?"

Josef wanted to throttle him, but what he'd said was true. The darkness of what he'd done, of the thief he was and would always be, overran his soul.

"You ought to give him another chance, Wil," the boy nearest Josef said. "It's his first time."

"All's fair in war." Wilfred stood with feet spread for a fight and crossed his arms. "Grindin' a Kraut to the dust sounds like war to me."

"Well, he's not won yet." The other boy punched Josef in the arm. "Mind how you go."

It was Wilfred's turn.

Josef was tempted to clap, to shout, to stomp and push his opponent over, but he stood still, sure that fate or God was dealing him the blow he deserved.

The first shot went outside the ring, neat as you please. Two more marbles and Wilfred would win. Josef couldn't watch.

"Oohh, too bad," the group commiserated. Josef opened his eyes. Wilfred's shot had reached the edge, but not gone across the ring, his tolley resting just behind the marble.

Wilfred paled.

Josef blinked. "So, if I knock his marble and his tolley out, that counts as two marbles? Then, there's just the one left."

"Aye," said the youngest boy in wonder. A

couple of the boys stepped back, eyeing Wilfred's fists.

"You daren't," Wilfred said, but he sounded worried.

"How could I?" Josef asked. "You've been so gracious as to teach me this game."

He knuckled down and sent Wilfred's marble and tolley flying past the ring. It was nothing to send the last marble out. No one cheered, but the boys huddled close, waiting.

Josef stood and stared at Wilfred. The relief of winning, of not losing Christopher's marbles, might have been enough, would have been enough, if Wilfred's eyes had not narrowed and he'd not spat, "Dirty Jew. Always cheaters, that's what me da says, and it holds."

Josef's heart raced in fury, but he didn't say a word. He bent and collected Christopher's marbles, one by one, and returned them to their pouch, placing the coveted aggie on top with a silent vow never to risk such a thing again. Then he rolled Wilfred's tolley between his thumb and forefinger. It would make a fine gift for Fräulein Claire.

He stood up and said, "Keep your marbles."

Wilfred's arms dropped to his sides.

"I'll keep this tolley." He tossed it in the

air and expertly caught it.

"Oh." A mix of dread and admiration swept the watchers. Wilfred's eyes widened in disbelief.

Josef walked away, determined to return the marbles to Christopher's room before the singsong and dancing ended.

"Wait!" Wilfred called. "Best two out of three! I challenge you!"

"As you said, they are not my marbles." Josef kept walking.

"I need that back! Stop! This is not over, you dirty pig —"

Josef knew he should keep walking, knew he should turn the other cheek as Frau Langford had preached often enough. But Wilfred had uttered the despised label once too often. Fury for what had been done to his father, his mother, to all those left behind in Germany and those with whom he shared refuge at Bluebell Wood rose within him. He stopped, stuffed the pouch of marbles into the maze, turned, then charged, a bull with horns bent, into Wilfred's stomach, sending the bigger boy flying backward into the dusty marble ring.

A fist-pounding, eye-gouging, nose-bloodying fight ensued, cheered on by every other boy who closed ranks around them. The noise and stomping egged Josef on. He pounded Wilfred's face, his chest, his neck. He gained a foothold and kicked Wilfred's knees with his boots, hard as he could, bringing the bigger boy's knees to his chin in a cry for protection, and calling grown-ups no one wanted into the ring.

The last thing Josef remembered was David dragging him — a wild tangle of thrashing arms and legs — from the ground, and the bitter tears streaming down his own face.

Chapter Twenty-Four

That night wasn't the first time Claire had despaired of squabbling children, but she feared Josef's fight might mark the end of the line with the villagers. Both boys were in need of Dr. MacDonald's attentions. Wilfred had suffered a broken rib, and Josef, two black eyes.

"The afternoon was going so well! The play was a hit, the food amazed everyone — what Mrs. Creedle can do with a ration book is beyond me! The dance was a true success. And your hamboning — they'd never seen the like." Claire's flood of words ended in a wail. She washed the last platter from the fete and handed it to David to dry.

"The afternoon was a smashing success with everybody — even the vicar's wife said so. And all boys fight, sooner or later," David defended, tossing his dripping tea towel over the hanger. "From what I heard, Josef had good cause to pummel his opponent."

"David! That's not the attitude we're fostering here."

"Did you hear what that Wilfred character said to him? He practically begged Josef to fight."

Claire pushed damp and disheveled hair from her forehead. "He can't give in to that. *We* can't give in to that. We're all foreigners here."

"That doesn't make us doormats. We're raising young men, not —"

"We're not raising them — we're housing them."

"No, Claire. Face it: the war is nowhere near over. We may be the only family, and this may be the only childhood, that any of these kids have left. It's up to us to make men and women of them."

She shook her head, her jaw tightening. "The war will end and they'll leave; they'll go back to their families, or what's left of them." Claire didn't want to pursue that line of thought in either direction.

"But we need to help them distinguish right from wrong, and I don't think that standing up for yourself is wrong."

"Your Mr. Lewis doesn't see it that way."

"What do you mean?"

"Lewis said, 'From the moment a creature becomes aware of God as God and of itself as self, the terrible alternative of choosing God or self for the centre is opened to it.' "

"I don't think Josef was choosing between God and self. I think he was standing up for himself and his family. But you're right. We all do it — we all struggle with self or God."

Claire nodded. "Lewis also said that the reason our cure of self-will is so painful is that it's like a death. I see it every day in the children — in their very faces as they wrestle with right and wrong."

"We're all children, then." David grinned, but his eyes were pinned to hers. "I didn't know you were listening that closely to his broadcasts."

Claire shrugged, turning away. "What you mean is, you didn't know I believed in God."

David said nothing.

"I'm not sure what I believe. But I've been reading a little. . . ." Claire wanted to change the subject. "About the children, you said, 'us' — that we're raising them — not that I agree. But does that mean you're staying?" She held her breath.

"I don't know yet. I don't know about enlisting. And I don't know if I can stay here, even if I keep working at the factory. I may not have a choice, once the village housing is finished. They're creating pretty much a company town for the workers."

"I've heard. Calgarth. It sounds like a million miles away."

"It's not." David ran his fingers through his hair and stepped closer. Claire loved those waves, thick and dark, hair that girls would fight for. "It's just down the road, not even a half hour by bus."

"They'll want you to stay there and save the petrol."

"Probably, and for security reasons. I'd come back often."

Claire bit her lip. She wouldn't cry. That was stupid. Of course David must leave. She turned away, needing to put some distance between them before she kissed him or cried. She could tell her movement confused him.

"There's one thing I'm a little concerned about, and should probably mention, especially if I'm not able to stay."

"And what's that?" She tried to sound light, and bit her lip again, blinking back the moisture in her eyes.

"The fete's brought the kids closer to one another, formed a camaraderie. For some of them — like Jeanine and Franz — it's the first time they seem to have found their place in the group or a place to shine. I think Jeanine will continue to blossom. Now that she feels free to frequent the piano whenever she likes, she'll have her music. But Franz, for all his surprising tailoring skills, might be a little left behind . . . no more costumes to create from abandoned drapes." She could hear David's half grin but still could not turn to look at him. "We need to find ways to draw him into the band, help him discover more skills, or encourage his natural interests. Josef and Gaston, for all their competitiveness, have formed an alliance. Franz stands outside that. I'd hate to see the little fellow shrink back into himself."

Claire sighed, forcing her attention to the subject at hand. "You're right. . . . I should have noticed, should have thought of him more."

"Well, you did have one or two things on your plate," he teased. "Maybe nothing to worry about, but he bears watching."

Claire could not help herself. She turned and smiled. "You really are the fatherly type, aren't you?"

David's color deepened. "Maybe the older brother type."

Claire felt her own blush rise. "It's late. I'll see you tomorrow." She didn't intend to meet David's eyes again. She wanted only to get away before embarrassing herself further, but he caught her by the arm just before she reached the kitchen door.

"Claire," he whispered. "It's been a good day. You pulled together a fantastic event for everyone and a lot of good connections were made. You can't control what every person does or doesn't do with their opportunities, least of all kids. You're not meant to."

Claire felt a lump rise in her throat, so thick it might have choked her if she hadn't pulled away.

Tired as she was, Claire couldn't sleep. By 2 a.m. she gave up the struggle and slipped from the house with her cloth-covered torch. Though barely a sliver of moonlight shone, her feet made their journey by memory. She inserted the key into the secret garden door, then found her tree and climbed it, its footholds now as familiar as objects in her room. Gaining her resting place, she leaned back against the trunk and tipped her head, immediately enveloped in the night sky awash with stars . . . millions of stars . . . millions too many to count.

There's comfort in knowing that something is so big, so brilliantly beyond me that I can't comprehend it, can't control it — that I need never try. This night sky will always be here, moving its pattern with the seasons but never leaving, never changing in its existence or its all-consuming beauty. If only life could be so clear, so stable, so sure.

Claire breathed deeply of the last of the woodbine honeysuckle and shivered in the cool of the night.

Chapter Twenty-Five

Josef's swollen eyes and purple jaw did not keep him from the first day of school. He didn't mind so much. It was a relief to be away from Bluebell Wood. He'd disappointed Fräulein Claire, and though she seemed to have forgiven him, he could not forget the shame he'd brought on the family.

It was to protect her and Frau Langford and little Aimee that he'd dug the Hitler holes. It was for Fräulein Claire that he'd wanted Wilfred's aggie. If he could not impress her with his military strategies and intent to protect her, he could have impressed her with the winning tolley. Now he daren't show her his prize. She did not approve his fighting and would not approve his stealing marbles. He could not blame her.

Josef sighed. At least he'd been able to retrieve and return Christopher's marbles, no questions asked. He wouldn't take them again. He'd lost his taste for gambling.

Josef's woeful distractions brought unwanted attention from Miss McCoy. He was kept after school that very first day to finish his arithmetic problems, wash the blackboard, and sweep the classroom floor. Josef didn't mind that, either. More than punishment for schoolroom infractions, the labor represented penance for those things he dared not confess.

He finished his tasks as shadows lengthened through the classroom window. With a freer conscience, he set off for Bluebell Wood.

Halfway home, just around the corner that freed him from the village and began the long stretch of narrow, winding road, Wilfred stepped out from behind a tree.

Charging Wilfred had been one thing when Josef stood on his own turf, full of fury for his family and friends. Now he saw the deepening shadows, the loneliness of the road, and that Wilfred was half a foot taller and twenty pounds heavier than he. Josef swallowed. His spit tasted of cardboard. "I've not got your tolley on me, so there's no need to ask." Not that he imagined Wilfred would ask. Josef gripped his lunch satchel and gas mask kit, praying the older boy wouldn't pummel him into the ground.

"I want to play again. I've got to win that tolley back."

"I'm through playing. As you said, they weren't my marbles. I shouldn't have taken them in the first place." Confession felt good to Josef's soul, and the vow helped him stand his ground.

"I might tell Lady Langford that you stole them."

Josef swallowed again. He didn't want that. But losing the marbles to Wilfred would be infinitely worse. "Go ahead, then." And he dared to walk on, past Wilfred, leaving the older boy standing in the middle of the narrow road.

"I've got to have it. I'll do whatever it takes to get it back."

Josef kept walking. He imagined Wilfred meant that he would beat him up, that he'd have to live under the threat of torture for the entire school year. Worse yet, Wilfred might take it into his head to torture one of the others, someone at Bluebell Wood that Josef cared about. That had been the tactic of the brownshirts in Germany. If they couldn't get you to do as they wished, they threatened your family until you complied. The ringing started in Josef's ears and he hurried his steps.

"Wait!" Wilfred called, but Josef kept going. *"Wait!"* He jogged to catch up. "It wasn't mine."

Josef stopped. "You stole your marbles?"

Wilfred had the decency to look ashamed. "The marbles are mine. The tolley belongs to me brother, Jim. It was our da's — a gift from his own da. Look, I should have used mine, but I didn't. I'll play you for it, or I'll trade you mine. It's just as good . . . well, nearly."

"Why did you play with it at all?" Josef knew why he'd taken Christopher's marbles. But why risk something so precious when you had your own?

Wilfred looked away, then scuffed at the dirt. "It was the first time any of us were invited to Bluebell Wood."

"You were showing off." It was a statement, one that Josef tried hard to center in his brain. Wilfred had wanted to show off in front of him and the others at Bluebell Wood, the ones he'd called "dirty Jews."

Wilfred shrugged. "I have to get it back. If you won't play, then trade."

"What?" Josef wasn't opposed to a good trade, especially if he could come up with a redeemable gift for Fräulein Claire.

Wilfred's eyes searched Josef's, as if taking

his measure. "I have somethin' . . . I mean, I can get somethin' really swell, somethin' nobody's ever seen before."

Josef huffed, certain Wilfred had nothing, and pushed past him. "*Ja, ja.* Telephone me."

"I mean it. Can you get out after eleven? After the Home Guard makes its rounds?"

"Are you crazy?"

"This is secret . . . top secret. Meet me tonight — in the cemetery behind the church. Bring the tolley . . . unless you're chicken."

Josef did not understand much British slang, but he understood the challenge. He was not a coward and would not be accused. He walked on a few steps, stopped, then partially turned. "Do not be late. Come alone."

Wilfred nodded — nervously, Josef saw, even in the dimming light.

Gaston turned out the lamp in the center of the room, then ran, diving into bed. He'd memorized how many steps it took in the blacked-out room and had never missed his cot. He clasped his hands behind his head and lay staring at the ceiling. The blackout curtains cut off the stars. It was like living in a cave. Only the breathing of the other boys told him anyone else was near. He could identify Bertram's breathing easily. He was his brother, after all.

At first he and Bertram had been alone in one room. When the German boys came, Madame Langford insisted they move to a larger room and all the boys share. She said it was a dormitory, like boarding school. Everyone had resisted at first, this mixing of French and German. But as the weeks and months piled onto one another, Gaston did not mind so much. Sometimes they stayed awake long into the night, telling one another stories to curdle the blood. Sometimes they spoke of their families. Often, each fell asleep with his own thoughts, his own memories to sort.

Gaston's eyes weighed heavy. It had been a long day, a good day, despite school and lessons, and owing especially to the evening reading. He loved to hear Mademoiselle Claire read. He loved everything about her — the way her hair fell across her forehead and over her eyes when she was perturbed or concentrating. He loved her laugh, which came too seldom. The way she spoke of Monsieur Arnaud might be a thing to be envied, but he saw, despite all she said, that she had eyes for Monsieur David.

He didn't mind so much losing her affections to such a man as David, but Josef's vying for her attention annoyed Gaston. He turned over. Josef wasn't worth thinking about, so why did such a thing keep him awake? He needed sleep for his English history test tomorrow. Why he needed to learn English history was beyond his imagination, but there it was, as immutable as Churchill.

Half an hour may have passed before Gaston counted the regular breathing, the sure sign of sleep, of Bertram, of Peter, of Franz. But what of Josef? Perhaps his rival had turned on his stomach.

Not five minutes later Gaston heard the slow cranking open of the window at the far end of the room. He felt the cool air for just a moment as the blackout curtain was pulled aside, long enough for a boy to slip behind and disappear.

Josef! Gaston nearly called his name aloud. More than wanting to report him or waken the others to join in the questioning, Gaston wanted to know what Josef was up to now. Wasn't he in trouble enough? What might possess him to steal out into the night after curfew? If Madame Langford or Mademoiselle Claire or even Monsieur David caught him — or the Home Guard — *ooh la la*! Gaston winced to think of the reckoning Josef would face.

Curiosity won. Gaston slipped from his bed, pulled on his pants, and shoved his feet into his shoes in one smooth motion. He took his jacket from the hook by the door and crept to the window. Peter turned over and coughed, his sleep interrupted. Gaston froze. He waited for the older boy's rhythmic breathing to resume.

By the time Gaston reached the window and slipped beneath the blackout curtain, he just glimpsed Josef's sprint across the lawn in the pale moonlight.

Gaston hoisted himself through the window and onto the ledge, closing the window behind him as best he could. Step by step he slid toward the ivy-covered stonework, grabbing the vines, catching his feet in the tangles, and climbed down. He and Josef had discovered the strength of the vines when devising plans of escape in case of invasion — a secret they would keep from the others until the need arose.

Gaston made it to the ground. Had Josef left the drive? Had he detoured to the maze? *Where would he go in the middle of the night? Why?*

By the time Gaston reached the drive, Josef was nowhere to be seen. Gaston stopped, steadied his breathing, and listened. Far off he heard the shuffle of gravel.

That meant that Josef was still on the drive. Gaston stepped onto the moss-covered shoulder and sprinted toward the road.

Josef waited in the black shadow of the church's spire, behind the cemetery gate. He was in no hurry to enter the Christian sanctuary of the dead.

Ten minutes passed. Tree limbs, now bare of their leaves, bent in the gathering wind, scraping the cloud-painted black sky, precursor to a storm. Perhaps this was a ruse, a prank on Wilfred's part to embarrass or frighten or chagrin him.

A sound — like a muffled cough — came from somewhere behind.

"Who's there?" No answer. Josef gulped. Louder, Josef called, "Wilfred? Is that you? Come out, like a man." Still no answer. Cold chills flew up Josef's arms and down his legs. Thunder rumbled in the distance. Lightning crackled across the sky, far away. Josef decided he'd waited quite long enough. Wilfred could forget his tolley.

Josef had just gained the road when Wilfred nearly bumped into him.

"You're late." Mostly Josef was relieved to see another human being.

"I had to wait for the Home Guard to pass on. He always stops for a cuppa with Da on his rounds. Did you bring it?"

"Did you? I want to know what you're offering before I agree."

"Follow me; I brought a torch to show you, but we need a place the light won't be seen."

Josef followed, feeling his way through the cemetery gate behind the church, not at all certain this was a good idea. And what about that cough? Did Wilfred have bigger boys lying in wait to jump him? He had no reason to trust Wilfred, except that the older boy had sounded desperate in his plea. Josef's jaw stiffened. He should have left the tolley at home, insisted that they trade in daylight. No one even knew where he'd gone or that he'd left Bluebell Wood.

"Here —" Wilfred broke Josef's train of thought — "behind the mayor's stone. This makes a little cove what you can't see from the road." He pulled something slim from his pocket and flicked on the torch.

"A pencil? You think I'm going to trade that tolley for a pencil?" Now Josef was certain it was a trick.

"That's what it looks like, what it's meant to look like. But it's more. Just look."

Wilfred pulled the eraser from its end. "This here is a compass."

"What?"

"A compass — it gives directions, north, south —"

"I know what a compass is!"

Wilfred twisted the pencil in a way Josef could not quite see, even with the torch. "And the barrel holds a map."

"*Ja,* sure," Josef said sarcastically.

"See?" Wilfred pulled an even slimmer cylinder partway from the barrel. "There's a map of Germany in here — but if I unroll it, I'm not sure I can get it back in. It's thinner than regular paper." He sat back on his haunches. "It's a spy pencil. For the RAF — if they get shot down in Germany. Looks like an ordinary pencil to the Germans, but our aviators break it open and the map helps them get to a safe route where the Underground can help them. The compass tells them which direction to go."

Josef was stunned. "Where did you get it?"

Wilfred did not answer.

"I'm not trading unless you tell me."

"I took it from my uncle's bag. I heard him talking to my da about it. They work at the pencil factory in Keswick, so I guess they're both in on it. Top secret, I heard them say — nobody's to know. So you can't tell anybody. It'd be treason."

"I'm not the one telling."

Josef sensed Wilfred's uncomfortable shift.

"You're not going to help the Nazis."

"No, I'm not." Josef warmed with that bit of trust.

"I told you it was good." Wilfred hesitated. "Is it a deal?"

It was a good trade. What did Josef care for Wilfred's tolley, anyway? But the pencil, a real live spy pencil, was a coup, even if he couldn't tell anyone.

Uncomfortably, the scrolled map inside the pencil casing reminded Josef of the mezuzah at home in Germany — the tiny rolled parchment inside the casing that hung on their front doorpost containing the words of the Shema from Deuteronomy, exhorting him to keep the words and commands of Adonai constantly in his mind and heart. He doubted Adonai looked kindly on the deal he was going to make or his motivation.

Then inspiration flashed through Josef's mind: a Christmas gift — an ordinary-looking pencil for Fräulein Claire, who loved to write, with a note coiled inside, or an intimate poem he'd write especially for her. That might please Adonai and would make her forget Arnaud and turn her eyes from Herr David. She need never know the pencil once held an aviator's map. He'd keep that forever, a fine wartime souvenir.

"*Ja,* okay." Josef pushed any twinge of guilt away and pulled the tolley from his pocket. They traded, hand for hand. To seal the deal, to make certain Wilfred would forever look on him as an equal, Josef stuck out his hand.

Wilfred did not hesitate, but shook it firmly. "Ta."

Josef grinned in the dark. "Ta."

Chapter Twenty-Six

Claire picked up two letters from the post office the first week of October. One was for Aimee, from Mr. Lewis.

"*The* Mr. Lewis?" Mrs. Newsome asked incredulously as Claire dropped the mail into the housekeeper's hands.

Claire didn't answer, but took the stairs two at a time to her room and locked the door. She'd been just as flabbergasted at Mr. Lewis's return address as Mrs. Newsome, until she'd seen the other letter, addressed to her, from Sylvia Beach, by way of Sylvia's parents.

Claire ripped her letter open. Sylvia wrote that she expected this would be her last batch of letters to get out of France for the foreseeable future, so she was writing everyone she could. The first part seemed nearly a form letter, probably copied from letters she'd written to other family and friends.

Between Sylvia's nationality and her Jewish affiliations — especially the hiring of an eighteen-year-old Jewish girl — the Nazis had pretty well finished Shakespeare and Company. They were compelled to declare themselves to the *Kommandantur* and to register once a week. Sylvia didn't know how long she could keep the bookstore open, or what the future might hold for her or their friends — so many of whom had moved away or emigrated to other countries — but wrote that she'd never be sorry she'd come to France. She finished the front page of her letter, "France is my home, my life."

Claire turned the single page over. There, everything became personal.

I am sorry to be the bearer of bad news, but Josephine has begged me to write you. Last week, she and her husband were shot by a German patrol while helping a local family. She said you would understand what that meant.

Arnaud was killed instantly, and Josephine severely wounded. She is in hospital but receiving poor care. The Germans let me see her only once. She was barely conscious and is not expected to live.

I suspect they have questioned her rather brutally. Her main concern was for you, Claire, and that I tell you she is so very sorry, and that she loved Arnaud with all her heart. She also said something I am not certain I have right: that Arnaud was not delayed, that his intention all along was to send you to safety.

I never quite understood why you left Paris so abruptly, Claire. Josephine said you were called suddenly away. I assumed that meant your aunt needed you, once I learned where you'd gone. Now I wonder if there is more to that story.

Know that you have my sincere sympathy. We will all miss Josephine, and Arnaud was . . . Well, he was our charming Arnaud, so full of life and fun. I know they were your close and particular friends. I remember the gay times you three enjoyed in the bookstore of an evening. Arnaud and Josephine seemed very happy, very much in love. I hope that knowledge will be of some comfort to you.

If I am able to send further word of Josephine's condition, I will, but do not expect it. I fear our mail, even to America, will be cut off very soon.

Claire dropped the letter, curled into a fetal ball, and wept.

■ ■ ■ ■

For four days Aimee clutched her letter to her chest inside her vest. *A letter! For me!*

Aimee had never received a letter. She had hoped for a long time that one might come from her maman or papa, that they might write and say they were coming to take her home. Perhaps they would write that they were coming to England to live, or perhaps they would just appear on the doorstep one day, having been smuggled into the country as she had been.

But after so many months, Aimee had stopped believing, stopped hoping, even stopped fantasizing that such a thing might happen. Madame Newsome said that her letters could not reach Paris now, because of the war. But Mademoiselle Claire had said they could go all over the United Kingdom. Aimee decided if she could not write her parents or they her, then she would write Mr. Lewis. She liked his voice on the wireless. He sounded like a kindly man, a grandfatherly man, a man who understood the ugliness of this war that tore families apart and the need for kindness among people. Madame Newsome said he was an author, like Mrs. Heelis. Mrs. Heelis appreciated Aimee's drawings; perhaps Mr. Lewis would as well.

When Aimee had drawn her picture for Mr. Lewis and Mademoiselle Claire had mailed it with a letter of her own explaining, it was like sending a note in a bottle on Lake Windermere. Aimee hardly imagined it would truly reach him, let alone that he would respond.

Then Mr. Lewis's letter came, and it was as if a new world opened — as if, in the moment Madame Newsome handed her the envelope, she'd stepped through glass doors into a world beyond her own, or fallen down the rabbit hole in Alice's world, from the story Mademoiselle Claire had read especially for her. The only person Aimee wished to share her letter with was mademoiselle, but she seemed terribly preoccupied and distressed.

So Aimee did not open her letter all that day or the next, or the next, though everyone from Mrs. Newsome to Madame Langford urged her to do so. She waited until the fourth day, until bedtime, until all the other children were tucked into their beds and she could hear their soft, whiffling breath. She even waited until she heard Mademoiselle Claire's weary steps trudge up from the library, and until she heard the latch click on her bedroom door.

Aimee slipped from her bed, clutching her now-wrinkled envelope, and padded down the hallway to Mademoiselle Claire's room. She knocked softly. No answer. She knocked again, this time a bit more loudly.

"Yes? Is someone there?" Mademoiselle Claire's voice came weepy and hollow from the other side of the door.

"*Oui,* mademoiselle. *C'est moi* — Aimee."

"Aimee?" Mademoiselle Claire swung open the door, swiping at moisture overflowing her eyes. "What is it? Are you all right? Is anything wrong?"

"*Oui,* mademoiselle, I am well, and, *non,* nothing is mistaken." Aimee hesitated again, aware that mademoiselle seemed burdened with her own troubles. But Aimee could wait no longer. She pulled the letter from behind her back. "Will you read it to me?"

Mademoiselle Claire's eyes blinked and blinked again. Her bosom heaved a sigh and a frown creased her forehead. She looked as if she would refuse, and then a sad smile slowly dawned in her weary eyes, a smile that rose the sun in Aimee's heart. "*Oui.* You haven't read it yet? No one's read it to you?"

Aimee shook her head. "I want only you to read it, *je t'en prie.* You helped me to write

Monsieur Lewis, to send him my drawing. It is for you and for me to know what he thinks."

Mademoiselle Claire tilted her head in the kindly way grown-ups did and reached for Aimee's hand, sending a thrill through the little girl. Aimee followed her into the room and to the pretty blue-and-wine-colored braided rug near the fire. Mademoiselle set pillows against the chair and invited Aimee to join her. She climbed immediately into Mademoiselle Claire's lap and tore open the envelope.

The letter was written on cream-colored stationery, very thin with little white space between the lines. Aimee gasped in disbelief. She shook the envelope and peeked inside, in case there was something more, then let out a disappointed sigh. "There are no pictures, mademoiselle! Not one!"

Mademoiselle, even through her watery eyes, looked as if she was trying not to smile. Aimee's back straightened, and she squirmed from Mademoiselle Claire's lap. *Do grown-ups understand nothing?*

"Wait, Aimee." Mademoiselle pulled her back. "Don't you want to know what he says?"

"What does it matter? I sent him my best drawing of the newborn lambs on the fells.

Perhaps he did not think it pretty."

"But he did. And he sent you a picture with his words — just like when we read stories at night. Lean in and close your eyes. Imagine what the words would look like in a picture. Listen to what he writes:

Dear Aimee,

I am very glad you wrote and sent me your fine drawing. I have always wanted to visit the Lake District in springtime and see the newborn lambs frolicking over the fells. Now, thanks very much to you and your drawing, I have. I especially liked how jolly the two in the meadow appeared, dancing on their hind hooves and tossing bouquets of tufted purple vetch into the air. The foxgloves made fine parasols, though I've never seen ones so big. Perhaps they grow that way in the Lake District.

I was not surprised to learn that the lambs in Windermere wear brown brogans. Those things seem appropriate for a mountainous region where it rains a great deal. I think your friend Mrs. Heelis would approve.

When I was your age, my brother, Warnie, and I created a world of creatures that walked about on two feet and wore clothes, much like your young lambs. We called our kingdom Boxen. All the animals spoke Boxonian. Being boys, our stories were consumed with battles and espionage by such creatures as sword-wielding mice.

Like you, I was inspired by Miss Beatrix Potter's (whom you now know as Mrs. Heelis) books of talking animals. She is a wonderful artist and storyteller. If envy weren't such a difficult character trait to overcome, I might envy your opportunity to meet with her and learn from her.

Keep drawing, Aimee, and keep faith. I hope the very best for your dear parents. I know they miss you very much. Let me know how you get on.

Yours ever,
C. S. Lewis

Snuggled on the rug by the fireside, her head on mademoiselle's knee, Aimee felt toasty and cozy. But that was nothing compared with the sleepy warmth that spread through her. *Content.* It was a word she'd heard from Madame Newsome — a good word, and it fit the moment.

The last thing Aimee remembered was Mademoiselle Claire lifting her up and pulling her head to her shoulder. She heard mademoiselle sniff back tears, but Aimee was too sleepy to speak. She reached for mademoiselle's cheek to comfort her and patted it with her hand, precipitating a fresh flow of tears. She hoped mademoiselle knew that she loved her.

Mademoiselle Claire smelled of lilac water, so that was what Aimee imagined as she was carried back to her room: lilacs and springtime, frolicking lambs and sword-wielding mice swashbuckling and victory-parading up and down the fells. Aimee's last thought was that Evelyn might make a very nice name for a little lamb sporting a yellow bonnet festooned in pink rosettes. She would draw her first thing in the morning. Monsieur Lewis might be interested, especially if Evelyn rowed across Lake Windermere and met a mouse prince in his land of Boxen. Mr. Lewis hadn't said if such a prince might be handsome. She would leave that to Evelyn to decide.

Claire rubbed the weariness from her eyes. Three in the morning, and she hadn't slept. For days and nights she'd wrestled with the ghosts that Sylvia Beach's letter had resurrected. *Arnaud — dead. Arnaud and Josephine — a couple — married.* It seemed an impossibility, and yet one she'd known might come, had suspected in the depths of her soul. And for all its horror, she knew the relationship to be true, to be right between them.

Even Josephine knew it would comfort Claire to know that they had truly loved one another . . . or was that Sylvia? Claire buried her face in her hands. She couldn't remember, couldn't sort it out. She didn't want Josephine to suffer, didn't want her to die, and yet, perversely, Claire wanted her to feel shame for taking Arnaud, for loving him when she'd known that was the dream Claire had nurtured. *Why? Why — any of this?*

For months Claire had hoped and waited for reassurance of Arnaud's love — reassurance that never came. And now, in one unexpected moment, it was as if all that waiting had been a dream, and her time in France, believing he'd loved her, a farce. Josephine, her best and closest friend, had betrayed her. Claire should be livid, but she realized at last that she wasn't. She wasn't anything. *Everything is so mixed up. I don't know what to feel, to think, only that I can't be loved. I'm not worthy of being loved by anyone. I knew this before. I've feared it always. Why am I surprised when the history of my life repeats itself?*

And yet, this evening Aimee had crawled into her lap and leaned her tousled head against Claire's heart, vulnerably offering her own heart. Aimee needed her, wanted her love and care. Aimee loved her; Claire saw this.

But Claire had almost pushed love away again. It wasn't the romantic love she'd craved from Arnaud, the thing she so desperately wanted.

Why do I do that? Why do I push away what's offered and crave what I can't have?

Because you're afraid.

The voice wasn't audible but spoke itself into Claire's mind as clearly as if someone had walked into the room and tapped her on the shoulder. *Of course I'm afraid. I'm terrified that if I love someone, they'll leave me — just like Arnaud, like Josephine, like my father did. Just like my mother, who was there, but never there, not really. I'm afraid of losing anyone I love, of being rejected, so I withhold love from those who want it and seek it where I can't have it. What kind of crazy, sick cycle is this?*

And then came revelation. *I don't want to live like that — like this! But I can't change. Help me! Oh, please help me!*

I love you.

Claire gasped. The voice in her head again — or was it her heart? — came so clear.

She turned off the light and lay back against the pillow. C. S. Lewis, in one of his broadcasts, had talked about God's rebuilding project — how you so want to be a decent little cottage, but He rearranges and knocks the house about in a way that hurts abominably, adding a wing here and a floor there, running up towers and making courtyards with the sole purpose of building a palace that He intends to come and live in. Claire certainly felt rearranged and knocked about. Dared she believe God loved her, that He wanted to build within her a place to live — a palace?

Claire punched her pillow and closed her eyes. The clock ticked on and on, each tick driving her eyelids wider. Before dawn she dressed and paced the floor. Finally, she scribbled a note and slipped it beneath David's door, then walked downstairs to wait in the library.

A half hour before breakfast, David opened the library door, his forehead creased in worry. "I just saw your note. Are you okay? One of the kids sick?"

Claire shook her head. "Nothing like that. I need to talk to someone." She couldn't keep the trembling from her voice.

David hesitated less than a moment before reaching for her hands and pulling her toward the settee. "Talk to me."

Claire swallowed. The knot in her throat had swollen thick. "I don't know where to begin."

"Your aunt told me a letter came from France a few days ago. She told me about your friend Arnaud." He spoke softly, kindly, still clasping her hands.

Claire couldn't keep the tears from spilling over her lashes. "He was shot and killed." The words still sounded foreign in Claire's ears, measured and far away.

"I'm sorry. I'm so very sorry." He rubbed one of her knuckles with his thumb.

"I've been waiting for him all this time . . . ever since I came to England. He and my best friend were — became a couple. I didn't know that before now."

"He was a fool, and a cad."

David's vehemence startled Claire. She'd thought he might belittle her, tell her she'd been living in a dream world all this time she'd imagined Arnaud loved her. She feared David might see her as a silly schoolgirl mooning over a teacher — an older man.

"Look, it would be easy for me to run the

man into the ground for the way he treated you. But we don't know what's happened there, what's happening now, and not knowing, I guess I shouldn't hang him." David rubbed her knuckle more fiercely. "I just hate to see you hurt, and I could do some serious damage to any man who does that, dead or alive."

Claire breathed. She'd loved Arnaud with all the love of her young heart, despite his long silence, despite his not coming for her, but it felt a relief to have someone champion her now.

"That's not really why I needed to see you. Something else happened," she whispered. In the light of day it seemed almost silly. Still, Claire knew she couldn't live with the uncertainty any longer.

David waited.

"I heard a voice. I mean, it was like someone spoke in my mind — a clear and deep impression, more than a voice — someone I don't know."

David's brow furrowed. "I'm not sure I understand."

Claire almost laughed in frustration. "Neither do I. I was hoping you might."

"What did the voice say?" David released one of her hands but kept hold of the other.

That small pulling away, the dropping of

one of her hands, made Claire feel less connected, more alone. She withdrew her other hand and wrapped her arms around her waist, wishing she'd not started this conversation. But she needed help, needed to talk it through.

In for a penny, in for a pound. "It said — it knew — I was afraid." There. As outlandish as it sounded, she'd said it. "It even seemed to understand my fear of loving Aimee, of loving anyone."

David's eyes probed hers. "Sounds like the Holy Spirit to me."

"The what?"

"God the Holy Spirit . . . our guide, our comforter."

"It came out of the blue," Claire whispered. "And then it said, 'I love you.' "

David smiled, his eyes shining. "Definitely God."

"But how do I know? How can I be sure — either that He is really there, or if He is, that He means this, that He wants me? How do I know He won't lead me to believe He loves me and then rip my heart and moorings away? Jerk me like a puppet on strings?"

"Like Arnaud?"

"Arnaud didn't —" She couldn't finish, but turned her eyes away. "Maybe I was the only one in love . . . or maybe I was in love with love. I don't know. But this is different."

"To get this love you want — to really own it — you have to surrender to God your greatest fear and trust Him, even for your greatest desire. Do you know what those are?"

"I can't trust anyone." It was an angry truth Claire clutched close to her heart.

David started to speak, but she rushed over his words. "If He loves me, why did Arnaud die? Why didn't He give me what I wanted?" Claire pulled farther away. "I don't know whether it's worse to believe or not believe. One might be ignorance, but the other is to live in terror that He'll take away whatever He's offering . . . or that He'll punish me because I can't buy into that. Worse, He might punish those I love — like Arnaud, or Josephine." The words choked her and the tears of confession, of release, came.

"That's because you don't know Him — yet. You're not seeing Him; you're looking at your circumstances and confusing those with Him. Life is hard. We all have circumstances."

Claire's defenses flew up. " 'Circumstances'? And what 'circumstances' do you have? Who has ever betrayed you by loving the person you love or by dying, by being shot in the street? Who has ever abandoned you the way my father abandoned me — disowned me? Or my mother, so caught up in her own grief that she had no time for me. She couldn't even leave off her drink long enough to come to my college graduation. She forgot!"

"I'm sorry, Claire. I'm so sorry. I know the pain of —"

"Of what? Of no one caring? No one wanting you? How would you know? How would you have any idea?" She spat the words. "Don't tell me you understand or that you know anything about abandonment. Don't tell me to trust this God of yours, because I know He'll let me down, just like every other person in my life."

"You're right about one thing." David's reply came in a whisper, through nearly clenched teeth.

"What?"

"Every person you ever meet will let you down. Arnaud is just the latest. They might not abandon you, but they will fail at some point to be all that you need, all that you want."

Claire felt the earth shift. This wasn't what she'd wanted from David.

"There is only One who will never leave

you or forsake you. There's only One who said and really meant, 'Though a mother forgets her suckling child, I will not forget thee.' There's only One ready to carry our wounds and forgive us our worst, and still love us with everlasting love." Tears filled David's eyes, but he didn't wipe them away.

What pain does he know? He knows something. Claire almost reached for his hand but stopped herself.

David searched her face so long she couldn't pull her eyes away. "You said your mother kept you at bay."

Claire nodded. "That was a polite description of our relationship."

"Mine didn't. The sun rose and set for her in our family — my father, my sister, and me — I thought."

"You're lucky. I didn't know you had a sister."

"My parents emigrated to the Appalachian Mountains soon after I was born."

"So you really are Scottish?"

"Aye." He smiled sadly. "My dad was a second son — not the firstborn to inherit the family estate. That went to my uncle. Dad had been a gold leaf worker in Edinburgh — leather bindings and front leaves of books, that sort of thing. An artisan. There was no call for such work once machines came on to do the work faster, more uniformly. That's why he emigrated, looking for a fresh start in the land of golden opportunity." David snorted. "There was certainly no call for gold leaf work in the mountains of West Virginia. No golden opportunity, either."

"What did he do?"

"Coal mines, and all that goes with them. Bent back, black lung. He was an artist, not a laborer, and the work belowground wore him down. He died when I was ten. My sister was six."

"I'm so sorry. I had no idea."

"We'd had a good life, the four of us. Poor enough, but that didn't matter. Food on the table and shoes beneath . . . sometimes." David stared into the lamp as if he saw his story written there. "But when Dad died, there was no income. I left school to go down into the mines, but Mother pulled me out, swearing she'd not lose another to the dark and dank."

"Did she go to work?"

"After a fashion." David looked at Claire, and then away, just as quickly. "She sold herself to the foreman of the mine."

Claire straightened, the breath pulled out of her.

"There was no work for women in the

mining towns. We were on the verge of being forced from our house. The mine owned everything, and we were in debt with the doctor, the company store, even the undertaker."

"I'm so sorry. It must have been awful for her." Claire didn't know what else to say.

David knotted and unknotted his hands. "She went to him two weeks after Dad died. Hardly the grieving widow. I suspected that there must have been something between them even before Dad died. Maybe that's not fair."

He stood and walked to the hearth, kneading the back of his neck. "She asked him to take us all in. I begged her not to, swore I'd find work. I'd already quit school. I would find something else if she wouldn't let me go to the mines — move to the flatlands, anything. I begged her to write Uncle Hamish — my dad's brother, the one who'd inherited. Surely he'd send money, maybe even bring us all back to Scotland."

"Did she?"

"She said Dad had died for her a long time before, when he first got sick, and that she had no claim on his brother."

"Do you think she was telling you the truth — about their marriage, I mean?"

"I believed her then, and hated her for it.

But what did I know? I was ten."

"So she went to live with — with the foreman?"

"We all did. He had the decency to marry her; I'll give him that. But he wanted none of me. I don't think he wanted Kirstine, either, but Mother would never part with her. He had Mother write to Uncle Hamish after all, tell him to take me. If Uncle Hamish hadn't, Jared Smith swore he'd have thrown me into the orphanage in Elkins."

"But she wanted you, surely. . . . She had no say." Claire tried to comprehend the woman's position, the idea of being trapped.

David turned to face her. "She didn't want me, Claire. I reminded her too much of my father. I begged her, day after day, not to marry Smith; then when she did, I begged her to leave him. She said she couldn't forge a new life by hanging on to the past, that I'd drag her down." Despite his clenched jaw, the muscle near David's eye twitched. "The way it was all arranged — so that I couldn't go back, didn't even know when or where I was going until I was actually on my way — I never even got to say good-bye to my sister. I never said good-bye, and I never saw her again."

"After this war, surely you can —"

"Someone — I never found out who — sent me a newspaper clipping two years later giving Kirstine's obituary." He choked on the words, stopped, took a deep breath. "She died of diphtheria. It sounded as if an epidemic swept the area. I wrote to Mother, but the letter was returned, marked *Refused* in her handwriting." David pushed long fingers through his thick hair. "All those years I waited for a letter, a word from her. I wrote her — and my sister, while she was alive — regularly at first. But every letter came back. The only word was when Mother wrote to Uncle Hamish telling him to make me stop writing, that he should see to it that I got on with my life. That I had no future with her or her family."

"I'm so sorry. Her husband must have made her do that."

"I wanted to believe that at first, but it made no sense. I even sent a letter to the house of a neighbor, a woman I was sure could get word to her privately. Now, with things I've seen, with what I know you've been through . . . I don't know. I sometimes wonder if she thought she was doing me a favor, sending me to a different life."

"What do you mean? How is that like me?"

"What if Arnaud sent you away, made you

think you had to go without him not because he couldn't get there or deserted you, but to save you? What if he intended to get you out of France all along because he knew what was coming?"

Time stopped for Claire. *That's what Josephine said. But I don't know. Is that possible?*

"Regardless, here we both are, and missing those we love. You miss your friends. I miss my sister."

"That's why you're so good with the children here . . . so compassionate. You understand them."

"I know what it is to be sent far from home and not be able to go back. I don't think any of these kids were sent away because they were unloved. They were sent to safety because they were much loved."

That was true. The children's parents loved them; Claire was sure of it. And if that was true, perhaps Arnaud had loved her, too, in his own way . . . like a parent? Claire cringed. Had she misread him? Had he misled her? There was no way to know now, no way to be certain. How was she to live with that?

After breakfast and before morning lessons, Claire made it up the stairs, her heart heavy and her brain spinning so much her head hurt. She closed her bedroom door, leaned her back against it, and slid to the floor, wishing so much that she believed in God enough to ask Him for help, for guidance, for information, for something to help her be strong and resilient and all she needed to be.

She wondered if she'd ever truly been in love with Arnaud or even wanted the life of Hemingway or Sylvia Beach and her friends. Or had she been mesmerized by their glittering lives . . . by their pursuit of fame, their tantalizing wit and charm and dreams of . . . of what? Red wine swirling in the bottom of cracked crystal? It had been like living in the pages of a novel being written — a novel that wasn't her own life or her own voice.

What exactly had she wanted when she'd thought their lives were the be-all and end-all of romance? Had she been in love with writing or with fantasy? Had she been in love with Arnaud or in love with love? What was love, anyway, and how did one get it, let alone give it? How did a person become worthy to achieve it?

Claire had no idea. She sat alone in the still-blacked-out room, not wanting to let in the daylight.

At last she stood. She might have no idea what love was or whom or how to trust, but she knew someone who might, someone Aimee had found a faithful friend outside the confines of Bluebell Wood.

Claire sat at her writing table, turned on the lamp, and drew stationery from the drawer.

Dear Mr. Lewis,

You don't know me, but I've read your book and listened to your wireless broadcasts each week, and you've given me much to think about. You've also been so kind as to write to a little girl I care very much about. Your letter has been an encouragement, a help to her in these uncertain times, so I hope you might be willing to help me understand. . . .

A half hour later she sealed the letter and set the stamp, half daring to hope for clarification, for a friend. When she drew open the curtains, daylight, and a flickering of anticipation, flooded the room.

Chapter Twenty-Seven

Claire knew that Rabbi Meir had sacrificed much in making the long journey to work with Bertram in his Hebrew studies, often staying overnight to avoid travel on Shabbat.

Peter had coached his friend in between — a beautiful thing to see. Bertram had worked willingly and hard. Claire marveled at how the boys had set aside their differences and even their national pride to work closely in pursuit of something higher, something clearly more important to each of them.

The day of the anticipated bar mitzvah at Bluebell Wood broke bright and cold, the skies awash in brilliant sunshine, billowing white clouds, and October blue.

Claire claimed a chair between Mrs. Newsome and Aimee in the library, her aunt conspicuously absent. "Where is Aunt Miranda?"

"She's done in, poor dear, and sends her regrets," Mrs. Newsome whispered.

"She's not coming down?" Claire knew her aunt had seemed more tired of late, the violet circles beneath her eyes darker. But she couldn't imagine that she would miss Bertram's bar mitzvah for anything short of catastrophe. Her eyes reached for Dr. MacDonald, who'd slipped into the back of the room at that moment, but he was focused on Bertram. What were Mrs. Newsome and her aunt not telling her? What had she missed, taken up as she was with her own worries?

"She spoke to Bertram this morning, in her room, and told him how very proud she is of him." Mrs. Newsome smiled through shining eyes. No one could have looked prouder than Mrs. Newsome, who sniffed repeatedly into her handkerchief as Bertram stood with the rabbi, surrounded by those who had come to love him.

Before Claire could think more of Aunt Miranda, the service began, and she marveled at the outpouring of love for this young man. To be loved by everyone who knew him — such a feat loomed unknowable, unachievable to her. *And yet Bertram's never asked for that gift. He simply receives it, all the while being himself.*

She'd asked Mr. Lewis to explain love: love from the God of the universe and love between people — what it meant, how it was done, how it could be earned. She'd asked him about Jesus and how His ransom worked. Her face warmed to think of the things she'd dared to ask. *He must think me ridiculously young and naive.* She almost hoped the letter had never reached him, that it had gone astray through some wartime mishap. But more than her embarrassment, her utter vulnerability, she wanted to know, and she hadn't known whom else to ask. Writing her questions on paper had seemed so much more possible than asking them to the face of another human being.

Claire breathed deeply. She so wanted to understand.

Though Claire could not translate a word of Bertram's melodic Hebrew chanting as he read from the precious yellowed scroll — the scroll the rabbi said had come from Jerusalem over one hundred years before — she grasped his mix of pride and fierce loss in performing the ceremony without his own father. Her heart ached for the fine young man.

She remembered what David had said about their raising the children, about being the only family they had now, and the reality that there was no way to know if the young people would ever see their parents again. Claire had not wanted to believe that, to own any of it. But now she swallowed the choke in her throat.

Until the war ended, Rabbi Meir had lamented, there would likely be no way to purchase a traditional prayer shawl — what he'd called a *tallith* — for the young man. Mrs. Newsome had kindly offered to whip something up on the treadle sewing machine for Bertram; she declared she would have been that glad to do it, and to add whatever knotted tassels they wanted. The rabbi and Bertram had respectfully declined Mrs. Newsome's offer, exchanging meaningful glances that Claire couldn't decipher.

What Claire had not expected, when the moment came, was for Peter to stand up and share his tallith — to cover his friend's shoulders with his own prayer shawl, the one inherited from his own presumed-dead father and grandfather. The two young men stood side by side, their shoulders touching and covered — brothers united in prayer before God and man.

Claire's heart lurched and her eyes smarted. *Perhaps this really is family.*

Dr. MacDonald congratulated Bertram

heartily and shook Peter's hand. He thanked Rabbi Meir for all he'd done and continued to do for the children, then waited for the meal prayer and for the gramophone music to begin before slipping from the festive bar mitzvah celebration in the dining room.

He walked swiftly up the stairs, paused outside Miranda's door, and tentatively knocked. He didn't want to wake her if she slept, but he would not allow the moment to pass. He'd waited too long as it was.

"Come in." The voice on the other side of the door came weaker than he would have liked. He steeled himself for a battle of wits while summoning every ounce of Scottish diplomacy he could muster.

"We missed you, Maggie. You'd have been proud of our boy — of all of them."

Miranda pulled herself to a sitting position in her bed, wrapping her bed jacket close about her. "Mrs. Newsome's already stopped in and told me of Peter's kindness. I'd no idea that they'd planned anything so symbolic. Such fine young men, both of them."

"Aye." He nodded, raising his brows, uncertain how to begin.

"Don't give me that look, Raibeart. I'm simply tired. I'd have gone if I could. I didn't stay away because of Christopher, if that's what you're thinking."

"That dinna cross my mind, my darlin' girl. I know you would have been there if at all possible. It's that that concerns me."

Miranda shifted in her bed and smiled faintly, unable to keep a trace of worry from her brow. "Old age? What can I say?" She attempted to laugh.

"You're not even fifty." He didn't smile.

"Nearly."

"What is it, Maggie? You must tell me what ails you."

"I don't know." Her eyes pierced his, but he saw that she couldn't hold the connection and looked away. "If I knew, I would tell you. I would do something about it."

"Would you?"

"Of course I would! How can you ask me that?"

"Because that's not been your response, not since Christopher . . ."

"Not since Christopher died. You can say it, Raibeart. Even I can say it now."

"That's something."

"Yes, it is. The children here have made that possible. I never imagined I could . . ." She looked up at him, her eyes pleading for his understanding. "They, and Claire, have given me —"

"Life?" he finished.

"A reason to go on — to want to go on . . . at least for a while."

"Then we must get to the bottom of this." He ignored her last phrase. "I know a doctor in London, at the —"

"I'm not going to London! I won't leave Bluebell Wood — not while the children are here, not while they need me."

"Maggie —" he sat on the bed beside her and took her hand — "I've done all I can for you, all you'll allow me to do. I've not got the equipment doctors there have, and if I don't miss my guess, you're going to need treatment I canna provide."

"You know what it is, don't you?"

He could not stand the stark fear in her eyes, nor could he abide the resignation that followed. "We won't know until we know. And we won't know until you have the necessary examinations and tests. The sooner we have a diagnosis, the sooner you can be treated."

"If it's — if it is what I fear, it would mean surgery." She looked away, withdrawing her hand. "I don't want surgery. I don't want to be half a person . . . half a woman." She blinked back tears.

It was all Raibeart could do not to beat his head against the wall and shout at her. Fear had wound its menacing tentacles through his gut over the past months. He'd made mental excuses when she'd not rallied from the influenza. She'd refused the more intimate examination he'd offered, but if not by him, it must be done by someone. Her life was worth far more than her pride. Of that he was certain; for that he was desperate. But anger and frustration would not work with his Maggie, so he knelt beside the bed, as if to plead. "You will never be less than you are, Maggie, darlin' — the most beautiful woman in the world. That's what you've always been and will always be to me."

"I need more time. Remembrance Day is almost here. I must stand for Christopher, and for Gilbert. And then, Thanksgiving. I want Thanksgiving here, with the children."

He pushed frustrated fingers through his thick silver hair. "And then you'll be wantin' Christmas, and New Year! Don't you understand, Maggie? Time is of the essence. It can make all the difference to — to —"

"Life or death?"

"To everything. To *everything,* my girl. Please . . . please, Maggie." He turned away, unable to keep his chin steady. He'd never crumbled before Miranda Langford, not in all the years he'd known her, not in all the joys and sorrows that they'd shared. But he'd never felt so desperate.

At last he felt her fingers trace his arm. He looked up, hoping against hope and reason.

"I'll think about it, Raibeart. I promise."

He took her fingers in his hand and brought them to his lips. "For love of all that's holy, don't take too long."

By mid-October the fells and valleys of the Lake District reveled and burned in color — shades of gold, orange, and rich mahogany amid evergreens and the earthy browns of autumn. Still, it was the first time Claire missed home. Growing up, she'd made an annual class trip to New England in the fall. She wished the children from Europe could see the northern Appalachians in their glory — brilliant crimson, pumpkin orange, and every rich shade of gold and butter yellow.

In Claire's mind, autumn was both a time of new beginnings and a time of mellowing, of drawing in — the new year of school, with its sheets of pristine notebook paper and the hope of stimulating classroom lectures, balanced by long evenings before the fire, cozy under a warm quilt, a mug of hot spiced cider by her side, transported lands away by a compelling read from a favorite author.

Mrs. Newsome, uncommon to her nature, declared it cruelty on students and teachers alike to keep the children shut up in the schoolhouse on glorious days, to expect them to attend to lessons when birdsong and the last of autumn's brazen leaf showers beckoned. It was far too easy for young minds to worry and wander home to France or Germany in this golden, melancholy time.

By late October hedgerows of the Lake District grew thick with wild rose hips, more than enough to route the Women's Institute into forming bands for collection. There was no time to lose, as long as the rose hips could be picked by the buckets full and processed in a timely fashion.

"We can make teas and jams — though not so sweet without the rationed sugar, I'm sorry to say. Above all, rose-hip syrup is essential to the war effort — all that vitamin C for the young ones." Mrs. Newsome instructed Claire as they prepared the dining room before the breakfast gong was rung. "They're best now we've had a bite of frost. Tell the children to pick only the bright-red ones, a mite soft, but not shriveled. Leave the rest for the birds and squirrels. Collecting rose hips is the perfect thing to get these youngsters out and about. I've spoken with the village teacher, and she's all for sending them out a day or two at the end of the week. Poor thing, she looks ready to drop."

"I know how she feels," Claire admitted, pushing a stray tendril back from her forehead, "but won't the board say we should have organized the event for a Saturday?"

"Pish-posh. I don't care what they say. Bureaucrats! The WI is intent on the collection and they'll be able to process them on Friday and, if necessary, Saturday. We have so few days with no rain. We must take advantage of each one! Besides, the board should try corralling eighty youngsters into a classroom built for forty-five! It will do them all a world of good — and you, too, Miss Claire, if you don't mind my saying so. You've grown rather pale of late."

"It's just so hard to keep everything going at once, to mind all the children and their needs."

"They look to you for everything now, don't they? I know my lady is not up to doing what she was," Mrs. Newsome confided.

"I've tried to take worry of the children off her," Claire said, setting the last of the silverware in place. "Is there something more you think I should do?"

"Not at all. You and Mr. David have done

a tremendous job in that way. She's just so very weary, and she sleeps more of a day."

"I could try to keep them quieter, I suppose, but —"

"No, Miss Claire; they're children after all, and I think their shouts and running laughter through the gardens are the best medicine for her spirits. I just wish I knew what more to do for her. She seems to be languishing, and I don't know why."

"What does Dr. MacDonald say?"

"I'm not privy to that. He comes and goes, frustrated and terribly worried, I can see, but he's said nothing to me and it's all beyond my ken." Mrs. Newsome nearly dropped the teapot, spilled some on the white damask cloth, and scolded herself.

Claire sopped up the spreading splotch as best she could and ushered the older woman to a chair. "You love her." Love was still such a mystery to Claire.

"Oh, my . . . ever since that first winter's day Lord Langford carried her over the threshold. Such a bride, she was . . . so young and inexperienced in every way." Mrs. Newsome shook her head. "Hadn't a clue or a care in the world but that she loved the master with all her heart. She gave him everything he longed for until he was called to war." She dabbed at her eyes with her sleeve. "You're the spitting image of her at that age, Miss Claire."

"Well, I am her spitting image if she hadn't a clue. I certainly don't."

"You're doin' fine. Better than you know. Even the doctor says so."

Claire doubted that. She wasn't like her aunt at this age in one way. She certainly had no husband to love with all her heart.

"Well, we may not be able to rally her ladyship," Mrs. Newsome clucked, "but we can rally these children. They all need a bit of cheering up. A day of rose-hip plucking in the October sunshine might be just the thing. Let's hope the weather holds."

Claire hadn't anticipated the joy and freedom to be found in such a day, or in the polite nods and occasional smile, in the few words of conversation here and there from villagers who'd attended the fete. It felt a new day to Claire, a new beginning. Mrs. Creedle had even packed a picnic lunch, and Mrs. Newsome included linen tablecloths to be spread across the frosted meadow. Bread and butter, a thermos of tea, and apples from the last of the harvest made a feast. Those venerable ladies even sent a jar of custard to pour over bread pudding. The children ran and laughed out loud for the first time in weeks. Squeals from games of tag and hide-and-seek rang through the valley and bounced off the fells.

But twice through the later afternoon, when their rose-hip-gathering party neared the woods, Claire felt as if someone were watching her. Once she even asked Jeanine if she'd seen anyone.

"There are dozens of women and children here whom I do not know, Mademoiselle Claire — whom none of us know, probably. How can you ask me if someone is watching?"

Claire swatted a bramble from her face. "Yes, of course. Silly of me." She laughed, as if it were nothing, a stupid question. But when she sensed the presence a third time, she felt tiny hairs prickle the back of her neck, just as she had that day she and Aimee had tramped home from Mrs. Heelis's house.

Claire counted the children from Bluebell Wood, to make certain all were present. Peter, it seemed, had strayed to the hedgerow on the opposite side of the lane and down quite a way. On closer inspection he was picking beside Emily, Mr. Firthman's daughter, who spilled over with giggles every time Peter whispered in her ear.

"Peter?" Claire felt as awkward as Peter's

guilty glance. "Will you help Mr. Dunnagan load the crates? I think they're rather heavy for him."

Peter's neck burned red. "*Ja,* certainly, Fräulein." He came away without a backward glance, but Claire noted the pout on the girl's pretty lips. She sighed. *Young love. What a disaster in the making, and what a muddle!*

By the time shadows stretched across the fells and darkened the hedgerows, Claire did not need to call for the children. Mr. Dunnagan's wagon groaned under the weight of weary and finger-sore children unused to the thorns of wild roses. Still, they laughed and mustered just enough energy to pummel one another with the last of their rose hips — hard-won ammunition which Claire and Mr. Dunnagan did their best to rescue. After all, Mrs. Creedle had promised a rose-hip tart for Saturday if they brought two buckets home after gathering enough for the WI.

At the fork in the road, Peter and Bertram stowed their crates in a wagon headed for the village and the WI, then bounded back to their group, waving good-bye to the villagers tramping homeward on foot. Claire didn't bother to count the tousled heads in

Mr. Dunnagan's wagon or walking beside. There was just enough time for a cup of tea before she and the children washed and dressed for Shabbat. She trudged beside the wagon, certain that if she sat down, she'd never get up again.

They'd almost reached the lane to Bluebell Wood when Peter asked aloud where Josef was.

"He's not with you? Gaston, where is Josef? The two of you were together, weren't you?"

"*Oui,* mademoiselle, but not for the last hour or so. He walked up the fell to pick a bouquet. He'll catch up."

"A bouquet?"

"Oui." Gaston looked disgusted. Claire deemed it best not to ask whom the posies were for. She'd sensed Josef's infatuation for some time but never encouraged it or called attention to the young Romeo.

"It will be dark soon," she worried. "I wonder if we should search for him."

"*Nein,* Fräulein Claire." Peter shook his head. "It is as Gaston says: he will catch up. He knows his way, even in the night. I will give him a shake when he comes for worrying his love."

Claire ignored Peter's grin and Bertram's snort.

"He will be late for Shabbat," Elise observed with a note of tattling. "Rabbi Meir won't like that."

"No, he won't," Claire agreed. Why couldn't she keep them all together and on task? Why hadn't she counted heads?

By the time they reached the kitchen and poured their tins of remaining rose hips into a large bowl for Mrs. Creedle, it was teatime. They'd not even washed, but Mrs. Newsome took pity on the "poor, hungry waifs" and fed them "just enough tea and biscuits to gather their strength for a wash. After all, they've been about a good deed today."

Claire marveled at the smiles Mrs. Newsome poured over the children. Happily, some spilled her way, or she might even be jealous.

A cold bath was better by far than no bath, and it felt good to wash the stickiness of the day from her hair and rub a bit of Aunt Miranda's lotion into her thorn-pricked hands and arms. Claire tied her wet hair up in a knot, securing it with pins, making it as presentable as possible. Rabbi Meir could be heard in the dining room below. It would not do to be late.

She was just on her way down the stairs, buttoning the last button on the cuff of her sleeve, when Josef tore through the front door and into the foyer, white as the goose down of her pillow. "Josef?"

But before he heard her, Peter had grabbed his brother by the arm and shaken him. "Josef, you're late! It's time for the lighting of the candles. Where have you been? Oh, never mind. Come in as you are. Rabbi has asked for you." He dragged a visibly frightened and dirt-streaked Josef into the dining room.

Claire paused on the stair, distracted. A compliant Josef was just as curious as a late one. She hurried down to the dining room. *Where has he been? And what became of his bouquet?*

Chapter Twenty-Eight

Mrs. Newsome shook out the tablecloth for tea with more vengeance than care. She simply did not understand young Josef. He and Gaston had been thick as thieves for months, ever since the digging of their Hitler holes. Mischief could be attributed collectively or divided between the two. But for the last week, ever since Friday's outing to pick rose hips, Josef had pushed Gaston away, wanting nothing to do with him — a fact that had obviously hurt Gaston, no matter that the boy pretended otherwise.

For that matter, Josef appeared to want nothing to do with anyone except Peter and little Aimee. He shadowed his older brother as if he might disappear at any moment, and Aimee had become to him as a bird in a gilded cage. Josef panicked if Mrs. Newsome did not have the child tied to her apron strings or if Claire did not have Aimee glued to her side in the library or the drawing room. He all but forbade Aimee to wander alone on the grounds or even to visit Mrs. Heelis in the company of Claire, a thing Aimee declared "Intolerable!"

Mrs. Newsome smiled to think Aimee knew the meaning of the word.

Just as worrisome was Mrs. Creedle's report of food missing from the larder.

"Half a joint! It's one thing when the scallywags nip a biscuit or two. I know you favor those two meddlesome boys, but this is not to be tolerated. I'd cooked that mutton yesterday for this noonday meal. It would have fed half the table! You must deal with it, Mrs. Newsome!"

Deal with it, indeed. Mrs. Newsome heaved a sigh. *Intolerable* — such a mild word for stealing. *In the old days — older than I — the boys would have been horsewhipped.* She wouldn't admit it to Mrs. Creedle, but she knew Gaston was not part of the conspiracy. This she could pretty well lay at Josef's door alone, though she hadn't caught him in the act. It was more a case of knowing where Gaston was when it had happened, and he could not have been the culprit. *But why is Josef stealing at all, and half a joint of meat, of all things? He eats his fill at mealtime. I've even given him a bit extra. It's not as if we starve the lad.*

"Oh, bother! I've laid the cloth wrong way round!" Mrs. Newsome clucked her tongue and pulled off the china and napkins to reverse the table linen. At least she hadn't laid the entire table.

The downstairs clock struck eleven. Josef listened for the even breathing of his brother and the other boys in the room, waited a minute more, then slipped from his bed, grabbed his shoes, and softly closed the door behind him. Already dressed, he carried his shoes by their laces around his neck and grasped his pillowslip stuffed with stolen treasures.

He dared not crawl through the window or shinny down the vine. He'd been caught once by Herr David doing that very thing and had no good explanation — not one he could give and not one Herr David would believe. The man was too smart to think Josef suffered from insomnia and needed a late-night stroll. He was more apt to believe Josef did it just because he could, or to prove that he could. But now he'd been warned.

Things were easier in that way since Herr David sometimes needed to work late and spent the night at the factory. The women were not so likely to be out at night to observe, or to keep watch in case of deserters or intruders, though Josef had no doubt Herr David had warned Fräulein Claire against him.

Intruders. Josef sighed. He'd been prepared for intruders or invaders. He and Gaston had formulated multitudinous and detailed plans patterned after the Home Guard's protection in case of invasion practices. But this turn of events he was not prepared for.

Josef crept down the stairs and through the front door, praying as he went. He didn't dare try the kitchen. Too many between the upstairs and downstairs had ears and eyes, even in their sleep. If he had to, he could pick the lock upon returning, but no one should be up at this hour, so leaving the door unlocked was probably safe enough.

Nights had turned cold, though rarely freezing. A sharp wind blew off the lake and tossed black silhouetted treetops, writhing like snakes, against the moonlit sky. If Josef believed in ghosts or banshees or Mollie Taggert's bogles, he would have been frightened. At least that's what he told himself as he stole through the maze, circled round the topiaries, and made his way to the woods paralleling the lane.

He kept to the shadows, despite his contention with tree roots and uneven ground, not knowing when or if the Home Guard might appear on their rounds. They'd recently restructured their patrolling sequence, believing the elements of uncertainty and surprise to their advantage.

Josef darted across the road and cut through the hedgerow. He climbed the fell to the high meadow, then followed the stream until he reached the field adjacent to the road where they'd all picked rose hips with the village children.

"Syrup and jam!" Josef spat the words. *If not for Frau Newsome and her syrup and jam, I never would have met that — that —*

He reached the bend in the stream as a bank of clouds freed the moon. Just as quickly a hand clamped over his mouth; an arm grabbed his chest and dragged him backward. It would do no good to kick or scream, but Josef did both.

"Quiet! *Dummkopf!* One word and I'll —" But the man with the sour breath and fierce but familiar accent didn't finish. He thrust the blade of the razor-sharp knife beneath Josef's chin. Josef had seen and felt the tip of that knife on the fateful rose-hip harvesting day, when the escaped naval officer had dragged him into the brush only moments after he'd wandered from the group. He made himself limp, which aggravated the man just as much. He threw Josef to the ground, kicking at his backside.

Josef fell on his pillowslip stuffed with all he'd been able to steal from the larder over the past three days.

"Yesterday you did not come!" the man accused.

"I could not get away. If I had come, they would have seen me."

"That is your problem. Not mine!" The man yanked the pillowslip from beneath Josef, sat down in the scattered moonlight to rummage through it, and wolfed the mutton joint, as if starving.

Josef thought that if anyone had followed him, it would surely result in the prisoner's problem, above all, but knew it best not to point that out.

"No one followed you? No one saw you leave?"

"Nein." Josef was sure of it, though part of him wished someone had seen, had followed, and would come to his rescue. But who? Who in all of Bluebell Wood could stand against this ferocious man? Herr Dunnagan? He was too old and feeble. One crash of this man's fist would kill the old groundskeeper. Mademoiselle Claire? Never! Peter? Peter was strong, but not

strong enough. The man had guessed that Peter was his brother and had vowed to kill him if Josef raised the alarm. He'd even observed Josef's care of Aimee — the little girl with the pink hair ribbons — and had threatened to harm her, small and innocent though she was.

"One or two less Jews, no matter" — that's what he'd said.

The man was a Nazi, Josef was sure — someone who'd signed allegiance to the government and Führer who'd been responsible for stealing away his father, the reason his mother had put him and Peter on a train bound for somewhere she'd never seen, to live out the war with people she didn't know. And now even his mother was probably gone — taken east to who knew where, to do who knew what. *Will I ever see you again, Mutti?*

Josef swallowed the rock in his throat and momentarily clamped his eyes against the pressure pushing there. He'd heard the radio reports. He'd listened to Peter and Bertram's talks when they thought the younger boys asleep at night, remembered what the grown-ups had whispered the day the foreign Jews of Paris were rounded up, but most of all he remembered the terror of the night his father was taken. Josef didn't believe in fairy tales. He would not tell one to himself, not even now.

Still, he thought of Pip, in the book *Great Expectations* that Fräulein Claire had read to them. Pip must have been just as terrified when he helped the escaped prisoner he'd faced in the graveyard, but he did it, and it turned out all right for him in the end — better than all right.

There was nothing for it but to "buck up" and face whatever came. That's what Herr David had said a man must do when faced with a challenge. Josef bit his lip. *With Herr David gone so often to the factory now, there is no chance of help. The outcome is up to me.*

Weary beyond words, and in bare feet with shoelaces slung over his neck, Josef slipped at last through the front door of Bluebell Wood just as the hall clock bonged two. He'd had a time convincing the German to let him live, promising that he would come again, that besides food he could procure civilian clothes and a map of the countryside that would allow him to reach the coast.

The only thing to do was to take clothes from the closet of the dead Herr Christopher, the ones he'd seen in his room when looking for marbles. The clothes had looked as if they could be about the size of the German. At least they were both grown men, and in the pictures Frau Langford kept of Herr Christopher, he'd looked lean and muscular.

Josef rubbed his sore shoulder. The German was definitely muscular, and determined to have his way.

But there had to be a way to bring the prisoner to justice, not let him escape. Herr Christopher, who'd wanted to fight the Nazis from the beginning, would have understood, would surely have applauded and helped him. If only Josef could think of a way to trick the man. But he was dangerous, so very dangerous.

A stray thought about a map and a convincing place to hide it — a map that just might lead the prisoner not to where the man hoped, but walking toward his capture — began to form in Josef's brain. He had carefully stepped over the third step on the carpeted staircase, which always squeaked, and was rounding the bend to go upstairs when he came face-to-face with a dark form. If he'd not been startled speechless, he might have yelped.

"Where have you been?" It was Gaston, quiet, whispering, immovable.

Josef tried to muster his bearings quickly,

knowing he must bluff his way past Gaston. "Out."

"Where?"

"Just out — that is all, not that it is your business." He tried to push past him but Gaston stood firm.

"It will be my business to tell Madame Langford what I have seen if you do not tell me where you've been, who you've been with, and why you stole a pillowslip of food."

In less than a moment Josef calculated the risk of including Gaston, the immense relief of sharing the burden, the hope that his clever friend might have another idea of how to bring the enemy down. But no, the sum always came out the same. The risk was too great. Gaston's life would hang in the balance — as well as Peter's and Aimee's. Josef could risk the involvement of no one else. So he lied. "I've met some friends. We've done nothing wrong. Just a lark — that's what the English call it, eh?"

Even in the dark Josef could tell Gaston did not believe him. "Who are they — these 'friends'?"

"It's secret. We've formed a brotherhood."

"A brotherhood?"

"Like Tom and Huck — the ones Fräulein Claire read to us about." Josef knew Gaston loved that story. They both did. His friend, his clever friend, so like Tom Sawyer, would understand this, and might believe it.

"I thought we were blood brothers — like Tom and Huck." Gaston's voice came thick but doubtful. Josef could hear the trace of hurt.

"We're here together because we must be, because we have no choice."

"Let me join the brotherhood."

"*Nein.* They are my friends."

"We are friends," Gaston insisted.

"I let you believe that because there was no one else. But we are not true friends, not really." This time Josef pushed past Gaston as easily as pushing goose down out of the way. His friend had lost his fight, his pluck, in a moment, and who could blame him?

Josef had just sent his only true friend a deadly arrow, a grievous wound. He swallowed the lump rising in his throat as he trudged up the stairs, leaving Gaston behind, speechless. *Perhaps my cruelty will save Gaston's life. But now I am truly alone.*

Chapter Twenty-Nine

Claire rallied her student troops after breakfast. If they left early enough, they could collect all the nature journal specimens they'd need for their projects and still reach Loughrigg Tarn in time to picnic, overlooking the lake for lunch. It was said that Wordsworth often walked five miles in the morning round Esthwaite Water before school. Even with the youngest children, Claire believed they should be able to tackle this smaller expanse by noon.

With such a schedule, they should surely be back in time for the Guy Fawkes bonfire before dark. Not a smidgen of light must be seen after sunset, and none of the children wanted to miss the rare afternoon bonfire, particularly the burning of Hitler's effigy, much to Aunt Miranda's dismay over the new twist on a bloodthirsty British tradition.

Bertram and Peter offered to carry knapsacks with the picnic lunch for all, but Claire felt it important that each child carry their own. Food had been disappearing from Mrs. Creedle's larder. If Josef and Gaston were the culprits, as the frustrated cook suspected, then Claire didn't want them pilfering food the other children deserved — especially the Grasmere gingerbread Mrs. Creedle had baked for their hike. If the youngest children needed help carrying their knapsacks later, the bigger boys could step in.

Claire made certain the younger ones were well bundled against the cold November morning, then gave them wide berth to spread out along the way, collecting leaves or rocks or bark or insects or fossils or feathers — any manner of things — for their journals. Even with the stopping and starting, the group reached the tarn with a splendid view of Lake Windermere just before noon. Claire called the children to open their lunches and to share their findings. But Gaston and Josef were not among them, nor was Aimee.

Twenty minutes before time to meet for lunch, Gaston split from the group and followed Josef. His former friend had been acting out of sorts all morning — petulant, pushing everyone to the extreme, even his older brother. That might not have been so unusual, Gaston thought, but Josef had also made a cutting remark to Aimee early in the hike, sending her in tears to Mademoiselle Claire. The little girl had not left her teacher's side for much of the morning — a fact that seemed to please Josef in a most perverse way, and infuriated Gaston. They had long ago sworn to protect Aimee from all harm. Who did Josef think he was, and more importantly, what was he about?

Though his words earlier in the week had pierced, Gaston did not fully believe Josef's story about other friends or larking about with them in the wee hours of the morning. He could not imagine that Josef had really made friends with Wilfred Cooper and his gang, despite the bigger boy's trade of the spy pencil. But who else was there?

Gaston had found the cache of stolen food beneath Josef's mattress but refused to tattle. Men did not do that, even when betrayed by their best friends. Josef clearly wasn't eating the food himself. If anything, he'd lost weight in the last couple of weeks and looked drawn and puny. He was hiding something; of that Gaston was certain.

So he'd watched Josef from the corner of his eye and had followed him each time they'd left the house or whenever his friend had separated himself from the group, to no avail. Today was the first time they'd been so far from Bluebell Wood. If there was any clue to Josef's secret to be discovered, Gaston stood ready.

Josef rounded a huge stone- and fern-covered outcropping not far ahead. Gaston kept just far enough behind not to be heard or seen. He waited half a minute, then rounded the outcropping in pursuit.

"I knew you were following me!" Josef lunged, pushing Gaston, quite off his guard, to the ground.

"Where are you going?" Gaston demanded.

"None of your business. Go away! Did I not make myself plain to you? I don't want you!"

"*Non* — you are not plain at all. You are hiding something, and I want to know what it is."

"Leave — me — alone! If I was hiding something, would I tell you? You would tattle in a moment. You are a little boy, nothing more."

Gaston stared at Josef, pushing away the sting of his words. "You are hiding something and you are afraid, Josef. Tell me what it is."

For three seconds or less Gaston glimpsed doubt and pain, even fear, flicker through Josef's eyes. And then it was as if someone had pulled a blackout curtain across the boy's pupils. Anger and bravado returned. "Go away, Gaston." He turned to walk away, then turned again. "If you follow me, I will see you, and I will beat you. I will have no mercy on a French Jew."

" 'A French Jew'?" Gaston mimicked. "That is a stupid thing to say. You are a German Jew."

"I am not the French, who turned on their own people."

"*Non* — you are the Germans, who started this filthy war!"

The glove had been thrown to the ground. Josef charged Gaston and Gaston bent his head to ram Josef's belly, sending him flying backward. As Gaston reached for him, Josef rolled to his side and threw a hard uppercut to Gaston's chin, sending his head reeling in a fearsome jerk.

All of Gaston's worry for Josef turned to adrenaline. He kicked and punched, but not as hard or as fast as Josef. Josef caught Gaston's arms and the two wrestled side to side, backward and forward, a blood-scraping dance at the edge of the woods. Tripping over tree roots, they parted only long enough to throw a powerful punch to one another's eye, to rip the shirt or send a kick to the kneecap of their opponent. Five minutes, ten — Gaston had no idea how long they pummeled one another. Finally, too beaten and bloody, too weary and weak to stand, they collapsed less than ten feet apart.

"Let that be a lesson." Josef could barely get the words out for his hard breathing.

"Oui — a lesson to you. *Espèce d'idiot!"* Gaston could barely speak through the blood from the loose tooth in his mouth. But the fight in him had gone out. As much as he'd hated Josef five minutes before, he was ready to get up, to shake hands, and to be glad they'd given and endured a good scraping. *Perhaps that is all that was needed,* n'est-ce pas? *To rouse the blood and give and get.*

Josef struggled to his feet. Gaston reached out his hand, expecting Josef to help him up. But Josef spit into Gaston's upturned face, grabbed his knapsack, and marched away.

Aimee tripped and slid down the fell, cutting her knees and both hands. The hill dropped steeply away, and the jagged rocks jutted into the path. She couldn't run as quickly as she wanted, or as quickly as Josef. She saw Josef reach the path, but he was far gone by the time her feet hit even ground.

Where could he be going in such a hurry?

Aimee had stood, horrified, at the edge of the tree line, watching Josef and Gaston beat violently on one another. What could possess her two valiant protectors to fight so? Why had Josef said such cutting words to her that morning, calling her a toddle baby who didn't deserve to go out into the big woods with the rest of them? Why did he tell her she was ugly and to keep far from him? It was not like him at all.

She'd wanted to rush in and stop their fight, but she was afraid of their wild punches. So she waited until Gaston stood, wiped the grit from his knees, and turned back the way they'd come. She wanted to go after Gaston, to comfort him. Perhaps soaking her pocket hankie in the stream and giving it to him for his mouth would help. But where had Josef gone off in a huff and a sulk? Was his mouth bloodied?

Mademoiselle would surely help Gaston, but who would help Josef? He'd been cruel to Aimee that morning, but what did that matter if her friend was hurt?

Aimee looked up at the fell she'd just clambered down. It was a long way to the top, and she wasn't sure she could find Mademoiselle Claire again. The path she'd taken was not familiar, either.

Aimee's heart began to beat faster. It wasn't pouring rain and it wasn't cold, but the same fear she'd felt the night she'd run away — the night Mademoiselle Claire and Monsieur David had rescued her from the cliffs near Madame Heelis's farm — crept into her mind and wound its ugly tentacles into her heart.

Today, Mademoiselle Claire did not know which way Aimee had gone, or that she'd gone away at all. Monsieur David worked far away at the flying boat factory by day. He could not come and search for her. Aimee looked backward and then forward on the path. She had no idea where she was or which way to go to find Bluebell Wood. All she could do was run in the direction Josef had gone and pray he didn't leave the path.

Claire might have been frantic for Aimee, but she knew that Gaston and Josef would protect her with their lives. All three had been missing for over two hours, but she could imagine they'd all traipsed off in search of something monumental for their nature journals, or become inspired over charcoal rubbings of fossils or tree bark and lost track of the time. She was glad they had their lunches with them.

"Mademoiselle!" Bertram all but dragged his brother by the scruff of his neck. "I've found one of them, but I think an explanation is needed." He deposited a dirty and disheveled Gaston at Claire's feet, but Gaston did not look up.

"Gaston! What in the world happened to your knee? Did you fall?"

When Gaston finally peered up, Claire gasped. A bright-red lump the size of a goose egg bloomed on the boy's forehead, and the beginning of two shiners surrounded his eyes. It was the bloody smear from his mouth that sent shivers up Claire's arms. "What happened?"

"It was . . . a disagreement, nothing more." Gaston spoke as if it hurt him to get the words beyond a thick tongue.

"A disagreement?" Claire couldn't imagine — and then she knew. "Josef? You fought with Josef?"

"Oui." Gaston did not defend himself, which concerned Claire more.

"Where is he?"

Gaston shrugged.

"Gaston, I said, where is Josef?"

"I do not know, mademoiselle. He wants nothing to do with me. I let him go."

Claire bit her lip. Josef would turn up in time. Even fear of punishment for fighting would not keep him away long. But something more worrisome niggled at the corner of her mind. “Where is Aimee? Is she with Josef?”

Gaston shook his head. “She is with you, *non*?”

“No, she is not.” Claire’s pulse quickened. “I thought she’d gone off with you and Josef.”

Gaston stood, clearly forgetting any pain or shame he might have expressed a moment before. “Aimee is lost?”

Claire groped for her bearings, did her best to keep her voice calm. “She must have just wandered off. I’m sure she can’t be far, but it’s getting late and I think we’d best all spread out and look for her. And keep an eye out for Josef. He’ll probably be able to find his way back to us, but I’m not sure Aimee can.”

Claire didn’t have to ask twice. Word spread through the small group quickly and they were on their feet at once, nature journals and picnicking forgotten.

“Let’s leave our knapsacks here. Go in twos and please stay together. Peter, perhaps you and Elise —” But Claire didn’t need to organize them. The children had already organized themselves, splitting off by twos, fanning across the high meadow and down the fell.

"Gaston, you stay here. If she comes back, she'll need to know we've not gone off and left her. If Josef returns, send him north to search, toward Peter."

"You should stay, mademoiselle. It is you she will want to find. I will go with the others."

"You are in no condition!"

"I am fine, and strong, mademoiselle. We will find Aimee and let no harm come to her, I swear."

But Claire saw the uncertainty in Gaston's eyes. That uncertainty clipped her confidence.

Chapter Thirty

Josef had run as fast as he could, but he was no match for the distance or how far the sun had crossed the sky. By the time he reached the appointed place, the German was gone.

If Josef believed the man had simply disappeared or found another way to the coast, he would have been relieved. But in prisoner's garb he would not stand a chance crossing farmers' fields, let alone tramping the road. The big circle on the back of his shirt and on his pant leg shouted, *Escaped prisoner!*

No. Josef had promised he could get him clothes, and since Josef hadn't appeared when he was supposed to, the man must have gone to Bluebell Wood. He knew the way. He'd followed Josef by night and knew.

Josef thought of frail Frau Langford, of feisty Frau Newsome and fussy Frau Creedle, of Nancy, with the game leg, all alone at the house. He had failed them. He had failed them all! His heart beat madly. Hot tears came though he despised them and swatted them back like so many spiders.

The only thing he could do now was run to the house and hope he could get there before the man, or at least distract him from his purposes while there — give him whatever he wanted and plead with him to go away. He would stand between the German and the ladies. Josef took a deep breath and began to run.

"Josef! Josef, wait for me!" Aimee's desperate plea came from the foot of the fell, just before reaching the glen and the cave beyond, where the man had hidden.

"Aimee? What are you doing here?" Disbelief and panic surged through Josef's chest, followed by a wash of relief that the man was indeed not there, that wherever he was, he hadn't seen Aimee.

Aimee's joyful smile pierced Josef all the more for his meanness to her that morning. However she came to be there, he would not abandon or hurt her now. "Come to me, Aimee!"

He would lose precious time hiding her before going home. *Perhaps I can take her to Mrs. Heelis's house, and perhaps Ruby can telephone for help. O Adonai in heaven, help me. I can't save them all. Save those I cannot save.* At all costs, he would save Aimee. He had sworn to protect her with his life — an oath between himself and Gaston. But more than that, he loved the little girl for her own sweet self. She was like a young sister to him.

One moment Aimee was running gleefully toward him and in the next her feet lifted off the ground and she flew through the air sideways, disappearing behind a hedgerow. Through the thicket Josef glimpsed prison brown. His heart leapt to his throat. He might have thrown up from fear had determination not gripped him first.

Josef raced back to the spot and froze. There stood the prisoner, one filthy arm wrapped around Aimee's chest with his knife at her throat, and the other pointing to Josef. "You betrayed me!" he hissed. "Who else is coming?"

"No one!" Josef could barely get the words out.

"You lie — again! Did I not tell you what happens to liars?" He jerked Aimee's head back and the little girl screamed.

"No! Wait! She must have followed me. There is no one else!"

"If you didn't know she followed you, how do you know there is no one else?"

"I swear it! Ask her!"

The man tightened his grip on Aimee's chest. "Who is with you?"

But Aimee was too frightened to speak.

"Speak up! Who is with you?"

"No — no one. I came for Josef," she whimpered, casting pleading eyes in Josef's direction.

"Let her go. She's just a little girl. I have what you want. I brought the clothes! Here! Here they are!" He threw the knapsack to the ground.

"Take them out. Show me." He still held Aimee in his grip.

Josef pulled Christopher's clothes from his knapsack, shook them out, and held them up for the prisoner to see.

The man seemed satisfied. "Throw them this way."

"Not until you let her go."

"Do as I say!" He tightened his grip on Aimee.

Josef knew the man could cut both their throats and be gone with the clothes in an instant. But he still needed the compass and map — the map Josef had copied and altered, and rolled tightly inside the spy pencil he'd won from Wilfred. His only chance was to delay the prisoner, to make him think they needed to go elsewhere to get the map. The man had not asked for the knapsack, and even if he did, he would never suspect that the pencil inside was anything more than it appeared.

"When you let her go. These clothes won't do you much good without the map."

"You didn't bring the map?" The fierceness of the man would make a warrior faint, Josef thought, but he could not afford that.

"You didn't give me enough time to steal one. I was lucky to get these. But I know where there is a map. It's not at Bluebell Wood. It's the map the Home Guard uses. That's the only one that will do you any good. They've taken down all the road signs, you know."

"Where? How long will it take you to get it?"

Josef considered his options, considered Aimee's options. He sat down on the grass. "I won't get it for you, not unless you let her come with me."

"I will break her neck."

"Then break mine, too, and add murder to your madness. You'll be picked up in no time once you reach the road. Civilian clothes or no, your accent alone will give you away, and you don't know where you are going. You'll walk straight into the arms of the Home Guard — or worse — just as the others that escaped with you. You said so yourself." Josef's heart beat wildly in his chest. Bravado dared everything, but it was his only weapon. Josef knew the prisoner knew he was right. He would have gone long ago if he'd found a way.

The man did not answer, but with steeled eyes grabbed Christopher's clothes, and dragging Aimee by the arm, stomped backward through the underbrush toward the cave. Josef followed, knowing this might be the end of the line for him and for Aimee, but he would not desert the little girl.

Inside the mouth of the cave, the German shoved Aimee against the wall behind him. While gripping the knife's handle between his teeth, he changed his shirt, keeping his eye on Josef all the while. When he stepped back to change his pants, Aimee scrambled forward, but he grabbed her, lifting her off the ground again as easily as a bag of apples. He tossed aside his prison garb. "We go together."

At least the escapee would not slit their throats and leave them in the cave. Josef swallowed. He could think of no means to change the man's mind, no possibility that he would leave them behind unharmed. He pushed the knapsack aside, hoping if it was found, someone would recognize it and understand what had happened. Maybe, as they traveled, someone would see them, report them, help them. It was Guy Fawkes Day, after all, and the English were mad to celebrate it out of doors. He would take the longest route possible to the Home Guard's underground tunnel near the lake. It wouldn't matter that the man learned of it, as long as he was caught, and wasn't there the remote possibility that it would be manned, or at least observed, especially if they reached there before nightfall? Josef prayed so. "Agreed."

It was nearly teatime. There would be no opportunity for bonfires. The children, having hollered themselves hoarse for Aimee and Josef, and having searched the fell and woods and fields for at least a mile's radius, returned at last to their starting point. Each one looked thirsty, exhausted, and frightened for their friends and sibling.

Claire knew she dared keep them no longer on the fells or they all risked being caught high up after sunset. The nights were far too cold for that, and the jagged rocks made for treacherous paths in the dark. Besides, she needed grown men with lights and perhaps a search dog.

How could I have let this happen? Why

didn't I keep better watch? Claire pushed the panic down, but it grated her mind and nerves. She needed help — more help than anyone human could give. Dared she trust God to hear her, to help her? Or was this, too, a case of Him pulling her near, then pushing her away?

She couldn't afford the luxury of doubt or fear to prevent her from crying out, begging for help; she loved the children too much for that. She prayed that Aimee was with Josef, and not alone. Wherever they were, if only they were together. *Please, God.* It was all she knew to pray. *Please help them; bring them home. Not for me, but in spite of me and my negligence. I'm so very sorry.*

Claire could have wept, but determined to keep a brave face for the others.

"If it's too cold for us, mademoiselle," Elise asked, "isn't it too cold for them?"

"Yes, it is, and for that reason we must hurry home now and get help to find them. They must have wandered farther afield than we thought."

"Don't worry. Josef is a good woodsman," Gaston manfully observed. "He'll take care of Aimee."

"If they're together," Jeanine reminded him.

"Oui." Gaston's confidence seemed to

fade, but he bucked up and smiled. “We will find them.”

Claire could have kissed the little Frenchman. She only hoped he was right.

By the time the weary, nearly frantic party reached Bluebell Wood, twilight had fallen and it would soon be dark. Mrs. Newsome’s irritation at their late arrival dissipated the moment she heard of the missing children. “I’ll telephone the constable and Sergeant Foley of the Home Guard. They’ll need to muster everyone they can find. Never mind the blackout — oh, I pray they’ll never mind it! Mr. Dunnagan’s brother, over Troutbeck way, has field dogs. I’ll have Mr. Dunnagan give him a jingle.”

“I’ll telephone David first. I know he will want to help, and maybe he can bring others from the factory. Can you telephone Ruby and Mrs. Heelis? I can’t help but wonder if Aimee might have gone there.” Claire forcibly pushed the terror of Aimee’s night on the cliff from her mind and desperately wished David were here now.

Within the hour fresh troops had been mustered and the weary searchers from Bluebell Wood nourished. The operator ran telephone searches through the village, but no one, not even Mrs. Heelis or Ruby, had seen either of the children.

The most worrisome news came over the telephone, from David, verified by Sergeant Foley. Three prisoners had escaped from Grizedale Hall more than two weeks before. Two had been apprehended and returned to the camp, but the third, considered the most desperate, had not been found. Sergeant Foley encouraged the inhabitants of Bluebell Wood to stay put, maintain the blackout, lock their doors, and leave the search to professionals.

"Now stop your fretting, Miss Claire," Mrs. Newsome cautioned. "You know that is the least likely explanation. I could box Ed Foley's ears for causing you such worry. They've probably just wandered off and lost track of the time."

Gaston understood Madame Newsome's hope but knew she was wrong. Josef, though he'd done his best to make a sworn enemy of Gaston, was the best woodsman of the lot and would not wander aimlessly away. He'd been on a mission when Gaston had challenged him — a mission with a very full knapsack. And the food — all the food Josef had stolen over the last couple of weeks — made no sense . . . unless he was running away for good and all, or feeding someone.

Gaston gulped. Josef had no reason to

leave his brother, his family at Bluebell Wood. It was all any of them had now. And he would not help an escaped German prisoner — not by choice. But if he was forced . . . ? Gaston remembered Josef's recent worry over Aimee, his obsessive need to know where his older brother was at every moment, his poorly explained reasons for pushing his best friend away. *Could Josef be protecting us? It would be like him.*

Gaston's mind filtered through the possibilities. Why, if Josef had been feeding the escapee and helping him, would anything change now?

Because Aimee saw them. Because Aimee is with them.

Gaston's mind reeled with what that could mean for the little girl. He swerved, nearly losing his balance. Bertram caught him before he fell.

"Gaston —" Bertram shook him — "what is the matter with you? Do you need something to drink?"

"Non," Gaston whispered, searching his brother's eyes. "I know what has happened."

Gaston poured out his tale to the group: everything he knew, and his fearful conclusion.

"Your imagination has gotten the better of you," Bertram scoffed. "You and Josef see

Nazis at every bend in the road, behind every bramble bush."

But Gaston saw that Peter and Mademoiselle Claire feared it could be so.

"If Aimee saw our fight, she might have followed Josef to comfort him. That is something she would do," Gaston declared.

"You said he started the fight. Why would she not comfort you?" Bertram challenged. "Why would she follow him?"

"Because she loves him . . . more than me." The confession cost Gaston, but he knew it was true.

"I saw Josef yesterday," Elise remembered.

"We all saw Josef yesterday," Jeanine ridiculed.

"*Non,* I mean that I saw him come from Master Christopher's room."

"What?" Madame Langford, pale, wrapped in her dressing gown, had descended the stairs and stood in the dining room doorway.

"You shouldn't be downstairs, my lady!" Mrs. Newsome fretted, quickly drawing Madame Langford to a chair. "I would have brought you anything you need."

"I heard the commotion. Aimee and Josef are missing?"

"Yes," Claire sighed. "We searched everywhere on the fells and all the way home but never found them. Search parties have gone out now, but Gaston thinks it might have something to do with a German escapee. There's still a prisoner missing from Grizedale Hall." Even as she stated the case, Gaston could hear the doubt in Mademoiselle Claire's voice.

"Elise, what did you mean about seeing Josef in Master Christopher's room?" Madame Langford had grown paler still.

Elise faltered.

"Please don't be frightened, dear. It's not tattling, and I won't be angry. Just tell me."

Elise looked from Claire to Madame Langford. "I saw him in the hallway, coming out of Master Christopher's room. He carried a bundle — it looked like clothes — in his arms."

"Clothes? What would he want with — ?" But Madame Langford stopped and looked at Claire, her eyes wide.

"A prisoner would need civilian clothes to escape," Peter said quietly, the worry in his face evident.

Claire reached for the back of a chair to steady herself. "If Aimee followed Josef," she began, "if she saw the prisoner . . ."

"If the prisoner saw her —" Peter went on. "Where? Where could they have gone? Where would a prisoner hide?"

"Think back," Madame Langford insisted. "When did Josef first begin taking food? When did he begin pushing people away?"

Claire's fingers went to her throat. "The day we all went to harvest rose hips. Remember? The rabbi was here and waiting to begin Shabbat services. Josef hadn't returned with us. You said he was out picking a bouquet . . . but he never brought the bouquet. And he was very late. . . . The look on his face, I remember."

"That would fit," Peter agreed. "He's been following me like a shadow since then."

"Then you think the prisoner's hiding place is in the vicinity of where you were picking?" Madame Langford kept them on track.

"*Oui* — perhaps," Gaston agreed. He remembered how tired and dirty Josef was when he'd crept up the stairs that night. The next morning he'd seen that Josef's shoes were muddied. "There is a stream near there. The man would need water."

"Mrs. Newsome, telephone the constable to search those woods. There's even a cave or two in that area — Christopher and his friends used to play there, even though they were told not to."

"A cave would be the perfect place to

hide, to sleep out of the night air," Peter agreed.

Gaston and Josef had not explored the depths of those caves, but all Gaston could think of was Tom Sawyer and Becky, lost in the cave, and a ruthless Injun Joe tracking them.

"Tell them to be careful. The man must be armed in some way for Josef to be so afraid." Claire looked near tears.

"I'll telephone straightaway, my lady." Mrs. Newsome was already in the hallway. "And then another round of tea is in order," she called behind her. "There'll be no sleeping tonight until those children are found."

Chapter Thirty-One

It was too dark to see; clouds had covered the moon and stars. Josef was tempted to grab Aimee's hand and run into the night. The prisoner, walking three steps behind, would never see him, but Aimee's pastel wool hat and coat, gifts from Mrs. Heelis, were visible even by the pale starlight. Aimee shone a beacon for the prisoner.

Not knowing what else to do, Josef continued to march toward the lake and the Home Guard's tunnel, walking slowly enough for Aimee to keep pace. The little girl must be dead tired on her feet, but she didn't whimper. Josef had taken the long way round, hoping the prisoner could not tell, hoping his sense of direction on land was poor in this foreign country.

Josef wished now that he'd told Gaston where he was going and why. If he and Gaston had not fought, Aimee would not have followed him, and Gaston would be the greatest help in bringing the enemy down.

Bring the enemy down — that's what I must do. Perhaps I can get him into the Home Guard's tunnel and trap him there. But what about Aimee? Would he believe she cannot go down? And if we go down there, no one will know where we are or be able to find us, even in the daylight. He could slit our throats. No one would know until the Home Guard comes again. And when will that be? They don't use the tunnel regularly, just often enough to be sure that it is supplied in case of invasion.

Josef had reached no conclusions by the time they reached Lake Windermere.

"At last," the prisoner huffed. "I was beginning to think you didn't know your way. Where is this tunnel with the map?"

"It will be harder to find in the dark. Do you still have the matches that I gave you last week? It would be much easier if we shone a light."

"And bring your Home Guard down on our heads? Do you think I am feeble-minded? I cannot tell if you are simply stupid or if you are extremely clever."

"If I was clever, I would not have helped you!" Josef shouted.

"Quiet!" The prisoner slapped Josef across

the mouth, knocking him to the ground. "Get moving, *Dummkopf*! Which way?"

Aimee began to cry. Josef struggled to his feet and wrapped his arm around the little girl, afraid the prisoner would strike her, too. Egging the man on was dangerous, but he'd hoped someone nearby might hear them. There was no one.

Josef marched forward, toward the old chestnut that marked the spot for the trapdoor. He and Gaston had been down a half-dozen times since Sergeant Foley's warning and were never spotted by the Home Guard. How he wished to be spotted now!

"Why do you hesitate? Where is it?"

"I told you, it's hard to find in the dark."

The prisoner grabbed Aimee. "Find it, or —"

"Here! This way! We've just passed it, I think."

"Surprising how quickly you think when this one's at risk."

How Josef hated the man. "Let her go. Let her go now, or I'll not take you a step closer."

Josef couldn't see the man's face, but he felt his indecision. Where such bravado within Josef came from, he didn't know. But it had worked before. It must work now.

The prisoner shoved Aimee toward Josef. “I’m losing patience.”

“This way.” Josef grasped Aimee’s trembling hand and led them all back toward the chestnut tree. “The trapdoor is just beneath the tree. We can’t see it, but if you feel around the base of the tree, there is a rope handle.”

As the prisoner bent, Josef pulled the hair ribbon from beneath Aimee’s cap and tossed it behind him.

“Why did — ?” the little girl began, but Josef squeezed her hand and she seemed to sense the message.

“Why?” the prisoner repeated, suspicious.

Aimee hesitated, but only a moment. “Why can’t we go home now?”

“That’s right,” Josef took up. “The tunnel is here. The map is there. You don’t need us anymore. Let us go.”

The prisoner smirked, searching the ground. “And have you alert the authorities?”

“I won’t!” Josef swore. “I haven’t told them about you all this time. Why would I now? I don’t want to be declared a traitor or a Nazi lover! Let us go.”

“You’re a convincing little demon.” The German stopped his search, said, “Ach!” and yanked up the trapdoor. “Get down there! Go!"

"She's too little. She's never been down and she won't be able to navigate the ladder."

"Then I'll throw her down." He reached for Aimee's arm.

"No! I can help her." Josef tugged her back.

"I thought as much."

"I don't want to go down there," Aimee cried.

"I'll help you. I'll go first, then guide your feet. Don't be afraid. I've got you." Josef stepped through the hole and found his footing on the ladder. "Come, Aimee. Come to me." He guided Aimee's footsteps.

"Sei schnell!" the prisoner commanded.

Josef guided Aimee until she was on the ladder in front of him. Together they descended. The prisoner's bulk shut off the little bit of starlight above. Josef grabbed a torch from the Home Guard's stash and shone it upward toward the prisoner, praying a patrol would see the light. The sudden brightness was blinding. He glimpsed fear and hope in Aimee's face and smiled at her, his determination renewed.

"Turn that off!"

"You need to see."

"I don't need to see, you scoundrel! You

are sly beyond your years. I will teach you to betray me."

Josef flicked off the torch. *Was it enough? Is anyone patrolling the lake? Did they see the light?* He pushed Aimee to the corner of the tunnel, far from the boots and menace of the angry man thundering down the ladder, and stood in the breach.

It was nearly midnight when David and Sergeant Foley telephoned Claire from the station. "We found the cave Lady Langford mentioned. It looks like someone has been living there awhile."

"And Aimee and Josef?" Claire hoped against hope.

"No sign of them. But we found a heap of prisoner clothing and a knapsack — might be Josef's. There's nothing but a pencil inside. The man must have been supplied with something else to wear, so Gaston may be right. It's too dark to see footprints now, but we can look in the morning, although I'm worried we've trampled anything of use. Mr. Dunnagan is bringing his brother's dogs up at first light. We hope they can follow the scent. There doesn't seem to be anything else we can do tonight."

"I can't believe that, can't accept that." Though Claire had no idea what more any of them could do.

"I'm sorry, Claire. Look, I'm coming to Bluebell Wood. I'll stay with you until we find them. And we will find them, I swear."

Claire couldn't respond beyond the lump in her throat. She hung up the phone. She knew they'd done their best, but their best wasn't good enough. Bringing the children safely, soundly home was the only acceptable solution.

"Mademoiselle?" Gaston stood beside Claire, though she'd not heard him come. He pulled her hand from the receiver. "They found nothing?"

"They found prisoner clothing, a knapsack — nothing in it but a pencil — and evidence that someone has been living there." Claire shut her eyes. "But no sign of Aimee or Josef."

"A pencil, you say?" Gaston's eyes lit. "Then I know the knapsack belongs to Josef! He would never give a German prisoner that pencil — it is most unique. But if the man left his clothes, he is on the move, trying to escape. He is using Aimee and Josef as his prisoners, what you call his 'ticket to ride.' "

Claire groaned, unable to stop hot tears or to keep the required stiff upper lip. "We don't know that. They could be anywhere."

"*Non,* Mademoiselle Claire. They are somewhere — somewhere a prisoner would want to go, somewhere he could find a way to escape the country, a way to return to Germany. He needs a map. We must think."

"I have no idea where he would find one, Gaston. It's like looking for a needle in a haystack." Claire knew Gaston was right. She felt it in her bones. It was all she could do not to vomit from fear.

"*Non,* you have no idea. This is true. But Josef would have an idea!"

"What do you mean?"

"The Home Guard is always afraid of the invasion, *oui*?"

"*Oui* — yes. What does that have to do with it?"

"They protect the lake most of all. They are always afraid that invasion will come from parachutists landing near the lake or flying boats on the water. They are on the alert for local German sympathizers giving signals there."

"I heard Sergeant Foley say so."

"Josef knows this. If he was doing as the prisoner required, he would lead him there — to the lake, and I believe I know where."

Mrs. Newsome had sent a reluctant but exhausted Lady Langford to bed hours before with a promise to wake her the moment they had news, but no amount of ordering, wheedling, or begging convinced Claire to wait for David.

"I'm not waiting another minute! It might be a wild-goose chase, but so far Gaston has been right. Telephone the constable and tell him to meet us with men at the lake at the Home Guard's tunnel. Tell them to call Sergeant Foley — he'll know where it is. Gaston and I will take the car."

"But cars are forbidden on the road until morning. There may not even be enough petrol in the tank!" Mrs. Newsome wrung her hands. The look on Claire's face shut her up. *What am I thinking? This is an emergency!* "Don't go alone. You'll need help, Miss Claire. You can't be rushing an escaped German prisoner. He's strong and desperate or he wouldn't have taken the children."

"I'm going after them. Don't say anything to Aunt Miranda until we know."

"I am coming with you," Peter declared. "Josef is my brother. Do not try to stop me."

"And I," Bertram affirmed. "If Gaston is going, so am I."

"I need one of you here with the others, in case the man might bring them here, might make some kind of demand. Bertram, please stay."

"Please — all of you — wait for Mr. David. He'll surely be here shortly," Mrs. Newsome begged. Could they not see how dangerous this was? But they all ignored her.

"The escapee would have been here already if —" Bertram argued.

"I can't take that chance. David and Sergeant Foley will surely bring an army of locals to help us, but someone must stay here with the women and children. I can't leave Aunt Miranda or the children unprotected."

Mrs. Newsome raised her brows, tempted to feel insulted by the omission and assumption that she couldn't take down a Nazi escapee, but decided even she might feel better with one of the young strong men about.

"Oui," Bertram acquiesced, but grimly.

"Thank you. Peter, Gaston — let's go."

"I do wish you'd wait for Mr. David!" Mrs. Newsome tried once more, hurrying to the telephone.

Claire didn't answer. She, Peter, and Gaston slipped through the front door, never minding the blackout. Mrs. Newsome, terrified for the three who'd just gone out into the night, could barely speak to the operator, whom she'd woken from a sound sleep.

The phone at the Home Guard rang and rang, but there was no answer.

"Please try again," Mrs. Newsome all but cried. "This is an emergency. We think we know where the children are, but if we're right, we need the Home Guard desperately."

The operator, who'd helped earlier with the telephone search, tried again, but to no avail. "I'm afraid they've all gone home for the night, Mrs. Newsome. Shall I ring Sergeant Foley's home?"

"Yes! Oh, yes, please!"

At last a sleepy Mrs. Foley answered. "Yes? What is it? Oh, no, he's not home yet. As soon as he comes in the door I'll have him ring Bluebell Wood. Oh, dear, Mrs. Newsome, they shouldn't have gone out alone. They should have waited for the constable or at least the Home Guard. Whatever possessed them?"

Mrs. Newsome hung up the phone. *Love possessed them. There is no greater love than to lay down one's life for a friend. Miss Claire is closer to following Jesus than she knows.*

There, in the hallway of Bluebell Wood, Mrs. Newsome knelt beside the phone and prayed to the God who'd always answered, seldom in just the way she'd asked or imagined, but to her and others' greater good. She prayed that He would see Claire and the children through, that He would bring Mr. David home quickly and alert Sergeant Foley and his men. She knew that God, in His sovereignty and omniscience, knew things she didn't. She prayed for the workings of miracles she could not now imagine. And then she prayed for the ability to trust Him, and to wait.

Josef sat in the corner of the Home Guard tunnel, his arm wrapped around an exhausted and frightened Aimee. How he wished he could soothe her, tell her that everything would be all right, that things, as Mrs. Newsome always said, would look better in the morning. But he couldn't.

By the light of the torch, the prisoner studied the map tacked to a board on the earthen wall of the tunnel. He was a naval officer, and no fool, Josef knew. He'd been lucky to string the man along for as long as he had. Once the man was convinced he had no more need of Josef . . . Josef didn't want to think what that might mean for him and for Aimee. The longer they stayed in the tunnel, the better the chance that the

Home Guard would eventually find them. If only he could think of something to keep the man here. . . .

Twenty minutes may have passed before the man stood back from the map and shone his torch in Josef's face. "Come here — now."

Josef repositioned Aimee's head on a lump of quilts and walked to the map.

"What is this, beside the lake?" The man pointed to a circled position on the map with the penciled name *Calgarth.*

Josef swallowed, feeling the lump in his throat grow thicker. "I don't know — just forest, I guess." It was the Sunderland flying boat factory and town, the place Herr David worked. The site used to build the flying boats that defended Atlantic convoys against German U-boats — something this naval officer would give anything to seek and destroy. If he escaped — *when* he escaped British shores — just getting the word to Germany could mean the end of the factory, the end of Calgarth, the bombing of the entire district.

"You walked us in circles to get here. You know the area well. What is this?"

Josef gulped. "It was dark. I couldn't be sure where we were."

"I don't believe you. You're a conniving

little Jew."

"I've done everything you asked."

"Well, I don't need you now."

Josef stared into the light, determined not to cry, not to show the fear the man desired. He returned to his corner and tightened his protective grip around Aimee's shoulder. "I told you we won't tell — we won't say anything."

The man grunted, turned the light to the map again, and yanked it from the board. He folded it into a small packet and concealed it inside his shirt. "I will see if it is only forest." His torchlight searched the room, landing on boxed and tinned food supplies. He rummaged through the stock, pulling out small packets, stuffing them inside his shirt and pants pockets. He opened boxes and tins, finally turning to Josef. "There is no compass here."

Josef thought of the compass on the pencil inside his knapsack, relieved he'd left it in the cave. He almost said he had one, that they could go back and get it, just to delay and perhaps appease the man, but that would put the prisoner nearer total escape and put him and Aimee nearer the man's final plans for them. A new idea occurred to him.

"You said you could get me one. You vowed."

"I thought there was one here."

The man stood, towering over Josef and Aimee, who had at last fallen into deep sleep.

"I know where I can get you one, but it will be risky. You have to let us go."

"Ha! You are not only conniving but stupid if you think I will let you go." The man pulled his knife from his boot.

"If you want the compass, you will. I can get one, but I have to steal it. If Aimee and I return home now, they will believe we were lost and stop looking for us. That will give me opportunity to steal one, and I can get it back to you tomorrow night . . . as soon as everyone is asleep."

"And have you turn me in? I think not. I have all I need from —"

Aboveground the trapdoor opened. A woman's voice called, "Josef? Josef, are you there?"

The prisoner flicked off the torch, dropping it on the ground, and grabbed Josef, holding the knife to his throat.

"Josef? I saw that light! Is Aimee with you?"

From the darkness a sleepy voice cried feebly, "Mademoiselle? Mademoiselle

Claire! I want to go home."

"Aimee!" Fräulein Claire's voice spoke deep relief. "We've been so worried about you. Both of you come up here, right away!"

"Tell her to come down here," the prisoner whispered in Josef's ear. "Tell her, or I will slit your throat and the girl's."

Josef's heart beat madly against his rib cage. *What is she doing here? Where is Herr David?* He could not risk Fräulein Claire. But he could not risk Aimee either. *Adonai! What have I done? Help me!*

The man thrust his arm against Josef's chest, emphasizing his threat. Josef could not speak. He could not bring her to this pit. "Tell her you've broken your leg, that you can't climb up!" the man hissed. "Tell her!"

"It's dark, mademoiselle! I want to come, but I can't see the ladder," Aimee pleaded from the darkness, her tearful voice filled with hope.

"I have a torch; I'll bring it down and help you up," Claire called.

The man reached for the torch at his feet, momentarily loosening his grip on Josef.

"No, Fräulein!" Josef gasped, kicking the man's hand as it grasped the torch.

He heard the knife hit the earthen floor, but the man grabbed his leg just as Josef lunged away.

"What's going on down there?" Claire called. "Is there someone with you?"

Silence.

"A bad man took us, mademoiselle! He's hurting Josef!" Aimee's voice quavered, but she called out bravely.

"If you value the lives of these children, Fräulein, come down here now, slowly. Are you alone?"

There was no response.

"Bring whoever is with you, or I will cut this boy's throat, and then the girl's!"

"We're coming. We're coming now! Don't hurt them. Please, don't hurt them!"

Josef's heart sank in defeat and rose in love for Fräulein Claire. Hot tears filled his eyes. He'd done all he could to protect her and Aimee, and now they were both in the clutches of the enemy.

In the bobbing of Fräulein Claire's torchlight, the prisoner grabbed his own torch. Her sturdy shoes stepped down the ladder, followed by shapely calves and the swish of her skirt. Josef could feel a change in the man's grip across his chest and knew her beauty sparked his interest. He hated him for that. Such a man had no right to look at Fräulein Claire in this way.

"Well, well, Fräulein," the man smirked.

But then a pair of boots and long pant legs appeared on the ladder. Josef dared to hope it was Herr David, that he'd come with Fräulein and together they would — "Peter!" Josef's relief at seeing his older brother was swallowed in his remorse that even Peter might be killed for his folly. But he sensed a panic in the prisoner.

"Who else is there?" he demanded.

Claire reached immediately for Aimee, who clung to her. "Who are you and what are you doing with these children?" Claire's brave face didn't fool even Josef.

"Let go of my brother," Peter insisted, walking forward.

Josef felt a slight shift in the prisoner's stance and tried to pull away, but the prisoner clutched him all the tighter.

"Stand back!" He held the knife against Josef's chest once more.

Peter stopped. The man's knife made all the difference in their confidence. But Josef also knew there was strength in numbers. His eyes slowly swept the group and looked up to the prisoner, then landed on Peter.

Peter blinked in understanding and stepped to the side.

"What are you doing? Get over there — with them!" the man commanded.

"Why? What will you do? Will you kill all

of us? And what of those who are coming behind us? Will you kill them, too?"

Peter's simple questions, as if he wasn't afraid, seemed to infuse strength in Claire, who stepped in the opposite direction. "Do you intend to add the murder of children to your war crimes? At least that will ensure you will not rot in jail. You will hang, and even your countrymen will despise you for your cowardice and cruelty."

Josef sensed the momentary uncertainty in the prisoner.

"We could let him go," Josef offered quietly, as if the tables had shifted, as if they possessed any power.

"Why would we do that?" Peter asked. "Others are on their way, even now. He will be apprehended and prosecuted."

"Kidnapping carries a heavy weight," Claire said, holding Aimee behind her.

"Then I have little to lose." The prisoner twisted Josef's arm behind him, enough to make him cry out. "Stand back! You will stay here."

"A wise choice," Claire said.

"But this wily one will go with me. If I am followed, I will kill him."

"He's young. He will slow you down," Peter spoke quickly, his German accent thick. "Leave him. Take me. I can guide you."

"*Nein.* This one is a compass. Stand back." The man pushed Josef to the ladder. "Up, slowly." He kept one hand on the ladder and the other on Josef's leg, turning only long enough to threaten the others with his knife. Josef climbed up the ladder, frightened but relieved to bring the man out into the open. Without the others at risk, he would have a better chance of escape.

Josef's head had just cleared the trapdoor when he felt the man yank his leg with a mighty jerk. Josef fell down the ladder, his head slapping against the rock, the earth, the ladder rungs, and into sudden blackout.

Claire could not let Josef disappear again, could not allow him to be taken. The second the prisoner's head had vanished into the upward tunnel she and Peter both lunged for his legs, wrenching him downward, beating his back, bringing Josef on top of them all.

But neither Claire nor Peter was a match for the man's brute strength or training. He turned on them in a moment, slicing the air near them with his knife. In the process he nicked Aimee's arm. The little girl wailed.

Claire, in fear and fury, flew at the man, screaming like a banshee. Peter yanked her back, but the knife found its target too soon.

Astonished, Claire fell backward. Aimee screamed. Peter caught her, and the man disappeared up the ladder.

"Go for help!" Claire pleaded with Peter. "Make all the noise you can. Rouse the neighbors — anyone who can . . ." But the darkness overtook her.

Chapter Thirty-Two

Claire woke in her bed at Bluebell Wood to find Dr. MacDonald standing over her, his weathered face wreathed in a benevolent smile. "You gave us quite a scare, lassie."

Claire's mouth tasted like gruel paste, her throat dry as old corn husks. It took her several moments to piece together all she remembered. "Aimee? Josef? Peter? Gaston? Are they safe?"

"Fine, lass, right as spring rain. They're downstairs now, nailing Aimee's mezuzah to Miranda's front doorpost. Seems the girl carried it with her from France and has been waiting for a home to attach it. Never mind, you'll hear all about that later. You've been out these two days. Josef got a nasty bump on the head but came round in no time. The others are none the worse for wear, only eager to know the moment their lady fair is awake. Quite the Joan of Arc you've become to them, I daresay."

Claire closed her eyes. "Hardly that. If I hadn't . . . Please, tell me what happened. I can't remember — Owww!" She'd tried to hoist herself to a sitting position, but violent pain wrenched her stomach.

"None of that, now. The devil plunged you with his lance, by all accounts. You'll need to lie still a few days yet and take life slowly for a time, let those stitches do their work. A nasty knife gouge, that, and none too clean, though no major organs damaged. I'm watching for any sign of infection. So far, all seems well."

"Is he still at large?"

"Ho, no! Well, of course you've not heard. Your Sir David's quite the hero. He'd gotten old Dunnagan's dogs in the dead of night and tracked the devil round the lake, met Gaston first and then the fiend head-on not long after he'd come out of that tunnel.

"The Campbell tackled the brute to the ground and knocked him unconscious. Young Peter heard the ruckus and together they tied him up. David carried you up the ladder of the Home Guard's tunnel himself. By the time Sergeant Foley and his men got there it was all over — crabbit they are that all the district knows of their secret tunnel! Had a few choice words for Josef and Gaston." The doctor laughed. "You young

Americans are alike — impulsive, won't wait for anything or anyone. Foolhardy actions on your part, but brave; I'll give you that."

"David carried me up the ladder?" Claire felt herself warm and wonder at the imagination.

"Aye." He smiled. "And all the way back to the car, then home to Bluebell Wood, stanching your wound with his shirt — which is likely what kept you in the land of the living. Quite the gallant knight, he was, and been worried sick for you. Wouldn't let another spare him a step. I've only just convinced him to leave your side for a needed shave and a rest. Says he must speak with you the moment you open your eyes. He'll be furious that you woke without him here." Dr. MacDonald chuckled. "He'll get over it, I'll wager, as long as you mend. And you will mend, provided you don't overdo and break open that wound. It's that serious; do you understand me, Claire?"

"Yes." Claire sighed, content, now that everyone was safe at last, to lie back on her pillow. "I'll be good, good as gold." In truth, she couldn't keep her eyes open. Deep weariness pulled at her bones and weighted her eyelids.

She was just drifting off when she heard

David's voice. "She's awake! Claire! Claire —"

But Dr. MacDonald shushed him, insisting, "Everything you have to say can be said later. There'll be all the time in the world for sweet nothings. She's going to make it."

"But I want — I need to tell her that —"

"Tell her later, when she's rested enough to know you're talking to her."

Claire's heart fluttered and she wondered what David wanted to tell her, what seemed so joyfully, manfully urgent. Somehow, even near sleep, she thought she knew. But sleep beckoned, and she slipped into dreamland, knowing that two men, good men who cared for her, watched over her.

When Claire woke again, her head felt thick and her mind cloudy, her vision unfocused. It was daylight, and the blackout curtain had been drawn aside. Still, the room lay dim, indicating late afternoon. Claire drew a deep breath and noted that the pain in her stomach no longer pierced, but sat dull and unmoving. *A good sign, I think.*

She squinted, then opened wide her eyes, taking in the familiarity of the room, wondering how long she'd slept, what day it was, what more had happened in her absence.

The last she'd known, Dr. MacDonald and David were in the room. She smiled, remembering Dr. MacDonald's words. What was it that David had so urgently wanted to tell her? David, who'd rescued her. David, who'd carried her home and sat by her bed until she regained consciousness. A small smile reached her lips, her heart imagining, hoping what he might say.

Her door opened, and in walked Aunt Miranda.

"Claire, darling!" Aunt Miranda smiled, her clouded eyes shining. "It's so good to see you awake!"

"Aunt Miranda." Claire, quickly past the disappointment of not seeing David first, hardly knew what to say. Her aunt looked as if she'd aged five years. Could she have been that worried for her, or was this the evidence of Dr. MacDonald's weeks of concern?

"Raibeart said you were out of the woods, but that we should let you sleep as long as possible. I just needed to see you — to know you're all right, and to give you a message from David."

Claire's heart flipped.

"He's been called away — government orders."

Her heart plummeted. "When will he be back?"

Her aunt sat on the edge of the bed and looked as if she might reach for Claire's arm, but pulled back. "We don't know. *He* didn't know, but thought, from whatever his superior said, that it might be some weeks. He said he'd hoped to talk with you before going, but Raibeart ordered that we not wake you. I hope I didn't wake you now."

"No, not at all." Claire swallowed her disappointment. She also tried not to stare at her aunt's hollowed eyes and cheeks, but pulled herself to a semi-sitting position.

"Be careful of those stitches. Raibeart said you mustn't pull." Her aunt braced the pillow behind Claire's back.

"It's better than I thought, though I'm not ready to run any races." Claire grimaced.

"I shouldn't think so. Healing will take some time. You'll have to be patient, even if that's a bit foreign to you." Her aunt half smiled.

"I'll mend. Dr. MacDonald said so." Claire couldn't keep her worries inside any longer. "But you . . . What's going on? What does Dr. MacDonald say about you?"

"I don't know what you mean." She laughed but paled. Claire waited. "Has our good doctor been speaking out of turn?"

Whether her aunt was miffed or not, Claire would not let the moment slide. "Something's wrong, Aunt Miranda; it's clear to all of us. I want to know what it is." When her aunt pulled her shoulders back, Claire knew the conversation was not going to be easy.

"I'm just a little tired; that's all. Nothing that won't ease now that you're doing better."

"Don't lay this at my door. You look terrible, and have for a month or more. You're getting thinner by the week." Claire could be just as demanding as her aunt.

"Well, no one can say you're free with your compliments." But uncertainty swept Miranda's eyes, and Claire knew her aunt was trying to decide how much to share.

"Please . . . please tell me. Nothing can be worse than not knowing." Claire reached for her aunt's hand. This time Miranda hung on tight.

"Can't it?"

"Whatever it is, please let me help you. We'll face it together."

Miranda raised her eyebrows but would not meet Claire's probing eyes. "I'm not sure I can be helped."

"Did Dr. MacDonald say that?" Claire felt

as if an anvil had been placed on her chest.

"No." Miranda stood and walked toward the window, her back to Claire. "He wants me to go for tests . . . and possibly treatment. He wants me to go to London, to a colleague he believes might help me."

"You're going . . . right?" But her aunt didn't respond. "Please say you're going."

"It's not so simple, you see."

"No, I don't see."

Her aunt's shoulders heaved. She turned, knotting and unknotting her hands. "There are things I must do, things I must take care of here."

"What? Tell me. I'll do them!"

"You're not to get out of bed — doctor's orders!"

"Promise me, the minute I get out of bed, you'll go."

"There are no guarantees that he can help me."

"There are no guarantees about anything in this life except that it will end," Claire pushed.

"Precisely."

"But it doesn't have to end now. Not unless that's what you want."

Her aunt did not answer, but the uncertainty in her eyes frightened Claire beyond anything she could remember.

"Please . . . please, Aunt Miranda. I love you. I need you. We all do. Promise me!"

Chapter Thirty-Three

November's winds swept the fells and lakes, bringing turbulent swells to the water's surface. Robust clouds purpled the skies with sheets of cold rain. Autumn's brilliant leaves turned rich auburn and deep, maternal gold. As the last leaves fell, swirling in snow-globe leaf showers, Remembrance Day came.

Mrs. Newsome handed round the poppies for each member of the household and staff to wear to services. Claire must remain home in bed.

But Lady Langford insisted on walking to the village church with the staff and family. She'd confided to Mrs. Newsome that though she'd not darkened its door since Christopher's funeral, she wanted to go to church now. This, she said, might prove her last opportunity to stand for her beloved husband's and son's memory. She would not miss the somber service, would not forgo this opportunity to honor Gilbert and Christopher within her community.

Mrs. Newsome understood, but such exertion on the part of her ladyship worried her. Claire had confided her conversation with her aunt, and Mrs. Newsome saw in Dr. MacDonald's eyes that every day delayed drew his love closer to danger's door. He'd begged and cajoled his Maggie to get on with the tests prescribed and pursue treatment. But it was Claire's begging of her aunt to do all she could to live a long and healthy life that had at last turned the tide. She could not refuse the niece who'd nearly died protecting them all, who lived and breathed in her image.

"I'll go the Monday after Thanksgiving — wherever Raibeart recommends — if Claire is well enough," Lady Langford had promised. Mrs. Newsome intended to hold her to it, and she knew Miss Claire would.

All the children attended church that morning with both the vicar's and the rabbi's blessing, each kissing their fingers and touching Aimee's mezuzah as they marched out and in the front door of Bluebell Wood — their own house of blessing. It was a day for unity, a day to remember those who'd fallen in battle for freedom, and a day to renew resolve for an uncertain future.

Dr. MacDonald forwent his own pew to support the ever-thinning Lady Langford in Bluebell Wood's pew, helping her stand, refusing to leave her side.

Mrs. Newsome shook her head. Why her lady had not swallowed her pride, or whatever kept her from claiming happiness, and married that dear man years ago, she could not fathom. *Such a waste of life and love. Such a pity not to enjoy what God has placed before us! What must the Almighty think of our ingratitude at His providences?*

She thought of her dear Thomas, long gone in the Great War. There'd never been another for her, never been an opportunity or interest. But what if there had been? Would she have taken that step forward? She didn't know, but yes, she thought she might. Living alone seemed a sad thing to her way of thinking.

Mrs. Newsome smiled, ever grateful that she did not live alone. She lived in a great house with a brood of children, as dear as any of her own she could imagine. Indeed, she prayed for their parents, and for sweet reunions at war's end, where the children rightfully belonged, but couldn't help her dread of that parting, or of their growing up and leaving to make their way in the world, if it came to that. Didn't every mother and auntie grieve the same loss when her children grew up? It was — would be — another station in life to embrace.

Embracing the death of Lady Miranda Langford, if it came to that, was another thing. Mrs. Newsome could not imagine this earth without her ladyship, or what she herself would do on such a day. Lady Miranda had become more like a younger sister than an employer to Mrs. Newsome — nearly blood of her blood. Mrs. Newsome was a praying woman, and if ever she had prayed, she prayed now.

Thanksgiving — quietly, closely, and warmly celebrated — came and went. David was still away. It was understood that his war work was crucial and hush-hush, but he and his infectious smile, and his lively hamboning of the year before, were sorely missed. Even Mrs. Creedle's miraculous savory turkey and sage dressing could not bring the needed life to the eyes and hearts around Bluebell Wood's full table, though there were many brave faces.

Miranda knew Claire's recovery was speeded by her own agreement to pursue tests and treatment. Claire's face held such hope for Miranda, but Miranda didn't feel quite ready, either to go and face her future or to say good-bye to her family at home — the family she'd taken too long to embrace as her own.

Very early Monday morning, before leaving for hospital as promised, before relinquishing her days and hours into the hands of medically minded strangers, Miranda Langford insisted on seeing her solicitor in her library.

After reading and approving the changes she'd asked him to make weeks ago, Miranda signed and set her seal firmly upon her last will and testament, sealed the envelope, and gave it to her frowning longtime family solicitor.

Far from embracing the role of fatalist, she maintained that it was only right to keep things up to date. She did not expect miracles on her behalf, but no matter what happened, she wanted to make things as easy and clear as possible for Claire, whenever her time came. Navigating Britain's death and estate taxes had proven overwhelming and nearly disastrous for Miranda, and they would surely prove a bear for Claire, an American citizen.

"Thank you, Mr. Peabody, for coming so early. I know this is an inconvenience, but I feel much better knowing my will is in your capable hands."

"I hope to see you soon, Lady Langford — soon and well."

She smiled. "You're very kind. You've always been very kind." It was a statement meant to graciously close the door, for neither the solicitor nor the locals had always been kind to Miranda. Perhaps her gratitude might help pave an easier path for Claire. "Mrs. Newsome will show you out," she told the man, who looked nearly as pasty white as she. "I'd like a few minutes to myself. Ask her to hold my tea, if you don't mind. I'll ring when I'm ready."

Mr. Peabody nodded in a half bow, straightened his shoulders, and walked crisply from the room.

Miranda imagined he'd hoped to see the last of the Americans with her passing. *We Americans spring like chickweed in the Motherland's gardens.* That had been her private joke with Gilbert. She sat back in her desk chair and smiled as the door closed.

Jokes with Gilbert were so long past. If Miranda held regrets, they were few. Only, if she could do life over again, she would have accepted Raibeart the moment he'd asked, when Christopher was young and in need of a father, when she was still young and in need and longing for a husband.

She should have let Raibeart into the private world she'd forged with Christopher. What joy it could have been for the three of them! He'd embraced the role of a dear friend to her and a kindly, guiding uncle to her son, but he could have proven so much more.

She'd been so concerned with appearances, so determined that she and especially Christopher be accepted in the village and by the community. Christopher's father and her husband, lord of the manor, hero of the Great War, could not be superseded by a mere Scottish doctor.

Could she and Christopher have left the manor tenantless to live with Raibeart in the village? Either scenario had seemed impossible. Langfords had owned and worked the land of Bluebell Wood for nearly six hundred years. There were standards to uphold, for love of Gilbert and for the sake of Christopher's future.

Just now all those high notions seemed empty, futile, especially since Christopher had been taken for good and all from his Hundred Acre Wood.

Miranda smiled through her tears. *The Hundred Acre Wood* — that's what Christopher had named their surrounding forest the moment she'd read A. A. Milne's books to him. Christopher Robin, Pooh, Eeyore, Piglet — they'd all become dear friends and intimates.

And so Bluebell Wood had remained the Hundred Acre Wood, at least until Christopher had grown a little older and she'd read him the many adventures of Robin Hood and his merry men. Then Bluebell Wood became Sherwood Forest to her brave, young Robin Hood. Once in a while, in childish enthusiasm, he had proclaimed her his Maid Marian.

Always, they'd kept the secret garden together. She knew that over the years, Christopher had savored treetop secrets there even more precious than her own among the sun-dappled roses and shaded lily of the valley. The garden at large was a private, magical world they'd shared.

Miranda sighed. Claire wasn't the only one who saw a story or line of poetry wherever she turned. Her niece was so much like her in all her literary dreaming. Miranda only hoped Claire wouldn't hold living, breathing love at bay for the sake of grief or fear of loss or abandonment or reputation, or for high hopes of a storybook romance that didn't exist, or any of the myriad feeble excuses her aunt had wasted life upon.

She hoped and prayed that Claire would cast aside her fear and embrace the real love offered her, both by her Savior and by a good man, perhaps even by David Campbell.

If David was that man, as she so easily envisioned, Miranda prayed that God would bless them with children who could imagine and create to their hearts' content within the walls of the secret garden, that they might spill over into the rooms and grounds of Bluebell Wood, making its walls ring with song and childish laughter, as they were meant to do.

Miranda set her pen in the inkwell. She was tired, clear through to her bones. She knew where her eternal home lay, not only where she would find the husband of her youth and the son of her joy but, even more, where she would at long last see face-to-face her loving Lord and Savior.

No more pain, no more sorrow — the invitation tempted. She prayed only that if she couldn't recover, the Lord would let her die with grace, with dignity. She did not want to embarrass those she loved so dearly. If Raibeart's test results and possible treatments didn't work — and she hardly dared believe they would — then Miranda hoped, even prayed, that she would die in hospital, not fade further before the grieving eyes of Claire and the children at home. She didn't want that. They didn't deserve that.

One last time she glanced around her beloved library, sanctuary and refuge so long dear to her. She stood and walked toward the fireplace, kneeling before her favorite armchair, just as she had done many times over the years.

She clasped her hands and poured out her heart to the One who loved and understood her best — her fears for the uncertain days just ahead, her every longing for the inhabitants of her home, and ultimately thanksgiving for each day's joy. All these she surrendered to the One who'd comforted and guided her each step of life's journey.

She asked forgiveness for giving in to the fear that had waylaid her so many times, for not grasping with both hands the joy He'd set before her on countless days, especially the earthly love of Raibeart, and for the years of wasted relationship with her only sister.

She thanked Him for the late-in-life love of Claire and the remarkable "apple of His eye" children entrusted to their care, for their unmindful awakening of her senses and rekindling of her heart. Raibeart had been right about that, too. She must tell him so.

Finally, Miranda stood, as ready as she would ever be to face this day. She wiped her tears and pinched color into her cheeks. Pasting on the bravest smile she could muster, she walked toward the library door.

On the other side, she knew, waited her good and patient Raibeart; her worried, loving Claire; and her precious Mrs. Newsome, faithful friend and protector for more than twenty-five years. Each of them would go as far as allowed with her into the unknown.

Once Aunt Miranda and Dr. MacDonald had left for London, Bluebell Wood seemed much bigger to Claire. Quieter, colder, bereft of sunshine.

At luncheon the children poked and prodded their food. Mrs. Newsome did not chide them, despite the waste. She seemed too distracted to notice, or too heart-heavy to care.

Jeanine looked down at her plate and spoke so softly Claire barely heard her. "It is like losing Maman all over again."

Elise began to cry.

Claire's eyes burned. She looked round at her table of war orphans — at least that's what she feared them to be based on all she'd heard in the news and from David. She realized that Aunt Miranda had become much more than an aunt to her, more like the mother she'd never experienced. Was she to be an orphan too?

Mrs. Newsome lifted her chin and tried to speak, but Claire saw that words and the British stiff upper lip failed her.

Such sadness would not do. Aunt Miranda would not want it, would demand she take hold and lead the family to higher ground. Claire cleared her throat. "Aunt Miranda would be appalled to think we've all given up on her getting well. She's gone to hospital to be cured. We must believe in that."

Gaston, ever the realist, looked at her as if she should be telling them all the truth and preparing them for the worst.

"No matter what happens," Claire continued, "we must pull together as a family. We *are* a family." She said it firmly, as if she meant it, and realized that she did. Ever since Josef had risked his life to save her and Aimee, ever since Gaston had seen beyond apparent cruelty and hurt to look into his friend's soul, ever since David had risked life and limb to rescue her and the children, she'd realized that these were far more, far dearer than wards or tenants or refugees to her. Claire swallowed the lump of fear that surfaced each time she remembered standing between the children and danger, each time she remembered lunging for the prisoner's legs as he disappeared up that ladder with Josef. No matter her knife wound, she would do it again, in a heartbeat. "Whatever the future brings for Aunt Miranda, or for any of us, we are, most truly, a family of strength and love. We'd best start acting like one."

One by one, the children blinked, looked up, or stole glances at one another. Bertram's shoulders straightened. Slowly, first Peter, then Gaston and Franz sat up. Marlene and Jeanine smiled at each other through worried eyes. Ingrid and Elise sniffled but raised their chins. Josef reached for Aimee's hand and squeezed it in comfort.

Mrs. Newsome sniffed and wiped her pocket handkerchief across her nose — at the table — and spoke with authority. "You're quite right, Miss Claire. We've every reason to hope for good things all round and enough love and courage to bolster one another on, come what may."

Elise stared at Mrs. Newsome's regained stiff upper lip until she giggled, and that set off a chain of grins and low chuckles, easing the tension wonderfully. Though Mrs. Newsome huffed and pretended to look offended, Claire saw the long-missing twinkle return to her eye for a moment.

A moment is one thing; a lifetime is another. Please, God, keep Aunt Miranda in Your care, whatever that best care is for her. You know we want her well and returned to us. But most of all, we want what is best for her. Help us to help each other through the uncertainty. Help us to be strong for one another, to love each other well, as You love . . .

Claire faltered, her mind and heart unable to utter the final word. Perhaps, even if the Lord couldn't accept Claire as she was, He would grant help on behalf of the children. After a moment, she concluded, *As You love them.*

CHAPTER THIRTY-FOUR

The children took turns writing daily letters to Lady Miranda, whom they each now called "Dearest Aunt Miranda."

Claire kept an ongoing journal for her aunt, reporting each day's activities and the children's exploits. She left it on the dining room sideboard. Anyone at any time could add a bit and send their love. By the time Claire posted it at week's end, the letter was fat despite paper rationing, and mostly a jolly collection meant to cheer Aunt Miranda. But there were the occasional smears — not so much from sticky childish fingers as from blotted tears. Claire knew her aunt would understand.

After a long and wearisome week, Mrs. Newsome had finally settled into her sitting room for a nice hot cup of tea, hoping to find some inspiring Sunday-evening organ music on the BBC, when her program was interrupted by a broadcast from America.

She listened, cup of tea in midair, unable to believe her ears. "Cheeky monkeys!" She slammed her teacup into its saucer, a thing for which she would have severely scolded the scullery maid. Paying no heed, she tore up the stairs to the library, rapped on the door, and entered without waiting for a word.

By the stricken face of Claire and the worried faces of the children, she saw they'd already heard.

"America . . . at war," Claire said, clearly dazed.

"The Yanks have joined at last." Mrs. Newsome spoke before she could catch herself. She knew she should be horrified and sorry for the terrible loss of life on the Hawaiian island — and she was — but she also gave thanks that the sleeping giant had been awakened. *Now they will help. Britain won't stand alone. Horrible as it is, how many Pearl Harbors have the Europeans seen in the last two years? It's nothing new to us.*

"I'll bring tea." Mrs. Newsome closed the door quietly, resorting to her standard cure-all. It would take them all time to absorb Mr. Roosevelt's speech, to form a plan of action. *Will Miss Claire feel the need to return home to her mother? Surely not now. We need her here more than ever, and travel is out of the question. What about Mr. David? Will he be required to return to the States and enlist? With my lady so ill and all these children, whatever would I do?*

The questions spinning round gave Mrs. Newsome a headache. *One day at a time, Lord Jesus. One day at a time. Sufficient to the day is the evil thereof. Oh, Father in heaven, let Hitler and his evil be annihilated. Let families and peace be restored. Let these dear children go home to their parents. Let Lady Miranda come home well and strong to us. And in the meantime, Father, I'll set a card on my sitting room mantelpiece as a reminder to hope: "America Is In."*

Just over a week later they lit the first Hanukkah candle. Peter presided over his new and intricately carved menorah. Although there was little joy and laughter, even from spinning the dreidel, Claire believed the growing number of lights and the miraculous hope of Hanukkah somehow helped their uncertainty and relieved the darkness. If God had performed miracles on behalf of the Jewish people so long ago, might He not perform miracles for Aunt Miranda now, for the parents of these children, for the people of Britain and

America and all the world caught in this horrible, messy war?

Rabbi Meir, who had come so faithfully each Shabbat to lead the meal and services, received a reduced petrol ration, like everyone else. The weekly journey was now too long. Bertram and Peter took turns presiding over the meal. Jeanine and Marlene took turns donning the veil and lighting the candles.

Some of the children accompanied Claire and Mrs. Newsome to church on Sundays. Mrs. Creedle and Mr. Dunnagan kept to the balcony, as was their custom. Nancy shared the pew with her mother, Mollie spent Sundays at home, and life at Bluebell Wood went on.

But life in the village had changed. Since the Americans had entered the war, a few locals, even the postmistress, actually welcomed Claire. Some gave her knowing nods, confiding, "It's high time." The growing level of acceptance lifted Claire's spirits, if only a little.

A week before Christmas a letter came from Aunt Miranda, in her own hand — a thing that had not happened since she'd left Bluebell Wood, so a miracle in its own right. The handwriting was shaky, the lines broken, but each word burned into Claire's heart.

My dearest Claire,

When I heard Mr. Roosevelt's speech, I could scarcely believe my ears. For all we've been so focused on Germany, I've given little thought to threats from Japan. But America's declaration gives me hope for a speedy end to this wretched war, and for the future of the parents of our dear children at home.

The tests here are uncomfortable, but that is all. It is the diagnosis of breast cancer and the coming surgery that are more daunting. Because of that, I must write plainly.

You will know from my solicitor that one day, perhaps soon, Bluebell Wood will be yours. It is all I have to give, my darling niece, and I give it to you freely, gladly, though I know it comes as a mixed blessing.

You will find joy and refuge there and, I hope, security for the family you choose. You will also find that while there may be a bit more appreciation just now that America is in, it may not last. Being an American in this ancient British village is not always easy. But you know that already.

Of all the gifts Bluebell Wood brings and of all the secrets it holds, the secret garden is my most precious offering. Don't pretend you don't know what I'm talking about. I know you found it in the first months you came.

Once I was miffed that you'd discovered my private sanctuary, but then I saw it as the natural order of things. Now, I am so glad to know it has proven a sanctuary for you, too.

While I'm able, I want to share its history with you.

The garden belonged to Gilbert's parents. They cultivated it and built the walls around it in the last century. It was their private family joy. Sadly, I never knew them. By the time Gilbert and I married, they were gone. Gilbert introduced me to the garden as a new bride. It was our bower all the months he was home, and I named it our Secret Garden.

It was the first place Christopher's baby eyes saw of the grounds at Bluebell Wood. We spent part of every day there that weather allowed, and each day I told my baby boy more about his father — every detail I could summon.

When word came of Gilbert's death, the garden became my refuge. Sometimes the joy and beauty of the place, the intense memories of the love Gilbert and I had shared there, were like the ripping open of a raw wound. So I locked the world and everyone in it from the garden, and in so many ways, from my heart. There were times I was tempted to close and lock the garden altogether — even from Christopher and myself — but Christopher loved it so, I couldn't bear to keep him from it. We kept it open until he went to Eton, at thirteen. And then I let the ivy grow over its walls and rarely visited.

I know Christopher found and created special places within the garden as a boy, just as I did over the years. You've discovered his tree. It's good to know that the joy of something he loved so well goes on. How I wish you could have known him! You would have loved each other dearly.

No matter what happens in the days ahead, my dear niece, the garden is yours now — forever and always. You know where the key is. You may do with it as you wish. Know that it comes with my blessing, precious Claire.

All my love,
Aunt Miranda

Two days later, before Claire could absorb the gift of the garden and the love she'd so lavishly received, Dr. MacDonald telephoned from London. Claire, in turn, reported the news to the children at breakfast.

"Dr. MacDonald said that the surgery did not altogether stop the progress of Aunt Miranda's cancer. Radiation therapy is needed — required — if there is to be any hope at all."

"And will this — this radiation therapy save her life?" asked Peter, ever insistent to pin down details.

Claire knew they'd all learned to cope without Aunt Miranda, but more than ever each one wanted her returned to them. She desperately wished that she could sugarcoat the truth, that she could change the truth. Still, these were brave children, what Mr. Dunnagan called salt. She must not deceive them. "We don't know. No one knows, and there are severe side effects from the prolonged exposure, especially since she's now so weak. Dr. MacDonald said there are experiments being done with new drugs that might help, but they're not well tested, and they hold great risk. He believes the radiation therapy in short bursts — shorter than the radiation doctor would prefer — is her best chance."

"Then she must do it," Gaston said stoutly.

"Will she?" Jeanine asked.

Claire saw the understanding in Jeanine's eyes that Aunt Miranda may not want to live more of this hard life, not enough to risk more pain, more treatments, or the questionable results. She hesitated.

"She must!" Gaston insisted.

"The decision is hers, Gaston, not ours."

"But she will do it for us, *n'est-ce pas*? She will do it because she loves us, because we love her!"

Claire hoped with all her heart that was true.

It was late. The children had hours earlier tumbled into bed, had been prayed over and tucked in for the night, and all who allowed it had been kissed on the forehead.

Claire waited up to listen alone to the wireless broadcast by President Roosevelt and Prime Minister Churchill, as together they addressed the world from Washington, DC. She agreed with both men as they encouraged the celebration of Christmas as a day of happiness and laughter, especially for the sake of children in a "world of storm." The prime minister implored listeners to "share in their unstinted pleasures before we turn again to the stern task and the formidable years that lie before us, resolved that, by our sacrifice and daring, these same children shall not be robbed of their inheritance or denied their right to live in a free and decent world."

Claire turned off the dial and sighed. The year ahead certainly loomed formidable, and the futures of the children uncertain.

She pushed aside the sashes and hair ribbons she'd spent the last hour braiding for Aimee and Elise's Christmas gifts. *So little for each child this year, and all made from bits and pieces and scraps.*

The shops were nearly bereft of gift items. Everything of practical use — from cardigans to writing paper — had been severely rationed. Food and goods had grown exorbitant in price, though having money wasn't really the issue. Unless you were willing to buy on the black market, so many goods were simply not to be found.

Coping with the children and their growing fears for Aunt Miranda was difficult enough. Claire held her own desperate worries close to her heart, doing her best to maintain a brave face.

Letters from faithful Dr. MacDonald, who shared loving messages from Aunt Miranda, helped. Aunt Miranda had grown too weak to write since the surgery, which made her gift of the garden letter, written over many days, all the more precious.

David had been gone for weeks, sent off by the Sunderland flying boat factory who knew where . . . all covert in wartime secrets. She'd not seen or heard a word from him since just after Guy Fawkes Day, the day of his wonderful rescue of her, even though she hoped he knew Aunt Miranda lay in hospital from her letters sent in care of the factory.

She missed him, much more than she could ever have imagined. She wondered if he was too busy to write, or perhaps restricted from writing personal letters for security's sake, or if he had formed some other attachment.

Claire swallowed. *What if he has? What if David has found another to woo and love? As Arnaud turned to Josephine?* She couldn't blame him if he had. She'd never encouraged David, not enough to let him know how she felt. Love was such a frightening thing, such a surrender of control, such a baring of the heart.

Claire had survived the pain of losing Arnaud, had survived the betrayal of her friend Josephine, had even survived the rejection of her own father and the neglect of her mother. Now, with Aunt Miranda standing on the brink of eternity, Claire did not think she could face the loss of David, too.

And yet she had no control over this. None. Once, David had asked about her greatest fear and her greatest desire. Though she hadn't formed the fear into words then, life without love, Claire now realized, was her greatest fear. Love and a place within a family were her greatest desires, had always been her greatest desires. And now she knew she wanted that with David, but was it too late?

She envisioned the years to come and saw herself standing gray-haired and alone — a perfect Miss Havisham from *Great Expectations* — in the midst of her secret garden, the door of her private sanctuary locked from the inside. The image made Claire shudder. The garden in every season was lovely, but standing in it, aging in it alone, was not the future she wanted.

According to Mr. Lewis, there was only One who could direct any real change in her life, in her being. According to him, she had important business to attend to before she could freely love others or freely receive their love. She pulled the letter from her skirt pocket — the letter she'd been thrilled to finally receive three days ago. She'd read and reread it, re-creasing its folds, keeping it close by, thinking about each and every line.

She'd asked Mr. Lewis about love and about Jesus laying down His life as a ransom for sin. That He loved made sense to her, based on what she'd read in the Bible Aunt Miranda had given her, but could it really and truly apply to her? Could Jesus have died for her, could He love her in that way? Or was that exclusively some corporate and economical payment of justice — a life for a life? Would He include her in His sacrifice, in His love, if He really knew her? Didn't she need to become better first?

Mr. Lewis had written as if there were no debate in the matter.

> I think every one who has some vague belief in God, until he becomes a Christian, has the idea of an exam, or of a bargain in his mind. The first result of real Christianity is to blow that idea into bits. God has been waiting for the moment at which you discover that there is no ques-

tion of earning a pass mark in this exam, or putting Him in your debt.

Such an awakened individual discovers his bankruptcy, and so says to God: "You must do this. I can't." Christ offers something for nothing.

We can't do anything to deserve such astonishing happiness. All the initiative has been on God's side; all has been free, unbounded grace. Our own puny and ridiculous efforts are as helpless to retain the joy as they were to achieve it in the first place. Bliss is not for sale, cannot be earned. Works have no merit, though of course faith, inevitably, even unconsciously, flows out into works of love at once. We are not saved because we perform works of love; we do works of love because we are saved. It is faith in Christ alone that saves us; faith bestowed by sheer gift.

The great thing to remember is that, though our feelings come and go, His love for us does not. It is not wearied by our sins, or our indifference. God loves us because we are a self, because He is love and that love pours out onto us . . . lavishly, as though God can't help but love us — His creatures — and delight, despite our own worst selves.

Could that be true? It was easy to see how He would — could — love the children or David or Mrs. Newsome or Aunt Miranda. They were lovable. But Claire? And if He really did love her, why didn't she know it, feel it?

At length Claire climbed the stairs, dressed for bed, and turned off the light, slipping beneath the covers of her bed. She stared into the blacked-out room, thinking more than praying. She wanted to sleep, to still the hammering questions and swirling storm of emotion. The clock in the downstairs foyer bonged one, then two. She listened to her own breathing.

In time, the surrounding darkness faded. In time, the outlines of furniture, barely visible, disappeared. In place of her room, she saw a pale-blue light reflected off of dense fog. A bell rang from some distant shore. She tasted salt air. Slowly, the fog dissipated.

Claire felt a slow movement beneath her, a movement that built to a sudden pitch. Her stomach rolled and flipped. Her fingers gripped like claws, intending to grasp the sheets of her bed, but the sheets had disappeared. Her bed became a small craft on a swollen sea — the craft smaller than Captain Beardsley's fishing boat, the sea far more treacherous. Lightning flashed across the water. A stiff breeze blew from the west, rising to a turbulent wind — sweeping, tossing her higher, higher, then crashing her tiny craft down again into roiling waves.

Claire's heart slammed against the walls of her chest. She and her craft took on water, began to sink, and she knew in her depths that her little boat, like all of her life, was out of control. In fear and desperation she cried out to the Lord. She cried, and He appeared.

Jesus stood at the helm of her small ship, both hands firmly grasping the wheel. He turned to face her and commanded, "Peace. Be still."

And it was. The winds and the waves stilled. The boat steadied and the storm in Claire's soul ceased.

Jesus gazed at her. He did not shift or flinch, did not turn away in disgust or indifference. And in those eyes, those wondrous eyes, she saw that He fully, truly loved her. Broken, fearful, angry, and despicable though she was — He loved her, and had died for her, too.

When Claire opened her eyes in the morning, her pillowslip was covered in tears — tears of relief and joy that had washed away stains and darkness and every form of despair she'd known.

Her circumstances had not changed one whit. Aunt Miranda still stood on the precipice between life and death. David was still far away, his feelings toward her unspoken and therefore unknown. The children stood in relentless need; there was no word regarding the fate of any of their parents. She knew nothing more of her father or even of her mother. Arnaud was dead, and Josephine — she knew nothing of Josephine. Claire had no idea how she and Mrs. Newsome would manage the children in the days and weeks and possibly years ahead. There was no end of the war in sight.

Her circumstances had not changed, but she had changed. Her mind, her heart had been transformed. She was free, unafraid, washed clean as never before. The words of a Scripture Lewis had written her came to mind: *"There is no fear in love; but perfect love casteth out fear: because fear hath torment."*

She'd long known that torment. But no fear in love? "No fear . . . I am loved." Claire repeated the words aloud, noticing how they tasted on her tongue — like honey, or the freshness of spring's first mint, or summer's honeysuckle.

Claire thought of her parents, of Josephine, of all the burdens Aunt Miranda had carried these many years. How she wished for them the joy and lightness she felt this morning. How she wished they could see the love and peace and complete freedom she'd seen in her Savior's eyes when He'd gazed into her own and taken control of her little ship, of her life.

Claire pushed the hair from her eyes and her eiderdown to the side. She planted her feet firmly on the floor and pulled aside the blackout curtain, allowing the sunshine of Christmas morning to pour into her room. She pulled out her best writing paper and took up her pen. There were important letters to write.

The first one began, *Dear Mother.* The second began, *Dear David.* The third began, *Dearest Josephine,* and the last, *My beloved Aunt Miranda.*

There was so much to tell, so much to share, so much to ask forgiveness for. There was even some to forgive. Beyond that, there was no time to lose, and none like the present.

Claire smiled, feeling a strong kinship to the reformed Ebenezer Scrooge on his first real Christmas morning. Her smile grew as she thought that someday all that had happened and would yet happen might make her own very good story, a great book.

Chapter Thirty-Five

Mrs. Newsome poured the last of the precious cocoa and cream into Aimee's breakfast cup, much to the astonished delight of the little girl. If Christmas Day was not the day to splurge on young ones, she didn't know when it was.

Mrs. Newsome and Mrs. Creedle had done all they could to make Christmas as happy as possible for Claire and the children despite the incessant and ever-more-stringent rationing. Mrs. Newsome knew her ladyship would want that. Even so, it was difficult not to be a trifle vexed with all the comings and goings and secrets running rampant throughout the household.

Miss Claire seemed in a highly excitable and happy state when she'd shouted from the upstairs banister that she would not be down to breakfast. Mr. Dunnagan had stomped through the kitchen — most unprecedented — at an unearthly hour and claimed double his breakfast plus a thermos of tea. According to Mrs. Creedle, he'd wanted it all packed in a sack to take away like a picnic lunch — a breakfast picnic by himself on Christmas Day!

Mr. David had telephoned at the crack of dawn, saying he was back in the area and asking if he might join the day's festivities, but please don't tell Claire. And Dr. MacDonald — well, she could make neither hide nor hair of his cryptic telephone message, only that he might arrive at Bluebell Wood in time for the noon meal.

"The children remain the most orderly of the lot — and that is a highly unusual state of affairs!" she remarked to Mrs. Creedle, who was beside herself with trying to "knit together a Christmas banquet from a sow's ear." Both women threw up their hands and went back to work.

Shortly before breakfast ended, Claire appeared in the dining room, wrapped in her coat and muffler, bright-eyed and rosy-cheeked, with a smile ready to take on the world. Mrs. Newsome could tell she'd been crying, but they appeared to be happy tears. She couldn't fathom what Miss Claire had to be so exuberant about, but it was a welcome change.

"Merry Christmas!" Claire cried, throwing wide her arms, as if to greet the day, the season, and all of life.

"Merry Christmas!" they all returned, glad in their faces to see Claire so cheerful, but clearly wondering at the mental state of their teacher and friend.

"I've a Christmas surprise for you."

"Presents on the tree!" Aimee guessed.

Claire laughed. "Yes, there are treats hanging from the tree, but we'll see those later. Don't expect too much," she cautioned. "War and hard times, and all that, you know. This is something else, something special, something lasting."

The children laughed, surprised by her enthusiasm, her good humor.

"As soon as you've finished eating, put on your coats and boots — wrap up warm in mufflers and gloves! It's freezing outside and we're in for a march!"

"You're taking these children hiking — this morning?" Mrs. Newsome gasped, horrified.

"The sun is shining, Mrs. Newsome. It's a brilliant morning!"

"Six inches of snow fell last night. Most don't have proper galoshes. Really, Miss Claire, I don't think you ought —"

"It's all right, Mrs. Newsome. We won't be gone long, and when we get back we'll all snuggle up in the library by the fire. It's well worth the trek; I promise."

Claire breathed a prayer of thanksgiving as she kissed her fingers and ran them over Aimee's mezuzah on the front doorpost — the first time she'd thanked God in full confidence for His love, His abiding care and blessing. Clasping Aimee's hand, she led her merry troop over freshly fallen snow and toward the maze. Icicles hung from the eaves of the house behind them, sun glistened off the snow-covered treetops, and heavy frost draped the looming topiaries in an air of grandeur.

At the far corner of the maze, Claire pushed through the thinned boxwood — something she'd reprimanded each of them for doing over the last year and a half — and came out onto a garden walk, stomping her feet. She cut across the lawns and into the edge of the woods, then followed the high stone fence around the secret garden's perimeter. When she reached the hidden door, she stopped so suddenly that two of the younger children bumped into her.

Claire gasped. Large footprints — a general scuffling — broke the snow at her feet. Who could have come here, and since last night's snowfall? Muffled voices came from the other side of the wall. Claire's confidence evaporated. No one should be here. No one should have access besides her and Aunt Miranda, and Aunt Miranda was lying in a hospital bed in faraway London.

The children, clustered uncertainly around her, inched closer.

"What is it, mademoiselle?" Gaston asked. "What is the matter?"

"Why are we here?" Elise wanted to know.

"Do you hear? Someone is on the other side of the wall," whispered Josef.

"The other side of the wall? How did they get there?" asked Jeanine.

"Shhh," warned Claire. "Let me think." But it was as if her mind had been wiped clean as an empty school slate. All she could imagine was to march in and face the intruders. She knew she should be worried for the small army of children at her back, but in fact, they bolstered her courage. Claire reached for the key over the lintel, but it was gone.

The audacity! Now she was thoroughly vexed. She pushed the door, and it creaked open on its great and rusted hinges. The voices stopped. Claire pushed in, Aimee behind her, both hands clinging to Claire's skirt. Claire scanned the garden, as far as she could see. No one. Not a sound.

"Hello?" she called. "Is someone there?"

No answer came.

Claire wound through the pathways toward the center of the garden. Gasps of wonder, sheer delight, and awe followed in her wake. She wished she could let down her reserve and turn to see their faces as they viewed the garden for the first time, but she feared what might lie ahead. She reached the last bend in the path, bringing her within view of the evergreen tree at the center of the garden.

But it was not the evergreen decked in snow that she'd expected. It was a regal Christmas tree, half decorated in blue and crimson and silver balls that shone, a near blinding light, in the morning sun. Claire recognized some of the ornaments from the tree as it had been decorated last year. But David was nowhere in sight. Unless . . . Her heart flipped.

"David? David, are you here?"

But there was no answer.

"Who's there? Show yourself!" Claire didn't know whether to be afraid or to cry.

A sheepish Mr. Dunnagan stepped from one side of the tree, removing his cap as he did so. A bleary-eyed and reticent Dr. MacDonald stepped from the other. Each man held an ornament for the tree.

"Dr. MacDonald? Mr. Dunnagan? What are you doing here?" Claire could not keep the disappointment or the confusion from her voice.

"Ever so sorry, miss. We meant to be done before you came." Mr. Dunnagan stepped back. "But she's a beauty, ain't she?"

The children swarmed gladly around the tree and their beloved gardener and their good, if sometimes gruff, doctor. But Claire stood motionless.

Dr. MacDonald handed his ornament to Mr. Dunnagan and stepped toward her. "Maggie — your aunt — sent me home on this mission. She wanted the tree fully trimmed for you when you came to the garden on Christmas Day. She was sure you'd come. I don't think she expected you to share it with the children — not yet, at any rate. I promised her I would trim it, and meant to get here yesterday, but all the trains were redirected for troop movement." He waited, but Claire could not say a word. "It is her Christmas gift to you."

"It's the same as last year." Overwhelmed by such love, especially when her aunt lay so ill, and confused that it wasn't David who'd decorated the tree the year before, Claire couldn't think what to say. She'd been so sure that last year he'd discovered and claimed her secret garden.

"The same as every year, according to Maggie. She said she and Christopher decorated it together. She wanted to pass this sacred tradition on to you." He stood back to admire the tree. "It's a wonder, isn't it? And to think she did this every year, even after she closed the garden, even after Christopher was gone."

"Were you part of their tradition?"

"Me? No." He looked somewhat crestfallen. "Maggie let no one but Christopher into her world in those days. It's you, lass, that's made the difference for her — in her. You, and these children, have given her back her life. I'm grateful to you for that, you know." He blushed and grinned just a little, returning to the tree and the children. "It means she's even noticed me standing at the gate," he called behind him.

"Rather late, though, isn't it?" Claire whispered, sad for faithful Dr. MacDonald, overwhelmed by the loving gift from her aunt at his hands, but disappointed that David had not been behind it. If he had known, if he had come, if he had decorated the tree, it would have been so romantic, so wonderfully, impossibly —

A low whistle came from just behind her. "Say, that's some swell tree!"

Claire's heart skipped three beats. She turned and looked up into the sparkling brown eyes of the man she dared to love. Did he feel the same? Could he feel toward her all that she felt? "Yes, it is. You've come." It was all she could say.

David pulled laughing eyes away from the tree and the children, who danced and marveled in delight over the precious ornaments in the great outdoors, torn between their beloved Dr. MacDonald and their snow crowning of dear Mr. Dunnagan, the grandest Ben Weatherstaff ever known.

Claire searched David's face until his eyes found hers. "Welcome home, David."

The old image of Miss Havisham standing alone in a locked and frozen garden flashed through Claire's mind. But in that moment the image cracked, splitting into a million pieces of sunshine as David grasped her elbows, pulled her close, and whispered, "Merry Christmas, Claire."

"The merriest," she whispered in return, gratitude and thanksgiving welling like a fountain inside her, spilling over, melting the snow of her worries, shooting up stars and rainbows and happily ever afters in her imagination all at once.

When he leaned down, cradled her face between his hands and kissed her, she knew this was no fairy tale, no exotic story. She was really, truly home.

Epilogue

June 1946

Three more Christmases and another spring came to Bluebell Wood and the secret garden before the war in Europe ended. Another year passed before Peter and Bertram, who'd come of age and enlisted late in the war, were free to return to their forever home at Bluebell Wood.

Golden daffodils and crimson tulips, pink-tinged wild cherry and delicate spring vetch blossomed to welcome the young men home, then faded into early spring.

By May, bluebells carpeted the woods once more in sapphire glory. Treetops filled with the sweet calls of linnets, buntings, skylarks, and redbreast robins. Burgundy and ivory peonies, lilacs in pristine white and every purple hue perfumed the air.

By mid-June, roses — pale pink, cream, and crimson — spilled over the fountains and arbors of Bluebell Wood, and lush, sweet, garnet-ripe strawberries swept the earth in ground cover. Even the stalwart purple foxglove rang its bells in preparation for the special day.

That same month, Claire's mother, who'd spent the last years of the war collecting and mailing care packages of clothing and chocolate for the children and coffee, lemons, and rationed sugar for the adults, came too. Through letters that began one special Christmas Day, mother and daughter had formed a truce, then a tentative understanding, and finally a relationship. At last the Atlantic was safe to travel.

Both bride and groom insisted their wedding day wait for their loved ones to share.

Lambs frolicking the fells were a good two months old the morning the tartan-clad piper took up his bag and pipes to begin the wedding march.

The bride, clad in a floor-length, pearl-buttoned and fitted ivory gown, but needing no adornment beyond her radiant smile, tucked her short train behind her, letting it trail down the steps of Bluebell Wood as she descended to meet her kilted groom. Together they stopped at the front door, touched their fingers to their lips, and ran them over Aimee's mezuzah. They thanked God for their home that had so abundantly received and given refuge and blessing, then marched through the porte cochere, down the drive, and through the maze. The proud groom winked, took a slight detour, and pushed back the thinning boxwood in the far corner, beckoning his bride to follow.

She rolled her eyes and grimaced, but only briefly, before following her mischievous husband-to-be through the hedge. They stepped onto the garden path, which had been mown and swept clean.

As they crossed the lawn, the couple was heralded by the morning *cheep-cheep* of two ochre-breasted robins, a cheering nuthatch with its *tuit, tuit, tuit,* and two bright yellowhammers demanding "a little bit of bread and no cheese, a little bit of bread and no cheese." When they reached the edge of the woodland, a painted lady butterfly fluttered her wings. Even a displaced lapwing, sporting its tiara for the day, mumbled its congratulations from atop the high garden wall. The couple laughed in return.

The bride, her eyes sparkling and cheek color high, tucked her arm a little tighter into her soon-to-be husband's, and they rounded the perimeter of the garden wall. Just before reaching the door of the secret garden, he stopped, pulled her closer yet, and turning her to face him, wrapped his strong arms about her. He leaned down and kissed her, a long and warm and very private kiss. "Are you ready, lass?"

Her breath came unsteady. She held back tears of long-awaited joy, smiled, and nodded, her heart too full to speak. But her eyes told him all he needed to know. Playfully, she pushed him back, nodding toward the garden and the guests who so patiently awaited them inside.

He grasped her hand and led her through the garden door. Lilies and roses, daisies, gardenias, rhodies, peonies, foxglove, delphinium, honeysuckle, and flowers of every fragrance and hue bursting in profusion, a kaleidoscope of color, greeted them — a magical, mystical garden in full bloom.

Every man, woman, and child who'd awaited this wedding stood from their wooden chairs and cheered the couple down the rose-petaled aisle, all the way to the center of the garden. The piper blew a last, long, plaintive note as the couple met the waiting vicar beneath the boughs of the evergreen, which had grown taller and spread wide over the years, so that it now formed a bower of blessing.

Claire imagined that in a way, the tree was a bit of Christopher, here to bless the nuptials. At least he was part of the memory that had helped to create this blessed day.

Aimee leaned close and whispered in Claire's ear, "Do you remember, in *Peter Pan,* how Mrs. Darling held one sweet kiss just at the corner of her mouth — a kiss no one could capture?"

Claire smiled, tucking her soon-to-be daughter's hand into the crook of her arm, and listened.

"I think Aunt Miranda holds that same kiss at the corner of her mouth, and I think Dr. MacDonald has captured it for good and all."

Claire almost laughed aloud for joy, squeezing Aimee's hand in silent agreement. As she watched her aunt and Dr. MacDonald take their vows before God and man, Claire leaned into her own dear husband, glad they had not waited till war's end to marry.

Aunt Miranda's surgeries, treatments, and recovery had proven long and brutal. She'd confided to Claire that it had taken her some while to accept that God did not plan for her to die with grace at this time, but to learn to live within His grace, His forgiveness, and with His unchanging, faithful, all-pursuing love. She had turned fifty the year after her surgery, and Dr. MacDonald had proposed on her birthday. Aunt Miranda took that as a sign for new beginnings — part two of her life's book — and said yes. In Aunt Miranda's acceptance and learning to live a life laced with joy, beneath the absolute singing of her Father in heaven, Claire had learned too.

But it hadn't taken Claire as long to walk into her future. The minute David had proposed, Claire had accepted and together they'd set the soonest wedding date possible. Though David had still worked and often traveled for weeks at a time for Short Brothers until the end of the war, they had married and made their home with a recovering Aunt Miranda and all the children of Bluebell Wood.

When David's war work had finished, he and Claire had opened a needed bookshop in the heart of Windermere. Josef, Franz, and Gaston stopped by after school to sweep the store's floors, unpack new merchandise, and take first peeks at new books. Ingrid and Elise dusted bookshelves and trimmed the bright-red geraniums and forest-green ivy spilling over window boxes in front of the shop. Each girl had claimed a private reading corner for rainy Saturdays. Ingrid did all the lettering for store brochures and flyers advertising special reading events. Whenever home from college, Marlene and Jeanine pitched in.

Claire and Aimee gladly labored together, reading to children during the after-school story hour, creating all the voices and drama that time and space allowed.

The bookstore specialized in British authors — Wordsworth and Carlyle, the Brontë sisters, Jane Austen, Thomas Hardy, Dickens and Shakespeare, as well as American authors whose stories the children of Bluebell Wood had read and loved. Mark Twain, Louisa May Alcott, and Frances Hodgson Burnett ranked high.

David created a special window display for the books of C. S. Lewis, to whom he and Claire acknowledged a great debt in their faith journey, and with whom Aimee and Claire continued to correspond, despite that good man's prolific writing and arduous schedule.

In the children's section, the books and prints of Beatrix Potter, the Lake District's most beloved children's author, held prime wall and shelf space. Sadly, Beatrix Potter Heelis — Aimee's beloved Auld Mother Heelis — had died of severe bronchitis in December of 1943. She did not see the war's end or the bookstore's opening.

Busy as life had grown, Claire continued

to write — journal entries for the Mass Observation Project and short stories. Her stories, published frequently in the UK and Canada, were billed as "moving" or "stirring," sometimes "gripping" and "heart-wrenching" — and all were taken from her real life with her real and unconventional family.

Over three hundred more children, mostly Jewish boys from the horrific concentration camps of Europe, had come to Windermere in the summer of 1945. With the war over and the Short Brothers' Sunderland factory at Calgarth closed, the boys were settled into the empty housing units of the estate to spend at least six months recuperating in the beautiful land of Wordsworth.

Josef and Gaston, and all at Bluebell Wood, had welcomed the boys with open arms.

Compassionate villagers of Windermere had donated ration coupons to collect extra food for the children. Once they collected enough so that each and every child could taste tomato soup for the first time.

Even Ed Foley, who collected cinema tickets once the Home Guard was disbanded in December of 1945, turned a blind eye when the boys snuck into the Windermere Cinema for free runs of Jeanette MacDonald and Errol Flynn films, or "borrowed" unlocked bicycles from locals.

Claire had long suspected that Josef and Gaston were as guilty as any of the Windermere Boys of such exploits.

Now that the war was over by a full year and they'd received word of the deaths of Aimee's parents, Claire and David's adoption proceedings had begun. The older children also remained with open offers of adoption if they wanted, and their home at Bluebell Wood was assured forever, even as schooling and searches for their parents continued.

Within the last month, a telegram had come from Paris, indicating that Gaston and Bertram's mother may have survived the war. The woman had collapsed after making her way from a labor camp in Poland, across Germany to France, and was now in convalescence in a hospital near Lyon. Identification was not yet certain. Each day all at Bluebell Wood prayed for the woman who'd survived the cruelties of concentration camp life and whatever horrors she'd endured on the road as a displaced woman alone. Each day Claire prayed for the Lord to sustain them all, come what may. She hoped with all her heart that the boys' mother was alive and could once again be well and hold her beloved sons. She saw that hope and also fear of the unknown in Gaston's eyes, doubt in Bertram's that it could be so. He'd seen too much of war and insisted on going to see the woman himself before he would believe she was their mother.

At the same time, Claire knew that her own heart would break to say good-bye to the young Frenchmen. They'd become as younger brothers — no, as sons to her. But she knew this time that she would not be left alone, that the God who had brought her beyond the darkest of her own demons would see her through the uncertain future. She was developing a history with this God, and knew she could trust Him. His mercies were truly new each morning, and great was His faithfulness.

Weeks after the wedding, Claire arched and rubbed her back. It ached more than usual these days. She pulled her journal and pen from her trench coat pocket and gingerly sat down on a wooden bench recently placed beneath Christopher's tree in the secret garden. She was no longer in condition to climb to her beloved tree house, even if the muse visited more clearly there.

In another month the new Dr. and Mrs. MacDonald would return from their prolonged honeymoon. Claire caressed her belly, hoping they'd come in time for the arrival of the next little resident of Bluebell Wood. Though the older refugee children may have temporarily outgrown the secret garden, this new baby guaranteed that the garden would ring with childish laughter for years to come.

There was, of course, no worry that the house itself would ever be empty or still. That was a covenant she and David, Aunt Miranda and Dr. MacDonald had made together. It would always welcome their wartime children home, and their children's children.

Claire stretched her arms skyward in thanksgiving for all that she'd received — the very desires of her heart — and breathed deeply, letting the world fall away and the muse come.

She placed the nib of her pen to her journal's page, ready at last to begin her novel based on early wartime life at Bluebell Wood. She did not hesitate, but scribbled those magical words she and Aimee loved best, the ones which always began the best adventures and were painted across the window of their family bookstore: *Once upon a time.*

NOTE TO READERS

Alarmed by the plight of young refugees fleeing gangs in Mexico to cross United States borders, and heart-heavy for victims and refugees worldwide who've suffered and continue to suffer under oppressive regimes, I looked for a moment in history to tell their tale as I wish it could play out. I didn't have to look far.

The *Kindertransport* of 1938–1940 brought ten thousand predominantly Jewish children to Great Britain for refuge from Nazi oppression. Accounts abound of men and women who rescued children through resistance, often at great cost to themselves — even life itself. But what happened next? What happened when those children entered countries of refuge without the parents who bore and loved them? I wondered about the average person and what role they might have played once the children were out of immediate danger . . . and what role we might play in the world's need today.

World news reported that in 2015, 51 percent of the world's refugees were children. Scripture tells us to care for widows and orphans. How do we do that from where we live, and as Christians, how do we reconcile this directive with the world's reality?

Most of us live quiet lives, rarely making decisions that change the world. But what if we could change the life of one person by providing a home and family for them? How would we cope with the everydayness, not to mention the prejudice, public opinion, injustice, necessary sacrifice, and potential crisis? Would we do it? Will we?

Knowing I would set this story in England's Lake District during World War II, I traveled to England and Scotland in 2014 with Carrie Turansky, my friend and writing colleague. We first toured southern England to see Tyntesfield, where Carrie's captivating Edwardian Brides series takes place.

For me, we traveled to Windermere and the Lake District to research Beatrix Potter and her renowned Hill Top Farm, to study the poetry and world of Wordsworth, and to learn just what happened to refugees and evacuees in the district during WWII.

As a result I learned more about the Short

Brothers' Sunderland flying boat factory and its village of Calgarth; camps for German prisoners of war, including Grizedale Hall; wartime homes for British evacuees and foreign refugees; the Keswick Pencil Museum and the famous spy pencil; the after-war arrival of the Windermere Boys (children deeply in need of rehabilitation who'd survived Europe's concentration camps); and so much more.

I ran my fingers over the desk where Wordsworth had carved his name as a boy, visited his burial ground, and fell in love with that poet's fields of golden daffodils, the heady perfume of lilacs, the glory of woodlands spread in sapphire carpets of bluebells, and month-old lambs tottering over the fells, butting tiny heads against their mothers' sides in search of lunch. We ferried across Lake Windermere, ate Grasmere's famous gingerbread, and took tea with jam and bread. Nowhere is the grass greener or the air purer than in the Lake District in springtime.

Beatrix Potter Heelis's Hill Top Farm, with its rooms and their contents reminiscent of her books, was a real treat. I bought my granddaughter a Beatrix Potter china tea set at its gift shop, a treasure and experience we'll share one day soon. During

WWII, Hill Top Farm housed British evacuees. Beatrix and her husband, William, lived their married lives at Castle Farm in Near Sawrey. For story's sake, I have the couple living at Hill Top during the war.

Our research trip culminated when we joined a ten-day tour of Scotland's "Highlands, Islands, and Gardens," hosted by Liz Curtis Higgs and guided by Karen MacCormick, tour guide in Scotland, and Beverly Henry, independent travel consultant. Forty ladies followed in Liz's wake as she inspired us through Bible study each morning, then led us through magnificent Scotland by day. We became the Scottish Standby Sisters — forty women who've kept in touch, standing by and praying one another through numerous illnesses, tragedies, griefs, and losses, as well as great and joyful healings and accomplishments. What a gift, and what a journey! As a result of that trip, I included in my story a good Scottish doctor, as well as memories of the terrible feud between the MacDonalds and Campbells.

During WWII, C. S. Lewis made a great contribution to the people of England through his series of BBC radio (wireless) broadcasts later compiled into his book *Mere Christianity.* Due to recycling efforts during the war, most of those broadcast reels were destroyed. One still exists. For sake of story, I did not chronologically time broadcasts or his early writings to the date of their publication or wartime events. The characters in this book, like so many living at the time, are challenged by those broadcasts and writings, their faith fostered or impacted. The letters written by C. S. Lewis in my story are a mixture of Lewis's actual writings and my own imaginings, inspired by his real correspondence. As part of my research, I reread many of C. S. Lewis's works, focusing especially on those written before and during the years my story covers. My son and I attended a theatrical production in DC portraying Lewis's journey from atheism to theism and then to Christianity. By all this research I was abundantly blessed.

Shortly after signing the contract for this book, I was diagnosed with breast cancer. Surgery, chemotherapy, radiation, and continued treatment ensued. Though I had the story planned, cancer treatments challenged my thinking, energy, stamina, and ability to write. I didn't know if I'd be able to think clearly enough to write this book.

Day by day the Lord brought me closer to Him, teaching me total dependence upon

Him and His grace — hour by hour, minute by minute.

He taught me to fight with a surrendered heart.

He taught me to trust not only that He loves me, but that I am enough for Him as I am — it's not about what I do or how I serve. He rejoices over broken me with singing, just as he rejoices over you.

He taught me not only to be prepared to die within His grace, but like Miranda in this story, to be willing to live within it, even when life is hard.

He taught me that everything in this life is only a precursor to all that will come, and that each day — now, as then — is an absolute gift from Him, to be treasured, cherished, and lived to the full.

He taught me to celebrate things that give me joy — worship, family, children, stories, flowers, music . . . All these are reflections of Him and His great love.

These lessons, as well as many favorite childhood memories and joys of parenting and grandparenting, have been woven into the pages of this book.

I hope it will bless you and warm your heart. I hope it will give you much to think about, to ponder in your own life: what you might do to reach and help those in need, and how you rejoice in and live deliberately each day — each beautiful, wonderful day that God has made.

In His love and by His amazing grace,

Cathy Gohlke

DISCUSSION QUESTIONS

1. What was your initial impression of Claire? Did that change at all as you got to know her?

2. Do you think the rejection from her parents made it more difficult for Claire to believe in and trust that her heavenly Father loved her? Have parent wounds affected your view of God? How can we separate the two?

3. When the story began, Miranda wanted to isolate herself. She wasn't initially happy with the arrival of Claire and the children. David Campbell, in particular, brought new life and new perspectives to Bluebell Wood. How did David's intervention both challenge and help Miranda? Claire? The refugee children? What does

that tell you about isolating yourself and your thinking?

4. How did Claire and others at Bluebell Wood help the refugee children cope with the loss of their families? Is there something more they could have done?

5. Some countries were more willing to take in refugees than others during the Holocaust and WWII. In 2015, it was reported that 51 percent of the world's refugees were children. Has this story fostered thought or given you insights into the plight of the world's refugees today? How should we respond to this crisis, especially given Scripture's directive to care for orphans? (See James 1:27.)

6. Both Miranda and Mrs. Newsome lost their husbands during the Great War. Contrast their forms of grieving and how they responded to life. What helped Miranda turn a corner in her grieving for Gilbert and Christopher?

7. What did you think of Miranda's longtime refusal to acknowledge the love and courtship of Dr. MacDonald?

8. Though Dr. MacDonald urged her to move forward, Miranda put off needed medical tests and treatments for a long while. Why do you think she did this?

9. As Miranda's health worsened, she prepared for the end of this life and even prayed that the Lord would allow her to die with grace and dignity. However, she eventually came to believe that the Lord was teaching her to live with His grace. If you were in her position, do you think that challenge would be difficult? How would you move forward?

10. Claire journeyed from unbelief, to blatant doubt, to skepticism, to fearfulness, to faith, to joy. What was the turning point in faith for her? Has there been a turning point in your faith's journey? What difference has it made?

ABOUT THE AUTHOR

Three-time Christy, and two-time Carol and INSPY award–winning and bestselling author **Cathy Gohlke** writes novels steeped with inspirational lessons and speaks of world and life events through the lens of history. She champions the battle against oppression, celebrating the freedom found only in Christ.

Cathy has worked as a school librarian, drama director, and director of children's and education ministries. When not travelling to historic sites for research, she, her husband, and their dog, Reilly, divide their time between Northern Virginia and the Jersey Shore, enjoying time with their grown children and grandchildren. Visit her website at www.cathygohlke.com and find her on Facebook at CathyGohlkeBooks.

The employees of Thorndike Press hope you have enjoyed this Large Print book. All our Thorndike, Wheeler, and Kennebec Large Print titles are designed for easy reading, and all our books are made to last. Other Thorndike Press Large Print books are available at your library, through selected bookstores, or directly from us.

For information about titles, please call:
(800) 223-1244

or visit our website at:
gale.com/thorndike

To share your comments, please write:
Publisher
Thorndike Press
10 Water St., Suite 310
Waterville, ME 04901